Mistress
by Mistake

Mistress by Mistake

MAGGIE ROBINSON

KENSINGTON PUBLISHING CORP.
www.kensingtonbooks.com

BRAVA BOOKS are published by

Kensington Publishing Corp.
119 West 40th Street
New York, NY 10018

All Kensington titles, imprints, and distributed lines are available at special quantity discounts for bulk purchases for sales promotion, premiums, fund-raising, educational, or institutional use.

Special book excerpts or customized printings can also be created to fit specific needs. For details, write or phone the office of the Kensington Special Sales Manager: Kensington Publishing Corp., 119 West 40th Street, New York, NY 10018. Attn. Special Sales Department. Phone: 1-800-221-2647.

Brava and the B logo are Reg. U.S. Pat. & TM Off.

ISBN-13: 978-0-7582-5099-5
ISBN-10: 0-7582-5099-1

First Kensington Trade Paperback Printing: May 2010

10 9 8 7 6 5 4 3 2 1

Printed in the United States of America

For John

ACKNOWLEDGMENTS

With love to my children, Christopher, Sarah, Jessie, and Abby, who are stupefied yet supportive that their mother writes sex scenes. Thanks to my agent Laura Bradford and my editor Megan Records, who made a dream come true. Extra-special thanks to my critique partners the Vauxhall Vixens, Tiffany Clare, J. K. Coi, and Elyssa Papa, who read every mistake I write and keep me from stumbling on the Dark Walk.

Chapter 1

Jane Street, London, 1820

"Honestly, Charlie! You're ruined anyway! What difference does it make?"

Charlotte felt the room spin every time her sister said the words "honestly, Charlie." Honesty had very little to do with Deborah Fallon. She was a mistress of prevarication. She was a mistress, period.

Charlotte Fallon looked at her sister, her beautiful, selfish, stubborn younger sister. The sister she was always trying to save in one manner or another, not that she'd been successful. Charlotte wished she had tossed her letter into the fire without opening it. "I should never have come."

"Nonsense. This is the ideal solution. Arthur wants to *marry* me, Charlie. I'm not getting any younger, you know. And neither are *you*. Surely you cannot stand there all stiff and disapproving and deny me happiness."

No one of importance had ever denied Deborah Fallon anything. One look at her cloud of black hair and mischievous sky-blue eyes, her bee-stung lips and spectacular bosom, and they had fallen at her feet. Since the age of sixteen, she had flaunted her assets and traded one rich man for another. Now twenty-six, she was still lovely and in possession of a very tidy fortune, even tidier now due to the recent infusion of money from the coffers of Sir Michael Xavier Bayard. He was expected to arrive in London from his Dorset estate any day now and fall into Deborah Fallon's bed. His own bed, actually. This house, every stick of furniture, every carpet, every lacy curtain belonged to him, as did the woman who was packing a sleek new trunk.

Charlotte Fallon did not belong to anyone. She also had black hair, only it was confined by hairpins and covered by a starched linen cap. Her sky-blue eyes were not mischievous at present, but dismayed. Her bee-stung lips were drawn into a frown, and her spectacular bosom heaved in indignation. "You cannot take Sir Michael's money and run off with Arthur Bannister!"

Deborah continued to fold clothes into the trunk. Charlotte took inventory of her sister's impropriety. Wispy, sensuous underthings trimmed with frivolous ribbons and bows. Low-cut silk dresses in every color of the rainbow. Embroidered slippers. Sheer stockings. Velvet jewel bags filled with precious stones.

"I shall leave you some of my wardrobe. And my pearl and sapphire necklace." Deborah sighed with sacrifice. "It's not as though I'm taking *everything*. I thought for a moment to take the paintings, but after consideration I just couldn't do it to the man. He is very fond of his art, even if they're only minor works by obscure painters. And I'll leave him *you*."

"I don't want to be left! You cannot just install me in your bedchamber and expect Sir Michael not to notice!"

"Of course Bay will notice. He's a very noticing kind of fellow. Those eyes! So black and knowing. They quite gave me shivers. But you and I are much alike, or would be if you didn't look like such a prude. Honestly, Charlie, where is the harm? He's a wonderful lover, and Lord knows you could do with a bit of amusement."

Charlotte felt a wave of revulsion. "You—you've slept with him already?"

Deborah tossed her black curls. "Don't be absurd. I never let him touch me. Not even a kiss. That's why he paid so much. I was absolutely unattainable without his contract. But," she said, closing the trunk latch with finality, "I'm on good terms with Helena Colbert, my predecessor. It was she who decorated this bedroom." Deborah looked around at the grotesquely chubby cupids that lurked on every surface. "Granted, she does not have much imagination, but she assured me bedding Bay was not a hardship. She said he's quite masterful."

"If that is true, why have you chosen Arthur?" Charlotte had met Arthur Bannister. Charlotte doubted Arthur could master anyone, let alone Deborah. He was the prematurely balding third son of an earl, obviously not destined for the clergy if he married her sister the famous courtesan.

"Arthur is very sweet. He loves me. His family will come round in time." Deborah gave her an assured smile. Everybody *always* loved her; it was inconceivable to her that one could not.

"You don't love *him*, do you." Charlotte did not tack a question mark to her words.

"Honestly, Charlie! What is love anyway? You thought you were in love and look how that turned out. You're thirty years old and live in the country with *cats*." Deborah pulled on her gloves. Pale yellow kidskin. How ridiculous for traveling, but they matched her slippers and flimsy striped dress. Charlotte envisioned her sister discarding the whole outfit in the carriage on the way to Dover just to ensure Arthur continued the journey. "We haven't much time. Thank goodness Bay's grandmother got sick and died and he was called away."

Only Deborah could say such a thing and look like an angel doing it. Charlotte wanted to throttle her sister's slender white neck. "You are attempting to perpetrate fraud, Deb. Theft. For all I know the man will lock me up in prison in your place before he finds you."

"Pooh. He's quite besotted with me. And even if he doesn't like you, you can explain this whole affair far better than I can in a letter. I should be quite thoughtless if I just left a note on the pillow."

An understatement. Deborah had always been thoughtless. She had broken her late parents' hearts when she ran off to London with George, although they did manage to spend the money she sent home at irregular intervals. Charlotte was ashamed to acknowledge that without Deb's help, her cats might go hungry. Of course, the cats weren't really her own. The half dozen or so were ferociously feral and only visited her out of habit, not gratitude. They would not dream of curling up on the hearth or resting upon her bed pillow or being helpful mousers. No, they yowled for their scraps and milk at the cottage kitchen door when hunting was poor or the weather problematic. They would be perfectly fine until she returned to Little Hyssop after she put her sister's ridiculous scheme behind her.

Deborah patted the feather bed. "Come. Sit down. I have many instructions to give you."

Charlotte blushed as brightly as a virgin, although she could not claim the title. Surely her sister was not going to subject her to courtesan lessons. She was most certainly not going to take Deborah's place in anything but conversation with Sir Michael, who was at least owed an explanation once he returned to town.

Charlotte reflected it had ever been thus—Deborah would do something impetuous and Charlotte would pick up the pieces. She dearly hoped that Deborah's new protector was not too badly smitten, for she was not good at mending heartbreak, especially her own. She listened with half an ear as Deborah recited a litany of practicalities and positions. Charlotte felt the beginnings of one of her vexing headaches. Any amount of time spent with her little sister was sure to produce such a result. She was never more relieved than when Irene, the young maid hired by Sir Michael to attend to whichever mistress was in residence, announced that Mr. Bannister was below and his driver on his way up for the luggage.

Charlotte was tugged downstairs and reintroduced to Arthur, who was a few years Deborah's junior despite the hair loss and beginnings of a paunch. These shortcomings were more than mitigated by the recent death of his great-uncle, who had remembered young Arthur kindly in his will. A pity that the old man had died after Deborah had come to her arrangement with Sir Michael Xavier Bayard. But then illness and another fortuitous death occurred, keeping the baronet in Dorset these past six weeks. Charlotte was afraid that Arthur Bannister had already slept beneath Sir Michael's sheets and could not like him for it.

"Come, my love. The carriage awaits, and I've a special license." Arthur patted his breast pocket smugly. Deborah said he'd spared no expense to make London's fairest Cyprian his own. By the time Sir Michael came home, she would be Mrs. Bannister. Of course, they were to travel on the Continent first, just to give his family and Sir Michael a while to calm down. Then Deborah would be mistress only of Arthur's late uncle's estate in Kent.

Deborah kissed her sister good-bye, and to her horror, Charlotte discovered her eyes were filling with tears. Truly, she wished her sister happy. If she thought for a moment that Arthur Bannister could control Deborah's dishonorable impulses, she might feel very differently about this hasty wedding. Deborah might make a poor wife, but at least one of the Fallon girls would be a bride at last.

Deborah left in a flurry of swishing skirts and lavender water. Suddenly the little house was quiet as a tomb. Somewhere below Irene and Mrs. Kelly, the cook-housekeeper, were engaged in dinner preparations for her. Charlotte didn't think she could eat a bite. A glass of sherry, on the other hand, would steady her nerves for the task ahead. She poured a healthy tot from a crystal decanter and drank it down in one gulp.

To think that her sister wanted her to become a harlot! As if she were at all suited to the position Deborah had cut out for herself almost a decade ago. To foist her on a stranger, to leave Charlotte holding the bag when Sir Michael returned made her heart skip erratically. She should have known to read between the lines of Deb's badly spelled letter. Anything Deb considered to be an emergency was really a catastrophe.

Charlotte poured another drink. It would not do to get foxed. It was a family curse. Both the Fallon parents had drowned their financial sorrows in a bottle, then drowned in reality when they had the drunken idea to go for one last midnight sail before their beloved boat was repossessed. Charlotte had disposed of their crumbling manor house, paid off their debts, and moved as far inland as she could. She had been scrupulous about sharing the pitiful proceeds with her sister. Judging from the contents stuffed in her trunk and stored in the country, Deborah had never needed a farthing. Her gentlemen had been generous from the start.

Charlotte sighed. Her sister had not been so very indiscriminate. She'd had only four lovers in ten years, each of whom had showered her with jewels, money, and clothing. Deb had not been able to wheedle anyone out of a house yet—save for poor Arthur. Charlotte should turn tail and go right back home. A note on the pillow would do as well as any stuttering excuse she could give Sir Michael for her sister's behavior.

She returned to Deb's bedroom to regroup, shoving a plaster Cupid away to set her drink by the bedside. Lord, but she was tired. The flying trip to town when she imagined her sister dying—or worse!—had sapped every bit of strength she had. And then to discover what Deborah planned—well, it quite took one's breath away.

She lay in the Cupid-infested room, nervously bunching the scarlet satin coverlet between her fingers. She would not unpack her own trunk but to pull out her tattered night rail and robe later. She could not move in and assume her sister's life. She didn't even want to consume her dinner. But an hour later, fresh-faced Irene was at the door informing her that supper was on the table. Charlotte imagined it tasted delicious, but was too distracted to tell. Despite her earlier pledge, she gulped a great deal of wine in order that she might actually fall asleep in her sister's bed. Woozy and warm, she allowed Irene to help her undress and bathe, then crawled under the covers, closing her eyes to the grinning statues. How Deborah had borne them for six weeks was a wonder.

She slept as if dead, having the most delightful tipsy dream somewhere past midnight. But when morning came and she found her nightgown hanging from a fat angel's head and a naked man with his lips planted firmly around her left nipple, she knew her dream was now a nightmare.

Bay had done his duty. When news of his grandmother's illness had arrived, he'd left immediately for Bayard Court, his oceanfront boyhood home. Grace Bayard had raised him, and he owed her everything. She'd been a little bit of a thing, but her tongue and wits were sharp, and she'd done her damnedest to set him on the proper path. It was not her fault that he had strayed more than a time or two. She had wanted to see him settled again and a father, and perhaps one day he would be. But at present he had the divine Deborah Fallon waiting for him in his little house in Jane Street, the most exclusive enclave of kept women in London. Deb was the third mistress he'd set up there. The first, Angelique Dubois, had not been much of an angel of any kind or even French, despite her name. His last lover, Helena Colbert, had served him well for a year, but things had wound down to their natural conclusion. His friend Viscount Marlow was happy to take her off his hands, gushing his gratitude in disgusting fashion at every opportunity.

Bay had been ready for a change, and his choice was the most alluring Deborah Fallon. Those full lips, those fuller breasts, those tip-tilted blue eyes. She looked like a naughty cream-fed kitten. She had some wit, and if she were a bit of a prima donna, it was only because she knew her own worth. Her last protector had to reluctantly marry to further the family line, and nothing he could say would make Deborah part of a triangle. She had her standards—her lovers had to be rich, of course, and completely unattached. Along with several others, Bay pursued Deb for weeks before he persuaded her to move into Jane Street, and he hadn't gotten to warm the sheets even once before he was called away.

He'd stopped at his town house to make himself presentable after his long journey, pleased to see that someone had thoughtfully hung a mourning wreath upon the front door. He was truly sad that his grandmother had passed, but she had been nearly ninety-five, a very great age. He was three and thirty—and would be happy indeed to treble that if he remained as shrewd as his grandmama up till near the end. She had fallen in her garden, tending to her beloved roses. The doctor thought she had had a series of small strokes, and by the time Bay arrived, she was sleeping most of her days away. She had rallied briefly at the sight of him, then went to bed one night and never woke up. Bay had stayed to see to the disposition of her faithful servants and shut up most of the house for the time being. He was a city man now. One day he might try to raise a family again in the stone manor house, but now he meant to raise his spirits in Deborah Fallon's arms.

Perhaps he'd been foolish to ride back to London. Every inch of him hurt, but he was damned if he was going to wait any longer for Deborah. He wondered how she'd amused herself while he was away. He let himself in to the dark house with his own key and climbed the stairs. He could have been blindfolded and still have found Deborah's bedroom. She had changed her perfume to a delicious harmony of orange and lemons, and her fresh scent filled his head. He stood by the bed, not wanting to startle her awake, dropping his clothing quietly to the floor. This was not how he pictured his first night with his new mistress, but he was stiff as a poker and could not wait to seduce her over champagne and strawberries.

Angelique's revolting cherubs were still gleaming in the moonlight. Helena had been too superstitious to remove them and had actually acquired several more. Poor Deborah had probably waited for him to return before she made any changes. He fully expected her to make the bedchamber her own, although the rest of the house was exactly to his taste.

Their liaison had not gotten off to a good start. The carters had no sooner delivered Deborah's trunks before he'd left her in tears in the marble hallway. He had sent letters and flowers weekly, of course, and news of his grandmother's death. In a foolish fit of lust he had discovered a ruby necklace in his grandmother's jewel case and sent it to London, with the under-standing that Deborah could wear it as long as she was his mistress. He was longing to see it around her white throat—it, and nothing else adorning her luscious body.

Grace Bayard was the rare woman who didn't care much for ostentatious jewelry, so he had never seen his grandmother wear it. He had buried her with the plain gold band his grand-father had given her eighty years ago, before he made his for-tune. Their marriage had not been an especially happy one. His grandmother had been practically a child when she wed, the fashion of the day. Her husband was older and ambitious, spending much of their married life outside England. Their long separation resulted in just one child, Bay's father.

Grandmama Grace had told him once his grandfather had given her the rubies to atone for some infraction. His grand-father, Bay thought, must have done something spectacularly bad, for the rubies were large and lustrous and very valuable, and the diamonds surrounding them not insignificant either. The collar with its enormous center drop was fit for a princess. Hell, fit for a queen. He hoped it had not been a mistake to gift them to Deborah temporarily. He'd have to tread care-fully when he discussed the necklace on the morrow.

He encountered an amusingly virginal night rail, which he made quick work of. She gave a pleased little sigh and wrapped herself around him. Her magnificent hair was in two school-girl braids—she certainly had not expected to entertain him this evening, and he was touched at her surprising modesty. And equally touched by her ardent, almost thirsty kisses. She tasted of vanilla and wine and smelled like a Spanish summer. She cupped his balls and brought him to her entrance and he slipped in without any hesitation. She was wet but very tight. Heaven. If she was a schoolgirl, he was as randy as a school-boy and didn't last long in her pillowing embrace. He'd spend more time tomorrow morning tending to her needs. He was known as a considerate lover, one of the reasons Deborah had agreed to be his mistress. Even his wife had no com-plaints while they were married.

Thoroughly spent, he passed a delightful night in his lover's arms. And when the first rays of sun had the audacity to slip through the shutters, he feasted upon her breast as if it were a banquet of cream and honey. She gave a low groan, but he didn't think it was in protest. The faint light showed him his mistress was not quite as young as she appeared to be six weeks ago—there were a few silver strands in her unraveling ink-dark braids. No doubt she resorted to artifice and would have corrected this had she known he was coming.

And speaking of coming, he wanted to seat himself within her again. Last night had been heaven, and now that the empty day was spread before him, the devil in him intended to visit heaven again and again. No, he was not sorry he'd paid the exorbitant price to secure Deborah Fallon's favors. If last night was any indication of what the woman could do when she was half asleep, he would cheerfully beggar himself. He was a lucky man indeed.

He licked her nipple to taut, pale pink perfection, wondering idly if he'd get a child on her someday. He'd been fortunate with his mistresses thus far, but he would do his duty by her if she bore his bastard. He was a gentleman, and that's what gentleman did. Somehow the thought of an infant suckling Deb Fallon's very tempting breast was unbelievably erotic. She would resemble a naughty Madonna, her black hair cascading down her ivory shoulders.

By God, she was making him lose his mind. The touch and taste of her was inebriating, clouding his judgment. One didn't keep a mistress for domesticity. One kept a mistress for sin, the darker the better. And if he knew anything about Deborah Fallon, she would complain loud and long caring for anything that was not her own luscious self. A baby? Proposterous.

As if she heard his thoughts, she stiffened beneath him. And then she screamed.

Ear-piercingly. Perhaps she had not recognized him when she awoke. But honestly, who could she be expecting? She was *his*.

He looked up at her, suspicious. She gave him a look he'd

seen only in battle, when the other side was hopelessly outnumbered, pushed beyond recklessness, and there was nothing
left to lose. He hoped very much that she was not sleeping
with a French bayonet beneath the mattress.

"You! You!" she sputtered.

"Yes, my pet, it is I. I know I gave you no notice, but thank
you for your very warm welcome last night. It was worth
every minute of the harrowing six weeks we spent apart." He
set back to flicking her nipple again with his tongue.

She hit him on the head with a fist. "Get off me! This instant! You are much mistaken, Sir Michael. I am not Deborah."

Was this some sort of fantasy? Perhaps she liked her love
play rough. To be the reluctant virgin, he the barbarian con-
queror. Angelique had liked to play highwayman and victim,
as he recalled. He was the victim, and a most willing one. He
stood, and he delivered.

"I shall call you anything you like, sweet, but please don't
strike me again. It's not a bit sporting when I don't know the
rules of your game. But I'm willing to learn."

"This is not a game, you stupid man! Oh, I do beg your
pardon! But you are under a severe misapprehension, sir."

She was scrambling under him quite provocatively. Her
skin was on fire for him, blushing most delightfully. And here
he had thought La Fallon cool and a little calculating.

"Hush, my dove." His lips captured hers and she squeaked.
Soon he would make her sigh again. See, she was softening
already. Her lips opened and he swept into the warmth. His
tongue tangled with hers in a dance as old as time. He was
fisting his cock to slide between her smooth thighs when she
bit him.

And drew blood. The taste of iron flooded his mouth.
Why, the little she-devil! He chuckled deep in his throat and
continued kissing her, showing her exactly who was in control, angling his cock into her so as to rub the top of her sex.
After a very halfhearted effort to push him away, she grew
as warm and hard as he, shuddering satisfactorily under him

as he applied more pressure to her clitoris with his cock and thumb. She kissed him as though they would both die tomorrow, her fingers exploring the bumps on his spine, the slash on his cheek, the cleft of his arse. Fingers that flew everywhere, whereas his never strayed from the pleasurable task at hand.

He could be patient. Last night had been a hurried affair but rather perfect nonetheless. He remembered the heat of her wet quim sheathing him, drawing him deep. Tempting as it was to sink within again this very instant, he focused instead on the kiss and the inexorable circling. He was good with his hands, even better with his tongue. But if he was any judge, she was close to coming, and any interruption and relocation would not be to either of their benefits. She was incredibly responsive, pure carnality wrapped in a small, plump package. He was unwrapping her, inch by delicious inch.

He felt her moment of capitulation as she stilled, then burned for him. Heat from her snow-white skin enveloped their bodies in all all-consuming blaze as she held him close. He swallowed up her cry, bore the frantic scoring on his back. Her legs fell apart in blatant invitation. He was not one to miss a cue, and took advantage of her total surrender by gliding home in a single thrust. Her legs laced tight around him, hips rising, heels spurring his every move.

Just as he remembered. Better than he dreamed. All those weeks away had heightened the anticipation, but nothing in Bay's experience could match the silk friction of being inside Deborah Fallon. No wonder she was the most sought-after courtesan in the ton. Her reputation didn't begin to explain her exquisite sexual artistry. She made him feel as if she'd just discovered sin and was making up for lost time, combining innocence and wickedness in the tantalizing twist of her limbs and her lush mouth.

He lost himself in another desperate kiss. It was so easy to lose himself with her, he might just disappear altogether. Bay reminded himself he had the upper hand—it wouldn't do to fall victim to the experienced wiles of his mistress. Bad enough he'd spent years in thrall to his wife. Women were all very good for amusement—and God knows he was seriously amused right now, seated in a shivering, shaking, quaking Deborah—but she was just a good fuck. Nothing more. But certainly nothing less.

He opened his eyes to break the spell, watched as she came apart again, her teeth biting her own lip in a slightly rabbity way and her dark lashes scrunched under questioning brows. Quite endearing, actually, and a sure sign that she had taken her pleasure again. As a gentleman, now he could take his. His balls contracted in undeniable need, his cock plunged on with ferocious insistence. Her tremors bore him in their tide, his mental reservations floating away. He was all body now, all male. All, when it came down to it, cock. There was nothing else of any consequence at the moment. He should, of course, withdraw, but her legs were locked around him and she must know what she was about. It would be a shame to break their unity. Criminal. His seed erupted. He shouted her name and fell on her as if dead.

The only sounds were their frantic gasps for breath and the ticking of a dreadful little angel with a clock in its porcine belly. Bay realized he'd better move before he squashed the life out of her, but truthfully, he could remain right where he was forever. Her citrusy smell was even stronger now, mixed with the scent of sex and sweat. He inhaled deeply, almost tasting the essence of Deborah Fallon. If she could bottle it, she'd make a fortune.

"Sir Michael."

He rolled off and grinned at her. "My dear Deborah, I think we might dispense with the formalities. I've asked you to call me Bay. That is what my friends and relations call me, and we are certainly friends, are we not?"

"No, Sir Michael, we are not." She reached for the sheet and tried to stuff it between them. He pulled it away from her easily.

"Don't cover yourself. I love looking at you."

She glared at him. "But I do not wish to be looked at. If you would just listen to me for a moment—"

He sighed. He hadn't counted on her being a talker, and certainly not so stern. Before they'd come to their arrangement, she was playful, flirtatious, like a fluffy black-and-white kitten. But it seemed her claws weren't retracted now. He hoped she would not be too tiresome. Even if she was the most skilled harlot he'd ever fucked, it would be a dead bore if she lectured him afterward.

He tried charm. "I am all ears. In fact, my angel, every part of me is at your disposal."

"Do not call me angel." She looked around the room with loathing.

"What shall I call you then, Deb?"

"*Not* Deb! That is what I was trying to tell you when you—when you—took such liberties with my person."

She was angry, beet red now, not a good color on her. Not any sort of color a man's mistress should have. He preferred her translucent white skin, so pale she glowed like a pearl. He'd never heard she had a temper. Vanity, yes. That was understandable. Perhaps a bit of pique when she wanted something and didn't get it soon enough. Perfection in bed, and *that* she'd already proven. Deborah Fallon was allegedly a paragon among mistresses. Everybody said so. Could it be she had the entire ton fooled? He was becoming irritated with her and himself at the moment. If he had wanted a shrew in his bed, he would have gotten married again.

"I was under the impression, madam, that my attentions were not unwelcome. You have accepted my astonishingly large bank draft and lived in my house for the past six weeks. You are wearing the clothes I bought you. Not at present, I grant you, but they hang in your closet. You have my grandmother's necklace and my good faith. Are you telling me you wish to renegotiate our agreement?"

"That is what I'm trying to tell you, Sir Michael. I am not Deborah Fallon. Deborah is my sister, and if I see her again I am very likely to strangle her on the spot."

"Rubbish. What kind of ruse is this?" Bay stared hard at her. She was Deborah Fallon, in his bed, well-fucked, his marks on her lush body, hers on his. The glossy hair, the blue eyes, the tits—he'd pursued the woman for months. Surely he could tell whom he was shagging. He watched as she stumbled out of bed and opened up the armoire. There was very little to choose from. Where the hell had all the gowns he'd ordered from Madame Duclos gone to? She reached for an ugly gray velvet robe, belted it tightly, and turned to him. Her braids lay like sentinels over her bosom daring any man to touch.

"My name is Charlotte. Deborah is my younger sister. I'm sorry to inform you she has eloped with Mr. Arthur Bannister. Perhaps you know him? Running to fat? Gormless? But recently he has come into some money, a house in Kent, and is stupid enough to want to marry her. She got me here under completely, *completely* false pretenses," she muttered. "I was meant to tell you what she had done and smooth your ruffled feathers. I suppose I have gone over and above my duty in that regard." She raised her chin, a rather charming chin with just the tiniest dimple. Deborah had no dimple there that he could recall.

He heard the unmistakable ring of truth in her voice. Good God. He had practically raped a stranger.

No, not raped. She had been willing. Twice. And this Charlotte so resembled her sister they could be twins. Bay shoved the enticing thought of the two of them in his bed out of his mind at once. He opened his mouth, but no sound was forthcoming.

She raised a white hand, a hand that not long ago had scored his back, sifted through his hair, caressed his stones. "Do not apologize for this morning. And I suppose last night. That wasn't a dream after all, was it?" she asked rhetorically. "We are both at fault. But in my opinion you are well rid of any association with my sister. She is not—thoughtful."

Bay barked out a laugh. The absurdity of the past few hours would not be duplicated if he lived to be his grandmother's age. "Nevertheless, I do apologize, Miss Fallon. It is *Miss* Fallon, isn't it?"

Charlotte nodded, looking acutely uncomfortable. Bay

frowned. "Forgive me for being so blunt. But you were not a virgin, were you? I would hate to think that this—this *mistake* resulted in your losing your innocence."

She stood very straight, her hands clasped tightly in front of her. "My innocence was lost long ago, Sir Michael. Now if you don't mind, I would like to wash and dress and make arrangements to return to my home."

"Of course. Allow me to assist you in any way possible." He reached for his discarded trousers. "I presume your sister made off with the clothes I bought her."

"She may have," Charlotte said evasively.

"What about the necklace?"

Charlotte went to the dressing table and picked up something glittery. She held it to the sunlight which was now slanting brightly through the shutters. "I should have known." She turned to him. "I'm afraid this is paste, Sir Michael. And the workmanship is inferior at that. I hope you didn't pay too much for it."

"*What?*" He strode across the floor in two steps and ripped it out of her hand. "No, not this bit of trumpery. The ruby and diamond collar. With a large pigeon's blood ruby drop at the center."

Charlotte bit her lip, reminding him of earlier. But the woman who had been so responsive—so *hot* beneath him—had disappeared behind a gray shroud. "I—I don't know. She packed several jewel bags, but surely she wouldn't take a family heirloom."

"Oh, wouldn't she," he said, grim. He began to pull open drawers. Empty, every one of them, save for one torn stocking, a packet of pins, a broken fan, and all the romantic letters he'd written to Deborah Fallon the past six weeks, ass that he was. "I'll be damned. Where else could she have put it? It's very valuable."

"Perhaps she hid it. To keep it safe." Charlotte was worrying the end of one of her braids. Unbidden, the image of it flowing down her back distracted him from his anger. Bay subdued the urge to grab a hairbrush and release all of that black silk.

Threaded with a bit of silver. Deborah Fallon wouldn't allow such impudence to take root on her head. What a fool he had been this morning. Ass. Ass. Ass.

"If you wouldn't mind delaying your departure, Miss Fallon, I'd appreciate your help finding my grandmother's necklace."

She looked frightened now. "What if it's not here?" she whispered.

No one could possibly believe La Fallon could prefer Arthur Bannister over him even if gormless Arthur had inherited a moldy old estate in Kent. Deborah would never be satisfied with so little. Unless Deborah Fallon was going to supplement their income with the sale of practically priceless rubies.

But everything had its price.

Damn it. The little witch knew her sister had stolen it. She had probably packed it in the valise herself. They were in it together, fleecing him, scheming to switch places, making him a laughingstock. Charlotte had been accomplished in her ardor. Virtually acrobatic. She was as much a whore as her sister.

He loomed over her. "Well, then, I suppose you'll have to stay until it's found."

Her succulent lips opened. He'd put them to good use later. "I beg your pardon?"

"You heard me. It seems the position of my mistress is currently vacant. You'll do in a pinch. Perhaps your sister will save you by returning my property. I'll have you prosecuted for theft and fraud if she doesn't."

Bay watched her fall to the carpet. How trite. She was a good little actress, he'd give her that. But the Fallon sisters underestimated him if they thought they could get away with this charade. He'd been burned once and still bore the scars.

Chapter 2

Charlotte stared at the ceiling. There were painted cherubs up there too, cavorting with something that looked very much like Satan in a white fur coat. She blinked and saw she had mistaken a cloud for the Prince of Darkness. She touched the back of her head and felt the lump forming. Mama had tried to teach her daughters the graceful art of fainting. Deborah had taken to the lessons like a duck to water, but Charlotte had discovered an actual blackout could not be choreographed. She had only ever fainted twice in her life and both times had cracked her skull.

She struggled to sit up. No, she was still mistaken. Satan was indeed here, minus the fur coat. In fact, Sir Michael Xavier Bayard was wearing nothing but a pair of buff trousers, his chest rather magnificent with a faint dusting of coppery hair. His arms were corded with muscles, his feet long and bootless, his smile terrifying. His eyes were as dark as the pit of Hell and trapped her in place. On the floor, on her sore bottom, with her old robe splayed open to reveal every inch of her legs and worse. She clutched the fabric shut. Too late. He'd seen it all before anyway. Those very legs had been wrapped around him in ecstasy not half an hour ago.

Oh. She was just as bad as Deborah. Worse. At least Deborah had some business sense before she entwined her limbs around a man. Sir Michael and the others had paid her a fortune over the years for the exclusive right to her body. Deb had once explained to an unwilling Charlotte that men didn't value what was free. She insisted on an outrageous sum at the beginning of each relationship, a generous monthly allowance, and, of course, shelter, victuals, clothing, jewels, and anything else she was able to inveigle. Both upstairs rooms in Charlotte's tiny cottage were crammed with the overflow of Deb's gentlemen's largesse. There were trunks full of clothes not a year out of season when they were stored, some of them never worn. Mother-of-pearl opera glasses, and Deb hated opera. Four full sets of bone china for twelve. A grotesque sterling silver epergne. Even a stuffed parrot, its brilliant feathers fading. If Charlotte sold every feather and bit of frippery, it would serve Deb right for landing her in such a pickle.

But apparently the money and assorted objets and even an offer of marriage had not been enough. Deb had taken this necklace that had Bayard so furious. Charlotte knew it. She might turn this house upside down, lift every cushion and carpet, but would find nothing. Deb did love her jewelry and had a keen eye. Enough to know the necklace she'd fobbed off on her sister yesterday was worthless paste. Charlotte was not at all surprised by yet more evidence of Deb's perfidy.

But to be charitable, there might be some mistake about the missing jewels' provenance. Maybe Deb thought the collar was an outright gift. Or packed it by mistake. Charlotte sighed. Most unlikely. Only a woman as hopeless as she would still be making excuses for her little sister.

The baronet was still fixing her with his gimlet gaze, as though he'd discovered a slug on the silk of his Persian rug. Charlotte stood up with as much dignity as she could muster.

"You cannot hold me against my will."

He gave her an insolent smirk. "I don't believe my company will be such a hardship. You enjoyed yourself earlier well enough, Miss Fallon."

"Don't flatter yourself! I was asleep the first time."

He lifted a dark eyebrow. "And the second time?"

"I tried to tell you!" Charlotte snapped. "But you kissed me." She felt herself flush. "And then I couldn't speak for the obstruction of your tongue in my mouth. You were so fast—"

"Hardly what a protector wants to hear, my dear. A mistress should use the word fast very sparingly."

"I am not your mistress, you insufferable man!" She fisted the worn velvet of her robe before she was tempted to hit him again and be charged with assault as well as thievery. "I am sorry my sister deceived you, but I assure you I had no part in the removal of the blasted necklace. I've never heard of it. Never seen it. I wouldn't know it if I stepped on it."

"You'd cut your pretty toes." He shrugged his very broad, bronzed shoulders. "Well, no matter. Unless you want to find yourself in Newgate, you'll fulfill your sister's end of our bargain."

"I am not my sister! I am not a courtesan—not a whore, Sir Michael. I am a respectable woman. A spinster. I live in a cottage in Little Hyssop. With cats."

His look was mocking. Perhaps adding the part about the cats was unwise.

"Can you prove you are innocent?"

"Can you prove I am not?"

He walked over to the dresser. "Perhaps not. But I can prove your sister is a thief, or at best mistaken or illiterate." He shuffled through the folded letters. "Ah, here it is. '*My dearest Deborah, blah blah blah*' I presume you don't wish to hear the evidence of my misplaced devotion."

Charlotte shivered and shook her head.

" '*I am sending this token of my affection by special courier. I regret to say the jewels are on loan only—they belonged to my grandmother and should remain in my family should I ever find a woman more tempting than you are to marry. I tell you true I cannot imagine such a creature, for you inflame me beyond—*'" He cleared his throat. "Erm, we'll skip that part."

"No," Charlotte said, her lips twisting in a smile. "I'm fascinated by this letter. I would never dream you were so eloquent, Sir Michael. Do go on."

He gave her a twisted smile back. "Very well. '*You inflame me beyond reason. I cannot wait to clasp the rubies and diamonds around your throat and watch as the candlelight reflects each facet on the marble whiteness of your body. For, my dearest Deborah, you shall need no other adornment than these borrowed jewels and the velvet of your own soft skin. It is my wish to fuck you until we are both quite exhausted, and then fuck you again. They say that sin deferred is sweeter sin, and so we shall discover for ourselves when I return to Jane Street. Do keep this necklace safe. Should you admire it, I will see if I cannot buy you some rubies of your own. Your most obedient servant, Bay.*'"

Charlotte's knees felt weak. Listening to his low rumble as he read his letter, she was reminded of throwing brandy on a well-banked fire. Heat and light sparked up in her blood. She closed her eyes, picturing a bloodred and bright white circlet around her neck, Bay's hands everywhere else. She swallowed.

"Well, what do you think, Miss Fallon? Your sister does read, does she not? I saw her once with a novel in her lap, but perhaps it was for show."

"She reads. We both do," Charlotte said faintly.

"Was my intent clear? I don't mean about the fucking part. I mean about the necklace." He scanned the lines again, enunciating each syllable. "'*On loan only . . . Remain in my family . . . Borrowed jewels . . . Some rubies of your own.*'"

"You were an idiot to send them to her." Charlotte collapsed on the dressing table bench, caught sight of herself in the mirror and suppressed the urge to jump out the bedroom window. She picked up her hairbrush instead, unplaiting her hair with her fingers.

"I quite agree. I imagine you think I'm a veritable beast as well, but you are my leverage. My bargaining chip. I'm sure your sister does not want you arrested."

Charlotte yanked on her hair. "I doubt she'll care. She cares nothing for anybody but herself. Certainly not poor Arthur. She's flown to the Continent, you know. I have no idea where. Or when she'll come back. With my luck, the packet has sunk and she and poor Arthur and your damned necklace are at the bottom of the English Channel."

He came up behind her, his sardonic smile reflected in the mirror. "Well, that will alleviate the necessity for you to strangle her."

Charlotte rolled her eyes. He thought he was so clever. So witty. He took the hairbrush out of her hand and began smoothing through the tangles. She kept her face impassive as the bristles stroked her scalp with the perfect amount of pressure. Sweep after sweep. One hand slipped up the back of her neck, the pads of his fingertips gently tickling. His rhythm lulled her. She lost count of the number of times the brush glided through her hair, her lids dropping in relaxation. He would have made a fine ladies' maid, if he hadn't had such magnificent masculine equipage.

"You have beautiful hair."

Charlotte made a face. "I'm going gray." She winced as he tugged a silver strand out and wound it around his finger. "See? Gone."

"And then I shall soon be bald." She met his eyes in the mirror. "This isn't right. Please don't do this."

He tossed the brush down with a clatter. "Fine."

"I don't mean brushing my hair. You cannot keep me hostage for my sister's sins."

His lips thinned. "How do I know they are not yours as well? The two of you no doubt colluded to trick me, steal from me, and make a fool of me. Deb is welcome to the money she took for services not rendered, but I want the necklace back. No, Miss Fallon, here you are, and here you will stay until we settle this. All cats are gray in the dark. Your duties will not be so very onerous."

Charlotte grabbed the hairbrush and threw it at him. His reflexes were excellent. Instead of it braining him, he caught it easily with one hand and pitched it against the opposite wall. He might have been playing cricket. "You will not attempt to do me harm again, do you understand? You've done enough."

Charlotte felt her fury bubble up. "I—I have not yet begun, sir! You are—you are inhuman! A fiend!"

"So I have been told," he said with a threatening smile. He pulled a watch from his pocket. "I shall return here at four o'clock. I had planned, you know, to spend the day abed with you. Lap perfectly chilled champagne from your skin and retrieve berries from—wherever. But plans change. I think you'll find me flexible."

"I don't care if you can bend like a sapling! You will not bed me, and will certainly not cover me in liquid and foodstuffs! I will not be here when you come back."

"Off to Little Hyssop? It sounds like a very small village. *Little*, in fact."

Damn her prideful tongue. She had told him where she lived. Charlotte had nowhere else to go and no money to get her there in any event. Deb had sent just enough money to come to London and Charlotte had been too stupid to ask for more yesterday in all the confusion. Charlotte turned to speak more cutting words, but instead watched Sir Michael pull his wrinkled shirt over his head.

She could charge him while he was temporarily blinded by linen and bludgeon him with a Cupid if she were quick. But his dark head popped out and her chance was lost. She really was going to kill Deborah when she saw her again, if she wasn't imprisoned already for killing Sir Michael Xavier Bayard first.

Four o'clock. That gave her hours. It was clear she could not pawn Deb's necklace, worthless as it was. Perhaps she could persuade the maid, Irene, or Mrs. Kelly to help her escape. There must be petty cash for the household stashed somewhere in a sugar jar. She would plead. She would beg. They must know what a wicked man their master was. And if he came to find her in Little Hyssop, she could shoot him with her papa's old blunderbuss and afterward say he was an intruder, his big body prostrate at her feet. She smiled.

"You should do that more often." Sir Michael spoke from the doorway, sinfully handsome even when dressed in clothes that had lain on the floor all night.

"What?"

"Smile. I was beginning to think you didn't have teeth. Oops, I forgot. You did bite me, didn't you? In several places." He ran a long forefinger down the column of his throat.

Oh merciful heavens. She had bitten his tongue in anger, but the other bites, love bites when she'd nipped his delicious salty skin, were done under the influence of an altogether different emotion. She was going to Hell with Satan as her tour guide.

Bay rubbed his forehead in impatience. Mr. Mulgrew droned on, oblivious to the fact that Bay longed to leap across his desk and shake the man. He stabbed an ivory-handled letter opener into his palm instead.

"Yes or no?" he asked, interrupting, watching a drop of blood rise. He hadn't intended such self-abuse. Charlotte Fallon was taking a toll on him. That is, her sister was. "Will you undertake the effort to find the Bannisters or shall I have to find someone else? I have a four o'clock appointment."

The large man flushed, adding to the high color he already sported from what had to have been several pints at lunchtime. Bay was beginning to think he had been ill-advised to seek Mr. Mulgrew's assistance, even if he had come highly recommended. After all, he'd heard wonderful things about Deborah, and look where that had led him—wrangling with a sodden Mr. Mulgrew, whose every breath bespoke middling-priced ale and fried fish.

"Beggin' yer pardon, my lord. My wife says I do go on."

"Sir Michael will do. I'm a mere baronet, not a member of the aristocracy."

"Indeed, indeed, your lordship" the man said, still fawning. "Ye haven't given me much to go on. The Continent is a mighty big place."

Bay well knew it. He'd tramped over half of it in the service of His Majesty until the Corsican upstart's defeat. Civilian life suited him very well, and he would be thoroughly ecstatic to rid himself of the sisters Fallon and enjoy the rest of his life.

"Bannister planned to marry yesterday. They might even still be in town. Look at ships' passenger lists. I don't have to tell you your business." Surely Deborah had not had the time to sell his grandmother's necklace already. And she would probably like to wear it awhile, even to her wedding. Odd that Deborah had not invited Charlotte, even if it was a hole-and-corner affair. Bay picked up a graphite pencil and began to draw the necklace on a piece of stationery. If he'd had time, he could have rendered the necklace in paint on watercolor paper upstairs. He was a fair artist, or had been before the art had been drummed out of him.

Mulgrew patted down the pockets of his tweed coat until he came upon his spectacles. *Good lord*. A private investigator who couldn't see. Bay handed him the paper anyway and watched the man hold it up against his nose.

"Hmm. Rubies and diamonds, you say? Worth a pretty penny."

"Quite. A piece like this doesn't come along every day. Canvass reputable jewelers, and disreputable ones as well. I don't care what happens to the Bannisters, but I want the necklace back."

Mulgrew puffed up. "See here, I don't do murder. Got a young family, I do. But if it's murder you want—"

Bay longed to bang his head against his desk. "You misunderstand me, Mr. Mulgrew," he said icily. "I had understood you were very good in the retrieval business, returning missing persons to those who mislaid them. I most assuredly do *not* want you to come back with Arthur Bannister and his wife cuffed to your wrists."

The man beamed. "Ah. Lord Egremont's wayward daughter. One of my most difficult cases. A regular she-devil, she was. But I am," he interjected hastily, "very discreet. I'll not breathe a word of this business with your ex-mistress, I swear. Doesn't do to have the world know you couldn't hold on to your woman. To be thrown off for a bit of sparkle, why, that's just sad."

Bay gritted his teeth. Sad didn't begin to cover it. "Thank you for your sympathy, Mr. Mulgrew." He slid the banknotes across the mahogany. The man was almost as expensive as Deb had been. Bay hoped he got a better return on his investment this time. He looked at his watch.

"I'll take the hint, Sir Michael," Mulgrew said cheerfully, pocketing the money. He extended a chapped red paw. Bay shook it. "Good luck to us both, then, eh? Hope I find your old doxy and you find a new one. But there's something to be said for marriage, you know. Kiddies. They settle a man."

On that unwanted advice, Mr. Mulgrew shuffled out of Bay's study, a burly bear who couldn't possibly go undercover and remain undetected for a moment. Bay wondered what his procedures were, but they didn't matter as long as the rubies got deposited in a safe. He went through a bit of correspondence, then ordered a bath, his second of this misbegotten day.

He supposed he was overly fastidious, but Bay had too often been walking dirt as a soldier. A hot bath, a close shave, and a bit of lime cologne made a man feel human again. As a considerate lover, he wanted to appeal to a woman's sense of smell as well as all the others. Charlotte would have nothing to complain about when she moved down his body.

He laughed. He certainly didn't intend to hold Charlotte Fallon to her sister's contract, but it wouldn't hurt for her to believe he did. Until he was certain she was innocent, he would torment her a bit. She was surprisingly passionate for a spinster with cats, and very beautiful, almost as beautiful as Deborah. Less polished to diamond-hard perfection, of course, but somehow more appealing for it. More real. Apart from the loss of the jewelry, Bay thought the sister switch would work out very nicely indeed.

Until he married again. Which he must do, if only to please Mr. Mulgrew.

Chapter 3

She had brought two dresses to London with her, and worn another. One was gray, one was gray, and another was a bluish gray that did something nice for her eyes. She selected the latter. Irene looked faintly horrified as she helped her into it.

"Are you sure you don't want to wear one of your sister's gowns? They are ever so pretty."

"Yes, and she took them with her." Deb did in fact leave four dresses behind. One had a tear at the bodice as though someone had been impatient to get at what was underneath, two were cut scandalously low, and the fourth was much too dashing for four o'clock in the afternoon. And cherry red. She might as way hang a HARLOT sign around her neck and parade through Covent Garden. Charlotte had never had seven dresses at her disposal in her lifetime and wasn't about to have her head turned now. Irene did something quite masterful with her hair and then Charlotte covered it with one of her starched spinster's caps. She'd packed six of those. Irene looked crushed.

If Charlotte had not been in such a hurry to rush to her sister's side, she would have brought her tatting with her. She longed to have something to do as she waited in the downstairs parlor for Sir Michael. She'd made enough lace to cover the altars of every parish church within a ten-mile radius of Little Hyssop, but she also quietly sold her best pieces to a London modiste that Deborah had recommended. Charlotte survived on the fashionable whims and trims of women in the ton. She wasn't quite in competition with blind French nuns, but if she did say so herself, her work was very fine. Her hands were uncomfortably idle now, and a little shaky. The gilt clock over the mantel ticked inexorably toward twelve and four. Charlotte searched the drawer in the card table under the front window and found a worn deck of cards. She could play solitaire and watch traffic on the street. Get her wits battle-ready when Sir Michael stalked down the sidewalk like the predator he was.

She wouldn't want to face him in a true battle. Deb had said he'd been in the army, and he still had a quiet fierceness about him that seemed quite deadly. He was tall, broad, and lean in all the right places, his chestnut hair still cropped close, his eyes so dark they seemed black. He was handsome without being a bit pretty and had the requisite saber scar on his cheek. She hadn't noticed any other scars, since she was shamefully too busy having one orgasm after the next and her eyes were shut. It surprised her that he had to pay a woman for companionship.

She began to turn the cards up on the table. The king of hearts was winking at her, wearing his crown, a smile, and nothing else. Charlotte rifled through the deck. All the kings, queens, and knaves were entirely nude. With a cry of disgust, she swept the cards up and promptly shoved them back in the dark.

What could she expect from a house on Jane Street? Even buried in the country, she knew all about it. Deb had been over the moon to acquire a protector who owned a house at this fabled address. The crème de la crème of courtesans resided here in this short cul-de-sac—a dozen houses, a dozen women who were perfectly expensive and expensively perfect. To be a Jane Street mistress was an affirmation of one's infinite worth. To be a Jane Street property owner was to be the envy of every man in the ton. Deeds passed only through death, extortion-ate fees, and occasional deceit. Charlotte wondered which way Sir Michael came upon his.

The dwelling itself was small and neat. There was a reception room and dining room on the ground floor, a smaller parlor, Deb's bedroom and dressing room on the first floor, and three rooms above where Irene and Mrs. Kelly slept. Charlotte's visit to the basement kitchen had been fruitless. Neither Irene nor Mrs. Kelly had any intention of helping her flee. They actually thought her quite mad to cast aspersions on Sir Michael's character, and had nothing favorable at all to say about Deborah. Charlotte had gone out to the well-kept walled garden and kicked a tree.

So here she sat in the front window for all the world to see, or at least the fallen women of Jane Street and their keepers. The irony was not lost on one of the Fallen Fallon sisters. Deb might have embraced her reputation, but Charlotte had spent the past ten years hiding in Little Hyssop, far from her crime. Her parents' untimely death had enabled her to start a new life, and now wretched Sir Michael Xavier Bayard, named for two saints but undoubtedly at Satan's right hand, had the power to ruin her completely.

She saw him immediately as he rounded the corner. Jane Street was within walking distance of the finer clubs and households in London, handy for a man to slip away to when his cards were unfaithful or his wife boring, or vice versa. Charlotte had to give her sister some credit. At least she did not bed married men. Sir Michael was therefore unattached. It was a mystery how a man his age had avoided the Marriage Mart for so long.

Charlotte left the window and arranged herself on a chair in front of the empty fireplace. It was very comfortable. She imagined she could be cozy sitting in it in front of a roaring fire this winter, tatting or reading away. But if she was still here by then, she really, really would kill Deborah. It was almost June. She had her little garden to tend and the cats to feed. How long would it take Arthur to slink back and face the wrath of his father, the earl?

Bay did not raise the knocker but entered with his key. She folded her hands in her lap and tried to look uninterested as he entered the room. She'd have to practice later in the mirror to perfect her most off-putting expressions. Supercilious. Arrogant. Condescending. Insolent. She would match him, look for look.

"What the devil do you have on your head, woman?"

"Good afternoon to you too, Sir Michael," she said primly.

"You look—you look ridiculous. Like an old tabby. How old are you, anyway?"

Charlotte selected 'superior' from her facial repertoire. "A gentleman never asks a lady her age." She decided to ignore his snort when she called herself a lady. He certainly was no gentleman, either. "May I ring for tea?"

"I don't want any bloody tea. Do you suppose I have any brandy left, or did Bannister drink it all?"

Charlotte felt her cheeks grow warm. Deb really did have a lot to answer for. "I know there is sherry." She had drunk altogether too much of it yesterday, plus the wine at dinner. No wonder she let a stranger make love to her in the middle of the night. At Sir Michael's nod, she went to the drinks cupboard and found the bottle and two glasses.

"You said your sister is younger. What does that make you? Thirty-five? Forty?"

Charlotte stopped midpour. "I'll have you know I'm only thirty!" At his triumphant smirk, she knew he had deliberately provoked her into revealing the truth. She handed him his glass, slopping a bit onto his immaculate bottle-green sleeve. Oops.

He did not seem to notice. "I'm afraid no mistress of mine, no matter how long in the tooth, will be permitted to wear a dust rag upon her head. Kindly remove it."

"I will not." Charlotte had made the cap and its lace trim, and if she did say so herself, she'd done a creditable job.

"You will. And that dress. Fit for the dustbin along with the cap. Did Deborah leave you nothing to wear? Madame Duclos sent me an astronomical bill." He crossed his leg and leaned back on the sofa, looking right at home. Damn the man.

She set the sherry down with a click on the piecrust table.

"I will not wear clothes that a man other than any future husband I might obtain has paid for. I have some standards, despite my sister's reputation."

"Well then." His dark brows knit, his lips pursed. "I also have standards, Miss Fallon. And I believe I have the perfect solution to our difference of opinion. You shall just have to go naked."

Charlotte yanked her fichu to her chin. "Never! You'll not see or touch my body again, sir. Unless I am dead and you are assisting the undertaker."

"A most unpleasant task. Some men might flinch. But I have been at war, Miss Fallon. I have seen my share of dead bodies. I allow as how it would be a shame to kill you in order to look my fill at your womanly form, but I've killed as well."

Charlotte spluttered. "First you threaten me with jail, and now murder if I don't do your bidding? You are a fiend!"

"This from a woman who uses her teeth and hairbrush in such unseemly, some might even say violent, fashion. You are a passionate woman, in bed or out, Charlotte, despite your futile attempts to appear otherwise."

"I have not given you leave to use my Christian name," Charlotte said, digging her nails into the padded arms of her chair.

"Come. You gave me leave to use your body last night and this morning. We have been intimate. We will be intimate again. Call me Bay, and I'll call you Charlotte. Although Charlotte is dreadfully dull." His face lit. "Why, *you* are the Charlie Deb was always going on about! The little minx. She used you to make men jealous, you know. All those girlhood adventures she'd regale us poor fools with. We thought you were some friend of Harfield's."

George. Viscount Harfield. Their childhood neighbor and Deb's seducer. To be fair, Deb had probably seduced him. She had been young and naive enough to hope for marriage. George quickly came to his senses once his father promised destitution and ruin, but he had kept Deb comfortably until he married six years ago. If Deb had a heart to break, Harfield had probably broken it. Since then Deb had gone through men, each richer and more influential than the last. Charlotte had never heard of Sir Michael Xavier Bayard, but he must have something besides his handsome face to have intrigued her sister.

"Charrrlie." Sir Michael—well, she supposed she'd have to think of him as Bay—rolled her name around in his mouth like a fine wine. "I like it."

Charlotte huffed. She was getting nowhere with him, losing ground every minute he sat sprawled on the sofa grinning at her. Everything she had planned all day to say was fragmented somewhere in the recesses of her mind. Snatches of "God-fearing woman" and "reasonable man" warred with each other, neither victorious. In the end, she kept her mouth shut, and opened it only to drink her sherry, which she desperately needed.

"Charlie, my dear, I thought we might set some ground rules for our association while we wait for your delinquent sister Deborah to return. Are you sure she made no mention of their exact destination?"

Charlotte shook her head. Silence was not golden.

"I am a reasonable man." Charlotte choked on her sherry and stared at him. Was he a mind reader as well as a satyr? "I will never expect you to perform acts which you consider to be repugnant. But I do have my favorite vices and will encourage you to become accustomed to them."

Charlotte's ears were turning red, she knew it. The rest of her was following suit. While Sir Michael—Bay, blast him—laid out his preferences in the bedroom, she felt like a fireball of mortification, soon to explode into thousands of crimson flames. Perhaps it was time to faint. A fake faint this time, of course, which might deter him from this litany of perversion and pestilence. Mama had always advised a swoon when one heard things one did not care to listen to. Tradesmen's entreaties, for example. Harfield's father, the Earl of Trent, when he discovered his son had run off with Deborah. The vicar's sermons afterward. Swooning was a useful feminine accomplishment, effective if used sparingly. But as Bay had done nothing yesterday to help her off the floor—had instead stared with lasciviousness at her exposed parts—Charlotte ruled out another drop to the carpet.

Bay waved his hand in the air. "Are you getting all this? You look a bit dazed. And red. I can repeat it all if you like."

That was it. She was done for. If she had to listen to one more word, he *would* be consulting with the undertaker. Best just to get on with it until she figured out a way to disappear. Mama said sometimes one simply had to close one's eyes and do unpleasant things in life. Charlotte suspected she was talking about the marriage act, but it was not as though she was saving herself for marriage.

"Very well. Let's go upstairs now and do it all."

Bay had nearly admitted that he was playing a joke upon her, that he'd engaged the services of a private detective, that she was welcome to return to Little Glossup or wherever she lived, when she tore the ugly little cap from her head and flung it in a corner. She lifted her plump white arms and pulled out the pins, and cascades of black curls helped cover her ugly dress. That was it. He was done for. He was now tangled in the sheets, panting like a madman. Who knew such crude talk could stir this little gray governess to the heights of decadent sensuality? He'd never been able to say no to a woman, more was the pity, and he couldn't find it in his heart to say no to Charlie Fallon. He wasn't sure he could sustain such dirty talk, but he was willing to make the sacrifice if it brought him more afternoons and evenings like this one.

She was exquisite. Now that he had seen her in daylight, he realized she was more rounded than her sister, her face softer. He had thought Deborah the fluffy kitten, but it was Charlie who was cushy, her alabaster flesh worthy of the Italian art he collected. He kept some minor works downstairs in this house, but the majority of his collection was in his town house a few long streets away. He was very fond of nudes, and he was very fond of Charlie Fallon. As long as she wasn't speaking or throwing things at him.

He had given her little to complain of. He'd even done some of the naughty things he promised to do when she had turned that alarming shade of red. She looked like a well-satisfied woman now, her upturned blue eyes glazed, her lips pink and swollen from his kisses. His hand remained on one full breast, his thumb stroking a berried nipple. If only she were wearing the ruby necklace, the picture would be perfect.

He suckled the nipple he'd readied between his fingers until she gave another groan. "I find I'm starving, Charlie. We'll both need some nourishment if we are to do all the things on my list. I'm going to have Mrs. Kelly prepare us a tray."

He got up and went into the dressing room. Parked in front of the fireplace was a copper tub, specially designed to hold two comfortably, three if he was in the mood. He pulled a black robe from the cupboard where he kept his spare clothes, and checked what had been Deborah's. It was empty. She had left just the few gowns in the armoire in the other room. He was damned if he was going to go to the expense all over again of dressing his new mistress, but he truly was damned if he didn't. Looking at Charlie in her gray gloom made his eyes hurt.

He slipped out of the bedroom past a dozing Charlie and went downstairs to consult with Mrs. Kelly. She was well-used to his erratic schedule and attire, and presented him with the week's menus for his approval without batting an eyelash at his dishabille well before sunset. He left orders for more brandy to be purchased and carried up a bottle of champagne and two glasses. He might be missing the strawberries, but he and Charlie had much to celebrate.

He paused on the stairs and examined a lovely little painting by an unknown artist depicting the seduction of a lovely little virgin. Her draperies were billowing in the wind, revealing her lovely not-so-little form. The expression of lust on her anxious lover's face told the whole story. Like the painted gentleman, Bay was thinking with his cock again, damn it. It was entirely possible that Charlie was as guilty as her sister in this whole affair. Just because she could make herself blush scarlet meant nothing. Their mama had probably taught the Fallon sisters exactly how to trap a man—fainting on cue, weeping, dropping handkerchiefs, showing more than a bit of ankle or bosom. What did he know about her, after all?

He'd made it his business to know all about Deborah, who had come to town with Viscount Harfield ten years ago. Bay had met her at a boisterous party once when he was home on leave and been stunned, like everyone else, by her wit and beauty. She seemed quite devoted to George until his marriage, but moved on with alacrity to Baron Perham, a widower with notorious sexual appetites. Perham was followed by Fellowes and Stuart, a young marquess and a younger duke respectively. Bay had felt some pride succeeding a duke. Deb could have picked anyone.

And then she picked Arthur Bannister over him.

Of course, Arthur had offered marriage. Who would have imagined the Divine Deborah interested in domesticity? And becoming a plain Mrs. at that. Women were a mystery that Bay had spent the past twenty years trying and failing to fathom. His wife was a prime example.

Charlie was no longer pinned to the bed like a sex-drugged butterfly but sitting in a chair, her hideous elephant-colored robe covering her lush curves. She had even tried to tidy her hair, but Bay recalled most of her hairpins were scattered downstairs on the parlor floor. He'd go down later and toss them into the street if he had to. Nothing should tame his kitten-like Venus, purring and clawing.

"I've brought us some champagne. Mrs. Kelly will bring dinner up later."

"To the bedroom?" Charlie sounded shocked.

"It will save us time. All those stair steps. Down, and then up again. This way we can get right back into bed when we're done. We might even bring a crumb or two along."

Charlotte screwed up her face. Her words yesterday indicated she was not amenable to lovemaking that incorporated food. He'd soon convert her to his way of thinking. The thought of licking honey from her—

"It's my turn to set some ground rules," she said, her voice brittle.

Bay set the bottle down. No point in popping the cork if she was in a mood. He could scarcely believe that this was the same woman whose every velvet inch had given him such recent satisfaction.

"I have agreed to your suggestions thus far, repugnant as they are. I also agree to wait here until Deborah returns, or until we hear from her so I can tell her you have kidnapped me."

"I believe the term 'kidnap' is incorrect. That usually involves abduction from one's home and the use of force. I found you in my bed, in *my* home, Charlie. Perhaps I should add trespassing to your other infractions. I have not used force. If anything, you have forced *me*. To hold me down like that while you had your wicked way—why, I couldn't escape without doing myself some bodily harm." He watched the beginnings of her rosy bloom. He counted the seconds until she was full vermillion.

"Nevertheless. I am here against my will. I'll honor my sister's covenant with you as she seems to have taken your property—accidentally, I'm sure—and I don't wish to go to jail in her place. But you cannot visit me whenever it strikes your fancy. We must work some sort of schedule for—for sexual activities. Every sixth Sunday of the month, say. That way I can mentally prepare myself." She shuddered as if his touch was anathema to her, which he knew it was most assuredly not from her cries of "Oh, God yes, fuck me!" earlier. "And I don't want to take meals with you. I don't want to take meals *on* you. If we are ever in the position to be dining together, we shall be sitting downstairs in the dining room, I at one end of the table and you at the other."

Bay stifled his grin, which would only inflame her further. She was adorable in her umbrage. He could play along for a bit. "Every *sixth* Sunday? Are you certain you can wait that long?" He tapped a finger on his chin. "And surely there can be no more than five Sundays in any given month. It's meant to be a day of rest, too. Our activities this afternoon were not precisely *restful*, Charlie. I declare you wore me right out."

"Every Saturday then."

"Every night of the week. Including Sunday. And possibly some afternoons when I'm not otherwise engaged."

She turned white for a change. "Monday, Wednesday, and Friday. Evenings only."

"Every weeknight. I'll give you weekends off if you behave yourself." He'd have to eat red meat and swill beef tea all Saturday and Sunday to restore his prowess for Monday. Charlotte Fallon was a tigress.

She looked as if she wanted to say more, a lot more. Instead she nodded curtly. "Very well. I am not hungry. Or thirsty. Kindly tell Mrs. Kelly."

Well, the pendulum had swung and the tigress was now a cranky cat with fleas. Bay couldn't bother to cajole her back to bed. Perhaps she was suffering from a bizarre brain manifestation that enabled her to turn from scorching hot to frigid, blushing red to icy pale, courtesan to spinster. There was a possibility he'd been unfair to challenge her with such suggestive suggestions and she was regretting her complicity. Too bad.

"I'll see you tomorrow evening, then. I'll just dress and eat downstairs if you don't mind. I wouldn't want to disappoint Mrs. Kelly since she's gone to the trouble of cooking us dinner. It doesn't do to annoy a woman with access to sharp knives."

Chapter 4

The nerve of him! He was still downstairs, smoking a cigar in the house instead of the garden if her nose was any judge. What had gotten into her? Well, besides him with his absolutely enormous member and his skillful tongue and fingers. Charlotte had never in her life behaved in such a fashion, wasn't aware that there was such a fashion in which to behave. She'd blocked out Deb's 'helpful hints' over the years, swearing never to lie with another man again after Robert. Two days on Jane Street and she was a confirmed slut. There must be something in the air.

She was so hungry she regretted turning away dinner. The house was small enough for her to smell it too, and each clink of cutlery and Bay's groans of pleasure and lipsmacking had driven her over the edge. He had been so audible deliberately, she was sure, making her suffer for her prideful refusal to share a meal with him. When oh when would he leave so she could raid the kitchen?

He was a fiend. An archfiend. A malevolent incubus dressed as a benign baronet, infecting society with lust and sin. Infecting her, anyway. She had spent the last ten years driving lust and sin right away with the biggest stick she could find. It helped that her heart had been shriveled. And that Robert was lost to her forever.

Charlotte hung her robe up in the armoire and lifted her nightgown from the shelf. She glanced at her satchel in the corner. She supposed she ought to unpack whatever she had crammed into it before she caught the London stage. When she was frantic to rescue Deborah. Ha. Who was going to come to rescue her? To get her out from under the thumb and every other inch of Sir Michael Xavier Bayard?

Charlotte put her few belongings in Deb's drawers. No, not Deb's. Deb had ceded her role as mistress quite permanently, and somehow Charlotte had been persuaded to assume it, with a fervor that she found incomprehensible and embarrassing. She loathed the man who called himself Bay, as if he were a tropical turquoise body of water or a chestnut horse or the howl of a demented dog. He had no hesitation to punish her for her sister's transgressions—if one thought that hours of sublime sensual pleasure was punishment.

Charlotte put an ear to the bedroom door and listened for any movement. A pleasant lingering of cheroot smoke drifted into her nostrils, but the house was dark and silent save for the steady ticking of the clocks. The timepiece in the cherub's stomach at her bedside told her it was gone on eleven. He must have left while she availed herself of the discreetly screened commode chair in the dressing room. Tiptoeing down the carpeted stairs holding a candle, she stopped at the painting of a half-clad virgin fleeing from a roué who bore no little resemblance to the picture's owner. She had seen that smile over her not long ago.

And then it hit her. Deb had teasingly spoken about making off with Bayard's paintings. Said they were valuable. Lord knows, there were enough of them all through the downstairs rooms. There were breasts and bottoms and nipples and nooks on every wall, some near to life-size. But the artwork on the stairs was a manageable size, as was the one hanging directly below it. Charlotte could take them down herself, cut the canvas from their frames, and sell them. All she needed was enough money to hide out for a few weeks. Not to Little Hyssop, but a completely foreign destination where she knew no one and no one knew her.

The pitfalls of her almost-midnight madness were immediately apparent. She would actually be stealing this time, and she could, she supposed, hang if she was caught. Bay didn't seem to be the type of man who forgave and forgot—look at what he was putting her through with Deborah's folly. If she suddenly appeared in some out-of-the-way country village, she might as well take out an advertisement in a newspaper. Strangers were always the gleeful target of gossip; she would not go unremarked. It had taken her years to worm her way into Little Hyssop's good graces, and she didn't have the patience now for the subterfuge. But the most troublesome aspect was if Deb contacted her—or even, miracle of miracles, returned the bloody necklace—she wouldn't know it. She might be on the run for the next six months.

The candle wavered as she heaved a sigh. She would think better on a full stomach. But when she reached the top of the steps that led down to the kitchen, she nearly tumbled straight down when she heard the laughter. *His* laughter. A little rough, as though he was unaccustomed to doing such a thing. Light and shadow flickered in the stairwell.

And then Irene giggled, a perfectly pure tinkly sound.

Good Lord. Charlotte's stomach flipped. He was having it on with the maid, who was almost young enough to be his daughter. Men were beasts, disgusting, diabolical dogs, and that was an insult to canines everywhere. When she heard Mrs. Kelly say, "That's quite enough for one night, Sir Michael. You want to keep us awake all night to have your fun, don't you? You'll get another chance tomorrow to try your luck again," she had heard enough. If Irene was young enough to be his niece at the very least, Mrs. Kelly could be his grandmother.

Clutching her candle with both fists, she flew down the stairs. Three pairs of eyes turned to her. Bay and his servants sat at the long pine table, the devil's deck of cards scattered on its surface. Mrs. Kelly had a little pile of walnuts in front of her, and Irene and Bay had nothing. Charlotte stared at them stupidly.

"Care to join me, Charlie? These two want to go to bed and deny me my revenge."

"Oh, go on with you, Sir Michael. Don't be a poor sport. What can I do for you, Miss Fallon? I hope you've changed your mind about a meal. There's some lovely chicken left, and cherry tart." The housekeeper rose from the table and headed toward the larder.

Charlotte's stomach rumbled. "No, no. I'm perfectly content, Mrs. Kelly. Don't trouble yourself. I heard voices and thought there might be an intruder." Her explanation sounded lame even to her own ears.

"Don't you be worrying about the safety of Jane Street, Miss Fallon. Sir Michael will be here most nights to protect you. And the Jane Street gentlemen hire a night watchman. No one visits who doesn't belong, if you get my meaning."

Oh, she got it. If people couldn't get in without an entrée, people couldn't get out without notice, either. She was already in a prison cell, only with tasteful décor—except for the paintings.

Bay stood, rolling down his sleeves. "Well, if I have no takers, I'd best be off. I'll see you ladies tomorrow. Late. I'm afraid Miss Fallon doesn't care to dine with me, Mrs. Kelly, but I'll probably rustle up a midnight snack. Good night." He blew them all a kiss and let himself out the tradesmen's door.

Mrs. Kelly's lips were set in disapproval. "That man needs to eat proper after all he's been through, Miss Fallon. He has a fool of a French chef at the other house. Muck and rubbish he cooks and calls it *gourmet*." To Charlotte's amusement, Mrs. Kelly pronounced the 't' at the end of the word. It was clear she disliked the chef and his language.

"I might change my mind about his dining here, then," Charlotte said, remembering the bit about knives. Mrs. Kelly looked sweet, but one never knew. "I'll go upstairs now so you can go to bed."

Mrs. Kelly clucked. "Oh, sit down, dearie. I may be old, but I'm not deaf. Your belly's empty. Irene, poke at the fire a little.

It gets damp down here at night, Miss Fallon, but Sir Michael likes to come down anyway. Reminds him of home."

Charlotte stacked up the naughty cards. "You've know him since he was a boy?"

"Oh, no. Not me. But my sister cooked for his grandmother for years before she passed. My sister, not his grandmother, although she's gone now, too. Irene, the milk jug if you please."

"It's terribly late," Charlotte said, upset she was causing so much trouble. "Really, I know my way around a kitchen. I can get my own food."

"Nonsense. Sir Michael has hired us to take care of you and so we shall. Sit."

Charlotte sat and swallowed. "You don't mind working here? Jane Street and its women are—are notorious."

Mrs. Kelly slathered butter on a chunk of bread. "Everybody needs to get by, dearie. Sir Michael's ladies have all been easy to do for, except your sister if you'll forgive me for saying so. I can't like it that Mr. Bannister came around."

"How did he get by the night watchman?" Charlotte topped a slice of chicken with a sliver of cheese and chutney, folded it into the bread and chewed. Divine.

"Came in the daytime, he did. That's the hole in their grand security scheme. As if men can control themselves and their tallywags until dark. Of course, most of the Janes respect the gentlemen who've set them up here and don't dally unless that's what their gentlemen want them to do so they can watch. But your sister had other ideas." Mrs. Kelly put the tart down on a linen napkin. "I suppose I can't really blame her. She saw her chance to catch a husband. Lord knows, Sir Michael might never marry again, and he's sure not to marry a whore. No offense."

Bread stuck in Charlotte's throat. "Bay is married?"

"Not anymore. The less said about that, the better."

Damn. This was not the time for Mrs. Kelly to rediscover her discretion. But the housekeeper kept busy and quiet putting platters and bowls away as Charlotte ate. Mrs. Kelly had already sent Irene off to bed, but was yawning herself.

"Please let me do the washing up," Charlotte said once she had drunk the last of the milk and eaten every morsel. "I live alone at home, you know."

"Well, if you're sure—"

"I am. And tell Irene not to worry about me in the morning. I don't need chocolate in bed or anything. You should both sleep in."

Mrs. Kelly snorted. "No chance of that. I've been rising before the cock crows all my life. But thank you, Miss Fallon. See you in the morning."

Charlotte stood in the dim kitchen. So Bay had been married. She wondered how and when his wife had died. If she knew, she might be able to make more sense out of the man, whose quicksilver moods were unsettling. Tonight with the servants he had been impish and youthful, but she had experienced his wrath and cutting tongue firsthand. She stepped into the scullery to scrub her plate and rinse out the glass.

What on earth was she thinking? Tomorrow she was stealing the man's paintings and running away.

Chapter 5

Mrs. Kelly had set forth to do some shopping. Charlotte had given her a list of her 'favorite' foods—things that would be a touch difficult or time-consuming to find, even in a metropolis as large as London. Mrs. Kelly's eyes crinkled when Charlotte claimed she was anxious to have a special late dinner with Bay to make up for last night. Mrs. Kelly, the romantic fool, was an absolute puddle when it came to the baronet.

Irene was more difficult to get rid of. She had a host of duties to attend to. Charlotte didn't expect a butler, but maintaining the house, even if it was small, was a lot for the two women. If she had stayed, she might have been tempted to pitch in. She gathered Deb had run them ragged.

Her mama would have been horrified to know how she lived in Little Hyssop. Even when her parents couldn't pay their servants' wages, they had plenty of them. Charlotte lived entirely alone within her garden gate. She swept her floors. She did her laundry. She cooked, preserved, pickled. She had been tempted a time or two to raid Deborah's Mistress Museum upstairs when her funds were low, but had thus far refused to pawn any of the treasures. Fortunately, she did not have such scruples when it came to Sir Michael Xavier Bayard.

Irene was out with her own list and Charlotte was armed with one of Mrs. Kelly's sharp knives. Her repacked valise was at her feet. Charlotte rolled the two paintings into it, fastened the latch, and looked around the hallway. A woman could feel at home here, she supposed. But she would be homeless for the indeterminate future. She'd get word to Deb somehow, if she could remember the name of the dead uncle's estate in Kent. Something End. It began with a B, although it wasn't Bannister. She wished she'd paid more attention when Deborah had lectured her.

Charlotte had done a very shameful thing packing, somehow worse than taking the paintings. Bay's letters to Deborah were tucked in her case. They were the closest thing Charlotte would ever get to a romantic correspondence, and she was impressed how someone like the fiend had such an unfiendish turn with words. The bit about the rubies reflecting the light was quite lovely. It was all wasted on Deborah, of course, who didn't have a romantic bone in her body.

Straightening her shoulders as she hefted the luggage, she was glad she'd been in too much of a hurry to pack much. The bag was light, and it gave her the perfect reason to send Irene off for necessities.

She knew exactly where to go. Her papa had kept the lines of communication open with a Mr. Peachtree, who at one time owned more of the Fallon objets d'art than the Fallons did. According to Papa, he was sharp but fair, and they had even become friends of a sort. Mr. Peachtree had an address she could recall at least, and she marched toward it.

Several hours later, Charlotte was sitting in her stocking feet in Mr. Peachtree's office. There was a hole that exposed her left pinky toe, which was mortifying. He had locked her old boots in his safe, after telling her to remove them. At gunpoint. Mr. Peachtree possessed a tiny silver pistol, but he assured her that size did not matter. The paintings were locked in the safe as well. He'd sniffed at Deb's paste necklace but threw it in for good measure.

He had repeated his scolding five times now by Charlotte's count. That he was a reputable businessman, that Sir Michael had a standing order to acquire Italian life studies, that he in fact had sold one of the paintings she brought to Sir Michael himself. That any dealer in London would know that Sir Michael was the owner of record and that she was a vicious little thief. That it was an excellent thing her parents had been dead these past ten years. That the only reason he had not called for Bow Street was the affection he felt for her papa all those years ago. How ashamed he would be to discover his daughter's dishonesty, not to mention her lovely mama, who had tried to raise her daughters as ladies despite the family's impecunity. One sister a whore, Mr. Peachtree had opined, the other selling that which did not even belong to her. Deborah, at least, sold only what was hers to sell. There were a few Bible verses tossed in just in case Charlotte didn't fully understand his diatribe.

Bay came at last, resplendent in a deep brown coat and buff trousers. His topboots were blindingly polished. Charlotte would bet her walnuts there were no holes in *his* stockings.

"Good afternoon, Peachtree, Charlie." Bay seemed unruffled, which frightened Charlotte to her core. Mr. Peachtree removed the key from his waistcoat pocket and walked to his safe. He presented Bay with the paintings, her boots, and the worthless necklace. Charlotte decided it was best just to say nothing until they were out of Mr. Peachtree's earshot. For then he would know her to be a thief and a liar *and* a whore. Mr. Peachtree had not believed for one minute that her 'cousin' Bay had deputized her to sell the paintings.

Charlotte buttoned her boots with trembling hands. Bay's civility was unnerving. She half thought he was going to get down on one knee and expedite the donning of her footwear. When she overheard him smoothly explain that his country cousin had misunderstood his intentions about the paintings, she didn't know whether to be grateful or thoroughly alarmed.

Mr. Peachtree returned the silver pistol to his desk drawer. "Then I do apologize, Sir Michael. I was under the impression Miss Fallon had no living relatives save her sister. Her father never mentioned you, you see. And when she came here looking guilty as a priest peeking under a choirboy's robe, I thought it best to inform you. Nervous as a long-tailed cat in a room full of rocking chairs, she was. I've seen my share of crooks in this line of work as you can imagine. I know the signs."

"You did the right thing, Peachtree. And I'm ever so grateful that the authorities weren't called. Wouldn't want to cause further family scandal. The Fallon sisters have always been a bit of a trial to us."

Mr. Peachtree glared at her in triumph but was wise enough not to speak.

Bay adjusted his gloves. "Do keep an eye out for me, won't you? I won't rest until I'm in possession of another Maniero. That man knew his women, what? Come along, Cousin Charlie. It's time for your medicine."

Charlotte followed him out of the shop with a sinking heart. Bay flagged down his carriage as it made its way around the corner with one hand, gripping Charlotte's elbow with the other. "Where precisely were you planning to go, Cousin Charlie? Little Jessup? France? You do know you could have booked passage to India and lived like a ranee for a year if Peachtree had fallen for your scheme."

"Deb said the paintings at the house were minor works."

"Ah. Deb. I should have known she had a hand in this. Charlie, you continue to disappoint me. What may be minor to Deb is still very major, I do assure you." He helped Charlotte into the carriage with unnecessary force.

"Then why do you keep such valuable things at Jane Street?" Charlotte knew she was being perverse. She'd never get Sir Michael to justify her theft.

"Because, my dear, until I met you and your sister, I never had any reason to suspect my mistresses of criminal behavior. Except in the bedchamber," he added wickedly, "at my direction. I spend a great deal of time at Jane Street. Why should I not surround myself with beautiful things?"

"I—I'm sorry. But I wanted to go home! I don't belong on Jane Street."

"You certainly don't, wearing that hideous hat and the abomination under it. I'm going to burn those caps."

Charlotte checked under the brim of her hat and felt the comfort of her very own lace. "You cannot! I made them myself!"

"Well, you won't be making any more. You won't have the time. Or the hands."

Charlotte had a truly terrible feeling. The Bible encouraged selling thieves into slavery, but the Qur'an advocated cutting off the hands of thieves. She had learned that at the Little Hyssop Women's Guild when that missionary came to talk. Either way, it would be no picnic for Charlotte. Surely Bay wouldn't be so barbaric.

"Wh-what do you mean?"

"I mean, my dearest Charlie, I'm going to tie you to the bed until I tire of you and untie you." He dipped a gloved fingertip into the indentation of her chin. "But I just don't see that happening any time soon."

Slavery, then. And it might even be somewhat pleasant.

Bay was beginning to seriously regret ever clapping eyes on Deborah Fallon. If he hadn't fallen a bit in lust with her some eight or nine years ago, envying Harfield his luck in having such a delicious little neighbor to run off with, he might not be saddled with her sour sister. To think that he had almost convinced himself Charlotte was innocent. As soon as his back was turned, she'd made off with more of his property. His grandmama's necklace was one thing, but his art—it soothed his soul. It was as necessary to him as breathing. It inspired him to see the perfect form of women, fleshy and dimpled, gilded with apricot and pearl. They were constant, caught in their prime, unchanging. Idealized women who didn't lie or steal or betray. The original models may have been whores, but the artists who painted them had found their purity and humanity. In this life when women—and men, too—were so undependable, Bay liked keeping company with his pretty two-dimensional strangers.

He wondered if he should take everything down and crate it to save himself the bother of hunting Charlie down again. No. Why should he? This was his house, arranged for his benefit. It was not as if she would have the opportunity to leave the house in the immediate future. The knots were quite strong on the silk ropes.

His grandmother always said he should have chosen the navy instead of the army. She loved the ocean at their doorstep and preferred a naval uniform above all others. But when Bay had purchased his commission, it was with the intent to get face-to-face with the enemy and slice his throat. Or have his own throat sliced. He was so angry at the time, he hadn't cared which. When one is twenty and brokenhearted, one thinks very foolishly, if one thinks at all.

He put his fingers in his ears as Charlie gave another bloodcurdling scream. He was very much afraid he'd have to gag her as well, or face the disapproval of his neighbors. The Marquess of Conover next door had not set up his mistress yet, however. There was still much to-ing and fro-ing with a swarm of staff and Conover's occasional supervision. Bay was more concerned with Lady Christie on the other side, who fancied herself a bit of a godmother on the street. She might not take kindly to Bay trussing his mistress on the bed, naked and extremely unwilling. He'd also taken a page from Mr. Peachtree's book and thrown her shoes out the window into the garden in the unlikely event she found a way to escape.

Ah, well. Charlie deserved the inconvenience. But he knew Mrs. Kelly was not absolutely on board with his method of bringing Charlie Fallon to heel, and poor little Irene was so shocked he'd given her the week off to see her mum. Bay would do for Charlie himself—wash her, brush her midnight hair, feed her Mrs. Kelly's delicacies. He supposed he'd have to release her so she could use the chamber pot. He was a man of some compassion, after all. And fastidiousness.

When he was done with her, she'd not think to lift so much as one of his teaspoons from the dining room sideboard drawer.

He checked his pocket watch. Just enough time to go home and bathe and dress for dinner. The spittle the little temptress hurled in his direction had dried on his lapel, but the fact that it was there at all irritated him. Perhaps she would be so hoarse when he came back, she couldn't put that lovely mouth of hers to speech. He had other plans for it entirely, and they did not include listening to any more of her surprisingly creative epithets.

"I'm off, Mrs. Kelly," he shouted down the basement stairs. "If you need some cotton batting for your ears, don't hesitate to visit the shops again."

Mrs. Kelly hurried up, wiping her hands in her spotless apron. "I do apologize again, Sir Michael. I had no idea Miss Fallon would be so duplicitous. To send me out for Grains of Paradise when ordinary peppercorns would do. I don't know when I've been so deceived."

"It's not your fault. The Fallon sisters may look like angels but they are as devious as the devil himself. Pay no mind to her caterwauling. I shall return for dinner. What's on the menu tonight?"

"Well, *she* told me it was to be a romantic supper." She ticked the items off her flour-dusted fingers. "There's to be oysters. Asparagus. Stewed celery. Salmon en croute. Chicken in ginger sauce. Almond torte. Fresh figs in cream. Chocolate petit fours. Raspberry fool. And of course, champagne. A whole case of it from some vineyard I've never heard of."

Bay grinned. The little witch had sent Mrs. Kelly out for foods commonly considered to be aphrodisiacs, and had planned for him to consume them all alone. Well, Charlie would be joining him tonight and reap the benefits of her recipes. Not that he would need any assistance in that area. When it came to Charlie Fallon, he was hard as marble, in body and in heart.

Chapter 6

The angry tears had left dry salty tracks on her hot, flushed face. Not that she was warm. In fact, her body was covered in gooseflesh as she lay, each limb staked to a carved bedpost by lengths of white silken rope. Trust Sir Michael Xavier Bayard to have implements of torture so handy. At least he had not blindfolded her, and there was no need of a gag anymore. After all her useless shrieking, she could barely croak out her displeasure at what the fiend had done to her. The evil little clock-cupid on the nightstand told her his arrival was imminent, which was a very good thing. If he did not release her to relieve herself very soon, this day would progress from folly to festering Hell.

How she ever thought his punishment might be amusing was a complete mystery. She had been robbed of her clothes and her dignity. He had set her spinster's cap on fire, causing the lingering malodorous scent in the bedchamber. He had opened the window to the little balcony to air the room and toss out her boots, and the gauzy lace was wafting in the twilight breeze. The air had also caused her nipples to peak into hard pink points. Her hair was a snarled mess from writhing in fury. Her mama would not know which was worse—her nudity or her dishevelment.

Yes, Mr. Peachtree was right. It was a very good thing her poor mama was dead. Mama had ambitions for both her girls. She was spared the knowledge that Deb did not get George to marry her after all and that Charlotte had somehow fallen even further into disgrace than her sister. Charlotte would consider herself lucky if she didn't wet the bed.

The thud of the downstairs door brought a surge of unbalanced hope. When the demon entered the room a few long minutes later, Charlotte gave him a pathetic smile.

"Please," she whispered. "Untie me. I need to use the chamber pot."

The fiend's dark eyebrow raised. "How am I to know your intentions are honorable? You may decide to bean me with it if I let you loose."

Oh merciful heavens. Surely he wasn't going to *watch* her. She shut her eyes to the frustrated tears that were welling up again.

"Oh, very well," he relented. She felt her bonds on her wrists loosen and abstained from grabbing his head and squeezing. Punching him in his handsome straight nose. Giving him a scar to match his other cheek. Instead she rubbed the feeling back into her hands and arms as he stood over her, looking at though he wanted to fry her with thunderbolts.

"I'll need your word that you'll not kick me or try to run away."

"I promise," she croaked.

When her legs were free, she hobbled to the dressing room door. There must be something in there she could use as a weapon—a hanger, a footstool. She'd spent the afternoon contriving ever more violent imaginary attacks upon his person. Although she had always thought herself a pacifist, it was easy for her to see now why people committed murder. But if he had been angry with her before, he was apt to be even more so if she attacked him physically. It would have to be poison. Slow. Painful. Her mama said patience was a virtue, and Charlotte's chance would come to bring Sir Michael Xavier Bayard to his knees.

She concluded her business and caught sight of herself in the standing mirror. Remarkably enough, there were no permanent signs that she had been held captive by a madman and come perilously close to losing her own mind as well. She simply looked well-tumbled. She sponged her face and body quickly, for who knew when she would be free again? Lifting her chin and straightening her spine, she returned to the scene of his crime, holding her hands before her.

"See? No weapons of any kind."

"I wouldn't say that, Charlie. Some might say just looking at you like that is enough to make a man lose all his sense." He pulled open a drawer and tossed her night rail at her. "See? I've relented already. Put it on. I had planned, you know, to keep you tied up and at my mercy for a week."

"A week!" she squeaked, scrambling into the threadbare lawn. It wouldn't afford much protection, having been washed so often it was practically sheer. If she could see the shadow of her nipples, then so could Bay. She clapped an arm across her chest.

"Yes. Consider the alternative. Death by hanging, and the ropes would not be silk, my dove. But I find I cannot do it."

She looked down at her bare feet. It was too much to ask for her boots back. "Th-thank you."

"Don't thank me quite yet. I'll come up with some alternative, but I find it's difficult to think on an empty stomach. In a few minutes Mrs. Kelly is bringing the dinner you so thoughtfully planned."

Charlotte realized she was starving. She'd been too nervous to eat much breakfast and had to watch Mr. Peachtree tuck into his lunch with one hand as he held his little gun on her with the other. He'd had difficulty cutting his meat, which only served him right. She heard the rattle of dishes as Mrs. Kelly climbed the stairs.

"Here, Mrs. Kelly, let me help you." Bay sprinted from the room to take the heavy tray from the housekeeper. Charlotte snatched a brass candlestick from the mantel, concealed it under her voluminous nightgown and sat down at the cozy little table in the corner. Who knew when she could access enough poison to fell a man Bay's size? Nothing ventured, nothing gained, her mama always said. Bay came back carrying a silver tray heaped with all the delicious things she had requested. Charlotte kept her lips pressed together so her drool would not escape.

Mrs. Kelly stood in the doorway, giving her an accusatory eye. "Sir Michael, I hope you don't mind I served these courses all at once. A woman my age can't be too careful on the stairs, you know. The desserts are downstairs chilling. Please ring when you're ready."

"I can go down and fetch it," Charlotte said, her voice scratchy.

"Aye, and stab me with one of my own knives and run off, no doubt."

"I'd never harm *you*," Charlotte said truthfully.

Bay began to place morsels of food on a plate for her. As if she were still in the nursery, he cut everything into bite-size pieces with the one knife that had come on the tray. Charlotte hoped she would be allowed a fork, but she was hungry enough to eat with her fingers and lick them off to get every last smear and crumb.

"I was going to feed you as you lay tied on the bed." He handed her a silver fork.

"I would have spit the food back at you." Charlotte shoved an inch of asparagus in her mouth. Crisp, the very *taste* of green. Divine.

"I was rather afraid of that. I don't know where you learned your manners."

"My manners are perfectly unobjectionable!" Charlotte said through a mouthful of salmon and puff pastry. Or they would be if she were not trapped here. Her mama had been a stickler for propriety. She watched as Bay held a rough shell between his fingers and slipped an oyster into his mouth. His eyes half closed, he swirled the meat around his tongue, making a little sucking sound. Perhaps it was he who had the abominable manners. She closed her legs together tight to stop the betraying ache between them. She knew perfectly well what else Bay could do with that tongue. And rather hoped he would do it again.

Mrs. Kelly had outdone herself on this lovers' supper. Each portion was small yet perfect—six succulent oysters each, one fillet of chicken, a tender salmon pie the size of her fist. Champagne fizzed in the flutes that had been wrapped in their starched napkins. Charlotte fingered the fabric. Should Bay destroy all her caps, she could fashion something out of the table linens.

The food was so delectable there was little opportunity for conversation. Bay reveled in each bite, pausing only to give her looks that were steeped in sin. When their plates were empty, he stacked the dishes on the tray. "I'll fetch the dessert. You won't do anything stupid, will you?"

Charlotte brushed against the cold candlestick that was lodged against one thigh. "Of course not," she said, as scornfully as possible. Let him think he had won her over with a hot meal and a few sultry gazes, not to mention the hours she'd spent lashed to the masts of the bed.

As soon as he left, she stationed herself behind the door, testing the weight of the weapon. Charlotte would need two hands for the job. She didn't plan to kill him, just whack him a bit to make him insensible so she could dress and escape. Then she'd have to make a detour into the back garden for her footwear. It was inconveniently dark now, but she supposed if she had to, she could run through the streets of London barefoot.

She racked her brain thinking of whom she might turn to in her hour of need. George, perhaps. True, he was very married with several children, but it was indirectly his fault that she was in Jane Street to begin with. If he hadn't ruined Deborah, she wouldn't have chosen a career as a courtesan and dragged Charlotte along with her.

She could never go to Robert.

Whistling! Bay was *whistling* as he came up the stairs. How very considerate of him to give her sufficient warning. She gripped the candlestick over her head. In a second it would come down on his.

"Charlie? How did you know my favorite—"

With a ferocious cry, she struck out. She would have been more accurate if only she had kept her eyes open, but she had ever had a distaste for blood and mayhem. She managed only a glancing blow on his shoulder, enough for the figs to bounce from their bowl and roll to the floor in a creamy puddle instead of Bay's body. She found herself pressed up against the wall by man and silver tray, the scalloped edges of which dug into her stomach. "Ouch!"

"I can see," said Bay, his face thunderous, "I was mistaken taking you at your word about refraining from stupidity. Let's see now. Perpetration of fraud and entrapment, two instances of theft, and now attempted murder. I begin to think you have a low opinion of me, Charlie."

"I wasn't going to murder you, just knock you out," Charlotte said sullenly. "It's only what you deserve, keeping me a prisoner here and torturing me."

"Torture?" His smile was wide and terrifying. "You haven't begun to see torture yet. Did I tell you I was a guest of some French outlaws for a week? A very long week. It was most instructive." With a vicious little shove, he pushed the tray against her, then brought it to the table. He popped a petit four into his mouth and chewed.

Charlotte stayed rooted to the floor, knowing if she tried to run he'd be on her in a minute. She realized she still clutched the candlestick in both hands. Bay was so confident of her clumsiness he hadn't even bothered to take it away from her. Lifting her chin, she glided across the floor to put it back on the mantel, lessening the effect a bit when she squelched a fig under her left foot.

"I want to be arrested," she announced. "Newgate will be a haven of respectability compared to Jane Street. Keeping company with the lowest criminals for a lifetime is preferable to spending one more day with you."

"You wound me." He was eating a slice of almond torte now, licking his fingers. "Care for some dessert? Mrs. Kelly really is a treasure."

"I want nothing from you but my freedom!" she cried.

"You are inhuman! I assure you I am completely innocent of conspiring with Deborah. And she won't give tuppence to get me out of here. She's got what she wants now. I doubt she even remembers she has a sister."

"Now, Charlie, you do yourself a disservice. I've only known you two days and I could never forget you. Take off that horrible nightgown."

"P-pardon?"

"Don't play deaf. Although I wouldn't mind dumb. No man wants a shrew for a mistress. The nightgown, if you please."

With great reluctance, Charlotte pulled it over her head and handed it to Bay. He balled it up and threw it out the window into the garden, where it could have a late-night assignation with her boots. At least he hadn't burned it. The room was only now beginning to smell fresh. She shivered again to be exposed to him so blatantly. She had never been naked with a man before, not even Robert.

"Lie down on the bed, Charlie. I'm afraid I'm going to have to tie you up again." The man had the effrontery to look regretful.

Charlotte bit her lip. "Please don't. I'll be good."

"I have no doubt of that. You are amongst the best I've ever had." He gave her a smug smile. *Beast.* Comparing her to other women. Hundreds of them probably, scattered throughout Europe. Everything was about sex to him. Just because he was so freakishly perfect and proficient—well, she would *not* succumb to his wiles, tonight or any other night. She would lie like a stick or a stone, completely insensate to his touch. She spread herself out on the white sheets like a pagan sacrifice, closing her eyes as he pulled each insidious knot tight.

She would not look at him. She would not speak to him. She would not—

"Oh!" Something cool plopped onto her stomach. If her breasts had not been so ridiculously large she could see what he had done.

"I'm a fool for you, Charlie," he said, his voice deliciously low. He bent over and began to lick the raspberries and whipped cream from her belly. She tried to lie still—she did, really, but when the tip of his tongue circled her navel, then dipped in, she jumped. Apparently finished with her stomach, he scooped more from the bowl and rubbed a dollop of pink on one nipple, then stood back to admire his handiwork.

"This is outrageous! This is wrong!"

"I quite agree. I'm missing something." He decorated the other breast as well, heaping a mound of raspberry-streaked cream on her aureole. Charlotte knew her nipples were stiff with cold and decadence. Bay then proceeded to warm her up, suckling the sweet mixture from her bosom as one sticky finger traced a lazy curve down her stomach to her curls. When she realized where he was going to put the raspberry fool next, her mouth opened in protest. Surely he would not do something so scandalous.

But he did. The wicked gleam in his eye matched the gleaming silver spoon as he dripped the tingly mixture between her legs. She gasped from the chill and knowledge of what would soon follow. Futile tugging on her bonds only resulted in his earthy chuckle.

"Better. Much better. Pink on pink. Lie still. If you can."

He held the spoon, empty now, and traced a pattern on her inner thigh as the raspberry fool slithered downward. The edge of the spoon tickled as Bay wrote his secret message. What was he writing? What was he waiting for? She wouldn't bother begging him to stop. She couldn't beg him to begin.

He took a step back, appraising her again from head to toe. She was open to him, splayed as wide as he could tie her without causing discomfort. She flushed, embarrassed that he would see just how anxious she was for him. There was no use in pretending she wasn't interested—her nipples were as rosy and firm as fresh berries. *She* was dessert, a banquet of carnal pleasures.

And then he bent to her. Finally. She had no choice but to accept his wicked ministrations, and she had no desire to do anything else. He parted her folds, slipping one long warm finger, then two, in and out of her passage as he laved her center. The cold of the cream, the heat of his mouth on her bud sent spirals of hunger deep within. And he was still dressed, denying her access to what she needed beyond need.

She shut her eyes and let him take her over the edge, not that there was any other place for her to go. She was at the mercy of a master seducer whose patient skill wiped away the reality of the room. There was no point to looking at a painted heaven on the ceiling when Bay was escorting her to his own particular paradise. Charlotte was aware of every lick and stroke, every breath, every ripple. Her skin was on fire, her voice hoarse. And still he did not stop, when one would have to be blind and certainly deaf not to know that she had been flung off the earth too many times to count. Even if her hands had been free, she could not have pushed him away for all the ruby necklaces in the world. The exquis-ite tug and tingle on her most private place went beyond any-thing she had ever felt. His lips, his teeth, his fingers worked in wicked concert. The man was a fiend. A talented one who knew precisely how to unlock the prim Charlotte from her prison and set her free. Too free. She would drown and dis-appear in her freedom, swept away by forces she'd never imagined.

The waves came hard, one after another until she lost her voice completely. How had she lived for thirty years not knowing such a thing was possible and so necessary? Two days with Bay had completely ruined her for her cottage and cats.

Mrs. Kelly's sister had made raspberry fool often when Bay was a boy, apparently using the very same recipe. He licked the familiar tart and sweet concoction from Charlie's soft white skin, savoring her shivers and his memories of innocence. He was no longer innocent, of course, which suited the occasion, for he was going to brand Charlie Fallon with his teeth and tongue. She would not think to brain him with brass candlesticks again, or run away, or steal from him. He intended to make her his slave to passion, and from her quaking and quick breaths, he was halfway there.

He shut his insistent erection from his mind, concentrating on her pleasure, lapping the cream from each fruit-stained nipple, drawing her flesh into his mouth, suckling. Her eyes were closed, but her lips were in their telltale position of transcendence. Little rabbit. He smoothed his hand down her body, combing his fingers through her springy black curls. The contrast between her midnight hair and pearl skin was totally erotic to him. She was a creature of extremes, going from governess to goddess. From rabbit to tigress. He spooned out more raspberry fool from the crystal bowl, coating her nether lips and her own berry within.

And then he feasted. Her tang mixed with the taste of the dessert nearly unmanned him. He buried his nose in her fragrant curls, inhaling raspberries and her citrus perfume. His patient sampling of her swollen center was rewarded as she strained against her bonds, crying his name at each orgasmic jolt. *This* was the true torture, to keep her flying higher and higher until she begged him to stop. And he would not. Could not.

When he was sure she had no more fight left in her, he cut the ropes, shedding his clothes before he disgraced himself like a schoolboy. She curled around him like a cat, every inch of her skin seeking his. His cock drove into her sweet heat and he kissed her, gifting her with her own essence. She shattered and he deepened the kiss, feeling that she was branding him now, making him a slave to *her*. He was plummeting, spinning, losing his bearings.

But now she caught him. Ensnared him in her honeyed trap. Anchored him inside her, her legs wrapped around him, hips soaring up to complete the job he'd started. Control had shifted, and it was she who drove him in deeper, she who held him so tight. She who robbed his mind and rocked his body like the expert she was.

Sex was supposed to be simple, elemental. But there was

something about Charlie Fallon that complicated their coupling. She was everything he loathed—a manipulative woman—yet he couldn't get enough of her. The taste of her, with or without raspberry fool. The feel of her. The orange-y scent of her, which made him hungry to kiss her everywhere all over again.

She was a thief. A liar. A whore. And right now, those words meant nothing at all.

Chapter 7

Charlotte's body felt like it had been brutally beaten, but the truth was she had been pounded with bliss all through the night. When she woke up, all traces of Bay and what they'd shared were gone, save for the smudge of chocolate frosting on the pillowcase. At some point, he had painted her lips with the corner of a petit four, then licked her clean. The leftover fool had not gone to waste either. His cock had looked a bit silly cloaked in pink fluff when she'd taken her turn to do the licking. She'd lost count of the number of times they had brought each other to exaltation.

Charlotte struggled to sit up. The tray, even the squashed figs, had disappeared. She must have slept like the dead. She *must* stop drinking, although each bubble of champagne had burst on her tongue like a delicious explosion. She and Bay had consumed a second bottle at midnight during a slight lull in the festivities. Charlotte was uncertain precisely when she'd fallen asleep, but judging from the brightness in the room, she'd slept half the day away.

She couldn't blame the wine for the abandon she'd exhibited. But she could blame Bay. The man was a tireless seducer. As his mistress, she was supposed to seduce *him,* but he had given her very little opportunity.

She was resigned now to her role, possibly reveled in it. Poor Deb did not know what she was missing. Marriage and respectability were all very well, Charlotte supposed, but she would not trade Deb's new life for hers. Who could imagine that Charlotte was the more wicked of the Fallon sisters?

Sighing, she got out of bed and put on her robe. There was fresh water in the dressing room, quite cold now, but that's just what she needed. She was significantly sticky. When Irene came up, she'd order a bath.

No. Irene had been given an impromptu vacation. Charlotte would have to haul the bathwater up on her own. She wouldn't want Mrs. Kelly straining herself. To lose a cook of her caliber would be a sin.

Bay poked his head into the dressing room. "Ah, Sleeping Beauty. Up at last."

Charlotte had not expected to see him. In daylight, their night seemed even more delectably decadent. "G-good morning, Bay." He was still wearing his black robe, but looked far fresher than she was feeling.

"Mrs. Kelly has breakfast for us in the dining room. Just come as you are. We won't stand on ceremony. Afterward, I'll bathe you."

Charlotte stared at him, shocked. She hadn't been bathed by anybody since she was a baby. Her streak of modesty, up until she had encountered Sir Michael Xavier Bayard, had been deep and wide. Surely a protector was supposed to go off in the daytime and protect his club or his finances or something, leaving his mistress to her own devices.

"That won't be necessary."

Bay approached her, a grin on his face. He picked a sugared almond out of her tangled hair and popped it in his mouth. "Oh, Charlie, it's very necessary. We both are disgracefully dirty. And as you can see, the tub is plenty big enough for two."

Good Lord. Was she to have no privacy? But perhaps he just wanted to keep an eye on her so she wouldn't try to bolt again. Her stomach rumbled and reminded her that the first order of business was breakfast. She'd think about the bath and bolting later.

Charlotte followed Bay down the carpeted stairs. Her boots were probably ruined after spending the night out of doors, and now she didn't have a nightgown either. There were any number of things she wanted to speak to Bay about, but her mama always said a man had to eat before he could think. The sideboard was spread with enough food to feed every mistress on the street. Charlotte helped herself to eggs, toast, and a bowl of stewed fruit. She watched Bay load his plate with a variety of meats and shuddered. There was no need of meat in the morning. Then the hall clock struck once and she realized he was entitled to whatever he wanted.

She had never slept so late in her life. She had never had so much reason to sleep late. Lifting her tea to her lips, she peeked over the cup's rim at Bay, who was reading a newspaper and enjoying a forkful of sausage. He looked handsome even ingesting pork products. Suddenly, he stopped chewing.

"The announcement is in the *Times*."

"What announcement?"

"'Lately, Arthur Alistair Bannister, Esq., Bard's End, Elham, Canterbury, Kent to Miss Deborah Elizabeth Fallon, by special license.'"

Bard's End! That was it. "Does it say anything else?"

"Not a word. No mention of his father the Earl of Cranmore and no mention of Jane Street for your sister, needless to say. I daresay the earl is having an apoplexy right about now."

"Arthur could have done worse," Charlotte said loyally.

"And could have done better, but let's not argue. I wonder where they are. Are you *sure* she didn't drop any hints?"

Charlotte had hardly paid attention as Deborah babbled on four days ago. Was it possible it was only four days? Quite a lot had transpired. The only thing she remembered definitively was 'the Continent,' which had comprised far too many countries in her geography book when she was a girl. She shook her head.

"Well, I daresay they'll turn up somewhere. I have half a mind to go see Cranmore." He tossed the paper down.

She pushed her eggs to one side, her appetite gone. "Why would you?"

"Perhaps he could talk some sense into his son."

"Oh, Bay. If you were to tell the Earl of Cranmore that his new daughter-in-law stole your necklace, she'd never get Arthur's family to accept her. Please don't."

"You are softhearted, aren't you? After what your sister did, I don't see how you can defend her. Unless—"

She saw the muscle clench in his jaw. "Unless I helped her trick you, you mean. When will you believe I had nothing to do with all this? I was just minding my own business, fast asleep—"

"In *my* bed."

Charlotte waved his words away. "Fast asleep and having the most beautiful dream. It has become a nightmare I cannot wake from."

His black eyes glittered. "A nightmare? I did not get the impression you felt that way last night. Or this morning."

Charlotte stood up. "Perhaps I became somewhat deranged after being tied up naked for hours, inhaling fumes from your assault on my headwear. I obviously lost my mind."

"I'll be happy to help you find it." Bay threw his fork down with a clatter.

"I doubt you could find anything as your head is wedged so far up your—" Charlotte gasped as Bay scooped her up and headed up the stairs. "Put me down!"

"With the greatest of pleasure. In my bed. Where you belong." She pummeled his shoulders but he just squeezed her tighter. Changing her tactics, she let her body go limp.

"Playing dead, are we? That won't last long."

He wasn't even winded carrying her, and she was no sylph. How she hated him. He didn't trust her, yet lusted for her. It made no sense to Charlotte at all. But soon she was too busy to analyze the mystery of his male mind, when there were other male parts to attend to.

He could feel her eyes as he plodded back and forth with the water pails. If they needed a bath before, it was now absolutely essential. The cloud of Charlotte's scent and sex was imprinted on him. He hadn't smelled this feminine since his army days in Spain when he'd been a guest at a very pleasant brothel. Those days were thankfully behind him. He'd survived without a scratch.

Except for the rakish scar on his cheek. He had received that wound not on the battlefield, but while home on leave. He'd been told it only enhanced his beauty, but beauty was as beauty did. He felt far from beautiful. There was something about Charlie Fallon that brought out the beast in him.

She very probably was innocent, at least initially. But she had made up for lost time when she tried to steal his paintings and cosh him on the head. He didn't trust her an inch. The only way to subdue her was to fuck her senseless, which he had done, and quite masterfully if he said so himself. He needed to find her sister and get Charlotte out of his house and back to Little Hiccup before he was saddled with her permanently.

He was afraid his little thief was addictive despite all her starchy primness, maybe because of it. Charlie Fallon almost seemed the sort of woman one might marry, if one were so inclined. But she hadn't been a virgin, so how prim could she be? If she had a sad story, he didn't want to hear it. The sooner he got rid of her, the happier he would be.

After his bath, he'd go home and see if there was news from Mr. Mulgrew. Right now, he was going to wash every glistening square inch of Charlie's skin. He arranged the bath table with soap, sponges, and pitchers. Rubbing his jaw, he decided he'd shave later at home. There was no point in letting Charlie near a razor.

She hadn't moved from the bed, but was not asleep. Her cornflower-blue eyes were focused on the ceiling, the tempera home to all the angels Angelique had insisted upon. It was not his best work, and his neck had gotten an awful crick painting it. How Michelangelo had endured the Sistine Chapel truly was a miracle. Bay would have been much happier with a mirror over the bed.

"Everything is ready."

Charlotte twisted the sheet around her. "You go ahead. I'll bathe after you finish."

"Indeed you will not." He strode over and lifted her from the bed.

"Oh, do stop carrying me around like a sack of coal! Am I to be completely at your mercy, even my ablutions?"

He dropped her into the tub with a splash. "Exactly so. You are at my mercy, and I will have my wicked way with you." She scooted to one end as he unbuttoned the placket of his breeches. Just holding her in his arms for a few steps had made him hard again.

She rolled her eyes. "Please. Not again."

"No? I'll give you the opportunity to change your mind." Her breasts bobbed in the deep tub, two snowy orbs tipped with pale pink. He climbed in and stretched his toes to tickle her sweet rounded tummy. "Come here."

"I'm fine where I am." She covered her breasts with her arms. Bay felt a pang.

"Very well." He picked up one bar of lime-scented soap, lathering his hands. He scrubbed his head, neck and face, knowing all the while she hoped he was getting soap in his eyes. He reached for a pitcher and rinsed, then stood, his feet planted firmly on the copper tub's bottom. He soaped his chest, his belly, his thighs. Charlie pointedly looked at the little marble fireplace. There was no flickering fire to watch, as it was a warm spring afternoon. He knew how he could get her attention.

Sitting on the broad edge of the tub, he stroked himself, his hands slippery with suds. His cock jerked to life, although the not-so-little fellow should be napping until next Tuesday after his recent workout. Bay closed his eyes, picturing Charlie on her knees before him, water beading down her breasts. He found his rhythm, honed by years of solitude and celibacy. He lifted one eyelid and saw her staring, her lips parted.

"Touch me, Charlie," he ordered, his voice rough.

She picked up the sponge, then dipped it into the water. Moving toward him, she dabbed lightly at his cock to remove the soap.

"Harder."

Her blue eyes widened. He was putting himself in her hands, literally.

She rubbed the sponge against his belly, then brushed along the underside of his penis with meticulous care. Circled the tip. Stroked his ever-expanding length. It was not enough. He needed more. He pulled the sponge from her fingers and tossed it aside impatiently. Her eyes darkened. They both knew what he wanted.

Soon she was in the position he'd imagined, her tongue hesitant as she trailed it along his flesh. He was not adorned with raspberry fool now, and he sensed she had little experience how to please a man this way. For a novice, her mouth was pure, fiery sin. The blush on her cheek showed a touch of reluctance, but the rest of her seemed disarmingly engaged. One small hand cupped his stones while the other held his cock firm. He murmured encouraging words to her until she enveloped him in her hot mouth and he couldn't speak any longer.

What wasn't surrounded by moisture was eased with warm strokes. She found her stride, teasing him, tormenting him, drawing him in so far until he struggled for balance. She was the embodiment of every man's dream. Or his, at any rate, and that was all that mattered. Her lips curled slyly around his cock, her breasts rose and fell with each gasping breath, her tongue was beautifully busy.

As if she knew he was close, she raised her eyes, the blue quite overtaken by black desire. She would deny him nothing. Wordless and grateful, his fingers threaded through the wildness of her hair as he selfishly held her in place. She startled only a little when he came, didn't disappoint him by trying to pull away. Through heavy lids, he watched the column of her throat as he spent. He'd never in his life seen or felt anything so sensual.

Ah. Yes, she was addictive. He was totally enslaved. He lifted her wet body up against his and kissed her, claimed her. Her dark lashes fluttered against her cheeks as he foamed lime froth along her curves, over her nether curls, into the cleft of her arse. Unsteady from the urge to taste her everywhere, he slipped back into the water, seating her back-to on his lap to wash her fall of ebony hair. She fitted perfectly, felt perfect against him, her softness yielding to the hard muscle of his body. She tipped her head back like a trusting child as he poured water over her. When she gave a little sigh of contentment, his cock twitched in response.

They sat together in their own liquid fiefdom, his thumb grazing her nipple as his other hand found her tickler plump and erect. He pressed and pinched, stroked and strummed until she broke apart. It seemed impossible so soon, but he was marble-hard. He lifted her hips and drove in, the cooling water sloshing onto the carpet. Without a word, he slowly raised and set her down on his shaft. She was pliant, yielding, all irritation forgotten. Her muscles contracted in a dizzying series of shocks, compelling him to spill into her with hardly any effort. She settled back against him, her body lax. The only flaws in the process had been that he was unable to kiss her mouth as he emptied himself, and that the water was now damned cold. She was shivering.

"We're turning into prunes." He kissed her temple, brushing away damp hair. It was springing up into a sable puff. Most reluctantly, he disengaged and turned her face to him. Blissful, her blue eyes sleepy, she placed her lips on his throat.

If only they could stay so at peace with each other. Bay knew it was unlikely. "I've got to leave you for a few hours. Take a nap, my dove, for when I come back I want you wide awake."

"You are a fiend." This time it didn't sound like an insult so much as a compliment.

He helped her out of the tub and wrapped a bath sheet around her. If he stopped to dry her off, he'd wind right back in her bed and inside her. For two middle-aged people, they were behaving like randy youths.

Bay dressed quickly in some spare clothes and headed home. *Home.* Odd. Now that Charlie was there, Jane Street seemed more like home to him than anywhere he'd ever lived.

Chapter 8

Bay's town house was a modest affair. As a single man he had no need for a vast quantity of bedrooms or servants. He'd lived in bachelor apartments when he sold out, spending most of his nights in the arms of either his mistress or a willing widow. He'd won the leasehold on Jane Street in a spectacularly lucky card game a little over two years ago. Lucky for him, at any rate. The Marquess of Angleton had been unhappy, his mistress even more so. Rumor had it she was so furious at Angleton for her eviction from "Courtesan Court" that she stabbed him with a fork. The man's hand had been bandaged for weeks. Puncture wounds were the devil to heal.

But last year Bay had felt the need for more permanence and privacy, a place to hang the collection of paintings that were stacking up against the walls in his bachelor quarters for lack of space. He couldn't spend all his time underfoot at Jane Street. Angelique and then Helena required their own privacy. Part of the mysterious allure of a mistress is that one didn't see them all the day as they did whatever mistresses do to kill time. Cleaning their teeth. Applying honey masques to their faces and lemon juice to their hair. Reading gothic romances. Clipping their toenails. The extraordinary observed doing the ordinary soon loses its appeal.

He had enjoyed bathing with Charlie, however. And brushing her hair. He wondered how she would spend the rest of the afternoon. She seemed bookish. Perhaps he could order a set of novels from Hatchard's for the house.

Bay's front door opened before he even mounted the first step. His old batman, now butler-cum-valet, actually closed the door behind him and rushed Bay off the steps.

"Trouble, Frazier?"

"Aye, Major. Your wife is in the parlor."

"I have no wife." He did, once. For a little less than five months. And then her dead husband returned very inconveniently, making her an adulteress and Bay brokenhearted. He'd been too young to marry anyway. Just twenty. Anne had been twenty-two and the loveliest thing he had ever seen. Black hair. Blue eyes. Skin as white as milk and as smooth as cream. One morning she'd been snuggled in his bed in Dorset; by the evening she was being escorted back to Whitley's estate by her papa. The scandal had been fierce. After a month of it, Bay had enlisted and directed his anger at the citizenry of France.

He placed a hand on Frazier's and squeezed to stop him from dragging him down the street. "Halt. I'll not run away."

"Now, Major, you told me after the last time that I'm to talk sense into you. I'm just doing my duty."

Bay pulled away and ran a hand through his still-damp hair. "How long has Lady Whitley been here?"

"Over an hour, sir. I tried to get her to leave but the b— woman won't budge."

Bay thought to reprimand Frazier for his hostility, but had learned when to pick his battles with the old Scot. To be fair, Frazier had every reason to dislike Anne. The man had dragged Bay away from enough bottles and beds after encounters with her. Bay had gotten better over the years, but Anne still had the power to make him feel like a jilted schoolboy.

"What does she want?"

"What she always wants, not that she'd bother to confide in me. You watch yourself, Major. Since that husband of hers died, she wants you back. And not just to diddle this time."

Bay shut his eyes, hoping his neighbors were not peering

out their front windows while he argued with his manservant. He was thirty-three years old. A decorated soldier, some might even say hero. The owner of three properties and sound investments. He was *not* going to let his past get the better of him, no matter how Anne's lips moved in entreaty or her lush body beckoned. He had a mistress for all that.

"Tell you what, Frazier. Station yourself right outside the parlor door. When you hear me say—" He paused. What would make a good code word he could work into conversation?

"Bloody cow," Frazier offered.

Bay cast him a stern look. "Hyde Park. Come in and tell me I have an urgent message. Speaking of which, any word from Mr. Mulgrew?"

"Aye. I meant to tell you that, too. Said he's been to see the earl, and he has a lead. Has a man on his way to France. He'll call on you tomorrow morning."

Damn. He devoutly hoped for Charlie's sake Mulgrew had not spilled the beans about Deborah taking the necklace. He'd definitely have to have a chat with Arthur's father now, on some pretext or other. They didn't precisely run in the same social circles.

Bay nodded and turned back toward his house. Frazier pulled on his sleeve again.

"Stay strong, Major. You've been in tougher battles."

Bay barked out a laugh. He'd almost rather don a uniform again than face Anne Whitley in his own parlor.

He straightened and slid open the pocket door. She really had not changed at all since the last time he saw her. Of course, that was only weeks ago, soon after Whitley died and before he went to Dorset. She looked magnificent in black, like the ultimate chess queen carved by a master craftsman. She looked even more magnificent out of her widow's weeds. It had not taken her long to shed them then, and would not take much to persuade her to go upstairs right now. Were he not so exhausted from his interlude on Jane Street, he might have been tempted for old times' sake. They had fallen into such a routine over the years that he almost dreaded coming home on leave. She was sure to find him, and he was sure to wind up right where he knew he shouldn't be.

But Whitley had been a bastard to her, or so she said. It had eased his guilty conscience some at the time to cuckold the man, but had not eased his heart.

"You look well, Lady Whitley. How may I be of service to you?"

"Bay, don't be silly! Come sit down right next to me. I have been waiting for you for ages and ages." She patted the sofa with a black-gloved hand, but she had removed her hat. Her hair was coiled neatly, wayward curls deliberately escaping around her heart-shaped face. Her eyes were the color of the autumn sky. He'd once placed a sapphire just their color on her finger.

"I'm afraid I'm not home for long." There was no sign of a chaperone. He took the red brocade chair opposite. Even from across the room he could smell the rose perfume she had always worn.

"Surely you have time for me." She smiled, both cheeks dimpling. She did not look like a woman of five and thirty, and knew it.

"What do you want, Anne? It's not proper for you to be here."

She frowned. "You don't sound very friendly today. I thought you'd be pleased to know I've come back to town. Whitley Abbey was so dull and grim. Even though I'm in mourning, I cannot be expected to deprive myself of every pleasure, can I?"

Good lord. She was actually batting her eyelashes, one finger tracing the neckline of her black gown. Surely she was showing too much daytime décolletage for a grieving widow.

Bay felt almost as though he were seeing her as she was for the first time. She was no longer the artless young widow he'd married and loved so desperately. Nor was she his erotic fantasy come to life after months sleeping on the ground and getting shot at. She was still beautiful, but he simply didn't feel the tug to his soul and his groin today that he always had. Could it be he'd finally come to his senses at last? Her years of reeling him in and tossing him back may have come to an end.

"You could have written. Then I could have written back telling you I have an appointment. In Hyde Park."

Right on cue Frazier blustered in. "Major, you've got an urgent message. There's no time to waste! You'll have to excuse him, Lady Whitley. I'll see you out."

Anne looked from one to the other of them and burst into a peal of laughter. "Oh, you two! Just like a French farce. You'll not fob me off with this nonsense. I'm not going anywhere, Frazier, and neither is Sir Michael until I've had my say. Go lurk somewhere else."

Frazier was brick red, but left, shutting the door with an ominous thud. Bay thought the walls were still vibrating as he lifted an eyebrow at his former wife. "It's for your own good, you know. You're risking your reputation to be here in a gentleman's establishment. Whitley's only been dead two months. Even if you've decided to become a fast widow, you're *too* fast for the ton."

"How sweet of you to care. You were ever discreet while you cuckolded Whitley. But he knew all about us anyway."

"Because you told him, Anne. To torture us both. I told you the last time we met that we were done."

Anne focused on her lap, smoothing the fabric of her dress. "Yes, you did. But I read in the paper this morning your new mistress is now married. How did that come about? You had such great plans for her, as I recall." She raised her eyes and smiled sweetly.

Bay should have known the announcement in the *Times* would be of interest to her. He relived the shouting match they'd had at the end of their affair in his mind, when he'd bragged about securing Deborah Fallon's services.

"Don't worry about me, my dear. I've made other arrangements already." Bay went to the drinks table and poured himself a whisky. He did not offer one to his guest.

"My, you work fast. Who is the lucky girl this time?" There was an edge to her voice that Bay found quite gratifying. It was well past her turn to be jealous.

"No one you've heard of." He took a sip of the amber liquid. He certainly wasn't going to explain the mix-up with Deborah and her sister.

"Does this one look like me too?"

Bay put the glass down with a clack. He was well aware he had a 'type,' a preference for fair-skinned women with jet hair and blue eyes. He'd told himself it was just a matter of taste, like choosing a raspberry over a strawberry. He preferred raspberries. Some gentlemen preferred blondes. He had been attracted to Anne because of her coloring, and did *not* choose his mistresses because they resembled his not-quite wife.

"Still keeping tabs on me, Anne?" He stuffed his hands in his pockets to control the shaking.

"Well, you've hardly lived a secret life since you acquired the house on Jane Street. Everyone knows your business there, and who you do it with. Jane Street gentlemen are the envy of everyone. And that's really why I'm here. I have a proposition for you."

"Make it quick. I really do have an appointment." *With the glass on the table and the bottle next to it.* Anne made him want to get foxed in the very worst way.

"When I lost our baby, I was crushed, Bay. A child would have made my marriage bearable."

"Not for the child." If Whitley had been cruel to Anne, he would have made Bay's son or daughter's life a living hell. It was for the best that Anne miscarried before she even knew she was enceinte.

"I would have done anything to protect your son, Bay. But it was not to be." She sighed, looking her age for the first time this afternoon. "I wanted a child then and I want one now. Whitley was apparently incapable. But I know you are not."

Bay's throat was dry. "What are you saying?"

"I'm asking you to help me. I want a baby, Bay, before I'm too old."

The room spun a bit. "You're mad!"

"Am I? I'm to be thrown out of the Abbey into the Dower House. Again. And it's in worse repair than it was thirteen years ago, when Clarence thought he inherited. Apparently, his wife finds me as much a distraction this time around as she did the last. I have no intention of living in that poky hovel this winter. I thought I might travel. While I'm abroad, I'll adopt a foundling to keep me company. Your child, Bay. Something we made together to remind us of what once was."

Bay picked up the whisky, draining the glass in one long swallow. "You can marry again once your year of mourning is over. Have a child with your new husband. It won't be me."

"I'm not asking you to marry me, Bay." Her lips twisted. "In truth, I wish to be no man's wife ever again."

"Not every man is Whitley, Anne." Whitley had become somewhat unhinged when he discovered the young wife he expected to be waiting for him had already remarried. He had survived a shipwreck, illness, and the perils of Africa, but could not survive the loss of his pride. Anne had suffered as much as Bay, if not more. It had changed her, although it had taken Bay years to see it.

She rose from the scarlet-striped sofa and picked up a feathery black bonnet. "Think about it." She tied the black ribbons under her chin. "You know where to find me. If you agree, I promise to never bother you again once we've achieved our objective."

When she left, he collapsed back into his chair. She was insane. She had to be. He was not a stallion to be put out to stud. And she was too smart to think he could simply father a child and walk away. Once she had known his every thought. He wondered if he had ever known hers at all.

After they had been forcibly separated, Anne had wanted to have her cake and eat it too. For years, Bay had begged her to run away with him. What was one more chapter to their book of scandal? They could have made a new life in the Americas, or settled quietly by the sea in Dorset again. But she was a viscount's wife and mistress of Whitley Abbey. In the grand scheme of things, Bay was just a good fuck.

Frazier entered the room, plopping down on the sofa as if he owned it. In a way, he did. Bay would not be here without him.

"I see you've still got your clothes on."

"Not for long if Anne gets her way," Bay mumbled.

"Well, you're a fine figure of a man. She'd have to be blind not to notice. But it's time you looked to your future, not your past. Settle down. Have some bairns."

"Have you been talking to Mr. Mulgrew?"

Frazier was the picture of innocence. "Why, yes. I told you he came to see you earlier."

"As it happens, you and Mr. Mulgrew and even Lady Whitley all have something in common."

"And what is that?"

"Mr. Mulgrew has advised me to marry. Lady Whitley just wants me to have a bairn."

Frazier drew his wild red eyebrows together. "I beg your pardon?"

"Lady Whitley is feeling the urge for motherhood. Apparently, I'm to be the father."

Frazier leaped up. "Never say you'll be marrying that woman! She's not good for you, Major! Oh, I grant she's an eyeful and an armful, but you want someone better than that. Someone who will stick by you and be true, not toy with your affections. Forgive me for speaking my mind—"

"As if I could stop you."

"—but that woman is not nice. Oh, she may have been when she was a girl and you married her. But look how she's treated you over the years, blowing hot and cold. Using you to punish her husband. Why, the man practically killed you once! And still, you went back every time she lifted her little finger."

"I loved her," Bay said simply. "She was my wife, no matter what the legalities were."

"Och, you loved what she did to your pecker. You were just a boy. What did you know about love? And then when you stared down death at every turn, it's no wonder you sought some comfort. But you've a fine life now, and a pretty new mistress from what I hear, though Mrs. Kelly says this one's a bit of a thief. You really do need a wife, sir. Someone to save you from designing women." Frazier paused to take a deep breath, but Bay had a feeling he was not done. "You're a smart lad. A good catch. You served your country well. The old scandal has died down by now. If you spent more time at parties and such and less time on Jane Street, I imagine you could catch yourself a wife by Christmas."

"I am touched by your confidence, Frazier. And who might this paragon be?"

His servant gave him a cheeky grin. "A blonde. With big brown eyes."

Chapter 9

Charlotte sat in the late morning sun, Bay's letters in her lap. He had not come to her last night, even though she had put on one of Deb's provocative dresses and waited with a saucy, mistressy expression on her face. His valet, Frazier, a short red rooster of a man, had delivered Bay's regrets in person, keeping his flinty gray eyes firmly on her face and not her bosom. He seemed to be checking her out anyway, then disappeared down to the kitchen to visit with Mrs. Kelly. By the time he was done, he'd know all about her ill-fated scheme to flee Jane Street. And how very wicked his employer was to tie her up and ravish her with raspberry fool.

Charlotte felt an unfamiliar ache of desire. She knew she should not like this captivity, but it was growing on her. Just like a pimple on her arse, it was inflamed and uncomfortable, yet she could not remove it.

So she had decided to torture herself further by reading Bay's love letters to Deb. Well, they were not exactly love letters, more like lust letters. There were twelve of them, two for each week he'd spent away. She was saving the ruby necklace one for last, like the last sugared rose on a chocolate gâteau.

She had arranged the letters in the order that they were written. Bay seemed methodical in dating each missive, his handwriting bold yet legible. She settled back on the iron garden bench and unfolded the paper, trying to block out the sound beyond the brick wall. A new garden was being put in next door, with workmen toting in almost full-grown trees and flowering bushes. Someone was spending a pretty penny to make the garden look as though it had been established for years. She had observed the activity from her balcony earlier, watching in appalled fascination as one of the laborers removed his shirt to reveal a large black cross tattooed on his brown shoulder. He made a total of two gentlemen she had seen shirtless in her whole life, and she'd only woken up on Jane Street for four mornings. Who knew what she'd see—and do—next? She blushed at her own daring and began to read.

To the Divine Deborah,

I arrived safe and sound at the old ancestral pile two days ago. I believe as a Dorset girl yourself you would be at home. The front lawn is the ocean, its sheep the whitecaps scattering on the beach below. It is always good to be back, although denying myself your company will take all my strength.

My grandmama is very frail as you might expect. She is ninety-five but once claimed she didn't look a day over eighty. The doctor has not given me reason to hope for her recovery, so I must warn you now to be patient. I am uncertain when I will return to Jane Street, but I hope you are settling in. Mrs. Kelly and Irene have been instructed to grant your every wish. Should you have need of a gentleman's assistance, my old batman Angus Frazier can be counted upon. Simply tell Mrs. Kelly to send for him.

I have been thinking about your mouth, Deb, your lips so full and plump. A blushing rose hue owing nothing to artifice, I believe. You have been cruel to me for weeks, forbidding even the most chaste of kisses. I assure you when you are in my arms at last, there will be nothing chaste about it.

> *I remain your most obedient*
> *and ardent servant,*
> *Bay*

Charlotte wiped the tear from her cheek. Deb did not deserve this letter. Here was Bay at his poetic and practical best. She tucked the letter into the pocket of her gray dress. As a concession to the absent Bay, she had left her cap in the drawer. Her hair, still scented with his lime soap, fell down her back like a wanton's. She picked up the next letter. It was shorter, but still managed to convey Bay's desire through his worry.

Dearest Deborah,

Just the briefest of notes to let you know you are in my thoughts even in this difficult time. The situation remains unchanged. I know one night with you will help me forget the nights we spent apart. I look forward to seeing you in the blue negligee that matches your eyes. And then I look forward to seeing you out of it.

> *Your obedient and hasty servant,*
> *Bay*

And Deborah had taken that negligee with her. Arthur Bannister was probably lifting its hem right now in some French coaching inn. For some reason that thought made her cry even harder. She bound all the letters up with a blue ribbon and shoved them into her pocket so as not to smudge the ink. She was bawling rather noisily now, oblivious to the sweating, swearing men next door.

Charlotte was not much of a crier. Even when Robert abandoned her, she had steadfastly refused to join her mama in wailing and woe-ing. The next month her parents were dead, and she allowed herself a few discreet tears in the churchyard. Deborah, hanging off Harfield's arm and looking perfectly beautiful in new mourning clothes paid for with Harfield's reinstated allowance, was making enough fuss for both of them. There were very few people to see or hear her—the Fallon family had fallen as low as one could go without actually being convicted felons. The people of Bexington were happy to see the back of them all. Harfield's father, the Earl of Trent, had purchased their house for a song and then flattened it, not that Charlotte would ever go back there.

And now here she was, living on the most notorious street in London, falling in love with a man who wanted her sister, a man who would send her back to her temporary cats as soon as he got his hands on his necklace. Charlotte sobbed and sniveled into her hands.

"My goodness. Whatever is the matter, my dear?"

Charlotte gulped, then quickly wiped her nose. The wooden door in the wall was open, not the side where the crew was hard at work, but the other. An elegantly dressed woman stood in the doorway, a basket with cuttings on her arm. She wore a spotless white pinafore over a teal silk dress. Her dark red hair was twisted up with aquamarine combs that caught the sunlight, and her gray eyes were wide with concern.

"Oh! I do beg your pardon for disturbing you."

"Nonsense. I hope you don't mind that I am disturbing *you*. Angelique and Helena kept the door unlocked so we could visit on occasion. I'm afraid I didn't have the opportunity to meet the other young woman who was here before you. I've been away for a few weeks. Sir Michael isn't cruel, is he? I have ways of dealing with that sort of thing, you know."

"Oh, no. No, he's not cruel at all." Only if you counted the way he had completely coerced her body to do his bidding so that she was a mindless puddle. Charlotte wiped her snot-covered hands on her skirt. "How do you do? I am Charlotte Fallon."

"Ah. You must be the Divine Deborah's sister. I never met her, but I did see her in passing. Now that I look at you, you are very like her, are you not? You might almost be twins."

"I am the elder by four years." Charlotte was finding this conversation terribly awkward. But really, this stranger was in the same boat as she was. Charlotte shoved her mortification in her other pocket.

"You have no idea who I am, do you, Miss Fallon?"

Charlotte tried to laugh. "You live on Jane Street, so I imagine I know part of your story."

"Ah. There you would be wrong. I am the Baroness Christie, but please call me Caroline. My husband, Edward, is Baron Christie."

"L-Lady Christie?" *And she had a living husband?*

"Quite. May I sit down on your bench? I'm afraid when I bent to pull up a few weeds I did something to my back."

Charlotte knew her mouth was still hanging open. "Of course!" she said hastily, scooting to one end. Bay's letters crackled in her pocket.

Caroline set her basket between them, the heavy scent of peonies wafting through the air. Charlotte fingered a warm silky dark pink petal. They were her favorite flower. The ones at her cottage must be in bloom too, only they were ivory. And drooping their heavy heads right now since she was not there to cut them.

Caroline rubbed the small of her back. "I'm most vexed with my gardener. A total case of while the cat's away the mouse will play. The flower beds are in a shocking state without my supervision. It's not as though the man has to take care of Christie Park, for heaven's sake, just a tiny city patch." She removed her gardening gloves. On her wedding ring finger were an enormous diamond set with smaller stones and a matching diamond wedding band. Charlotte tried very hard not to gape. "Anyway, a bit of history. My husband and I separated five years ago after an unfortunate misunderstanding. Unfortunate for me, at any rate. He purchased my accommodations without my consent, naturally. I have tried to make the best of things. Of course in the eyes of society I am quite ruined, but there's no reason for me to waste my time or tears, although I can tell you I once did. What has upset you so much, Charlotte?"

"I—I don't really know. I've had a bit of a misunderstanding, too. My sister, the infamous Divine Deborah, ran off to get married. She *is* married. She left me here to explain the situation to Sir Michael, but somehow things have gotten a trifle out of hand."

"The old bait and switch. I once knew a pair of sisters—the Condon girls—who were forever doing that to their beaux. Men never knew which one of them they were kissing."

"I assure you I never meant to even kiss him. I most certainly didn't intend to take Deborah's place in Sir Michael's bed. It just—happened. I am—I was—a respectable woman. Mostly." *But not lately.*

Caroline laughed. "Aren't we all? If you need a friend, I'm right next door. I receive every Thursday afternoon. Most of the girls stop by if they are not busy with their gentlemen. You should come and meet your new neighbors."

Charlotte felt her world tilt a little. The baroness was a most unconventional woman. She watched as Caroline rose from the bench with a wince. "It's a hot brick in bed for me this afternoon. And *that* is all that's been in my bed for five years except my cat Harold, in case you were wondering."

Charlotte stuttered over her good-byes. There was a crash and a curse on the other side of the wall. "The Marquess of Conover," Caroline whispered. "Known as the *Mad* Marquess. They say he lost his soul in the desert."

"Does he have a tattoo?" Charlotte whispered back.

"I'm sure I couldn't say, but it wouldn't surprise me. Thursday, then. Anytime between three and five. I look forward to seeing you."

Dear Lord. She had just been invited to sip tea with Cyprians. Her mama would have fainted—gracefully—dead away.

Chapter 10

Bay was beginning to think his luck was finally running out. He stood in front of his shaving mirror, blotting up the blood that coursed under his chin to his bare throat. He was clumsy this morning—a sleepless night lubricated with a bottle of whisky accounted for the tremor in his hands. His black eyes looked even blacker than usual, surrounded as they were by darkened circles. He should have allowed Frazier to finish shaving him, but wasn't in the mood for the lecture.

Nor had he been in the mood to see Charlie last night. His reluctant mistress was proof that he had somehow, somewhere gone far astray from the ideals he had when he was twenty.

At twenty, Bay had believed in love. That marriage was forever. That he would somehow avenge the death of his child.

But his life had gone on, loveless, childless. No matter the risks he took, he survived them. He'd had no thoughts of marriage or other children for years, just careless pleasure. Now he had a chance to change that. And he wouldn't.

Not with Anne. She still stirred his blood, but he couldn't give her what she needed.

Frazier rapped on the door and pushed it open. "Don't bite my head off. Your Mr. Mulgrew is here, Major."

"Bloody hell. I haven't even had breakfast." Not that he was remotely hungry.

"It's noon, sir. Time to be thinking about lunch. Shall I stash him in your study and bring in a tray?"

"I suppose." Bay pulled a clean shirt over his head, taking care for it not to touch his chin. He applied some sticking plaster, dispensed with a neckcloth, and shrugged into a dark blue jacket. Each step down the stairs rattled what was left of his brain.

Mr. Mulgrew was in his same tweed coat, a squashed hat on his lap. "Good afternoon, my lord. Sorry I was unable to come any earlier."

"Thank God for that," Bay murmured. He didn't bother to correct the man again about his title.

"I expect your man told you I was by yesterday. Had a nice chat with the old Earl of Cranmore. He seems to think his son and the missus have gone to France."

"Well, that would be the logical destination. You didn't, I hope, say a word about the necklace?"

Mr. Mulgrew looked aggrieved. "I'm a professional, your lordship. Said I owed his son some money and wanted to repay it, kind of a wedding present, don't you know. Seems that Arthur has a school chum with a château, or what's left of it, in the Loire Valley. The Vicomte Bienville. Beans."

"Pardon?"

"The friend. Known as Beans. You know these silly nicknames boys pick up in school. If my given name were Patrice I might prefer Beans, too. So I'm sending someone to Patty's house in Vouvray with a message from Cranmore. And you, of course."

Bay imagined Mr. Mulgrew had accepted a second fee from the Earl of Cranmore, but that didn't matter. "When will you know anything?"

"Not for a day or three yet. I'll keep you posted. If you don't mind me saying so, you look a touch peaked this afternoon. Steady habits, sir, steady habits. A pint at lunch is fine, but you've got to watch out for overindulgence."

"I'll keep that in mind." Just then Frazier entered with a

tray. Bay hoped the coffeepot would provide a cure for both his hangover and Mr. Mulgrew's unsolicited advice. There was a thick beef and cheese sandwich on a plate. Bay's French chef would never have assembled such a prosaic meal.

"Apologies, Major. Monsieur David has gone to get a tooth pulled. I hope this will do."

Mr. Mulgrew looked at the sandwich with some respect. "I'll leave you to your luncheon then. Good day, Lord Bayard."

Bay rolled his eyes to the ceiling and took a bite. It would do. It would have to.

Charlotte had washed her face and hands, and was now lying on her bed, a cool cloth across her eyes to reduce the swelling and redness. She had looked an absolute fright in the garden. What must Lady Christie have thought of her? Granted, the baroness was liberal in her thinking, but no one could excuse Charlotte's shameful tangle of hair or her tear-stained face. Charlotte had braided and pinned up her hair, covering it with her usual cap. Bay must be tired of her already, as he hadn't come last night or even early this morning. Why should she try to look alluring? She was an old maid and might as well face the facts. Just because the fiend had tapped into her heretofore hidden reservoirs of passion didn't mean he was in the water doing the breaststroke with her. Men were as easily aroused by a naughty painting of a female as the female herself. Charlotte was just a living painting in Bay's collection.

She had almost convinced herself of her utter worthlessness when she heard footsteps on the stairs. She flung the wet cloth from her face and sat up against the pillows, steepling her fingers on her lap. She knew she resembled a woman in prayer, and she was. She prayed he would send her back home and extricate himself from her heart. She could not afford another ten years of useless regrets.

Bay entered, minus the usual spring in his step. He was

pale and drawn, his eyes shadowed. He was ill! That's why
he hadn't come to her last night. If she were home she would
give him her special infusion of herbs from her garden. Perhaps that marquess next door had a few leaves she could
snip. His garden seemed to have everything.

"Are you unwell, Bay?"

"Not you, too. I should have come out with a sack over
my head." Instead of sitting down on the bed with her, he
went to one of the chairs at the fireplace. "Take off the stupid
napkin, Charlie. I told you I won't stand for it."

His words were rude, but there was no fight to him today.
Charlotte fiddled with the strings under her chin. "How was
I to know when to expect you? Our original agreement was
for every evening, but then you said you were coming last
night and didn't."

Bay raised an eyebrow. "Missed me, did you?"

"Certainly not," huffed Charlotte. "Mrs. Kelly was disappointed, that's all. Dinner was most delicious."

Bay stretched his long legs out in front of him. Although
his face was careworn, he was dressed to sartorial perfection
as usual. "I drank my dinner, I'm afraid. Had an unexpected
encounter with a woman from my past."

"Oh?" Charlotte pretended disinterest, but her heart kicked
up a bit. She imagined there were a great many women in
Bay's past.

"You've had lovers, Charlie. What's your past?"

"I've hardly had *lovers*," Charlotte snapped. "You make it
sound like I'm a concubine. And I can't see why it should
concern you. We hardly know each other."

Bay stared at her and then threw his head back, laughing.
She was pleased to see the melancholy wiped from his face,
but did not want to be the butt of his joke. "What I mean to
say is, we may know each other in the Biblical sense, but you
know nothing about me and I know nothing about you, except you keep a series of mistresses. And you were in the
army." *And you were married and are surprisingly poetic.*

"Exactly so. I thought I'd remedy that situation this afternoon. Say, ten questions apiece. You may ask me anything you like and I shall do the same."

"How will I know you'll answer honestly?"

He waggled a finger at her. "Come, come, Charlie. I am not the one here whose honesty is in question."

"Up until I had the misfortune to meet you, my honesty was never in question." Except the once, and she had paid for that lie a long time.

"I'll begin. I quite thoroughly researched Deborah, you know. I do with all my mistresses. As you were thrust on me so precipitously without proper vetting, I must rectify that."

"*You* were the one who was thrusting, as I recall," Charlotte said tartly.

"Be that as it may. I was under a misapprehension, as you well know. Now then. Where shall I begin?"

"How about 'When would you like to go home, Miss Fallon?' The answer, in case you're interested, is 'Right this very minute.'"

"That brings your questions down to nine. There's no point in talking to yourself, you know. You'll never get anywhere."

Charlotte aimed a little fringed pillow at him but missed. "How can you be so annoying?"

"Tsk-tsk. That's eight left for you now. And the answer is, most people don't find me annoying at all. My grandmother loved me."

"She's dead."

"Ouch. You are cruel to remind me of my loss." He looked sincerely upset. Charlotte longed to throw the Cupid-clock straight at his head next.

"How many men have you slept with, Charlotte?"

She bit her lip, hating to give him the satisfaction. "Two."

His face betrayed nothing. "Your turn."

"How many women have you slept with?" She didn't really want to know, but it was the only thing she could think of. She already knew his middle name.

Bay made a pretense of counting on his fingers. After more

than a minute passed, he grinned and her fury mounted. "Rather a lot. But a gentleman does not kiss and tell. I never keep more than one mistress at a time, if that is what's worrying you. You'll have no competition."

Odious, insufferable man. As if she cared what he did.

"Who was the woman from your past yesterday?"

"You're out of turn, Charlie." His voice was level, but she knew she hit a nerve.

"I'll forfeit another question if you answer now."

He had the oddest expression on his face. "My wife."

Black spots danced the mazurka before Charlotte's eyes. At least she was on a bed this time and wouldn't hit her head on the floor again when she fainted.

He'd done a stupid thing telling her that way. He found a balled-up wet cloth and wiped her brow. Her eyelids fluttered. He could see each tiny blue vein against the parchment of her skin. She was like his own version of Snow White, minus the dwarfs, of course. Bay was not completely perverted, although he'd indulged in a ménage à trois ou quatre a time or two to try to drive Anne out of his mind. It hadn't worked, but had been pleasant in its way. Seven dwarfs would be entirely out of the question, however.

He unbuttoned her bodice, watching the pulse leap erratically at her throat. Lord, he hoped she wouldn't expire in his bed. It would do his reputation no good. And he would miss her.

She'd slept with two men. He assumed she had counted him in that number, although sleeping had little to do with the flames of the past four days. He wondered that they had not combusted, both of them just a shower of sparks scattering on the rumpled sheets, scorching tiny black holes in the linen.

She really was nothing like Deb, although even Deb had been nothing like the *idea* of Deb that circulated in the ton. The Divine Deborah had been with just four men as far as he knew. Five, probably, if one included gormless Arthur, who had made inroads with Deb while Bay was in Dorset. But an hour in Deb's company made one feel as if one had been in her bed. She touched, flirted, teased. Befuddled, really. A man felt blessed that she had given him the time of day, and the exaggerations grew.

Charlotte did not have a coy bone in her body. She was a sharp-toothed spinster that someone had hurt. Bay did not want to add to that hurt, nor did he want to get rid of her quite yet. He was the worst sort of cad. He'd driven her to desperation and theft. But he'd make it up to her, and soon.

"Wake up, Charlie. Or I'll take advantage of your unconsciousness."

"Just like the first time, you fiend," she mumbled.

Ah. There were her teeth. "Exactly. I'm going to sit you up now." He pulled her up onto her pillows. She was as limp as a stuffed doll, still unnaturally pale.

"I didn't mean to shock you." He smoothed a wrinkle in her bodice and she slapped him away.

"Well, you did." Her blue eyes were icy. "Deborah never, ever consents to sleep with married men. You tricked her and me. Bad enough I'm now fornicating, but you have made me an adulteress!"

"Let me explain."

"What is there to say? Yesterday you spent the evening with *your wife*! I sat here like an idiot waiting for you. I'll not be party to breaking some poor woman's heart."

Bay smiled. "I don't think you need to worry about Anne. She can take care of herself."

"What do you know? You're a man! You've no notion how women are dependent on the occasional goodwill of their fathers and husbands. We cannot keep our own money, own property, vote. Even our children don't belong to us. Oh my God. Do you have *children*?"

He gripped her hand hard. "Charlie. I misspoke. I am no longer married. In fact, I never *was* married. The ceremony was invalid, as the bride had another husband. We thought he was dead but he was not. She went back to him and I went to war."

"Oh." She chewed her lip, processing what seemed even to

him to be the plot of some gothic novel. Whitley Abbey with its gargoyles had served as the perfect setting for sin, seduction, and intrigue. Viscount Whitley had been the perfect villain. Absently Bay rubbed at the scar on his cheek. Most people took it for a war wound, but it was not.

"It was long ago. But Anne and I—we've kept in touch on occasion. Her husband died recently, and she—" He could not possibly repeat the reason Anne came to him. "She needs a friend."

"Do you still love her?"

He stood up abruptly and went to the fireplace. "Is this one of your six questions?"

"I don't know. I've lost count."

How to answer? A part of him would always love Anne. He had worshipped her, growing up not far from her family's estate. Then she had made her brilliant marriage when she was just sixteen. She disappeared, becoming sought-after words to him in the gossip columns his grandmother read. 'Society rejoices as Young Lady W— has returned to Town, having found rusticating at W— Abbey a bore. She and Lord W— were seen at the Somerset soiree Thursday evening.' He finally had his chance when she returned home five years later, beautiful and tragic and lonely. He'd fought his grandmother tooth and nail for permission to marry before he came of age. If only he'd waited a few months, his life would have been far different.

"My answer would be complicated if I could give it, Charlie. I'm not sure I know it myself."

"Never mind then. It's none of my business, really." She had drawn herself up in a little ball, her arms wrapped around her ghastly gray skirts. He would have to do something about her clothes eventually. If she stayed.

He returned to the bed, removed one hand from her knee and massaged her knuckles. "I've told you my tragedy. Now tell me yours."

She pulled away. "It's hardly a tragedy. I was engaged once, or thought I was. And then I wasn't."

"What happened?"

"Deborah, in a way. She ran off with Harfield. Robert was disgusted. I think at first he hoped Deb would marry George and add to our consequence, and when that did not happen he suddenly discovered his morals and became very priggish. And then my father made a truly bad investment that affected my dowry. My fiancé decided not to align himself with the disgraceful Fallon family."

"After he had taken your virtue."

Charlotte flushed. "Yes."

"Any number of times."

Her blush deepened. "Yes."

"The bastard."

"I could not agree more, but Mr. and Mrs. Chase were in fact married."

"Robert *Chase*?"

Charlotte shrank away into the headboard. "Do you know him?"

Bay's fists bunched up. If Rob were standing in front of him now, he would not be standing long. "Dorset is not so large. We've run into each other a time or two." He cupped her cheek. "I wonder how I could have missed the Fallon sisters."

"We lived in a tiny village. Bexington. George's father was the largest landowner, and an absentee landlord most of the time. There was very little in the way of social life. And my parents' precarious financial position didn't allow trips to Dorchester, let alone London at the end, when I might have made my debut. Anyway, I've not lived in Bexington for a decade." He sensed her uneasiness talking about her home. She switched the topic. "How long have you been back in England?"

"I resigned my commission after Waterloo. Took the long way home by way of Italy."

"Where you bought your naked ladies."

Bay grinned. "You don't approve of my taste in art?"

"I suppose it is easier to indulge in carnal pleasures surrounded by nudity rather than the martyrdom of saints."

He looked around the room. "Or angels. I confess when Angel—when the statues first made their appearance, they had a depressing effect upon my ardor."

"I doubt anything could depress you long, sir. In my limited experience, you seem randy as a goat."

"A goat? A goat!" Bay put a hand over his heart. "I don't know when I've been so insulted."

"I believe it's a classical reference to the god Pan, who was admired for his masculine attributes," Charlotte said, her pursed mouth prim. He wanted to kiss her and make her unpucker.

Bay leaned in toward her. "Do you admire *my* masculine attributes, Charlie?"

She blinked her eyes at his closeness, then gave him a clear blue gaze. "I believe I do. And that's all the questions I'm willing to answer today."

He traced her lush mouth with a fingertip. "That was a very good answer, Charlie. I may even forgive you for calling me a goat. If I remember my mythology correctly, Pan fucked every one of the maenads. Orgies left and right."

"They were madwomen. Drunk," whispered Charlotte, her lip trembling against his finger.

"Whereas you are so very sane and sober. Even more of a challenge, I expect. Let me drive you a little bit mad, Charlie." He kissed the corner of her mouth as she turned it up in a rueful smile. They could help each other forget the past for a while.

Her hands brushed through the bristle of his short crop, circling gently. "What have you done with your horns?"

"Gone the way of my cloven hooves. Help me with my boots and you'll see."

Chapter 11

This was such a mistake. Bay was not only in lust with Deborah, but was still in love with his wife. Anne. Possibly Charlotte had supplanted Deborah, simply because she was present in his bed while Deb was who knows where. Charlotte was handy. Available. And absolutely aching for the friction of his fingers on her body. From the way his mouth was coaxing hers, Charlotte had every reason to believe he was as fully engaged in this exploration as she was. His lips and tongue were in concert, advancing and withdrawing with tender ferocity. Charlotte felt as if she was being eaten up, bite by bite. Soon she would disappear.

And then Bay could go back to his wife.

Bay's wife didn't need a friend. She needed *this*; every woman did. This skillful assault on all her senses. The taste of coffee on Bay's tongue, his ragged inhalations, the hardness of his cock. The scent of lime and sweat on his skin. Watching as his dark eyes shut in blissful release. Any woman who had given herself to Bay would want to do so again and again. Charlotte was a prime example. No matter how successfully she argued with herself, as soon as he stepped across the threshold, she lost her wits and found her wantonness.

Anne had been married to Bay, had experienced his lovemaking innumerable times. How she must have suffered when she went back to her undead husband. How Charlotte would suffer when she went back to her old life.

Bay had guided himself in her, gliding in and out with a twist that drove her mad. He was Pan, her cloven-hoofed devil, playing her body's music to a crescendo. Her nails dug into his back as she spiraled up off the bed, legs stretched taut. He collapsed on her, then rolled her to her side, still connected in the most elemental way. She quaked against him, her skin slick and burning. He kissed the perspiration from her hairline and the tears from the corner of her eyes.

"You aren't unhappy with me?"

Charlotte shook her head. "No." She would not tell him what she felt. She scarcely knew herself. Half the time she wanted to throttle him and the rest—well, they had just done the rest.

"I don't want to, but I may have to go away for a few days."

Her heartbeat slowed. "To find Deborah?"

"Yes. The man I hired has a lead. I don't want to leave it to chance."

Charlotte pulled back. "You've hired an investigator?"

"Several days ago. The sooner I get my necklace back, the sooner you can go back to Little Sickup. I know this has been wrong, Charlie. Keeping you here. I didn't mean for it to go this far." He tucked a strand of hair behind her ear. "I was angry at first. You'd agree I had some cause?"

Now he was asking her to condone what he had done to her. She could not. Worse than tying her up, he had turned her to mush with one touch, deconstructing all the barriers she'd thrown up since Robert. She was an idiot. She could remain his captive forever, *wanted* to stay on Jane Street as long as he'd let her. But it seemed she'd been handed her congé. Charlotte covered herself with the sheet.

"I'll go with you. If you have difficulty with Deborah—"

He put a finger to her lips. "No. I'm sure she'll see reason. Or Bannister will. It will be different being in France without any worry that my throat will be slit. I don't suppose Deborah is handy with a knife?"

"I daresay Deborah's weapon of choice is her body," Charlotte said quietly. As was Bay's. He'd tied her in knots using no rope at all.

He kissed her nose as if she were his niece. "I'm off then. I'll write. If you don't mind staying here another few days, I can escort you safely home when I get back."

Charlotte couldn't watch him get into his clothes. She stared instead at the angels on the ceiling, playing lutes and floating on clouds, their wings tipped in silver and gold. Heaven above looked very happy, but somehow Charlotte found herself in hell.

Bay marched with purpose in his step. He had a thousand things to do. Pack. Arrange for his passage. Look up Vouvray on a map. It was for the best. He hadn't really made his mind up to go until he saw her tears. They could not go on this way. If he left, he could kill three birds with one stone. Charlie could get her life back, he'd find the rubies, and escape from Anne's clutches all with one dash across the Channel. He didn't believe for one minute that Anne would hang about Whitley House less than a mile away waiting for him to call on her. She was probably bullying Frazier right now to let her in the front door. And he wouldn't put it past her to try the tradesmen's entrance. Monsieur David had a Frenchman's appreciation for a beautiful woman, toothache or no.

He stopped dead on the sidewalk. He was no coward. His years in the army had proved that, along with the jumble of medals he kept in his cuff link box. He didn't need to run after Mr. Mulgrew's associate—he might pass him en route and never know the necklace was in the man's pocket. He was a total stranger. He certainly didn't want to see the familiar face of Deborah again, although he would like to thank her for leaving Charlie in her place.

Two months ago he had made up his mind to resist Anne even if she was free. *Especially* since she was free. It was time to cut all ties with her. He would not bind himself to her with a child. There was a raw spot within knowing that their love was responsible for her miserable marriage, but he couldn't change the past. Or relive it.

He'd go home, have dinner. Another sandwich if necessary. And go back to Jane Street to surprise Charlie, sleep-warm and slumberous. He'd have to arouse her slowly so she didn't clout him with a stone cherub. She seemed remarkably predisposed to violence.

A dowager wielding an unnecessary umbrella gave him a glacial stare as she passed, maid and footman in tow. Bay snapped out of his reverie. Gentlemen just didn't stand around thinking on street corners. Most gentlemen of his acquaintance avoided thinking at all costs no matter where they were. But there was an insistent little voice in Bay's head that urged him to start thinking, stop coasting, pay attention. If only that voice had spoken a little louder, he might have noticed the man following him.

He said he would write. Charlotte got out of bed, legs cramping from her acrobatic endeavors. She slipped into her robe and picked up the dress that Bay had flung with such abandon. Thankfully he had been too intent in ravishing her to search her pockets. She pulled out the little stack of letters. At least she would have something with which to compare his words to her. When he had written to Deborah, he had not yet taken her to bed. Yet his desire was all too clear. How would he express himself to Charlotte, whose body he now knew better than she did herself? He had made it his mission to explore every nook and cranny, and she had been a willing accomplice in his amatory expedition. She felt mapped, surveyed, each inch measured to scale.

She realized now the furtive fumbling with Robert was no proper introduction to the sex act. For one thing, she had never seen all of him, just the odd thigh, a flash of white buttock, a smattering of dark chest hair when he took the time to remove his cravat. Their encounters were by their very nature hurried and clumsy, laden with guilt on her part and excess enthusiasm on his. Deb had been starry-eyed describing what George did to her, but Robert was no George. And he certainly did not hold a candle to Sir Michael Xavier Bayard.

Charlotte had felt her emotions waver at twenty. Deb had happily disposed of her virginity and was living like a princess in London, certain that George's father would come around eventually. Her misspelled letters were filled with exclamation points and descriptions that made Charlotte blush to her toenails. She didn't understand half of what she read. She and Robert had an understanding from the time they were children, and their relationship in no way resembled what Deb had with Viscount Harfield. A chaste kiss here, a brush against her hip there. It was all very tame, and Charlotte decided she wanted more.

Robert trained in his father's solicitor's office, doing whatever work his father chose not to do, while she tatted tablecloths for her hope chest. He asked her to be patient about their marriage, but was impatient himself when it came to anticipating the wedding night. His kisses were soft and thrilling, his desire so flattering. She felt *something* in his arms that needed investigation. Part of her hoped that once she gave him her virtue, he'd toss away his objections and marry her at once. She knew she could economize; living with her parents had given her that dubious advantage. But after months of groping each other in carriages and caves, Robert broke it off. A country solicitor, he said, not meeting her eyes, could not afford the scandal of her sister or the poverty of her parents. Should she discover she was with child, she was not to look to him for support, for he would deny their association. Charlotte had stood with her mouth open, very likely looking like a dying carp.

So that was very much that. Charlotte's mama had taken to her bed with a case of brandy for a week, and she hadn't even known the worst of it. Three weeks later, Charlotte's parents went for their moonlit sail. She sometimes wondered if their accident had been deliberate—that their troubles had simply overwhelmed them—but she never let herself dwell on that particular possibility. When the Earl of Trent made his offer on the house, Charlotte snatched it and reinvented herself far from Bexington and Robert and scandal

Her cottage in Little Hyssop was tiny and slapdash, but it was all hers. She doubted Bay could have stood straight under its low sloped ceilings. People in the village called her *Mrs.* Fallon, the unfortunate fictional Mr. Fallon having drowned along with her parents. Thus widowed and orphaned, she engendered some sympathy and enjoyed a degree of freedom. All in all, it had been a nice little life, if a bit boring, until Bay decided to hold her hostage on Jane Street.

Charlotte climbed back up on the bed and flopped down on her stomach. Reading Deb's letters was just like scratching an itch. One knew one shouldn't, but one did it anyway. This time she would *not* cry or feel sorry for herself, for she would be getting a letter of her own soon. She skimmed through a few until she read Bay's terse note announcing his grandmother's death. There were no sensual overtures in this one. Charlotte wondered if Deb had even bothered to send a note of condolence. She picked up the next letter.

Dearest Deborah,

The church was very crowded today. My grandmother Grace would have been pleased, I think, to see old friends and enemies, though she had precious few of those despite the sharpness of her tongue. Pointed as it was, it was often accurate, and one ignored my grandmother's advice at one's peril. They say it's very common when man is faced with his mortality to seek comfort in the arms of a woman. I hear many a babe has been conceived on the eve of a funeral. If you were here tonight, we could test that legend. While I am sadder even more than I expected, I am also grateful to be alive, and long to show you just how very alive I am. I will be thinking of you the whole night through.

Yours affectionately,
Bay

Charlotte swallowed. She didn't believe Bay meant to get Deborah with child. One didn't impregnate one's mistress if one could help it. But she suddenly realized they had taken no precautions the past few days. Bay had already shown *her* exactly how alive he was, and what if there was a child growing inside her? She tried to count back to her last courses, but never paid much attention to the calendar. There had been no need since Robert. She'd made a lucky escape there.

Her mama always said not to borrow trouble. There was no point in worrying herself when there was absolutely nothing she could do but wait. And anyway, she was old, well past her prime as a woman. She had the silver hairs slithering like snakes on her head to prove it.

She returned Bay's letters to the empty drawer and sat at her dressing table with a hand mirror. Gritting her teeth, she began yanking out every one of the coarse gray hairs that had plagued her for the past ten years. If only it were so simple to uproot her fears. And her desires.

Chapter 12

Monsieur David had recovered sufficiently to present him with a raft of palatable delicacies for his dinner. Bay had taken his time digesting, one eye fixed upon the case clock in his study. For good measure, he unpocketed his pocket watch at intervals and double-checked the time. When he was satisfied at last that Charlie should be sleeping, he stretched, rolled down his sleeves, and put his jacket back on. He left the desk in its disordered fashion, ledger books and pens strewn on the surface; he could set it to rights tomorrow when he returned from Jane Street. He had waited long enough.

The evening was mild, the skies clear, the walk was short. Spring had come to fashionable London in bursts of flowering trees and blooms in window boxes. Bay took a deep breath of night air, inhaling the sweet smell of flowers, so different from the miasma of other parts of the city. Like a naughty boy, he plucked a lilac branch from behind an iron fence, then a few buds from a stone pot that flanked some nob's doorstep. Armed with his improvised bouquet, he would lay it on Charlie's pillow in a few minutes.

His cock twitched impatiently. Miss Charlotte Fallon had an unpredictable effect on him, despite her fusty caps and tart tongue. And while she was far from the strumpet he first thought her, she had proved to me a very satisfactory bedmate. If he ever ran into Robert Chase again, he'd thank him before he planted him a facer. To the best of his knowledge,

Bay had never taken a woman's virginity. He supposed he must when he married again, and the prospect did not fill him with any particular thrill.

But he was sure he'd manage it better than Robert Chase.

Poor Charlie. Seduced and abandoned. Robert was married now, to a viscount's pretty daughter who had been possessed of a good dowry. Quite a step up for a simple country solicitor. The offices Robert shared with his father were far grander now, as was their clientele. Bay had attended the wedding with his grandmother a few years ago, more as friends of the bride's father than the groom. The elder Chase had served Grace Bayard well enough in local affairs. He wondered if Robert's wife knew of her husband's dishonorable use of his childhood sweetheart. Robert had never once uttered Charlie's name in his presence during their years at school together, but he had bragged long and at length of his other conquests. He must not have had anything yet to brag about with Charlotte Fallon.

Bay again marveled that he had never stumbled across the Fallon sisters. They had lived not twenty miles away from Bayard Court. Of course his old friend George, Viscount Harfield, had stolen Deborah right out of the schoolroom ten years ago, while Bay was busy battling Napoleon's forces in Spain. As a youth, he might have passed Charlotte on market day in Dorchester and never noticed—he'd only had eyes for Anne then anyway.

But now he definitely had eyes for Charlie, his very unlikely mistress. He was in hopes he could persuade her to remain in that position for a while yet, for as long as it was mutually agreeable to both of them. Bay was confident he held more attraction than Little Hyssop, whose very name was ridiculously prosaic. Despite her best intentions, Charlotte was more poetry than prose, her curvy body a heavenly cushion of carnality. Yes, Deborah was to be congratulated on her marriage and leaving him her sister in his bed.

His thoughts were entirely focused on what he planned to do with Charlie within the next hour. He didn't hear the stealthy shuffle behind him, but could not ignore the three large men who blocked his path as he rounded the corner on Jane Street. Surely hiring three night watchmen was a bit of overkill. None of them was familiar, either. He hoped he wouldn't be dragged off by his ear. He most urgently needed to see Charlie.

"Good evening, gentlemen," he said, his voice breezy. "I'm Sir Michael Bayard. Number Eight."

"Evenin', guv. Sorry about your whore. We got other plans for you tonight."

Bay opened his mouth, but the crack to the back of his skull made argument difficult. He pitched forward, grabbing at the lapels of one of the toughs, taking him down to the pavement.

" 'Ere now!"

The man smelled of tobacco and ale and serious body odor. Bay couldn't quite get his hands around his throat, but his fists seemed to be working. Knowing he was outnumbered and outfoxed, he rolled off and tried to stand up, only to be clubbed down again. His last sight was a pair of scuffed boots before a hood came down to cover his face. When he was hit for the third and final time, his world became permanently dark.

The gray morning light revealed to him that he was in a rather shabby bedroom. Naked. Tied to a bed.

The irony was not lost on him. How on earth had Charlie managed to hire those goons and teach him this lesson? He had apologized to her. A sincere apology. As far as he knew she had no access to any funds, unless she had promised one of the paintings as payment once he was safely out of the way. From his brief impression of them, they did not seem like art collectors. And how had she time to make these nefarious plans, when he had kept her so busy in bed over the past few days?

She must not have been 'waiting like an idiot' last night but deep in league with the bastards who had given him such a headache. Bay wrinkled his forehead and could feel the dried blood pulling tight against his skin. Charlie Fallon was a bloodthirsty little bitch. How could he have let himself be deceived by her? His first instincts had proved correct.

The whole while these thoughts were jumbling through his head, he strained against his bonds. The rope was nothing like the silken cords he used on Charlie, but rough hemp that cut into his wrists and ankles. He would have cried out, but the filthy rag that gagged him make anything but muffled grunts impossible.

No doubt the little minx thought she was clever to torture him thus. She underestimated him. He'd been a prisoner of the French for a mercifully short week, and they had not taken kindly to his activities before he was captured. It was true he bore no outward physical scars from that encounter, but his injuries were nevertheless acute enough for him to be in-valided home for a while—just long enough to be nearly dis-patched more efficiently by Anne's husband. Bay had been foolish enough to see if after all the humiliation he'd suffered if his manhood was still intact, and Anne was as ever his partner of choice. The whole affair had been hushed up, though the mark on Bay's face was a daily reminder of his foolishness.

By his estimate, he had been unconscious for four or five hours at least. More than a blow to the head had probably been applied. He inhaled deeply, wondering what he had been subjected to that incapacitated him, and hoped that his body was free of any drug. He bit into the rag, tasting its vileness, but didn't detect poison. He wasn't dead yet. But Charlie Fal-lon would be swinging from a noose as soon as he freed him-self from his own ropes.

He squinted around the room, looking for anything that might be put to use to get himself out of here. His clothes were nowhere in sight, nor were there any useful guns or swords mounted on the stained brown wallpaper. It seemed he was left with his wits, scattered as they were, and his furi-ous desire to escape. They would have to be enough.

The house was dead quiet. Bay listened hard for any noise of the neighborhood, but the shutters appeared to be nailed closed. There was absolutely nothing for him to do but lie here and wait.

Frazier would know something was amiss when he didn't come home. Even if his batman thought Bay was with Charlie, he would eventually trot round to Jane Street for some gossip with Mrs. Kelly and a piece of her famous strawberry pie. There were bills and business to attend to. Bay had left a very atypical mess on his desk last night that Frazier would notice immediately. If Charlie was still in residence, Frazier would frighten her into telling him the truth about his whereabouts.

But Charlie had probably bunked it, leaving her henchmen in charge. Bay devoutly hoped they hadn't forgotten about him, leaving him to lie in his own squalor for days, if not forever. This would be a most unpleasant and embarrassing way to die, trussed up like a plucked Christmas goose in a dirty oven.

He'd only kept Charlie tied up for a few hours, if one didn't count their raspberry fool interlude. If she was aiming for parity, he would already have been released. And as far as he knew, no dessert of any kind had been applied to his body. In fact, he was getting rather hungry.

Being a practical man, he shut his eyes against the feeble rays of light. As a soldier, he'd learned to sleep under the most primitive of conditions, hungry or not. This imprisonment would rank above a wet Spanish ditch, he reckoned. At least he was on a mattress, musty as it was. He'd need his rest before facing his jailors. If they came.

Charlotte rose early, wandering about the house as the morning drizzled on. The day was as gray as her spirits. She missed Bay, and when he got back, their liaison would be over. He would bring her home in the most discreet fashion, she was sure. He wouldn't drop her in the middle of the Little Hyssop green from his shiny new carriage. Probably trusty Frazier would be deputized for the last leg of their journey, in some conservative vehicle, Mrs. Kelly or Irene along for the ride for propriety's sake. Her neighbors would be agog anyway. Charlotte wondered what she would tell them about her visit with her sister that wouldn't betray her with suspicious blushes.

Yes, Charlotte's little adventure was almost over. She should be overjoyed. Instead she found herself wiping a tear from her cheek, earning her a scornful look from Mrs. Kelly as she charged through the house with a feather duster.

Charlotte felt useless and morose. She stared out onto the street from the front window, seeing no gentlemen creeping out of love nests or wicked ladies strutting down the sidewalk. But there was a break in the clouds, so she decided to get some fresh air in the back garden and escape Mrs. Kelly's disapproval. The foolishness of her actions was born upon her when she sat down on a damp bench, jolting her bottom with uncomfortable wetness. Just one more reason to feel sorry for herself, and her tears began to flow in earnest. For a woman who prided herself in not giving in to morbidity, she couldn't seem to control them or the accompanying blubbering.

"Not again."

Charlotte looked up to see Lady Christie in a lavender day dress and gave her a wobbly smile. "You must think me a veritable watering pot."

"What *I* think is of no import. What has the man done now?" She handed Charlotte an exquisitely embroidered handkerchief and joined her on the bench.

"Oh, you shouldn't sit! It's very wet."

"Pooh. I have a hundred dresses, not that my husband has bought them for me. I have a little sideline that keeps me in pin money. But do tell me—what has upset you today?"

"S-sir Michael has left. Gone to France." Charlotte hiccupped.

"Well, that's a good thing, is it not? You won't have to service his needs in your sister's place. Although—" Lady Christie raised an elegant copper brow—"it's my understanding that Sir Michael is more than adequate in the bedchamber."

Charlotte felt her crimson flush. Was there no privacy of any kind on Jane Street? All this garden-door hopping made it easy for the courtesans to confide in each other, not that Lady Christie was a courtesan. Charlotte wondered if Lady Christie's Thursday teas were another source of information for her. Perhaps the mistresses brought rulers and anatomically correct drawings with them to compare notes. That thought was quite shocking and compelling at the same time, and Charlotte giggled.

"There, that's better, although I don't know what brought it on." Lady Christie stared hard at her, but Charlotte was not going to confess.

"I am—I am to go home once Sir Michael completes his mission in France."

"My dear, surely you've been told, the war is over."

Charlotte snorted. "Not Bay's. He'll have to wrestle a valuable necklace away from my sister. She's apt to give him a scratch or two. She's *very* fond of a bit of sparkle."

Lady Christie's hand flew to the pansy-shaped diamond and enamel pin on her bodice. The stone in the center was large and brilliant, the purple petals each lined with tiny diamonds. "As am I. There's no point to jewelry sitting in a dark safe the year long. Edward used to argue with me over it. Now, thank goodness, I don't have to listen to him drone on and on. He was *such* a bore. Tell me, how did your sister come by this necklace?"

"It was on loan from Bay. Sir Michael, you know. She packed it with her in haste—oh, who am I kidding? She took it and Bay wants it back. It was his grandmother's. At first he thought I was in league with Deb, but I feel sure now he knows I had nothing to do with her taking it. We began on a very bad footing. But I have come to—to *care* about him. It's only been a few days, and I'm angry with myself for letting my guard down so easily."

Lady Christie sighed. "Poor thing. No matter how we resist, there are men in this world who manage to worm their way into our hearts. Bastards, all of them. Shall I ask about for another protector for you? Sir Michael will be sorry he let you go."

"Oh no!" The very idea made Charlotte go hot all over again. "I am not that sort of woman. If you only knew how boring *I* am. I live in a tiny cottage in a tiny village. I tat."

Lady Christie patted her hand. "Then you definitely must come to tea. It will do you a world of good. The Janes will perk you up."

That was the second time Charlotte had heard the women of Jane Street referred to as "the Janes." Such a plain name for a group of exotic, erotic women. In for a penny, in for a pound.

"I'd love to come."

"Excellent!" Lady Christie rose, shaking her soggy skirt. "I believe I'll have to change. The blue with the sapphire choker will be just the thing. See you tomorrow, my dear."

"Thank you, Lady Christie."

"Please, please call me Caroline. We are to be great friends while you are here."

She swept through the wooden door, her exit made a little less regal by the sodden patch on her backside. Charlotte needed to change herself, then figure out a way to spend her days waiting for Bay to come back.

Could she persuade him to keep her on Jane Street? Charlotte knew she wasn't the usual run of mistress. She hadn't heard of half the things on Bay's to-do list, although they had proved very pleasant. She was a fast learner. The raspberry fool was proof of that. Her mama would be appalled, but Charlotte hoped Bay would change his mind. She was perfectly content to remain in Bay's bed, or against a wall, or on a carpet, or in that wicked tub. She was completely fallen into folly and felt fine, if a bit alliterative.

Bay jerked awake hearing footsteps beyond the door, although they were not the heavy thud of boots like his captors had been wearing. He stilled his body as a jingle of keys preceded the turning of the lock. The room was still gray and dim, but he had every intention of showing Charlie Fallon just what he thought of her by the contempt in his eyes. Although perhaps the contempt could wait—he had an imperative need to relieve himself. How that was to be managed if she refused to untie him didn't bear thinking on.

The door edged open slowly and a veiled female figure, garbed head-to-toe in black, glided in, stopping just short of the bed. Bay took a deep breath. No whiff of oranges, Charlie's signature scent. Instead, he detected roses. *My God. Anne.* It was Anne who had arranged for him to be beaten and secured to this bed. Anne, who did not want to take no for an answer. Anne, who had obviously lost her mind.

His own mind raced, reevaluating every thought he'd had since midnight. Of course it was Anne, who had a substantial widow's jointure from her husband, arranged in the marriage settlements long before Whitley discovered Anne had been unfaithful. She had the money to hire the thugs. To rent a house in which to keep him imprisoned. He most certainly was not at Whitley House, or anywhere near Mayfair if his reliable nose still worked. The roses blended with cabbages and sewer. He grunted around the gag. She lifted her veil, looked him up and down, gave him what he knew to be a well-practiced smile.

"I'm sorry to be so late. I only just got word of last night's success."

Anne held her black-gloved hands primly before her. There was no attempt to remove the rag from his mouth or untie his bonds. Certainly no attempt to clothe him or cover him with a blanket. He lay naked, feeling himself flush in anger and embarrassment.

"You were not especially amenable to my proposal the last time we spoke. I thought I'd take this opportunity to change your mind." She reached for him with her black kid gloves, enveloping his cock in their warmth. Despite his every effort, he responded to her expert touch.

"How gratifying." She bent, teasing her lips against him for a fraction of a second, then set to work with her hands.

He screwed his eyes up, thinking of Spanish ditches and cold rain. That week he spent truly imprisoned by a small group of renegade French soldiers. Maggoty bread. Lying in his own piss and shit. Getting cleaned up only to be beaten and bloodied as the men took turns holding him down. His grandmother's funeral and old Mrs. Poole, who brought her smelly, snappish dog into the church. The winter morning he had to shoot his favorite horse as he lay heaving in snow, his eyes so trusting as Bay stood shaking over him. Learning of the loss of his child. It was useless. Anne stroked him until he spent onto the filthy sheets.

"I will send one of the men up to assist you. Or maybe several. They told me you put up quite a fight last night."

He had no recollection of it, just the humiliation of being bested on the street by some brutes. All his years of fighting, of killing, and his instincts had gone soft. It seemed his instincts were the only soft thing—to his horror his manhood had been rigid as he allowed Anne to manipulate him to ejaculation.

"I will be back tomorrow. And I'll speak to someone about tidying up this room. Its condition is not ideal in which to conceive our child. Just a month, Bay. That's all I'm asking. If we cannot accomplish the thing, then I'll let you go back to your little whore on Jane Street." She left the room, the key turning with finality in the lock.

A month. A month tied to this bed. Charlie thought he was in France, and would never question his whereabouts. Frazier might, if Charlie encountered him belowstairs and asked about his trip. His batman would know not so much as a shaving brush had been packed. Bay's fate depended upon the accidental meeting of his mistress and his manservant. It was not good enough. With a muffled howl of frustration, he waited for what was to come next.

Chapter 13

Charlotte wondered what one wore to a Courtesan Tea. Probably not one of her gray gowns. Definitely not a little white linen cap. She fingered Deb's cherry-red dress, rather stunning in its naughty way. Charlotte was surprised Deborah didn't take it with her until she tried to wrestle it on. Charlotte was a good stone heavier than Deborah, and this dress was *very* tight, too tight even for her sister. Deb had always liked to be comfortable. Charlotte had always liked to be safe. Well, to hell with comfort and safety. For one afternoon, she would flaunt her body with the other birds of Paradise. She would just not be able to eat much at Lady Christie's or the seams would split.

The afternoon had turned very fine after this morning's rain. It seemed no expense or trouble was spared for the party. Charlotte had watched from her bedroom window as Lady Christie's servants had set out little linen-draped tables and chairs in the back garden, placing standing umbrellas about for shade. Silver tea and coffee services gleamed in the bright sunlight, and fine bone china place settings adorned the tabletops. There were several guests already partaking of tea and conversation, Lady Christie flitting among them like a periwinkle-blue butterfly, a pearl and sapphire necklace about her throat. Undoubtedly real, unlike Deb's. Lady Christie had rescued her garden from its neglect and, like her, her roses were in healthy bloom.

It was a pity that Irene was not here to dress her hair into something suitably courtesanish. Charlotte did the best she could, raising her arms over her head as the sleeves pinched. She gathered her gloves and her shawl for the short walk through the garden door, leaving her battered straw hat behind. She had noted most of the other guests had opted not to wear a hat, and those that did would laugh out loud at her ancient bonnet.

"I'm visiting with Lady Christie, Mrs. Kelly," she called down the kitchen stairs. "Right next door. I promise I'm not running off."

Charlotte waited patiently until the housekeeper was at the bottom of the stairs. "You can check up on me through the garden door."

Mrs. Kelly sneezed. "Dratted pepper. Don't spoil your appetite. I've a delicious dinner planned."

"You do know that Bay—that Sir Michael has gone to France, don't you?"

Mrs. Kelly frowned. "First I've heard of it."

"He mentioned it yesterday. I'm sorry. I thought he would have told you."

"So that explains why he didn't come last night and you've been so mopey."

"I have not been mopey!" Charlotte cried. "Well, maybe a little. And you won't have to worry about me anymore once he returns. I'm to go back home."

Mrs. Kelly sneezed again. "I can't say I'll miss you, although you're a sight better than your sister."

"Thank you," Charlotte said dryly. "I don't think I'll be gone all that long."

Mrs. Kelly gave her a baleful look. "You look a proper tart."

"Yes, well, that's the point, isn't it? I'm meeting the other mistresses. I thought you had some sympathy for the women of Jane Street."

"I do, when they're honest."

Charlotte sighed. She really didn't know why she was bothering talking down the stairs to the housekeeper anyway.

"I am honest, Mrs. Kelly. Usually. I only acted out of desperation to leave. I'm not pinching any more paintings."

"You'd best not." Mrs. Kelly looked ready to arm herself with one of her vaunted knives and turned back into the kitchen.

Charlotte nervously tugged on her gloves, then nervously tugged up the bodice of her dress. She did look like a tart. Her arms were ever so much better covered than her breasts. But for this afternoon, she was a Jane, an acclaimed courtesan of "Courtesan Court." She would mix and mingle with *really* fallen women, not novices such as she. An opportunity like this didn't come along every day, certainly not in Little Hyssop. She went out into the garden, lifted her chin and marched through the wooden door.

"Charlie, my dear!" Caroline gave her a hug. Charlotte was pleased to see her new friend's dress showed even more shocking cleavage than her own. "Red suits you. How I love the color, but one is never supposed to wear it when one has red hair as I do. At least that's what Edward always said." A brilliant flash flew across her face. "But really, why should I care what Edward thinks? For these six years, I've denied myself red gowns. Well, to hell with that! Tomorrow I shall go to Madame Duclos and order an entire new wardrobe! Red. Vermillion. Rose madder. Scarlet. Alizarin. Crimson. Ruby. Cardinal. Ah! What fun I shall have! Come and meet some of my other guests."

Charlotte was dragged to a table where two girls sat, one, a dark Spanish beauty named Victorina Castellano, the other, ethereally fair Sophie Rydell. They were a study in contrasts even beyond their coloring. Victorina was animated and voluble, peppering Charlotte with questions in her charming accent. Sophie was quiet, delicate, and terribly refined. Both were considerably younger than Charlotte's thirty years.

"It was so kind of Lady Christie to invite me." Charlotte fiddled with a sterling fork. She had answered Victorina's questions as best she could. Both young women were now aware of the accidental aspect of her residence on Jane Street.

"If you are still here next Wednesday, I host a card party," Sophie said. "You are most welcome to come."

Next Wednesday seemed a long way off. But Bay might even be back by then if all went well, and then she might be gone. "Card parties, teas. It seems you all are a very congenial group here on Jane Street."

"It is all Caroline's doing," Victorina explained. "I think at first, she was bored, missed the company of her friends in the ton. Her husband the baron made her the insult, putting her here. But she is a woman of strength. She will not just sit back and do nothing. Twiddling her toes."

Sophie leaned across the tea table and whispered, "Thumbs, Vicky. We help her keep busy. We tell her *everything,* and she puts it in her books."

Charlotte was confused. "Books?"

"Do not worry. She changes things all around, the names, the hair colors," Victorina said. "But her novels, they are very popular. Always the strong, rich man and the innocent girl fallen into sin against her will. A happy ending every time." Victorina looked a bit wistful.

Good Lord. Charlotte did not want to read the book about the wrong sister sleeping with the right man. It had all the earmarks of a best seller. She swallowed her bite of muffin.

"Don't forget the sex scenes." Sophie smiled wickedly, dropping her refinement. "Caroline has a way with words. Women from all strata of society buy these books to learn our sensual secrets. Caroline says we are performing a public service, really."

Victorina's dark eyes flashed. "And when a Jane Street gentleman misbehaves, Caroline turns him into a villain. He finds it very difficult to find a new mistress, afterward, I assure you. Lord Pope now resorts to desperate girls on the street. He even had to sell his house. We all know about *him.*"

Charlotte had never heard of these books. From their description, they were not apt to be available in the Little Hyssop lending library. She resolved to ask Caroline about them at the earliest opportunity. She was introduced to four more mistresses during the course of the afternoon, and broke her vow, eating a great many tiny finger sandwiches and biscuits. She would have to waddle home carefully and ask Mrs. Kelly to push back dinner a few hours. When she bid good-bye, she was surrounded by a symphony of silk and perfume, kissed on the cheek by every courtesan and given open invitations for advice of all kinds. She had enjoyed herself immensely, shutting away her mama's objections completely from her head. These women could help her devise a strategy to stay with Bay. It was time to be wicked.

Bay lay on fresh sheets. He was somewhat fresh himself, having been permitted to wash, surrounded by four men, one with a pistol, two with truncheons, and the fourth a pair of fists that looked like hams. He had not been especially cooperative yesterday when he was helped to the chamber pot, nor when his hands were untied so he could eat the swill that had been prepared for him. His captors were so irritated with him that they had neglected his breakfast and luncheon today, but remembered to tie him fast to the bed after his ablutions, his naked body once again exposed in the dim light. Because they had not trusted him with a razor, his face was itchy with bristles. They had shoved something vile down his throat a little while ago, and his body felt weak as a kitten, his mind numb around the edges. They had not bothered to gag him again. His tongue was too clumsy for speech at any rate.

But he was alert enough to know he waited for Anne. He imagined her lifting her black skirts and mounting him. He would have no choice but to serve as the sacrifice on her altar of parental ambition.

If this situation were not happening to him, Bay imagined he'd think it amusing. He was a love slave, or a sex slave at any rate, love having little to do with anything anymore. Desired so ardently, he had nothing to do but fuck, with no real effort on his part. No words of promise, no casual caresses, no finesse necessary. Only his cock need function, and after yesterday's embarrassing loss of control, it seemed his member had a mind of its own despite Bay's abhorrence. He knew, though, that once Anne trapped him into fatherhood, he would have to marry her again. He could never permit his child to disappear in the arms of a madwoman.

He drifted off to drugged sleep, finding critical thinking far too difficult. When she came to him, he was too far gone to respond, either verbally or physically. Whatever they had given him rendered him incapable despite Anne's every merciless effort. Furious, she struck his face and left the room shrieking for her goons.

He had been given a reprieve. A day at least for this lassitude to wear off. Tomorrow he'd have his wits about him. For now, he'd just go back to sleep.

Bay had no notion of the time. He was washed again, begrudgingly fed, and much more lightly drugged. They had put something in his coffee, he knew. His eyelids were heavy, although his limbs had been livelier when he was permitted to get out of bed. His jailors were taking no chances on his reflexes. Bay wondered if Anne was aware that they still dosed him. He was not looking forward to her frustration if he failed to perform today.

Anne would never let him contact Frazier. She disliked the man on principle, and would be suspicious that they had some sort of code word between them. Bay only wished that were true. He and Frazier had a very conventional war, with no need of secret ciphers. Bay's one brief foray into espionage—reconnaissance, really—had cured him forever. Frazier had helped get him out of that debacle, and Bay knew he could count on his batman to get him out of this. If he could get word to Charlie somehow, she might be bright enough to read between the lines.

Charlie knew his writing. He'd read her that letter about the necklace, and he would bet his walnuts she'd read every single bit of Byronic drivel he'd written to Deborah during the six weeks he was in Dorset. He could easily imagine her coming to his rescue and knocking Anne on the head with a blunt object. But Anne was so unstable he wouldn't want to place Charlie in harm's way. Charlie could go to Frazier, however. Bay would make sure of it. Frazier would be delighted to take Anne on, blunt object or bare hands.

When he heard the jangle of keys, he shut his eyes and feigned sleep. Anne entered alone, the swish of silk the only sound in the grim little room. He felt her rub at his beard. "My. Your beard comes in quite red. I shall have someone shave you tomorrow."

Bay groaned as if he were dreaming.

"Don't tell me those fools have miscalculated again. Wake up, Bay." Her voice was sharp, insistent. Bay wondered how long it would take her before she lost her temper again.

He kept his eyes resolutely closed, evening his breathing. If she hadn't touched him, his plan might have worked.

But touch him she did, with the friction of her gloved hands relentlessly working through his reservations. He would not "wake" for this, not participate willingly in this travesty. Not give her the satisfaction of his conscious complicity. She abandoned any preliminaries of kissing his lifeless lips or cuddling in his leaden arms. He lay absolutely still as she slid onto him, the fabric of her skirts teasing his skin.

There had been a time when being inside her was all he ever dreamed of. He supposed he was now being punished for all those years of adultery—when he should have accepted his lot and moved on, away from Lady Anne Whitley.

An image of Charlie flashed in his mind, her bare silky white skin above him, her full breasts bouncing as she rode him. Her delighted, astonished smile as she watched their bodies join. The arch of her back as she reached her peak. The fan of her thick dark lashes on her love-flushed cheeks when she gave herself up to sensation. He felt the tension in his balls release as he spurted into Anne, seeing Charlie all the while.

But he said nothing, played possum, biting his tongue bloody so his ragged breaths would not reveal he was fully aware of what had transpired. Anne had collapsed upon his sweat-slick body, the scratchy starched ruffles of her dress irritating him.

"You cannot tell me you are still asleep," she purred. "You are as magnificent as ever."

He did not respond. Would not. The entire affair was a form of necrophilia. Their love was dead and no amount of her sexual scheming would revive it. As long as he was being drugged, he would milk it for all it was worth.

He heard her sigh, and then she pinched his nipple rather viciously. It was all he could do not to cry out. He gave an experimental snore instead. Very lifelike, if he did say so himself.

"Damn it. You'll be awake tomorrow. I'll see to it," she mumbled, gathering herself up and off the bed. "But it doesn't matter if you speak. I've gotten what I wanted."

She slammed the door behind her, rattling the glass behind the shutters. His child would be conceived in this hovel. How would he explain it?

He wished he had a blanket to cover his clammy skin. He'd have to ask for one tomorrow, which meant he'd have to wake from this nightmare and try to reason with Anne. If he could convince her that he agreed with her plans, even, God help him, welcomed them, perhaps she would let him move about freely. He'd jump out the window if necessary, no matter how high up he was, and take her with him.

Yes, tomorrow he'd talk, cajole, flatter, and lie.

Less than twenty-four hours passed before Bay had his chance to test his dissembling skills. His grandmother Grace had always seen right through any falsehoods, but he was trusting Anne to be so delusional she'd fall for his charm. This time when she entered, he met her eyes and gave her a seductive smile.

"I had the most marvelous dream, Anne. You were in it, and I was in you."

Even in the dim light he could see her blush like a schoolgirl. She was not veiled today, but wore an elaborately feathered hat that she was unpinning. She placed it on a rickety dresser and pulled a chair close to the bed. Bay wondered why she was not removing all her clothing but could not, in fact, complain.

He injected as much casual disregard into his voice as he could. "I wonder if you would permit me to get a note to my mistress. She thinks I went to France. I told her I would write, and if she doesn't hear from me, she's apt to wonder."

"So your letter was mislaid. It happens all the time. The mail service between here and there is very unreliable." Anne shrugged, toying with the locket at her throat he'd given her all those years ago. He wondered if the lock of his chestnut hair was still within. She had been partial to his curls once, which was one reason he had Frazier shear them off now every month.

He altered his tactics. "At least let me get rid of her, Anne. She's probably costing me a bloody fortune on Jane Street. I'll be most happy to see the back of her. She's been trouble from the moment I set eyes on her."

Anne's eyes narrowed. "You know I'll read anything you write."

"It will all be perfectly innocent." Bay swallowed the lump of hope forming in his throat. "You know you've convinced me, Anne. I don't need a mistress when I have you." He plastered a false smile on his face.

"I don't think I should trust you."

"I only need one hand to write. Keep me tied, Anne, if it worries you. I don't plan on going anywhere even when you let me loose. Why should I when I'll finally be with the woman I've always loved?" He hoped she wouldn't see how preposterous his sudden change of heart was. But she seemed disconnected from reality. She probably thought he was only giving her her due again, as he had for all those hopeless years.

"Truly? Do you mean it?" She sounded now like the girl she once was, the girl he had once nearly given his life for.

"I do. In fact, I'm willing to say 'I do' again, Anne. There's no reason we cannot marry now."

She wrinkled her nose. "I have no wish to marry you or anyone else. I told you that. I have my own funds, and you would only take them away."

"Don't be absurd. You know I have no need of any fortune you might have. We could hammer it all out in the marriage settlements."

"You did not feel this way a few days ago. What has made you think differently?"

"You have, my love. I'm assuming yesterday was no dream. While I regret I was not a more active participant, it can't escape your notice that I climaxed. And how I want to again." God, he was making himself sick, but if he could get her to release him—

"I'm afraid you'll have to wait a few days. My damned courses arrived early this morning."

Bay sent a prayer up to a benevolent God. "I am sincerely sorry you are unwell." He remembered how she would take to her bed with brandy and a hot brick. It must be costing her something to make this visit.

"Let me think on your proposal. You'll have to stay here where we can keep an eye on you."

"Really, Anne," he said huffily, "I'm a man of my word. I want nothing more than to have a life with you again." He sounded so sincere he was beginning to convince himself.

"I'll tell Karl to bring up some paper tomorrow so you can write to your little doxy. But I warn you, I'll be reading it."

"As you wish. I've nothing to hide, Anne." And a day to plan the most important letter of his life.

Chapter 14

Mrs. Kelly came into the dining room bearing a rather grubby note. Charlotte put her fork down. The truce between her and the housekeeper was fragile at best, and right now Mrs. Kelly was frowning at her with some ferocity quite putting her off her coddled eggs.

"A letter for you, Miss Fallon. From Sir Michael, I believe. The urchin who delivered it to the kitchen door didn't say and didn't even wait for a coin. Now before I give it to you, you must promise me that you'll be up to no funny business. I've got to leave the house for an hour or two on some errands, and Sir Michael will have my head if you get up to your old tricks." The woman actually held the letter behind her back, as if withholding a sweet from a child.

A letter of her own! She had practically worn holes in Deb's dozen letters, mooning over Bay's unexpectedly romantic turns of phrase.

"I promise I will be right here when you come back, Mrs. Kelly. Is there anything you'd like me to do for you while you're gone?" Charlotte asked sweetly.

"Laying it on thick, aren't you? I suppose if you want fresh flowers for your room and the downstairs parlor you might cut some." She placed the letter on the opposite end of the dining table and left the room. Shortly thereafter, Charlotte heard the slam of the back door as the woman left for the market.

Charlotte was up in an instant, all thoughts of finishing

breakfast gone. Her fingers trembled as she broke the red wax seal on Bay's letter.

Dear Deborah,

Charlotte sat down on a dining chair so fast she nearly fell. Dear Deborah! Dear *Deborah*! How could the man write such a thing? She was tempted to tear the paper into a million little pieces, then stomp on them. Even if he were distracted by travel, he should know her name. He'd shouted it loudly enough when he emptied himself inside her time after time. Her face grew hot and her pulse quickened in anger.

I hope this letter finds you well.

No, she was most assuredly not well. And if Bay had been here with her, he would not be either, with her hands fastened around his throat.

*Please keep it with the others I have written you.
Frannce is very hot. I have seen your sister and the
emerald necklace is safe. I have gotten tied up and have
to delay my return home, so see Frazier for the money
to go back to Little Turnip where you belong. Bring
this letter to him as soon as possible and he will
know what to do.*

Sir Michael Xavier Bayard, Bart

Charlotte let the letter slip from her fingers. This was the worst letter in the history of human correspondence. He might have dismissed her gently, thrown in a compliment or two before he so brutally told her to get out of his house. Little Turnip! Yes, she would go back to Little Turnip at the earliest opportunity, and hope the man never remembered the real name of her village. If she never saw him again, it would be too soon.

To think that she thought they were coming to an understanding. An accommodation. She had convinced herself that being Bay's mistress was something she could live with, at least for a time. Deborah had been right for a change—Charlotte *was* in need of amusement, although ravishment was perhaps the more accurate term. She had spent the past ten years being so damned good it was almost a relief to succumb to Bay's seduction.

What a fool she had been. Still was. She should not be allowed to ever leave her cottage in Little *Turnip* again, for she could obviously not navigate in the wider world. She had been duped by a devil, and he was so stupid he couldn't even spell France.

Charlotte looked at her plate of eggs, longing to throw them against the flocked wallpaper. That would be highly unfair to Mrs. Kelly. But damn it, she was in the mood to break something.

An insidious idea popped into her head. Why not? At least she would be sparing Bay's next mistress the repugnant remains of Angelique's and Helena's tenure on Jane Street. With determination, she marched up the stairs.

The clock would be the first to go. Let the next poor girl measure out her days waiting for Bay by some other means. She gathered up a few smaller statues from the bedside table and went into the garden. She pitched the Cupid-clock against the brick wall and smiled as it shattered, springs and metalworks flying into the air. It was child's play to hurl the others quickly after it.

The splintering sound was most satisfying. "There! That will show the bastard!" Her blood was buzzing so loudly in her ears she almost missed hearing the hesitant voice of the woman next door.

"I say, is something wrong? Are you all right?"

"I am now." Charlotte straightened her little lace cap and wiped a flake of plaster from her cheek. It was a pity she did not have protective spectacles. Having to squint her eyes closed as she heaved each angel to its destruction lessened the satisfaction to some degree. "Who's there?"

"Your neighbor. I'm Laurette."

"How do you do? I'm called Charlotte. When he remembers my name," she muttered.

There was a long silence, and then a tentative question. "Are you going as mad as I am?"

What an extraordinary thing to be asked. But then Charlotte's entire life was extraordinary at the moment. She would not be surprised if pigs flew or the mountains came to Mohammed, rock by rock.

"It depends how mad you are. I have always thought of myself as being the steady and sensible one, but lately I have reason to doubt. This is rather absurd, talking through the wall. There's a wooden door, you know." Charlotte heard the rustling of leaves. "I imagine it's covered over on your side, but I'll rattle the knob."

"There is? I'll have to cut back some of the ivy," Laurette said. "Hold on." After some vicious snipping sounds, the hinges creaked but the door didn't open enough for Charlotte to pass through.

"Bother. Can you push?"

"I can try." Charlotte giggled, filled with a kind of giddy anticipation. She had enjoyed meeting the other mistresses, and this one sounded charming and intelligent. "If this doesn't work, I suppose I could always come round and ring your doorbell."

"That would take all the adventure out of the endeavor. Here, I'll pull, you push."

After a joint effort and a sore shoulder, Charlotte slipped through into the most magical garden she had ever seen. Put the bastard Bayard's totally in the shade. There was every kind of flower she knew and many she didn't. Tiny yellow birds trilled and dodged overhead. A fountain bubbled. It was dazzling.

But Laurette was not. Laurette did not look like anybody's mistress, or at least not a Jane Street mistress. She was pretty enough, but frazzled. And she was old, at least Charlotte's age. Her wavy blond hair was pinned back in a messy lump, and she had thousands upon thousands of freckles. Charlotte's mama would have attacked her with a crate of lemons.

"Oh! How absolutely lovely this is!" Charlotte gazed around the garden. "I watched them put it all in from my bedroom window, you know. They all worked like fiends. Even Lord Conover dug right in." She lowered her voice. "He removed his shirt. You are a lucky woman indeed."

Laurette snorted. "He *is* a fiend."

"Oh, my dear, you've no idea of a true fiend. Sir Michael Xavier Bayard's portrait is right next to the word in Dr. Johnson's dictionary."

"Then why—" Laurette colored. "Forgive me. It's none of my business."

Charlotte sat on the stone bench and lifted her face to the sun. Her mama was not there to warn her of freckles, although Laurette served as a living example of complexion misfortune. "It's rather a long, sordid story. Let's just say that one's family obligates one to do things that are distasteful if not downright repugnant."

"Exactly so. How long have you been in residence?"

"Long enough. It seems like I've been here forever. An eternity. But at least I won't have to look at the damn cherubs any longer."

"Pardon?"

"You heard my little fit. The smashing and the screaming. I just broke what are no doubt valuable but entirely vulgar little naked statues that belonged to my predecessors. There are still more in my bedchamber. Would you like to help me finish off the rest?"

Laurette looked a bit frightened of her, and no wonder. It was not at all ladylike to destroy property, particularly when the property was not your own. Charlotte gave her a benign smile. "Truly, I am not usually so bloodthirsty, not that there's any blood in gilded plaster, mind you. But when you see them, you'll understand. Come."

Laurette nodded toward her house. "I'm not sure—they might miss me."

"Oh, you poor dear. I've heard all about the strange and mysterious Conover. I saw the *tattoo*. Is he keeping you a prisoner, then?" Maybe they had more in common than she thought. Under house arrest. Sisters in forced seduction, although if she were honest, there had been times when she was forcing Bay.

"No! Not really."

"Well then. Come along."Charlotte looped an arm through Laurette's. "Is he stingy, your Lord Conover? Your dress looks seasons old."

Laurette laughed. "That's because it is. It's my own. I assure you, Conover has filled my closets. I just chose not to be tempted today."

"Very wise. I myself will not wear what Sir Michael has bought." Bought for her *sister*, not that she was going to tell anyone that at first acquaintance. It was all too sordid for words. "It drives him to distraction." She'd leave one of her spinster's caps on his pillow as a parting gift.

They ducked into the kitchen entryway. "My servants are out, otherwise I would not have had the courage to kill all the little angels. Follow me." Since the Painting Incident, she had been watched like a hawk by Mrs. Kelly. Charlotte had sworn she had learned her lesson. Being tethered to the bed had its charms, but was not to be repeated if she could help it. But in a day or two she'd be on her way with the full approval of Sir Michael Xavier Bayard.

Laurette stopped in her tracks to admire the artwork along the hallway. It was Charlotte's opinion all the subjects could do with more clothing. She was getting very tired of plump breasts and buttocks, but she knew now Bay's collection was famous. Bay knew his nudes. And every art dealer knew Bay and knew his pictures. She was lucky he didn't clap her in Newgate after her abortive attempt at theft, but his punishment had been almost as bad, minus the rats. The paintings would continue to hang on the walls, taunting her and making her nipples stiffen with cold just looking at them.

"None of them are my doing. Sir Michael is quite the connoisseur. He has excellent taste in all things, except mistresses. What they did to the bedroom—well, you shall see for yourself."

When they stood in the doorway upstairs, Laurette gawped.

"You understand, don't you? How can one possibly live in a room where so many plaster eyes are on one? And they look far from innocent. They are not proper angels. See their leering little faces?" Charlotte poked a dimpled cheek and shivered.

"I'll help you. A pity we cannot borrow a wheelbarrow and roll them down the stairs."

"I daresay the exercise will do us good, but I'm grateful you're here. We'll have the job done in half the time." Charlotte gathered up her skirt and started depositing the little Cupids in the fold. Laurette followed suit.

It was a heady experience, dropping the plaster angels on their heads and shattering them on the bricks. Wings flew everywhere. Charlotte imagined each tiny neck was Bay's as she strangled the statues first before she dashed them to the ground. Laurette was getting into the spirit quite nicely, whooping with sympathetic vengeance. She taught Charlotte how to skip the smaller angels like stones. Laurette showed an excellent arm bouncing each baby to its doom.

Eventually the angels had all gone to heaven. Charlotte and her new friend were glowing with perspiration where they weren't coated in dust. The brick path looked like a battlefield, the odd elbow and foot blown off by the enemy and scattered. Charlotte sent Laurette back through the wall so she could sweep the bits of plaster under the foliage. Before she left, Laurette invited her for tea tomorrow, which would make a nice farewell party from Jane Street. She was not about to be rushed out before she was ready, Bay be damned. What difference did a day or two more make, when he was undoubtedly in the arms of some French floozy?

Charlotte was nearly ready to go next door when Mrs. Kelly knocked at her bedroom door. "Lady Christie is downstairs, Miss Fallon."

"She is?" This was most unexpected. Such a flurry of friendship for her, when she had spent most of the past ten years in solitude with her undependable cats. She tied her battered bonnet over her usual cap. Perhaps it was time to give them up, but they had annoyed the annoying Bay so very, very much. It was too bad he would not see her one more time.

She followed Mrs. Kelly downstairs. Caroline was sitting in the parlor, frowning over a little notebook in her lap. She was crossing out something with a silver pencil.

"Caroline! I didn't expect you, but I'm so happy to see you."

"Are you going somewhere? My, forgive me for being blunt, but that is an atrocious hat."

Charlotte flopped down on the settee beside her. "I know, but it's all I have. I've been invited to the Mad Marquess's house. His mistress Laurette and I engaged in a bout of vandalism yesterday." Charlotte proceeded to tell Caroline the particulars, and to her discomfort, watched Caroline take notes as she did so. She was very much afraid that an obituary for the cherubs was being written, to be included in a future volume of Lady Christie's shocking novels. Charlotte's fit of pique would be made famous, or more accurately, infamous. Hopefully no one in Little Hyssop would ever connect the quiet Mrs. Fallon with the wild woman who smashed statues on Jane Street and slept with her sister's lover.

"Fascinating. This Laurette sounds like a splendid girl. Do you think I might come with you?"

"I suppose. She seems quite lonely. She hasn't a thing to do but wait for Lord Conover to come. And when he does arrive, she wishes him to the devil."

Caroline raised an eyebrow. "Another unhappy mistress? You two will give Jane Street a bad reputation."

"You needn't worry about that. There will be no gloom cloud over Number Eight. I received my congé in yesterday's mail. I've sent for Bay's Mr. Frazier and will meet with him tomorrow. The sooner I can make arrangements to leave, the better."

Caroline's pencil rolled onto the floor. "But no!"

"Oh, but yes." Charlotte felt her lip tremble.

"And I was just getting to know you." Caroline patted her hand. "You understand I'm fond of all the girls here—most of them, anyway. I've had to be careful of Lucy Dellamar, though. Things seem to disappear when she comes calling. The odd silver teaspoon, the brooch I left on my dressing table, that sort of thing. It's said her protector keeps her on a very short economic leash, so the poor girl is probably only supplementing her income. One day her sticky fingers are bound to get her in trouble. If only she would come to me, perhaps I could help her. I try to help them all, you see." Caroline twisted a rather spectacular topaz bracelet over her glove. "But the Janes are not quite the thing. You seem so nice and normal. Refined. It's been a while since I had such a friend."

Charlotte swallowed back her tears. "But I'm a fallen woman."

"Well, all of us have made a mistake or three, I expect. Your family was gentry, was it not?"

"Yes, but at the end we were quite ruined. When my parents died, they were one step away from the workhouse."

"Then we have something in common. My father always had more pride than pounds. Papa would have been thrilled to know Edward proposed. Our relatives found bailing him out over the years tedious in the extreme. Papa spent every bit of mama's settlement money and then some. He's dead, else he would be hovering about wondering why I have not found a rich lover by now to spot him a monkey."

"Why haven't you?" Charlotte asked.

Caroline looked uncomfortable. "I'm sure I don't know. Perhaps one day I will. It's not as though I haven't had offers." She changed the subject abruptly. "Let's not keep Laurette waiting. If you are leaving, I shall have to replace you.

Charlotte laughed. "Fair weather friend! I think Laurette is as ill-at-ease here as I am."

"I got used to it," Caroline said softly.

They did not go next door via the garden gate but instead stepped out onto the short street, turned right, and lifted the shiny brass star and moon knocker. The butler opening the door was a foreign fellow, very elegant and correct. He announced them both and Charlotte watched Laurette blanch. Charlotte should have sent round a note explaining that she was bringing another guest. Her manners as well as her morals had gone missing.

But Caroline took charge as usual. In the very short time Charlotte had known her, Caroline seemed a force to be reckoned with. Caroline was already holding Laurette's hands in hers, beaming a smile at her. "Do forgive Charlotte. I invited myself. Your arrival on the street in the Mad Marquess's house has caused quite the commotion, and when she said she was coming to tea, I couldn't resist. I am Caroline Christie."

"How do you do, Lady Christie?"

"Please call me Caroline. The less we hear of my husband's name, the better." She settled herself on the settee, smiled, and patted a pillow. Laurette had no choice but to sit beside her while Charlotte arranged her dull gray skirts on a chair. Laurette's hands were twisting nervously in her lap. "I told you you'd scare her," Charlotte said. "Would you like me to pour, Laurette? I'm quite used to Caroline now. She's been a lifesaver."

"Don't worry, I shan't reveal a thing to any of our other neighbors. I can be discreet if I care to be."

Laurette looked shocked. "You *live* here on Jane Street?"

"Indeed I do. My husband bought my house five years ago when we separated. He thought to make a point, you see, to let me know what he thought of me. But I find the street suits me very well."

"Caroline lives next door to me. She heard me in my garden crying one morning and we've been friends ever since," Charlotte said. "I seem to be a noisy neighbor." She winked at Laurette and passed a cup to Caroline.

"All men are beasts. I am sorry I missed the demolition of those deviant little angels. I should have enjoyed getting my hands around their scrawny necks."

"It *was* fun." Laurette grinned.

The ice broken, they spent the next hour filling Laurette in on the personalities on the street. Charlotte was almost sorry she would be leaving. But leave she must. She left Caroline and Laurette deep in gossip. She was going home to pack—again. This time she would not be secreting paintings into her luggage. Tomorrow morning Mr. Frazier was coming to make the arrangements for her return home. She would be in her cottage before she knew it, her contact with "Courtesan Court" over. It was time to go back to boring.

Chapter 15

Charlotte fidgeted with the strings of her cap. Mr. Frazier was frowning over the letter as though he were teaching himself to read. Perhaps he was not going to help her leave Jane Street after all. He had been most suspicious when she presented him with Bay's orders, and had not believed her until she fished the letter out of the drawer in her room.

He was scratching his red head, reading the hideous thing for perhaps the sixth time.

"I dinna like it." His Scots brogue had become more pronounced the longer he sat in the parlor.

"Well, I didn't care for it much either," Charlotte said with asperity. "Yet you cannot argue he wants me gone and he wants you to help me."

"Hold on now, lass. When Mrs. Kelly sent word to me yesterday you wanted to see me, I was baffled. I thought the major was here with you all this time."

"As you can see, he is not. Has not been for days. He's gone to *Frannce*," she spit, sounding the extra "n." The man couldn't even spell the name of the country he fought against so many years.

Frazier shook his head. "He has not. Not an article of his clothing is missing. Not a comb, not a stocking. His valise is in the attic." He paused. "His desk is a mess, too. The major is quite orderly. He'd never go on a trip without tidying up. Or saying a word to me."

"Well, obviously he has. He can always buy toothpowder and a change of smallclothes on the road. Perhaps he lucked out on a quick passage." Really, would the irritating man not fork over some money for her so she could get out of here? Charlotte was not asking him to accompany her.

"Think now. What were his last words to you?"

Charlotte huffed. "He told me he'd hired an investigator to find my sister. And the bloody necklace."

"Mr. Mulgrew. And the rubies, yes. Why then, Miss Fallon, does he refer to the necklace as emeralds?"

"I could not tell you. He ranted about them enough to me." And wrote about them with eloquence.

"He mentions other letters. Is this one anything like the ones he wrote to Deborah?"

Charlotte felt the wash of color creep up her neck. "No."

"He calls you by her name, too. There's something fishy about all of it."

"Be that as it may, he wants me to go home and has asked you to help me. *As soon as possible*," she emphasized.

"Aye. And did you contact me the day you received this?" His hound dog brown eyes bore into hers. She shifted uncomfortably in her chair, remembering her first reaction to Bay's letter. All the shattered statuary and the resulting euphoria. Calling for Mr. Frazier was the last thing on her vengeful mind, and then Laurette had invited her to tea.

"Practically. I had an engagement yesterday."

"So he's been waiting for us to come to his rescue." Frazier placed the letter on a table, then stood up, fists clenched.

"What on earth are you talking about?"

"Miss Fallon, forgive me so for saying so, but you're a slow top. Does the major not know your name?"

Charlotte snapped back at him. "He had an arrangement with my sister first. I'm sure one mistress is much like another in his world."

"Nay. The major is a most particular man. See here, he calls you by the wrong name, gets rubies mixed up with emeralds, talks about Little Turnip. I assume that's not the name of your village?"

"No, but he was always making fun of it. And don't forget, he can't spell either. But he's made it plain he wants me out of his life."

Frazier picked the letter up again. "F-R-A-N-N-C-E. I'll be damned."

Charlotte was quite sure he would be, working for the odious Sir Michael Xavier Bayard.

"Good God. *She's* got him."

"My sister is many things, but she's a married woman now. I doubt Bay is so attractive she's thrown over Arthur on her honeymoon."

"No, you little twit." He buried his face in his hands. When he looked up his eyebrows resembled deranged caterpillars. "Och, forgive me. It's Anne. Lady Whitley. She's sunk her claws into him again somehow."

Charlotte reared back in her chair. "His—his wife?"

He snorted. "He'd never write a letter like this if he could help it. The major has a way with words. Always lets the ladies down gently. This—this proves that he's not himself."

"He's run off with his *wife*? All the more reason for me to leave. Please, Mr. Frazier, I beg you. I simply want to go home. I have no money. None. If you don't help me, I'll have to resort to stealing the paintings again. Surely Bay would not approve of that." Charlotte leveled a stern eye at the man, but he paid no attention to her.

"No, no, lass. He would never run off with Anne. Not again. He's taken the devil's own time to learn his lesson, but he's done with her."

"That's not what he said. He told me his feelings were—complicated. That he was trying to be her friend. Maybe the friendship has turned into something else after all." She watched as Frazier's face turned as red as his hair.

"I canna believe it! I willna believe it!" He pointed a stubby finger at her. "You stay right here. I'm off to see that Mulgrew fella, find out what's become of his man and the damned necklace. See if he knows whether the major made it to France."

"I don't want to stay right here!" Charlotte shouted. Without thinking she gripped an empty Chinese vase and hurled it against the wall. Frazier didn't flinch.

"Spirited, are ye? We might need some of that spirit before this is all over." He stepped closer to her, lowering his voice. "Now, see here, Miss Fallon. I know the major, have known him more than a dozen years. He's in trouble. If you thought about it past your pride, you'd see I'm right."

Charlotte shut her eyes. She didn't want to hear the reasonableness of his words or see the sincerity on his face. It was true when they parted, Bay had promised to escort her home himself. But rich gentlemen were a fickle lot—the letter made it clear he had changed his mind and was without a doubt happily sporting with some French tart. Or two. All the mistakes were probably made in a drunken haste to get back into bed.

But what harm did it do for her to remain here a little longer, until Frazier was satisfied that his employer had in fact meant every word? The Jane Street house was loaded with every luxury, and Mrs. Kelly didn't seem quite so disposed to poison her now. She had met congenial neighbors, and, if she were honest with herself, she didn't exactly have a lot to go home to.

"Very well. It's your hide. Do what you must to assure yourself of Bay's intentions."

Much to Charlotte's shock, he patted her on the head. "Thank ye, lass. I'll return as soon as I can with news. Please tell Mrs. Kelly all of this, every bit. Show her the letter and tell her my concerns. She might have a word or two to cheer you up."

Charlotte doubted that. She watched as Frazier sprinted out of the room. Reluctantly she got up and picked up the dreadful letter. She reread it with fresh eyes.

Dear Deborah,

I hope this letter finds you well. Please keep it with the others I have written you. Frannce is very hot. I have seen your sister and the emerald necklace is safe. I have gotten tied up and have to delay my return home, so see Frazier for the money to go back to Little Turnip where you belong. Bring this letter to him as soon as possible and he will know what to do.

Sir Michael Xavier Bayard, Bart

She still didn't see Frazier's point of view. The letter was as straightforward as ever to her. My word, Bay even talked about the weather. How banal. But she dutifully went down the stairs to explain the situation to Mrs. Kelly as instructed.

The older woman was rolling out a pie crust. Charlotte took the rolling pin from her as the cook fished her glasses out of her apron pocket and continued to smooth the dough on the marble slab. She was a dab hand at pastry herself. Her pies always sold well at the Little Hyssop parish fair.

"Hmm." Mrs. Kelly looked up. "Sir Michael says he's tied up. Don't you feel his choice of words is rather significant?"

"I'm sure I couldn't say." Charlotte would not soon forget her delightful humiliation, but she was not about to discuss it with Bay's servant.

"I agree with Angus. There's something off about the whole thing." She carefully folded the letter and put it on the kitchen table. "When you told me he'd gone to France without a word to me, I confess I was surprised. He's a thoughtful boy."

"Bay is hardly a *boy*," Charlotte reminded her.

"When you get to my great age, you'll sing a different tune. He'd never leave Angus behind if he were to go on a trip of any length, either. There is a mystery afoot here."

"Pooh." Charlotte rolled the pin with a violent flourish. "If he's not in France, then he's with Lady Whitley. Either way, I'm still stuck here against his wishes. And mine. But it's no skin off my nose if Mr. Frazier is reprimanded. What kind of pie are we making?"

"Chicken. Be a dear and fetch a potato from the barrel, will you?"

The two worked in companionable chatter preparing Charlotte's lunch. Charlotte was treated to secondhand anecdotes from Bay's youth, gleaned by Mrs. Kelly from her sister's letters. Her descriptions of Bay's grandmother made Charlotte sorry that she would never meet her. No wonder he wanted the necklace back as a reminder of his formidable grandmama. When the pie emerged from the oven, pastry browned and gravy bubbling, Charlotte shared it with Mrs. Kelly right at the basement kitchen table. The hatchet and knives had been buried.

Anne had not come yet today, for which Bay was grateful. His captors had loosened the ropes somewhat after Anne complained yesterday that his skin was rubbed raw. He was on a strict schedule like a nursing baby. Meals were delivered at regular intervals, he was released—and surrounded—as he relieved himself to the taunts of the four grubby men who guarded him. The rest of the time he was left to stare up at the cracked ceiling. If Bay were to take up his paintbrushes again, he would paint a vision of hell to rival the heaven of Charlie's bedchamber.

He had failed there. Evidently she had not realized his intent when he wrote that horrid letter, nor, apparently, had Frazier. Perhaps she hadn't even shown it to him but dusted off to Little Lockup in a huff. It was going on three days since the missive was delivered, unless Anne had simply lied and thrown it away. Bay had been so sure Frazier would be suspicious of his sudden disappearance and come looking for him.

Ah, well. He supposed he'd better get used to his situation. Eventually he would escape. He had to. The thought of being bound to Anne for a lifetime was too terrible to contemplate. The shadows from the slatted shutters told him it was late afternoon, too soon for a night's sleep. He made himself drift off anyway, half-listening for any movements in the house. It was

remarkable what utter boredom led to. Bay had already exhausted his repertoire of remembered poetry and Bible verses. It
was safer to doze, dreaming of being in Charlie's arms.

He was awakened from his pleasant dream by Anne's leather-
gloved hand on his bare chest. The room was in full darkness
apart from a tallow candle that glowed on the crude table.

He made himself sound petulant. "Where have you been?"

"At the most dreary of musicales. Nothing very tonnish.
I'm in mourning, as you know, but my great-aunt invited me
to hear her protégée. The shrieking set my eardrums on fire.
How have you been occupying yourself, Bay?" she asked
with a catlike smile.

"Anne, there really is no need to keep me shackled. I could
have accompanied you to hear this songbird. I'm sure we
might have found an alcove or a balcony where we could
have made our own music." *Laying it on thick*. He watched
her preen in the candlelight.

"There, there. Perhaps in a week or two, when you've
proved your ardor again." She traced his mouth with a fingertip. "Somehow, I'm not quite convinced by your words. Perhaps a kiss will help persuade me?"

She was bending over him, her cloying rose scent filling his
nostrils. He opened his mouth to protest, but it was quickly
covered by hers. She tasted of sherry and determination. He
allowed the kiss to last far longer than he wanted, participat-
ing with his own desperate earnestness. She must be convinced
of his intentions—it was the only way he could win his freedom. At last she settled back on the edge of the mattress, her
face flushed.

"Can we not end this nonsense, Anne? I want you. I want
to be inside you."

"Soon. Another day or two, I promise."

She left, blowing out the candle on her way out the door.
Once he heard the front door close and her carriage move
down the street, he let out a bellow. Let her goons think he
was frustrated that he hadn't fucked her. Bay knew otherwise.

* * *

The pounding woke her from a sound sleep. Charlotte threw on her gray robe and stumbled down the stairs. Mrs. Kelly was snoring unaware in her room. Irene was due back any day, but would have been no more prepared to answer the door at this hour than Charlotte was.

"Who is it?" she shouted over the incessant thudding.

"Angus Frazier! Open the door, Miss Fallon!"

Charlotte turned the large brass key and pulled the handle. Angus nearly fell into the hallway. His hair and eyebrows were standing at red attention, wild, and his clothes were in a dreadfully rumpled state.

"She's got him! I followed her tonight to a mean little house in Islington."

Charlotte could barely understand the man's Scots burr. "Come in, Mr. Frazier, and take a breath."

"I havena time to breathe! Anne Whitley has got the major locked up in a house with four guards!"

Charlotte blinked. Frazier rather resembled a charging bull. "Come into the parlor. I'll get you something to drink—some sherry or brandy—and we can talk about this sensibly."

"There's no sense to be made of it!" He paced the hall, slapping his hand on the wallpaper so Bay's paintings jumped. "I went to see Mulgrew after I left you this morning. He's had word from his man on the Continent. Your sister turned over the necklace—only after her new husband showed her some gumption from what I ken—and he's on his way back to England with it. Mulgrew was all set to report to Major Bayard with the news when I went to his offices. He knew nothing about the major turning up in France, so we went down to the docks. Major Bayard never booked passage *anywhere*. Mulgrew and I both checked. He knows what he's about, Mulgrew does. So then I went to Whitley House this evening, watched as Lady Whitley went off in her carriage to her aunt's. Hung about until she left. And did she go home?" the man barked. "No, she didna! I attached meself to the carriage like a barnacle and we wound up at a wee shabby house. Two strong lads let her in. There was talk about the 'prisoner' misbehavin' right there on the front steps for all the world to hear. So she goes upstairs. I watched the candle flicker until I saw a dim light in the front room upstairs. Mind you, the shutters are closed right and tight. I crept round to the alley, and three of the blokes were smokin' and laughin' at the fourth, who's wearin' a sling and looks mad as hell. They kidnapped him, Miss Fallon! The major is tied up at Anne Whitley's mercy!"

Charlotte sat down on a stair step. "Mr. Frazier," she said softly, "there might be some other explanation. Did they mention Bay—the major—by name?"

"They didna have to! Who else could it be? That Whitley woman wants Major Bayard's seed, she does. He told me so himself."

"I beg your pardon?" Charlotte wished someone would bring *her* a large glass of brandy.

"That woman came to the major's house days ago with some crazy idea that he get her with child. I fought with him over it."

"Bay wants to *marry* her?"

"Och, no no. But if she falls pregnant, he would wed her all over again, poor fool."

Charlotte wrapped the robe tightly around her, feeling suddenly chilled for such a warm spring night. "Mr. Frazier, forgive me, but none of this makes any sense at all."

"You're tellin' me." He stopped pacing and ran his hand through his hair, upending it further. "I'll get hold of Mulgrew at first light tomorrow, see if he'll help us. We've got to get the major out of there."

Charlotte shivered. "You keep saying 'we.'"

He glared at her. "You won't help? You're happy enough to live in his house and eat his food, aren't you?"

Charlotte felt her face go warm. "You may not know this, Mr. Frazier, but I was an unwilling participant in this folly, and I've begged and begged you to help me go home. For all we know, Bay and Anne have a little love nest and don't want to be interrupted. The men you saw could just be ordinary servants."

"Not bloody likely. They're hired thugs. I've seen their like all over Europe. You'd know I'm right if you saw them." He smacked the wall. "Maybe you should see them. Divert them while I get the major out of there. We'll talk to Mulgrew and see what he thinks."

Charlotte stood up. "Now see here, Mr. Frazier. If these men are so dangerous, I hardly think I can be diverting enough. I'm not exactly a femme fatale."

Frazier looked her up and down, as if seeing her for the first time. Charlotte was acutely aware of her old gray robe, her braided hair, and her nightcap. "You'll do. Now go back to bed and rest up. I'm going back to Islington to keep watch. Someone needs to have a clear head tomorrow." He slammed the front door behind him.

Charlotte leaned against the wall. Her head was most certainly unclear tonight. Mr. Frazier had convinced himself that Bay was in danger, when in reality the man didn't even know if Bay was in the house that Anne Whitley visited. Just because Frazier and this Mr. Mulgrew couldn't find evidence that Bay went to France didn't mean that Bay wasn't someplace else enjoying himself in high style. There could be a hundred different explanations for his whereabouts.

Heaving a sigh, she mounted the stairs. Fat chance she would get back to sleep tonight, although Mrs. Kelly was still snoring away in her attic room, each rippling snort a testament. Mr. Frazier was a difficult man to sleep through, with his shouting and slamming. Charlotte thought he was a difficult man to ignore, no matter the time of day. Tomorrow would come too soon.

Chapter 16

Despite Charlotte's misgivings, she fell back asleep, drifting into sensual dreams. In no time at all, Mrs. Kelly was shaking her awake.

"You've got company downstairs. Angus—Mr. Frazier and another gentleman, Mr. Mulgrew."

Charlotte groaned. "What time is it?"

"Just on seven. Why didn't you get me up last night?"

Mrs. Kelly's tone was accusatory. She obviously believed Bay was being held hostage by four ruffians under the direction of Lady Anne Whitley. Charlotte was not yet prepared to agree.

"I'll dress as quickly as I can. Please go downstairs and offer them breakfast."

Mrs. Kelly looked even more aggrieved. "And just what do you think they've been doing this past hour waiting for you, Miss Slugabed? There's no time to lose!" With that warning, she turned on her heel as quickly as an elderly cook could and left Charlotte with a basin of hot water. Within fifteen minutes Charlotte was dressed in her usual gray, a neat cap covering her curls. She could do nothing about her pale lips or shadowed eyes, but perhaps a cup of strong tea could clear her thoughts. She followed the masculine bellowing down to the kitchen. Mr. Frazier was even more disheveled and agitated. He paced the room while a very large man sat placidly drinking a cup of coffee at the table. The only sign of the early hour was a stubborn cowlick of grizzled gray hair that stood up on the back of his head. He rose the instant he saw her.

"Good morning. Mr. Mulgrew, I presume." Charlotte extended a hand. He clasped it briefly between two huge ones. A *prizefighter*, Charlotte thought, looking at his genial face with its broken nose, or a man very unlucky with someone else's fists. Mulgrew caught her stare and rubbed his nose reflexively. "The Duke of Egremont's daughter," he said, sheepish. "One of my most famous cases, but alas, the little b—er, witch had a spectacular right hook. Angus has convinced me his lordship has fallen into a spot of trouble."

"Sir Michael," Charlotte corrected.

"Aye. Too bad my assistant is still in France, or we'd have better odds." He squinted at Charlotte, then took out a pair of spectacles from his tweed pocket. "I can see it, Angus. With the right attire, Miss Fallon might be the answer to our prayers."

Charlotte rolled her eyes and was saved from speech when Mrs. Kelly slapped a plate of toast and eggs on the table.

"Here is the plan, Miss Fallon. Mrs. Kelly here is going to beg for an interview with Lady Whitley, keep her at home as long as she can. You and I and Angus will go to Islington and break into the house where Lord Bayard is being held."

"Sir Michael," Charlotte muttered through a mouthful of poached egg.

"Right. You'll be dressed as a strumpet, o'course, and go round the back door, keep the boys occupied while Angus and I do the rescuing."

Charlotte's toast lodged in her throat. After an alarming series of coughs whereupon Mr. Mulgrew was prompted to pound her rather forcefully on her back with one of his large red hands, she was able to object.

"Look here. Why don't *I* go see Lady Whitley, and Mrs. Kelly bring round a basket of food for these men? That makes much more sense to me."

Angus's bushy red brows drew together. "Hmm. That's not

a half-bad plan. They were complaining last night about the local pie shop. Rosemary, no one would suspect you of anything underhanded, and your cooking is ambrosia from the gods. What do you say?"

Mrs. Kelly pinked in pleasure. "I'll be happy to go into the gates of hell itself if it will mean saving Sir Michael from Anne Whitley. My sister never did care for her."

Mulgrew clapped his hands. "Excellent. One of us can help you tote in the victuals. Let's say Lady Whitley is supplying the house for a few days or so. It would only make sense for you to have a helper." He looked across the room at Angus, who despite his bright red hair, was a much less conspicuous figure than Mulgrew. "You can wear a cap. One of those chef things. Let me in when the coast is clear and then we'll see what's what."

Charlotte swallowed her tea, hoping she had chosen the less dangerous mission. Bay's staff did not think highly of Lady Anne Whitley. She admitted to herself she was curious about Bay's choice of a wife, even if the ceremony had not been altogether legal. She watched as Mrs. Kelly spun around the kitchen, tucking food into boxes and baskets. Mulgrew pulled out a watch. "Can you be ready by ten o'clock, Miss Fallon? Too early to be calling, but also too early for Lady Whitley to be out and about."

"I'm ready right now."

Mrs. Kelly paused from wrapping up a round of cheese and frowned. "Oh, no, dear. You want to make Lady Whitley jealous and keep her off balance. You are Bay's mistress, after all. She won't ever believe he offered you his protection if she sees you like this. You look like a Sunday school teacher."

"I *am* a Sunday school teacher," Charlotte grumbled.

"The red dress," Mrs. Kelly said firmly. "You can wear that again. Shocking, it is. I'll help with your hair. You two"—she pointed at Frazier and Mulgrew—"pack up the rest. Go into the wine cellar, too. I'll fix those brutes a lunch they'll be too drunk to remember."

Charlotte was pushed upstairs by Mrs. Kelly before she

had a chance to wipe the breakfast crumbs from her lips. She was stuffed into the red dress again, her bosom glaringly obvious for daytime. Mrs. Kelly was a bit of a miracle worker with her hair, creating an effect that looked like she had recently risen well-satisfied from bed. Charlotte owned no appropriate hat for a visit to Lady Whitley's, but Mrs. Kelly went upstairs and came down with ribbon, a length of tulle, some fringe, and a paste pin that she somehow twisted around Charlotte's head. In addition, she brought cosmetics left over from Bay's former mistresses that Irene had squirreled away in her room. Charlotte's lips and cheeks were rouged, her already dark eyelashes blackened, and the corner of her mouth patched. Mrs. Kelly could have rivaled any dresser on Drury Lane. Charlotte scarcely recognized herself.

"Is—is not all this a bit much?"

"Exactly so. You look a proper whore now, Miss Fallon, if you don't mind me saying so. Lady Whitley will be outraged you've come to call, but won't be able to resist quizzing you. And if Angus is right, she must have made Sir Michael write that letter to get rid of you. You're going to tell her you're not leaving Jane Street until you hear it from his own lips." She yanked down Charlotte's bodice another inch. "There. Perfect."

Charlotte felt a bit faint, and not only because the dress was so constricting. It was decided that they would go in two vehicles, with Mr. Mulgrew dropping Charlotte off in Mayfair before journeying on to Islington. He peppered her with instructions, reminding her of the day not so very long ago when Deborah lectured her about Bay. A great deal had happened since then.

Self-conscious, she stepped out of the hack, wrapping her shawl as high as possible. Whitley House was a middling-grand property, with as stiff-necked a butler as she had ever encountered, who opened the door before she had trod on the lowest step. It was clear he admitted her into the hallway with great reluctance, confused by her cultured accent, which clashed so with her attire.

"Please inform Lady Whitley that Miss Charlotte Fallon has come to call." Charlotte looked down her nose at Denning, the butler, no mean feat as he topped her by several inches.

"Your card, miss?" he held out a white-gloved hand.

Charlotte's homely reticule was quite empty save for a vinaigrette, a handkerchief, and the cab fare back to Jane Street. "It is too early for calling cards, sir, as you must know. Were it not a matter of the gravest urgency, I would not dream of disturbing her ladyship at this hour," Charlotte bluffed. The fringe on her headdress wavered as she spoke.

"May I inform Lady Whitley of the nature of this so-called emergency?"

"You may not," Charlotte snapped.

The butler sniffed. Charlotte found herself shut up in a little room off the hall, no doubt intended for pesky tradesmen or those seeking charitable donations. She tossed her shawl aside and sat in the only chair, a spindly affair designed to hasten one out of Whitley House as quickly as possible. The room was white, bare of ornamentation. Charlotte wished for a mirror to see whether her eyelashes were flaking black bits onto her crimson cheeks. Her face was so hot now rouge was completely superfluous. She fished out her handkerchief and wiped away the worst of her maquillage. She had been doubtful she should appear as sluttish as Mrs. Kelly had painted her. Bay was a man of taste and restraint. Her lips twitched when she remembered exactly *how* restraining he could be.

There was no way to measure the time she sat, save for the increasing wetness under her armpits and at her hairline. The longer she waited, the more nervous she became. She thought of her sister, ever at home in any circumstance. Deborah would have no difficulty dealing with Anne Whitley. Deborah would be saucy, flirtatious even with another woman. She was capable of great charm, and was diamond-sharp in intelligence, even if their schooling had been less than lengthy. Deb *did* read, hung on to every word her powerful protectors had uttered. She could hold her own in any conversation when it suited her to appear intelligent. Conversely, she could seem to be the merest bit of attractive fluff if the situation called for it. Which Deborah should she channel, Charlotte wondered. Gradually, she sat taller in the uncomfortable chair.

Her composure faltered a bit when Lady Whitley opened the door. To say she was shocked was an understatement. It was almost as if she was looking in a distorted mirror. Anne's black hair, blue eyes, and buxom figure were very like Charlotte's own. No wonder Bay had selected Deborah from the bevy of available courtesans. He was reliving his time with Anne with each mistress he chose. The woman confirmed it with the first words out of her mouth.

"I see Bay is running true to form. You look like all his other Jane Street whores. Angela and Helen or some such. But neither of them had the gall to come to my home. What is it you want?"

Charlotte detected a certain wariness behind the rudeness. She swallowed and stood, throwing back her shoulders and thrusting her exposed chest before her. If she was not mistaken, she was slightly better endowed than Anne Whitley.

"Thank you for agreeing to see me, Lady Whitley. I didn't know where else to turn. Bay has told me so much about you, you see. So many . . . wonderful things. I'm very worried about him." She rubbed her hands together nervously, giving credence to her words. She was Deb at her most helpless. Perhaps Lady Whitley would take pity on her.

Anne looked about the little room, as if she wished to conjure up another chair. "Let's discuss this in the parlor."

Charlotte followed her across the hall to a lovely white and blue salon with touches of black lacquer, a setting that showed Lady Whitley to great advantage. She realized, however, that there was a newer Lady Whitley somewhere in the country, who was probably planning to redecorate first thing. In the meantime, Anne sat regally on a blue wing chair and indicated Charlotte should do the same opposite. A china clock on the black marble mantelpiece chimed the half hour.

"I have very little time. I repeat, why are you here?"

Charlotte's mission was to keep Anne Whitley away from Islington as long as possible. If the woman could hire four thugs, she had resources to hire even more. Mr. Frazier and Mr. Mulgrew needed time.

"This is a very beautiful room, my lady. Very tasteful. It suits you." Charlotte gave her most deferential smile.

"Come to the point, Miss Fallon."

Flattery was not working. Charlotte placed a hand over her heart and looked as pitiful as possible. "Very well. I don't wish to shock you, my lady, but I have nowhere else to turn. I'm quite alone in London, you see. Without friends or family. I'm very much afraid that Sir Michael is missing. I am in hopes you might know his whereabouts."

"Missing? How absurd." Anne arched a perfect brow. "He's in France, I believe. Didn't he write to you?"

Charlotte stuck to her script and wiped an imaginary tear from her eye. "No, ma'am. I've received no word at all from him."

"Impossible! I know for a fact—" Anne flushed and closed her lips. Charlotte knew then that Anne was hiding something. Whether Frazier's fears were grounded or not, something was off.

"He promised to write, he did," Charlotte confided, batting her thickened eyelashes. "His letters are a perfect treat. How he does go on in the most romantic fashion. But then, I expect you know that." Bay had probably written hundreds of letters to Anne over the years.

Anne plucked at her skirt. "Perhaps he is just very busy."

Charlotte shook her head, fringe flying at the corner of her eye. Really, she wanted to rip Mrs. Kelly's concoction right off her head. "His manservant, Mr. Frazier, came to me yesterday. It's most unlike Bay to travel anywhere without him. It's his opinion Bay has met with foul play."

Anne tittered. "How ridiculous. The man has just gone off on holiday. And," Anne said, looking disdainfully at Charlotte, "before he left he told me he was quite committed to *me*. He intends to end your association, Miss Fallon. He has no need of a mistress any longer."

Charlotte's heart fell. The dismissive words of Bay's letter came back to haunt her. But if she accepted Anne's version of events, she would have no reason to stay here. "I don't believe it. I can't believe it. He couldn't be so cruel after all we've meant to each other."

"I watched him write the letter himself! He has broken with you completely and wants you to go back to Little—Little, oh, it's some sort of vegetable." Anne's eyes glittered in triumph.

If Anne was present when Bay wrote the letter, then he certainly was not in France. "But I never received a letter. I won't leave until I read it from his own hand," Charlotte said stubbornly.

"What if you heard it from his own lips?"

Oh dear. Surely Anne didn't intend to drag Charlotte to Islington and interrupt Bay's breakout.

"I—I suppose."

"Wait right here. I won't be but a few minutes."

Charlotte couldn't give Anne the opportunity to warn those who were keeping Bay prisoner, for she was now fully convinced that's exactly what the situation was. There was something entirely mad about Anne Whitley. She reached out a hand and Anne recoiled.

"What do you mean to do?"

"Why, send for Bay, of course! I do know where he is, actually. We've had a little interlude away from that interfering Frazier. And you. Bay will come here and tell you to go and leave us in peace." She gave a ghastly smile and left Charlotte seated on her chair.

Oh, but she had muffed her mission. She looked around the room wildly, hoping to find a spare pistol or brass candlestick. Disappointed, she set to praying that Anne's messenger would arrive once Bay was freed, tripping over the subdued bodies of the four guards. Bay would come here and straighten all this out. There was nothing to do but continue her conversation with God as she waited for Anne to return.

And when she did, Charlotte was dismayed to see that it was Anne who had discovered a spare pistol and had it pointing straight at her ill-clad head. Charlotte's conversation with God took on more urgency.

"We'll just see which one of us Bay chooses," Anne said, smug. "This might help him make up his mind a little faster."

Mrs. Kelly put the empty wine bottle down. Never had she enjoyed herself so much in any kitchen. An enormous spread of food covered the dinged table. Chairs were overturned, and three large men were trussed like chickens on a spit on the floor. The wine bottle had assisted one man into unconsciousness after he made an especially rude remark. The fourth man was currently being divested of his clothes upstairs so that Sir Michael would have something with which to cover his body when he returned home. There wasn't time to search for his own things.

Angus and Mr. Mulgrew had been mercilessly efficient in dispatching the brutes as they sat at the table like slavering wolves. Mrs. Kelly liked to think that her rabbit pie had a hand in bespelling them into letting down their guard. They had dutifully helped her bring in the food from the carriage, allowing Frazier to disappear upstairs in all the confusion. She had their full and undivided attention as she had unpacked the victuals from their containers, chatting artlessly as Frazier let Mr. Mulgrew in. When they both returned to the kitchen, each was armed and definitely dangerous. Before any of the villains could think to move, Mr. Mulgrew had shot one in the foot and asked who would like to be shot next. There had been a scuffle anyway, several more shots, and quiet at last. Angus had packed lengths of rope in the boxes, which he used to lash the fellows together in a bloody heap, their own neckerchiefs serving as makeshift gags. Mr. Mulgrew had gone to fetch a constable. Mrs. Kelly surveyed all the wasted food, but she was not about to try to save any of it. She hoped the men had got their fill, for it would be a long while before any of them had a decent home-cooked dinner again.

She turned at the clunking and shuffling on the stairs. A pale Sir Michael came down, supported by Angus. He looked rather ridiculous in the shabby clothes that hung off him, and smelled worse, but she flew to him and gave him a kiss.

"Ah, Mrs. Kelly. You are a sight for sore eyes." One of the men growled from the floor, but stopped when she gave him a dark look. "I say, is that your famous apple pie?"

"We havena time for you to eat, Major. The sooner we get out of this hellhole, the better."

"Pish posh, Angus. We've got to wait for the constable anyway. Some cheese to go with it, Sir Michael?"

Mrs. Kelly watched as he forked a huge wedge into his mouth. "Heaven. These gentlemen were not very adept in the kitchen."

Bay polished off the plate and was about to ask for another when there was a knock at the kitchen door.

"Blast. Mulgrew wouldn't knock. It can't be him. Hand me one of your guns, Frazier."

Bay positioned himself against the wall. "Mrs. Kelly, you answer it. Don't open the door too wide—we don't want our guest to see the trash on the floor."

Mrs. Kelly opened the door a crack. "Yes?"

"Message from Lady Whitley for a Mr. Smith."

"And who might you be?"

"I'm James. The second footman at Whitley House."

Bay leaped forward and dragged the young man in by his neckcloth. James's white wig took a tumble, revealing soft yellow curls beneath.

"I say!" James sputtered. "Unhand me!" He caught sight of the gun and fainted dead away.

"All looks and no backbone," Angus Frazier grumbled.

Bay eased him down. "Tie him up, too. He looks like an innocent lamb, but one never knows." He scooped up the letter that had fluttered to the floor and broke the seal. "It seems I am to be temporarily released and escorted by Mr. Smith and his cronies to Whitley House. We've just anticipated the orders by a few minutes."

He toed James with a borrowed cobbled boot. "Out like a light. I hope Anne's carriage is waiting. I confess I'm rather anxious to see her again."

"You're not going alone!"

"Come now, Frazier. I don't believe I'm in danger any longer. I doubt she's enlisted the Whitley House staff in this farrago. You stay here to protect Mrs. Kelly. If any harm comes to her, I could never forgive myself. Not to mention I would waste away to nothing. My French chef cannot hold a candle to her in the kitchen. When Mulgrew returns, explain the situation." Bay put the pistol into the pocket of the tattered jacket. Crime must not pay very well—there was a hole in the sole of each oversized boot as well.

Bay didn't want Anne arrested, even if she was the mastermind of this kidnapping scheme. If he could persuade her to begin her travels on the Continent early—as in immediately—he would consider himself satisfied. For all that they had meant to each other once upon a time, he was willing to forget the past few days. Although he couldn't chalk up her actions to an odd form of grief for her detested husband, he supposed she did grieve—grieved for what had been between them so long ago, when they were young and so besotted with each other. Well, Bay had been besotted anyway. But he was clearly over that now.

Anne's driver cast him a skeptical glance as he strode toward the carriage parked on the street. James had been foolish enough to come in a crested conveyance. Every neighbor would soon be talking of the doings in the house. The driver snapped to when he heard Bay's orders delivered in his impeccable upper-crust accent and recognized him as the gentleman his mistress had dallied with over the years. Clothes here did not make the man.

Frazier had told him Charlie had been sent to make sure Anne was kept away from the fracas. He hoped she was safely back on Jane Street by now. As much as he longed to make love to her one more time to erase the shameful memory of Anne, it was his duty to return her to her home in Little Dustup. She had been abused quite long enough.

Now he'd have to go through the whole tedious process of finding a new mistress. Or perhaps he should settle down with a wife as Mr. Mulgrew suggested. The thought of some dewy-eyed virgin held no appeal. He was too old for a schoolroom miss. A virtuous widow then, someone young enough to bear him children and know her way around the bedchamber. Bay imagined that given time, he might work up some enthusiasm for the project. A fleeting thought of Charlie's black hair tangling down her white back gave him pause, but he pushed it away.

He hadn't been to Whitley House since shortly after Anne's husband died. He had resisted her entreaties then, and would have no hesitation after the business of the past few days. Bay was prepared to threaten her with arrest, even if he had no plans to prosecute. It would be folly of the first order to expose what she had put him through. He could imagine the knowing smirks every time he set foot in a ballroom or cardroom if it was learned he'd been kept a naked captive by a woman for close to a week. The gentlemen would wonder at his objection, for Anne still cast her spell on society. The women would see him as weak, to be subdued so easily by one of their own. It would be pointless to mention the four toughs who had made his life a living hell lately.

The carriage came to a neat stop and Bay hopped down, nearly tripping in the large boots. The rank scent of his borrowed clothes permeated his nostrils, but his own clothes had disappeared, probably sold off to buy a pint. Anne would be surprised to see him arrive in this condition, and without his guards. He was looking forward to seeing the shock on her face.

But the shock was his once Denning announced him and shut the parlor doors. Charlie sat, pale but composed, on a blue wing chair as Anne held a gun neatly in her lap.

Anne's nose wrinkled, but the pistol did not waver. "Bay! What are you doing in those dreadful rags? And where are my employees?"

"What is the meaning of this, Anne?" He hoped his voice did not display his own dread.

"Why, I thought you'd be pleased to see me. And this little trollop. Tell her, Bay. She didn't get the dratted letter, or so she says. Tell her what you told me. That you love me and that we're together now."

Bay kept his face impassive, but casually felt for the comfort of Frazier's gun in his pocket. He had put it there without thinking once the footman fainted, never believing it would be necessary to come to Anne armed.

"Let her go home, Anne. Home to pack. I can't believe she's still lurking about Jane Street to begin with." He watched as Charlie's white face crumpled. There would be time later for apologies. He had to get her out of here as quickly as possible.

"There! I told you so," Anne said in triumph. "And I've changed my mind, Bay. I *will* marry you, and then our child will have a normal home."

"Child?" Charlie whispered. "You are enceinte?"

"Not yet, but I will be, I assure you. Bay is everything a man should be, but then I suppose you know that."

"All very flattering, I'm sure," Bay drawled. "But let the little whore go, sweetheart. She means nothing at all to me. Why, she's just a poor imitation of you. The hair, the eyes— I've been a sad fool for you since I was a lad. Let's go upstairs, love. I'm in sore need of a hot bath and a change of clothes. Your men seem to have misplaced mine." He walked slowly toward Anne, smiling. "And put the pistol away, Anne. We don't want anyone getting hurt, even inconsequential courtesans."

For a fleeting moment, Anne clung stubbornly to the gun. He fixed his face into what he hoped was lustful admiration.

"Your little trick convinced me, my darling. You've brought me to my senses. *All* my senses. There's never been another woman who could hold a candle to you. I cannot wait to have you in my arms again."

He didn't turn when Charlie gave a strangled cry, didn't hesitate as he heard her fleeing footsteps, didn't start to breathe until Anne's pistol joined the other in his pocket. "There now, that's better." He laid a finger on Anne's cheek. "Let me just make sure the whore has enough money to leave. I won't be but a moment."

Anne frowned. "Let Frazier handle that."

"Have a bath readied for me. I cannot come to your bed like this. I'll be right back, I swear."

He kissed her then, hoping his lips and tongue could lie. Anne clung to him despite his filth, wasting moments better spent chasing after Charlie. At last he disengaged and walked calmly out of the room, as if he had all the time in the world. Once he shut the door, he plunged down the stairs and out into the street.

There was no splash of red anywhere, just the dull gray of fashionable stone houses marching up the street. *Blast.* Could she have found a cab already? Though Jane Street was not all that far from Whitley House. She might be on foot. Bay bolted down the sidewalk, giving no thought to the image he presented, disreputable jacket flying behind him, pistols clunking into his hip. He'd better do something about that before he shot off his own foot. Pausing to stuff the guns into a planter filled with scarlet geraniums, he turned the corner and was rewarded by the sight of Charlie's determined back.

"Charlie!"

Her tulle headdress had unwound. Batting it away, she continued her furious pace.

"Charlie! Please stop!"

She didn't, of course, the stubborn minx. He hadn't run like this since he was a boy, but he caught up to her, pulling her into his arms. Tears had coursed down her face, spoiling her makeup, but she was the loveliest thing he'd seen in days.

He didn't appreciate her fists, though, beating a tattoo on his chest.

"Let go of me! Have you come to insult me further?"

"Hush, love. Listen to me. Anne is quite mad. Surely you know that. I said what I did so she'd let you go."

Her hands stilled, then she pushed him backwards with all her might. Bay stumbled in his awkward boots and found himself ignominiously on his arse in the middle of a Mayfair sidewalk.

"Since the first moment I laid eyes on you, my life has been nothing but one catastrophe after the other! I *am* going home! And nothing you can do or say can stop me!" The fringe wound around her head quivered in indignation.

"Whatever you want, Charlie." Bay made no move to get up. Exhaustion was catching up to him. A couple walking toward them crossed the street in haste. He and Charlie as currently attired made an unlikely pair to be in this part of town. If their public disagreement wasn't over soon, a constable was sure to come and end it for them.

"I sat there for *hours*. She kept smiling, pointing that gun at me." Her voice shook.

"I know, Charlie. She's mad. I just said so. I'm sorry you got in the middle of my mess. I had no idea the lengths to which she'd go."

He watched in dismay as Charlie stepped forward to walk down the street. But then she pivoted.

"Was Frazier right? Did she keep you a prisoner?"

Bay sighed. "Does it matter? You're free now. I'll give you whatever you need to get back to Little Hyssop and more."

Charlie raised an eyebrow. "You *do* know the name of my village."

"Of course I know it. But it's so much fun to tease you."

Charlie growled. Bay thought if she had a parasol she might have bashed him on the head. He supposed he'd better get up. The sidewalk was meant for walking, not sitting, although truthfully his legs didn't want to cooperate. He'd been inactive and useless for days, save when they let him up to relieve himself. The last time he had any range of motion at all, he'd managed to dislocate one of the thugs' shoulders. There had been unpleasant consequences for him, but it had been worth it.

"Look. Go straight to Jane Street. Tell Frazier I said to give you all you ask for."

Charlie snorted. "As if he'll believe me. He doesn't like me at all."

"He likes Anne less, I assure you. Tell him I'm dealing with her, and that I'll be home tonight. And get him to send a new suit of clothes to Whitley House, would you?"

Charlie gaped down at him. "You're going back there? You're as unhinged as she is!"

"Very likely." He pulled at a loose thread on the cuff of his jacket. "I cannot apologize enough for what you've gone through. Everything, not only this business with Anne." He looked up, hoping to see a softening in her countenance. He was disappointed. Charlotte Fallon was still a little Fury, and he wished he could kiss the contempt from her lips. "Go home, Charlie. God be with you always."

For a moment, Bay thought she would speak. Instead, she pulled the trailing fabric from her head. Bay watched it float down to the sidewalk, the paste pin twinking in its folds. She turned away, her spine stiff. He sat until her red-clad figure disappeared around a corner. Slowly pulling himself up, he picked up Charlie's headwear and stuffed it into his pocket. He retraced his steps, stopping only to retrieve the weapons from the geraniums and layering them in tulle.

Chapter 17

The tomcat's yowl awakened her. Soon he was joined by the female's grating song. It was still fully dark, damp and grim with the torrents of rain that had fallen for days. The weather had matched Charlotte's mood perfectly. Since her return home, she had been unable to appreciate her snug little cottage or the sudden profusion of flowers and vegetables in her garden. Instead she saw bare whitewashed walls and a tangle of weeds that would have to wait until the sun shone. If it ever did. Perhaps Deb had left some paintings upstairs with which she could beautify her humble house. No nudes, of course, although absolutely anything could be in the crates that Deb had shipped to her over the years. Charlotte should sit down and write to her, offer to send everything off to Arthur's estate in Kent. Bard's End. She knew that now.

She wondered if Deb had even returned home yet, or was still honeymooning with her new husband. Charlotte's precipitous disappearance from Little Hyssop had been duly noted and remarked upon. When accosted in the village shops, Charlotte staunchly told the tale of her sister's wedding, not that she had witnessed it. She discovered she had a flair for dissembling, right down to the color of her sister's wedding gown (rose pink, she decided, mostly because it would be her own choice in the unlikely event she ever married) and choice of flowers (white lilies, for the same reason). This fictitious version of her London trip seemed to satisfy the local tabbies,

who always had time for a good gossip, even if the protago-
nists were unknown to them. Charlotte had trudged home
with her meager supplies, the brim of her old straw hat dripping rainwater, but she was not struck by a bolt of lightning
for telling her lies. Despite Mr. Frazier pressing quite a lot of
money into her hands, far more than she asked for, she had
set it away for a rainier day and was determined to resume
her quiet life on her restricted budget.

Now she really was a whore, bought and paid for, even if
she didn't intend to touch all the pound notes Mr. Frazier had
conjured unless major calamity befell her. The money was sitting in a chipped ginger jar on her mantel. No self-respecting
thief would be tempted to remove such pottery from the
premises. She supposed if the cottage ever caught fire, she'd
force herself to rescue it.

Having a bit of a financial cushion was a help. She might
not be able to depend on Deb to keep herself and the cats afloat
now that Arthur controlled the purse strings. And Deb had
been indifferently generous anyway, depending on the gulli-
bility of her past patrons. Months could go by before she remembered that she had a sister buried in the country. The last
ten years had been a test for Charlotte to live within excep-
tionally modest means. The little she got for her lace had put
food on the table, although it was not generally known in
Little Hyssop that Mrs. Fallon supplied the ton with trimmings
for their unmentionables and evening gowns.

Despite the early hour, Charlotte rose. There was no point
in tossing and turning while Tom was fornicating under her
bedroom window. The blasted cats had been contentious
ever since she returned, punishing her for their abandonment.
When they weren't rutting, they were strutting and slinking
and squalling around the kitchen door like beggars. Maybe if
she tossed a few sardines into the dark, the racket would
quiet down.

Charlotte opened her wardrobe and reached for her gray
robe. Her hand brushed the cherry-red dress that she had un-
accountably packed when she left London. She would never

wear it again, of course. Little Hyssop was not the type of town that would sanction a scarlet woman. In fact, as today was Sunday, she would be on her knees in church in a few hours, praying for forgiveness. She had been foolish in the extreme—again. God must be very displeased with her, for surely she was old enough and experienced enough to know better now than to fall for the blandishments of an attractive man. She heaved a sigh. Bay was very attractive indeed.

Her little bedroom was just off the kitchen. It suited her to live all on one floor; it was cheaper also to heat just the downstairs rooms. She felt her way through the shadows, the coals a faint spark in the stove. She stuck her head out the kitchen door and was rewarded by a blast of wind and needling rain. Hard to believe that June was here when she had to race barefoot across the cold wet grass to the privy. She wasn't about to ruin her slippers, but hoped she would not step on anything untoward in the gloom. The scent of battered roses climbing the little shed was pleasant and masked the fact that she needed to order lime the next time she went to the shops. She rationalized going outside this morning was much like a shower bath, freezing though it was. She lingered a bit on the path, letting the rain sluice down her face and throat. The cats were silent at last, probably languishing in the afterglow under the hydrangea bush. Sardines would be superfluous.

Once indoors, Charlotte stripped off her wet robe and set to stirring up and adding to the coals. She pulled a stool in front of the warming stove and brushed her hair, rebraiding it. When the flames licked up, she lit a fat tallow candle on the center of the table, filled the kettle, and made her tea. She was going to the early communion service. By all that was holy, she should not even be *thinking* about tea. But she was chilled to the bone. She allowed herself one small lump of sugar only, breaking the bad habit of three on Jane Street. Charlotte had a dreadful sweet tooth. Mrs. Kelly had aided and abetted it.

As the sky lightened, Charlotte blew out the candle and toasted her forbidden bread. She ate it minus butter and jam as penance. If she cleaned her teeth thoroughly, Vicar Kemble might not realize that she had broken her fast. It wasn't as if she weren't going to Hell anyway. Eating breakfast was a very minor transgression. She pinned up her still-damp hair and dressed in a gray dress in the gray light. It was her turn to do the altar flowers this morning. She had been smart enough to pick them in a brief break in the rain yesterday afternoon, and pails holding drooping blooms were lined up along the edge of the carpet of her snug parlor. She fished out the flowers and laid them in a flat basket, covered her hair with her usual cap and battered hat, and marched down the lane to the church, gripping an umbrella tightly in the wind. Her skirts whipped about in the mud. Her person would win no prizes today for beauty, but her flower arrangements would speak for themselves.

Once inside the hushed, cool church. Charlotte shivered and grabbed the empty brass urns off the altar and took them to the vestry. As good as his word, the vicar had left a ewer filled with water, and she poured it carefully into each container. She heard the thud of the church door and waited for Vicar Kemble to shout out a good morning, but curiously she heard only booted footsteps on the stone aisle and the scraping of a kneeler. An early bird sinner with plenty to pray for, she thought, and continued her task. The rain spattered against the roof and pinged against the wavy glass window. The world outside was a blur of gray and green. It was good to be home, doing something familiar in a familiar place. She didn't miss Jane Street a bit. Or Bay either.

Her cottage garden had blossomed quite happily while she was away in London. She buried her nose to inhale the rich scents and stepped back, giving the vases a critical eye. Too much yellow on the left. She ruthlessly ripped some buds from the coreopsis stalks. There. Perfect balance, a rainbow of colors and fragrance. Lifting one heavy vase she carried it to the altar.

The top of a gentleman's head was just visible over a high-backed pew toward the rear of the church. It was too dim inside to distinguish its color—darkish, some sort of brown. She didn't wish to disturb him in prayer, so tiptoed quietly over the flagstones to get the other urn. When both were in position, she herself slipped into her regular spot, tugged her gloves back on, and closed her eyes. Just last week she had been staring down the barrel of a gun. She was still alive. Pinching herself just to make sure, her lips moved in the silent repetition of the Lord's Prayer. She leaned back, relaxing into the pew. A few neighbors came in and nodded to her, then Mr. Kemble, who flashed her a bright smile and disappeared to change into his cassock.

The steady rain drummed on the slate roof throughout the brief Holy Communion service. The sound was as lulling and peaceful as a prayer. Charlotte nearly dozed off through the reading, and had to pinch herself again. She needed her wits about her to instruct the children who would be coming for Sunday school. She rose to take communion, joining the few others before the altar. Mr. Kemble paused, then looked over their heads to the back of the church. After a moment, there were crisp footsteps against the stone floor. Charlotte didn't turn out of politeness, but expected it was the same man who had come in while she was busy in the vestry. He knelt at the opposite end of the communion rail, his face shielded by the very topiarylike hat of Mrs. Beacham.

A stranger then with the few faithful who came to early services. Charlotte peeked around the corner of her own bonnet again, but was rewarded with only the sight of Mrs. Beacham's truly extraordinary hat. Receiving her wafer and sipping from the chalice, she returned to her seat. Curious now, she observed the broad shoulders clad in dark brown superfine, the unscuffed boot soles. Whoever the gentleman was, he had money.

She watched as he tipped his head forward. There was something about the close crop of hair—

Bay! Charlotte dropped her Book of Common Prayer. It fell with a clunk that reverberated through the near-empty church. Hastily, she bent to retrieve it, staying low as he walked back down the transept. Her blood rushed to the surface of her skin. She needed to leave at once.

Mrs. Kemble was more than capable. She could deal with the children for the Bible lesson in the rectory when they came. Half of them were hers anyway. Perhaps the rain would keep the others away. Charlotte inched down the pew, heart beating rapidly.

Mr. Kemble stepped down from the altar and made his way down the aisle. "The grace of our Lord Jesus Christ and the love of God, and the fellowship of the Holy Ghost be with us all ever more. Amen."

Charlotte shot up as the bells began to ring, her heart racing. Bay was waiting in the vestibule, a tall beaver hat rolling in his hands. He was deep in discussion with Mr. Kemble. His face lit with mischief when he saw her. Charlotte clutched at her umbrella and prayerbook, wondering which would do more damage wiping the smirk off his face.

"Ah! Mrs. Fallon! The flowers are as ever lovely," Mr. Kemble boomed. "This gentleman was just remarking on them. I told him you have one of the loveliest gardens in the village. Puts Mrs. Kemble's to shame, it does."

"Th-thank you, Mr. Kemble," Charlotte stuttered.

"I would so love to see it. Gardens are a particular interest of mine," Bay said smoothly. "One might say they tie me in knots."

"B-but it's raining!" Charlotte glared at him. Let Mr. Kemble think of it what he would.

"A little rain never harmed me. I'm used to much worse, I assure you. Kidnap. Torture. I was an army man. Mr. Kemble, perhaps you would do me the honor of introducing me to this young lady."

It was on the tip of Charlotte's tongue to give him a rousing set-down. Young lady! She had more gray hairs after her time with Bay than ever. He was not going to charm her ever again.

"Certainly, sir. Sir Michael, isn't it? Haven't a head for

names, I'm afraid, a failing in my line of work, but I do know Mrs. Fallon's. Pillar of the church. She made the altar cloth too. Mrs. Fallon, may I present Sir Michael—" The vicar looked helplessly at Bay.

"Sir Michael Xavier Bayard. It is a pleasure to meet you, *Mrs.* Fallon."

Charlotte flushed and fidgeted. "How do you do?" she asked her feet.

"Very well. Do say you can give me a tour of your garden before I am obligated to leave your charming village. Perhaps you have time now? Good morning to you, Mr. Kemble. Excellent service." Bay put his gloved hand on her elbow and practically shoved her out the open door. In one fluid motion he took her umbrella and popped it open over them. Charlotte had no opportunity to beg off teaching Sunday school. She could only hope Mr. Kemble would make her excuses to Mrs. Kemble since it seemed she was practically being carried away by a forceful man with a heretofore undeclared passion for gardening.

"Why are you here?" Charlotte blurted.

He looped his arm through hers. The comfort and warmth of it was most unsettling. "London was a bit of a bore. I thought I'd go home for a bit, actually. To Bayard Court. It's right on the coast, you know. June. Summer. Swimming and boating. I was rather hoping to persuade you to join me."

Charlotte escaped his arm. "Don't be ridiculous! Our association is over. Completely over." Charlotte stepped in a puddle and lurched sideways. Bay tugged her close, saving her from going down in the mud.

"I don't see why."

"Oh, don't you? I'll have you know I was telling the truth when I said I was a respectable woman! This is my home, and I'll not give the gossips any reason to talk. How dare you come to church?"

"I dare because I worry about my immortal soul. And yours. I often go to church."

Charlotte snorted.

"I do, no matter your rude noises. My grandmama insisted upon it. You still think me a fiend, don't you?"

Charlotte decided it was best to remain silent. She didn't trust herself to speak coherently. They continued on the path. It seemed Bay knew exactly where he was going, which made her even more nervous.

Bay peered through the sheets of rain. "Little Muckup is a quintessential English village, isn't it? It must be lovely on a sunny day. Thatched cottages. Climbing roses. And you, on the altar guild, arranging flowers and tatting lace. How homely. There are cats too, as I recall?"

She couldn't resist elbowing him in the ribs.

"Don't mock me! I'm very happy here! And you will ruin everything!" They turned into her lane. She would not let him into her home, she *would not*. He could wander around the garden in the wet all day to lend credence to the fiction that he was some sort of horticulturist. If any of her neighbors were nosy, they would not see Sir Michael Xavier Bayard cross her threshold for any reason whatsoever.

"I have been completely discreet. I put up at the Pig and Whistle last evening and didn't overindulge, although the local ale is very good, I must say. Even when the landlord— Mr. Braddock, is it?— tried to pry my life story out of me, I resisted all his efforts. I even asked your vicar to introduce us this morning. No one will have an inkling of our earlier association."

"Association!" Charlotte stamped her foot, splashing more mud on her skirts. "You blackmailed me into becoming your mistress! I trust you got the necklace back?"

They were at her gate now. One of the cats darted under a bush. Unfortunately Charlotte could detect the very distinct aroma of cat arousal. Bay seemed oblivious. He passed her the umbrella, put a hand in his pocket, and pulled out the most magnificent rope of rubies and diamonds she had ever seen. The umbrella tipped. Charlotte shut her mouth before the raindrops fell in and she drowned.

"You can see why I was anxious to have it back, I trust. Mr. Mulgrew returned it to me the other day."

"Uh." How absurd she was being! As if jewels meant anything to her at all. She was not Deborah. No indeed. Her head would not be turned by sparkling cold stones—

Unbidden, Bay's written words snaked into her head.

I cannot wait to clasp the rubies and diamonds around your throat and watch as the candlelight reflects each facet on the marble whiteness of your body. For, my dearest Deborah, you shall need no other adornment than these borrowed jewels and the velvet of your own soft skin. It is my wish to fuck you until we are both quite exhausted, and then fuck you again.

She edited out the "dearest Deborah" part, feeling gooseflesh wash over her body. It was just the chill from the ever-present rain, she assured herself, nothing more. She had read those foolish letters one too many times if she could quote them so readily. Why had she packed them into her bag and not left them at Jane Street, shut tight in a dark drawer? She would burn them in the stove today. Yes, she would.

Bay wiped a raindrop from the tip of her nose and righted the umbrella. "We're getting soaked through, Charlie. Do you think I could beg a cup of tea from you? Perhaps a bit of bread? It's hard to believe that summer is right around the corner."

He was talking about the weather, impudent man. As though they had some sort of normal relationship. A relationship not predicated on bullying and sinful sex and sheer terror.

Charlotte's lips thinned. "You must leave. I understand the Braddocks put on an excellent spread at the inn."

Bay tsked. "Here I've come, all this way to see you, and you want to cast me off. I confess, Charlie, I'm wounded."

"Good! You have been nothing but a pebble in my shoe, Sir Michael, since the instant you—you—"

"Brought you to heaven beneath all those cherubs? I do remember, Charlie. There was no talk of shoes and pebbles, but rather a lot of charming undulating and heavy breathing. And love bites." He looked so very self-satisfied she wanted to shriek.

"I propose," he continued, "that we start again. As if that week we shared never happened. Why, I met you in church just this morning and inquired after your garden. A hobby of mine."

"You never mentioned it before," Charlotte muttered.

"There are a great many things you don't know about me," Bay smiled. "Come, *Mrs.* Fallon, you'll catch your death out here in this drizzle. Surely you can spare me some hot water and a few tea leaves."

"If I give you breakfast, do you promise to leave me alone?"

Bay shook his head. "I never make promises I can't keep." He pushed the gate in and made for her front door. "A cheerful red. Matches your roses. Did you paint the door yourself? I expect it's unlocked. I thought about coming by last night, you know, but it was too reminiscent of our earlier introduction. And we are starting fresh."

Charlotte found herself running after him. He turned the handle before she could make the pretense of fishing a key out of her pocket.

"Ah. I was right." He ducked under the lintel. He was almost too tall to stand straight under her cozy ceilings. She hoped he'd knock himself unconscious. "Delightful. All this lace. I suppose you made it yourself?" He was standing in the center of her little parlor, hands in his pockets, no doubt checking to see if the blasted necklace was still there. Why on earth did he have it on his person? She supposed he didn't trust the Pig and Whistle clientele, which was ridiculous. Visitors to Little Hyssop were pure as the driven snow. Except for him.

"Where is your wife?" she asked, acid dripping from her tongue.

"Lady Whitley is on the Continent. I hope she doesn't bump into your sister. The resemblance might unhinge her."

"As if she's not completely unhinged already! The woman

held a pistol to my head! And had you beaten and kidnapped!"
Charlotte could still see faint traces of bruising under Bay's
chin and around his left cheek.

"I do apologize. Sincerely, Charlie." His black eyes bore
into hers. She turned away.

"It's warmer in the kitchen. If you're not too grand, you
can sit at the table in there."

"I'm not too grand," he said softly. "Mrs. Kelly's sister always welcomed me in hers when I was a lad."

"Well, you're overgrown now. Mind your head." As if she
cared whether he hurt himself, although it would be a chore
to drag his body outside into the mud.

Bay ducked under a beam and found himself in a square
snug room. The old stove threw out welcoming warmth. Filthy
weather had followed him ever since he left London. He dearly
hoped once he got to Bayard Court the sun would shine and
the sand would run hot between his toes. Frazier, Mrs. Kelly,
and Irene had already been sent ahead to open the house and
alert the skeleton staff at his grandmother's house that he
was on his way. After his little adventure in London, it was
time for a change of scenery.

He envisioned a picnic with Charlie, her black curls released
from that dreadful little cap and blowing in the sea breeze.
The secluded cove at the bottom of his cliff was perfect for
bathing. Her pearly skin would shimmer in the sunlight, her
spectacular breasts bob in the sea. She would be his own particular mermaid, and he most willing to crash against her
rocks, lose his trousers to frolic in the surf with her.

"Do you swim?"

She was slamming tea things together, mulish. "Of course.
But I am not," she said as she hacked into a half loaf with a
deadly looking knife, "going to Bayard Court or anywhere
else with you."

"I'll give you five thousand pounds."

The knife clattered to the floor. He knew he was utterly

mad. The plan was to woo her away from Little Pileup gently, and he'd just baldly offered her a fortune—an insane amount, five times the amount he'd given Deborah to seal their deal. What had come over him? Charlie had. She had come over him, under him, virtually into him. He wanted her as he had not wanted a woman since Anne. It had been impossible to shake the thoughts of her away, and Lord knows, he had tried.

At first he'd been unable to get the image of her frightened white face out of his mind. He saw her sitting frozen in that blue chair, her scarlet dress like a splash of blood. It had taken him hours that day before his heart beat normally, but then he'd had his hands rather full encouraging Anne to make her travel arrangements. His subsequent guilt over Charlie proved to be overwhelming, and he decided he must make more of an effort to make things up to her for Anne's insanity. Charlie had taken such a paltry amount from Frazier and deserved so much more for the trouble their acquaintance had visited upon her. He consulted with his banker, planning to soothe his culpability with cold, hard cash.

But then Bay saw her in his mind's eye when she wasn't frightened, when she was pink and warm and honeyed in his arms, when she was shuddering in pleasure, weeping his name as she crested beyond her prim propriety. This image swiftly overtook the first, and had haunted him in his lonely bed for several nights. He decided to see her himself and make sure she was all right. It was the gentlemanly thing to do.

Only he had the most ungentlemanly thoughts. Even with her nasty gray dress and grim face, he wanted to find the nearest feather bed and kiss her senseless. Everywhere.

"You are absolutely mad. You cannot buy my company, not for any price." She flew around the kitchen with even more irritation than before, embarking on a long litany of his deficits. Bay sat back in his humble chair watching her with appreciation. It was not every nearly virgin spinster who would turn down five thousand pounds. So eloquently, too, although he stopped paying attention somewhere around the ninth or tenth "fiend." Charlie was a most unusual woman. He was right to come, even if his noble impulses were now tucked into a pocket and the devil was stirring in his trousers.

"Well?" she asked somewhat shrilly.

Bay gathered himself from his fantasy. "I beg your pardon. What is the question?"

"Milk or lemon? If it's lemon, I haven't any. I'm sure they have lemons at the Pig and Whistle. Barrels of them." She slopped a white pottery mug of tea on the table. The Welsh dresser had some lovely blue and white dishes, but he had been given this rude, misshapen cup with a significant and deadly looking chip right where he might place his lips.

"Just sugar, Charlie. I'll need something sweet if I'm to sit here being harped at."

"Harped at? I've not *begun* to harp!" She shoved a sugar bowl at him and tongs clattered after it. "You will ruin me! There are probably twenty people staring out their cottage windows waiting for you to emerge. I don't know why I let you in, I really don't." She sat down abruptly and covered her face with her hands.

They were a bit rough, he noted, probably from the gardening and doing for herself in her little house. He should have known that first night when he felt them on his back and buttocks that they were not the hands of a cosseted mistress. But he'd been rather too busy to think.

"Charlie," he said carefully, "there is no reason for you to be upset."

"No reason? Because of you I was almost killed!"

"Well," he replied, dropping a small lump of sugar into the mug, "I suppose I could say the same. But here we are, sharing a comforting cup of tea." He stuck his finger in and swished, as she hadn't provided him with a spoon. It was tepid at best. She really must be trying to rush him out of here.

Charlie got up and went to her sideboard. She took down a fragile cup and saucer set and poured her own cold tea, still looking troubled. He wanted to ease the little *v* that appeared between her dark brows, lift the clouds from her blue eyes, turn her rosy lips up in a smile. "Six thousand," he said.

Charlie choked on her tea. She set the china down with a crash. "Have you not heard a word I've said?"

Bay smiled. "I'm afraid not. I was too busy watching you storm around the kitchen in high dudgeon. You are very captivating when you're angry."

Charlie gave a disgusted sniff. "Please. Do be original."

"It's true. You are so full of pique and passion, you've made an indelible impression on me. I would not be here otherwise."

"Let me see if I understand you. You will pay me *six thousand pounds* to go to Dorset with you."

Bay folded his hands and nodded. This was not entirely how he wanted to woo her to Bayard Court for a romantic interlude. Offering money was so crass. But he was in sore need of comfort, and it seemed Charlie was the only one who could provide him succor. She was not the only one who'd been terrified recently. The sooner he wiped Anne Whitley from his consciousness, the happier he would be.

"You truly have six thousand pounds to throw away for a few days of sexual congress?"

"I had hoped you would spend the summer with me there actually," Bay said calmly.

Charlie got up as if she were sleepwalking. She came back to the table with a jar of golden plum jam, centering it in front of her. Bay's stomach rumbled. Surely she was not going to eat without offering him anything. The knife still lay on the floor where she had dropped it earlier. He rose, picked it up, and sliced another piece of bread. "Where do you keep your cutlery?"

She pointed silently to the Welsh dresser. He opened a drawer and took out a spoon from the modest collection of coin silver and tin. Grabbing two plates, he went to work making a jam sandwich for each of them. He gobbled his in three bites while she stared at hers as if she wasn't quite sure what it was.

"Why?"

Bay swallowed the last chunk. The jam was delicious. He'd seen the plum trees in her front garden. He actually did have an interest in gardening; he was Grace's grandson, after all. This jar was probably the last of the previous summer's bounty. A few more mysterious glass containers were lined up on the dresser. Charlie probably put them up herself. "Why what?"

"You have your pick of any lightskirt in London. You own a house on Jane Street, for heaven's sake, a guarantee that you can attract the most discriminating whore. And I know there is such a thing. I got to know the neighbors a bit. It was—they were astonishing."

Bay smiled to think of Charlie in the midst of a group of courtesans. He knew there were regular entertainments on Jane Street. He just hadn't imagined his Charlie being entertained.

"I prefer you, Charlie. We were becoming well used to each other, and not in any sort of boring way, I might add. If you are worried about your reputation, don't be. Bayard Court is somewhat isolated. Frazier and Mrs. Kelly and Irene will be on hand to provide discreet service. I let most of my grandmother's staff go when I shut up the house—and found them all employment, so you can wipe that sneer off your face, *Mrs.* Fallon. The neighbors will respect that I'm in mourning and not expect me to partake in the social scene, what there is of it. We'll have time to get to know each other better."

"Whatever makes you think I want to get to know you better?" Charlie's face was bright red again, not a good omen.

Bay shrugged. "You must admit we were getting on quite well toward the end. I was on my way to visit you when I was kidnapped that night, you know."

"Rubbish. You were going to France to see my sister."

"No. I changed my mind. I decided to let Mr. Mulgrew's operative earn his fee. I didn't want to leave you, Charlie. Didn't want to leave your bed."

She was silent, her hands trembling around the teacup. She must have heard the sincerity in his voice, must understand that he wasn't ready to leave her behind in Little Fillup forever just yet. A summer idyll would be just the thing for both of them. They'd had a difficult time and deserved some restoration of their spirits. Even if it cost him the earth.

A part of him wished she'd come even without the enticement of a fortune. He glanced around the simple room that was dominated by the large stove. A streak against the whitewashed wall showed where the stove smoked, but the rest of the kitchen was spotless. A gleaming copper teakettle sat atop its surface. The space was cheery without being one bit ornate, much like the parlor he'd had trouble standing upright in. Perhaps her head wouldn't be turned by money—she was nothing like her sister.

"You tempt me," she said at last.

"Good." He grinned at her.

"Oh, not *you*," she said scornfully, finding her bite. "It's nearly impossible to turn down that kind of money, as well you know. I could do a lot of good in the village."

"I mean the money for you, Charlie, for your future."

"Little Hyssop *is* my future. It's not as though you're offering me marriage."

A prickle of unease swept from his neck down his spine. Of course he couldn't offer to marry her, not that she wouldn't make some man a happy husband. Judging from the condition of her cottage, she was an excellent housekeeper, not that any wife of his would ever have to lift a finger—his nabob grandfather had ensured that. And he knew from experience her performance in the bedchamber was every man's dream. She's certainly bedeviled his nights since they'd been apart.

She stacked and carried her dishes to the slate sink. He pushed his arctic tea aside and stood. "Think about my proposition, Charlie. I'll be at the Pig and Whistle until I hear from you."

She continued the washing up, not acknowledging his departure. Fine. Let her stew over it for a day, a week, however long it took. He'd wander about the countryside on his garden tour until she came to her senses and into his arms.

Chapter 18

Charlotte spent a sleepless night, counting the raindrops as they fell on her roof. The man was impossible, the devil himself, to taunt her with such an enormous amount of money. She would be set for life, never wondering whether she should sell one of Deb's castoffs, never tatting another inch of lace if she didn't want to. The banknotes she had in the ginger jar could fall into the fire and she needn't deign to singe her fingers to rescue them.

A summer by the sea as well as a fortune—she realized she missed her childhood home, hearing the slap of waves against the rocks, feeling the sharp wind against her face, seeing the gilded ribbon of moonlight on the water on a calm night. When her parents had drowned, she'd turned her back to the ocean, hating what she once had loved. But a decade had passed. She would love a beach holiday—she'd even contemplate going for a sail should the opportunity present itself.

But if she had felt guilty taking money from Mr. Frazier, however could she reconcile herself to Bay's offer? She would be a true prostitute, bought and at his every beck and call. No one could possibly refuse any demand he made after he had paid such a wicked sum. She would be completely at his mercy. The situation was absurd.

Let him cool his heels at the village inn. He'd soon grow bored waiting to hear from her. He'd simply have to find another woman to captivate. She would not succumb to his allure. Not again.

Grumpy, Charlotte tumbled out of bed and straightened the covers. She always made the bed first thing. She had her routine, and she stuck by it. Today was Monday, which meant she would clean her clean kitchen, then walk to the village shops. It had turned out to be a fine day for a change. She could finally get at her overgrown garden this afternoon, work up a sweat, and work out the irritability she still felt for Sir Michael Xavier Bayard. She wrapped her hair in a clean kerchief, tied an apron on over an old brown calico work dress, and entered her kitchen.

She stopped still. There on the table was Bay's mug, the tea still in it. She had been so distracted when he left yesterday, she'd gone straight into her parlor and wound lace on her bobbins, weaving and twisting and pinning the thread to her pillow until her hands cramped and it was too dark to see. She'd gone to bed without supper, her toast and the jam sandwich the only thing she ate all day yesterday. She was famished.

Sweeping the mug off the table, she opened the back door and tossed it into the garden, where it bounced along the lawn. It wasn't fit to be used anymore. She sometimes kept spare coins or pins in it. Perhaps Bay had swallowed one.

She stoked the stove, adding a shovelful of coals, boiled her water, scrambled her egg. When she finished breakfast she tidied the kitchen and set to scrubbing the stubborn long gray stain on her wall. If she had six thousand pounds, she could buy a new stove that wouldn't smoke. If she had six thousand pounds, she could hire Mrs. Finch from the village to scrub walls and sweep floors while she read one of Caroline's naughty novels in her back garden.

No, she was not going to do it.

She made herself presentable for her walk to the shops, gathered her basket by the front door, and went outside. Her plum trees were bursting full with green fruit. In a few weeks it would be time to make jam. If she were at Bayard Court, all those delicious plums would drop to the ground for the birds and the worms, and then what would she have for her bread come winter? She'd miss the raspberries and blackberries too. She'd been in the middle of making strawberry preserves when Deb's letter had come, so at least there was that, although she'd promised a dozen jars to Mrs. Kemble for the church fair in August.

But if she had six thousand pounds, she could buy jars of jam at any church fair.

Charlotte mentally slapped herself. She had her pride. She had her dignity. She had her modesty, what there was of it. It was one thing to be an accidental and then blackmailed mistress, quite another to acquiesce to the position in broad daylight.

So preoccupied with her born-again virtue, she nearly walked right by Mr. Trumbull's bentwood gate before she noticed the old gentleman hailing her. He was crouched over his stick, a smile splitting his wrinkled face. Mr. Trumbull's pride and joy was his garden, although he'd had to cut back its size severely the past few years since his wife had died. His roses in particular were to be admired. Because he was quite lame, Charlotte often shopped for him as well when she went for provisions. She had an eye for a bargain, which suited them both in their straitened circumstances.

"Hi there, Mrs. Fallon!"

"Good morning to you, Mr. Trumbull. I'm on my way to the shops. May I get you anything while I'm there?"

"No need, no need. I have an acquaintance of yours here who has already been and back. Turned up on my doorstep bright and early this morning. Good fellow. Wouldn't take a penny for his trouble but wants some China rose cuttings in exchange. Told him he was getting a bad bargain—why, he bought me so much I don't believe I'll live long enough to eat it all."

Charlotte's heart thudded. "An acquaintance?"

"Aye. Said the vicar introduced you in church yesterday. Sir Michael Bayard. Military man, but now he's a man of leisure, going about the country looking at gardens. He's planting a memorial to his old granny. Fond of roses, she was. Don't quite know what brought him to our neck of the woods, but I'm happy to help." Mr. Trumbull grinned in pride, revealing several yellow teeth. "He's out back, clearing out all the brush that got away from me. Can't do what I used to, and that's a fact."

What on earth? Why was Bay working at her neighbor's, if not to spy on her?

"I would hardly call Sir Michael an acquaintance, Mr. Trumbull. He wanted to see my garden after church yesterday, but the rain prevented it. He admired the flowers I did for the altar."

"I'm sure they were lovely as always. Didn't get to see them myself, you know. Too wet. Makes my old bones ache. Vicar Kemble came round last night after evensong, so I reckon I'm still in good standing with the Lord. I'll tell Sir Michael you'll receive him after you get back from your errands. He's got a powerful interest in your garden. Keeps peeking over the wall. Seems to like your Cuisse de Nymphs." The old man chuckled at the name. Thigh of nymph roses did sound naughty. Whatever one called them, they were a beautiful, lush, blush rose.

Charlotte couldn't very well forbid a garden tour today. The sky above was a brilliant blue. And even if she lingered in the five tiny shops in Little Hyssop, there was no way she could postpone the inevitable without attracting suspicion. One could only stare at thread so long, or debate the virtue of one lamb chop versus one pork chop. The thought of eating a chop of any kind made her nervous stomach nauseous. "Please tell Sir Michael I have time to see him at four o'clock. I suppose I can spare him a cup of tea."

The old man nodded. "That'll give the boy a chance to clean himself up. He's a handsome one, Mrs. Fallon. I suppose you noticed that yesterday," he said, his rheumy eyes twinkling. For an ancient, nearly blind man, Mr. Trumbull was entirely too astute.

"I had not noticed," Charlotte said, nose in the air. "The only man I ever noticed was Mr. Fallon, God rest his soul." Her imaginary dead husband had taken on rather mythic proportions in the ten years he'd been invented. Charlotte sometimes wondered if she'd gone a bit overboard. No man could ever measure up, but that had been the point. She'd been successful turning away the handful of unsatisfactory suitors who'd shown any interest in a pretty young widow. She was not about to get mixed up with another Robert, for all men were Robert at heart—ambitious and fickle, always looking over the next garden wall.

She bid Mr. Trumbull good-bye and walked into the center of the village. If Bay were coming at four o'clock, she'd better have tea for him, this time hot. There was no time to bake biscuits, so she purchased a half dozen at the baker's, as well as a fresh loaf of bread. She'd lay out the good dishes, and over a proper table she'd have a civilized conversation, refusing politely to join him and wishing him well in the future. With any luck, he'd pack his bags and rose cuttings and leave Little Hyssop early tomorrow morning and she would never, ever see him again.

Charlotte spent the remainder of the afternoon readying herself and her house for the unwelcome visitor. Perhaps she was foolishly vain, but she put on her best navy blue dress trimmed with her own lace and tied a new cap over her curls. The tea table was set in the parlor with her mother's transferware, starched napkins covering neatly cut sandwich triangles and cookie rounds. The kettle was simmering on the hob in her little fireplace. The house was still a bit damp and cold after the week of rain. To steady her nerves, she picked up her bobbins and clicked away until she heard the knock at the door, precisely as her mantel clock sounded the first of four chimes.

Bay stooped a bit as she let him into the narrow hallway.

He was so very much taller than she was, a fact that had made her feel safe in his arms. But safe she was not—her heart would be at risk if she agreed to his plan.

He bent to kiss her cheek and she darted away. "Mr. Trumbull might be spying in the bushes," she said lightly. "Thank you for being so kind to him."

"He's a nice old gent. Here. This is for you." Bay handed her a lumpy parcel wrapped in brown paper.

"What is it?"

"Open it and see."

Charlotte frowned. "You needn't give me presents. I'm not going to accept your invitation, and nothing you can give me will induce me to change my mind." She tore off the paper only to find the same cracked white mug she'd tossed out the kitchen door. Stuffed inside it was a red velvet drawstring bag.

"I rescued the cup from your back garden. There it was, like a snowball in the grass. I agree it is far too unsafe for ordinary use, but it served as a vessel for my other gift."

Charlotte put the mug down on the hall table, opened the pouch, and gasped.

"This time, I won't want it returned," Bay said, his voice as dark and smooth as chocolate sauce. "You deserve it after all the trouble it's caused you. I meant to give it to you yesterday, but the circumstances did not seem propitious. You were so very angry you might have strangled me with it."

Charlotte felt witless. The rubies and diamonds lay heavy in her hand. If she had been dazzled yesterday by the necklace, today she was spellbound. He couldn't really mean to give it to her after all the fuss he had made about Deb, could he?

Her lips felt numb. "But it was your grandmother's."

"Yes, and she wasn't all that fond of it, to be frank. She never wore it. Its history is not one of undying love, I'm afraid. My grandfather was a bit of a rascal. He made his fortune in the Orient, breaking all sorts of rules. One of them was his marriage vows. The necklace was a gift given out of guilt. I suppose I'm simply continuing the tradition. I truly regret all the indignities I've subjected you to. But I can't regret meeting you, Charlie. You've gotten under my skin."

"Like a rash?"

"Ah. A tongue as sharp as an adder's. That's what I like about you. Is your offer still on for tea? I've worked up a powerful thirst hacking and pruning away."

Bay brushed by her and made himself comfortable in a faded chintz-covered chair. She had no choice but to follow him into the parlor, the rubies weighing down her every step. She dropped the necklace in his lap. "I can't possibly accept this. You know I can't."

"Why not? You've earned it, Charlie. Every stone."

Suddenly dizzy, she carefully poured the steaming water into the teapot and set the kettle on a trivet before the little fire. She sat at the tea table, busying herself with strainers and rattling cups, wishing she was in her homey kitchen where Bay hadn't quite *loomed* so. It wasn't as if he was trying to intimidate her—he was sitting back, relaxed, a composed dark presence against the flowery slipcover. His hair seemed a little longer and less kempt. She thought she spied a coppery curl sprouting at his temple. His square jaw was shadowed with the beginnings of his beard, and for an instant she wanted to reach across the table and touch the stubble for herself.

"Bay," she said in impatience, mostly with herself, "I have told you time and time again I am a virtuous woman. Or I have tried to be. I made a mistake when I was a girl and I have been paying for it every day since. I don't need jewels or money for the life I live now. Mr. Frazier was more than generous when I left London. I cannot become a rich man's plaything, even if *you* are that rich man."

Bay took a sip of tea. "Then you do like me a little bit."

Charlotte felt the heat in her cheeks. "What I feel or do not feel is not at issue."

"Charlie, feelings are everything. Life is short, you know. If you didn't know it before you met me, you must be convinced of it now. A woman like you shouldn't go through the rest of your life buttoned up and covered up. It's a—it's a *sin.*"

"I am not my sister!"

Bay put his cup down and leaned forward. He looked suspiciously earnest, his dark eyes flashing. "No, you are not. You are better. Full of life and real passion, not someone who plays a role. Deborah is all glittering surface. You glow from within, Charlie. I was a fool not to see the difference earlier." He paused, letting his compliment sink in. He really was a master of persuasion. If one weren't mesmerized by his good looks alone, his voice could lull one into complete submission.

"If you are so determined to bury yourself in Little Wallop for the rest of your life," he continued, "how can it harm you to spend three months in the country with me? Think of it as a last fling. A final farewell to the woman we both know you are. I'll spoil you as you deserve to be spoiled. You won't have a care. Then come back and do your good works with my money. Wear my necklace beneath your spinster's night rail, where no one will ever see it."

Charlotte shivered. She felt like a snake in a basket, twisting to the snake charmer's hypnotic music. She should have some riposte—something sharp and off-putting so he would swallow up his tea and go away for good. Instead of biting him, she bit into a sandwich, struggling to keep her throat from closing.

"I've spoken to my banker. Whether or not you agree to come to Dorset, I've arranged to have a substantial sum transferred to you. You've succeeded in making me feel penitent— and I'm a man who rarely regrets anything, Charlie. But I wronged you and want to salve my guilty conscience."

So, he offered a fortune either way. She *had* been wronged, from the moment she woke with his lips suckling at her nipple. She'd been stripped of her freedom, although it had been a more than pleasant imprisonment. Terrified by his crazy wife, too. To be bound in his arms again would not be a hardship.

She'd had so little love in her life, not that Robert had truly loved her. Not that Bay did either. Both men had loved her body though. She was still young enough to feel desire, despite years of enforced purity. Could she survive her next thirty years without wishing for one more night with Bay?

She could have one more night. One more afternoon, anyway. She could allow him to make love to her right now, and focus on every kiss, caress, stroke. Store them up in her memory bank for the frigid winters ahead, like the pound notes in her ginger jar. Say good-bye to him once and for all.

Give him some small value for the money he seemed determined to bestow upon her. Give herself the gift of one last fling, as he put it. To feel him over her and in her, his hands and tongue and teeth imprinting themselves and anointing her.

She stood up and he quickly rose, concern on his brow.

She licked her lips. "I cannot give you three months, Bay. But I will give you three hours. Now. It's all I dare." She reached out to him, her hand trembling.

He pressed a kiss to her hand. "What if I can convince you to spare me a little more time? A month, say?"

"You can try." Charlotte felt the corners of her mouth turn up. She must be mad, as mad as Anne Whitley, but he was so effortlessly tempting.

"I shall rise to your challenge. In fact, I'm rising now." He pressed her palm to his breeches. She had done that to him without an ounce of flirtation. How very odd. "See? I've been hard for you since I walked through the door. Go close the curtains in your bedchamber. We wouldn't want to shock Mr. Trumbull."

Charlotte was shocked herself. But she threw her caution out the window and pulled the curtains in her mind shut and led Bay into her bedroom.

He untied her stupid cap. It was criminal to cover such hair. Glossy, rippling waves escaped down her back as he carefully removed each pin. She stood still, her eyes downcast as if she was afraid to meet his. Her lashes seemed unnaturally dark on her pale cheeks.

She was afraid of him! Afraid of herself, too, of what they had together. He would have to warm her up gently if he would have any hope of convincing her to parlay three hours into thirty days. He looked forward to sparring with her for a month, both in and out of bed. He could be persuasive, verbally and physically. She would fall from her pedestal into his arms.

But in truth, it was she who had persuaded him to follow her here without any effort at all.

Her room was small, simple, virginal, the bed snowy with white linen, every corner tucked. He would soon alter that. His bed at Bayard Court was a massive Elizabethan affair, a tester bed with fringed brocade bed hangings that could accommodate a small family. He could see himself and Charlie tented within, the shadows abetting their happy sin. Today he'd have to control his impulses to roll around with her wildly or they'd wind up on the rag-rugged floor. He unbuttoned her plain navy dress and wished she'd at least reach for his cravat, but she was still as death. Like a Christian martyr waiting on a china plate for the lion to come for supper. This would never do. She was as solemn as a nun. Had she forgotten already that it was her idea to bring him to bed in the afternoon? He had merely come to tea, expecting another set-down.

He stuck one finger under her armpit and wiggled. She flinched, bit her lip but said nothing. He applied more pressure, this time with both hands, and she let out a little scream. Her dress dropped to the floor. She toppled backward on the bed as his fingers continued their tickling mischief. She was laughing and writhing now, helpless. Her face was rosy with some anger, and—yes—enjoyment.

"Stop this at once!" she cried before shrieking. She batted at him ineffectually, her breasts rising and falling beneath her chemise and corset. Her lips opened in further protest. He had to stop their mutual torment, so he kissed her, as he had wanted to do from the first moment he nearly decapitated himself entering her cottage.

She tasted of cress and butter. Sweet tea. So sweet. Soft. He cupped her face with one hand as he untied her laces with the other to free a plump breast. It was perfect in his hand, the creamy weight temptation itself. He'd missed the scent of oranges, missed the velvet of her skin. Missed everything about her, even her bad temper and hideous caps. He thought about confessing, but he'd already pled his case. It was time to use other methods.

His tongue was useful, circling around a darkening nipple. He feasted, deliberately savoring each second buried in her lush bosom, indulging himself, and, he hoped, her as well. He knew success when he heard her sigh and felt her fingers slide through his hair. The taste of her filled his mouth, more delicious than all the store-bought biscuits in the world. He felt her melt as he suckled, her legs part. He tugged up the hem of her chemise and headed homeward, skimming her smooth skin with his fingertips. Her white thighs, the sensitive spot behind her knees, her beautiful belly—they would be tended to later. All he wanted right now was to touch her hot core. Get inside her and never leave. Make her beg for him to stay tonight, and then go away with him forever tomorrow. He dipped a finger into her dark curls, slipped between her nether lips. She was already silky, slick, welcoming.

But he could wait, though not for long. He set to abrading the inch of swollen flesh at the apex, for her pleasure and his. He would benefit from every touch, every tensing, every letting go. She shuddered under him as he worked her clitoris to rigid attention, much like his own cock, which was near to bursting in his breeches.

He drew her nipple between his teeth as he circled harder and felt her world shift. She cried out, her nails nearly piercing his shoulder. He chose to withstand the sting and soldiered on, nipping, soothing, and smoothing her as she came apart. Charlotte let loose a string of somewhat colorful descriptions of all the things he had already planned to do.

He heard her orders, and he was an obedient sort of fellow. So much for gentling her into submission. She was as wild and needy as he was. He had to have her, had to feel her tight and wet around him now. This very minute.

Apparently she felt the same way. There was no time for finesse. There wasn't time to remove his jacket or even her shift. Between the two of them, two pairs of hands desperate, the placket of his breeches became undone and he sheathed himself within her in one very firm stroke. She spasmed around him, all warm honey, her hips lifting and driving him further inside. He was so lost he forgot to kiss her, just shut his eyes and plunged deeper, the exquisite friction almost too perfect to bear. She rose up against him and lured him down with a nip at his throat.

The heat between them danced across his skin. He opened his eyes thinking to see his jacket in flames, but saw instead his lover, her hair a tangle, her ivory skin flushed, her mouth open in joyous surprise. His tongue swept in and she returned the parry, as though she was starving, tasting him for the first time and could not get enough. He could kiss her forever, drink in her sweetness. Their coupling was so right, so thoughtless, really. He needn't worry about position or mindless patter—she opened to him willingly and matched him each time he thrust. Then she rippled all around him, riding the crest of her orgasms, making quick cries between kisses. It had been like this from the first night, when she thought she was dreaming. Perhaps it was he who was dreaming now, for surely this was too ideal to be real.

But reality did intrude on this come-to-life fantasy, so he withdrew and spent on her belly. He lay pressed close, their heartbeats skipping between them. Her white breast spilled over in his hand, its nipple peaked and pink. The weight of his clothes was suddenly onerous—he should be with her, flesh to flesh. He'd taken her like an impatient brute, but judging from her lazy smile, she didn't mind.

"I'm sorry I was so precipitous. I didn't even remove my boots."

She touched his scarred cheek. "We still have most of three hours." Her voice was playful and sultry, even if she had reminded him how very fast he had taken her. How very fast she had brought him to completion. But it had been as good for her. Next time he would make it even better. He rolled away and tugged at his neck cloth, which had disentangled enough for her to mark him with a lovebite. She sat up and drew her shift over her head.

Her body was even more desirable than he remembered. She glistened with a sheen of perspiration from their lovemaking, and her scent, far from disturbing him, made him want to taste her all over, lick up each drop of moisture. He watched as she used the garment to wipe away the sweat and semen. If they had been on Jane Street, they could have bathed together, which reminded him he was overdressed for the occasion. He removed his wrinkled clothing, returned to the mattress and to his absolute astonishment, watched his cock recover some of its audacity.

He sensed her regaining her propriety, moving away from him both physically and mentally. Her face had lost some of its sly softness, as if she was awakening from a reverie. He meant for her to go back, for them both to go back where the world was as small as the bed they shared, and life was as simple as a good fuck. He would force her from her prudery, and with luck, would be on his way to Dorset with her in the morning. He tipped her back against the pillows and trailed his tongue from the hollow at her throat to her delicious hot slit. She would not say no. She could not say no. She was his, every inch of her, at least for a little while.

Chapter 19

Bay's carriage rolled through the drive, the open fields of tall grass on either side flattened by the brisk wind. Ahead was a large stone manor house overlooking a gray-green sea. Storm clouds hung low on the horizon, promising to continue the bad weather that had followed them all the way from Little Hyssop. A few stunted black trees sprung up here and there along the lane, but mostly the green of the ground met the sky and the ocean as far as the eye could see. Charlotte took a deep breath, devouring the smell of salt air and rain. She was home for the first time in a decade, not all that far from the beach she played on as a child. Bay had promised her sailing and swimming, as well as days and nights of his masterful loving.

No, not loving. She mustn't be foolish. Mustn't make more of their mutual lust. And lust it was. It was as if she had shredded every admonition her poor mother had ever given her. "Don't. Don't. Don't." So many sentences her mama uttered began with those words, or "a lady never . . ." A lady would never give her body to Bay with heedless abandon in coaching houses and carriage rides. A lady would never rest on a pillow on her knees as she took her lover's member in her mouth. A lady would never feel jubilant as she cradled and suckled him to lose all control. A lady would not crave the taste of his enslavement. Charlotte was ashamed of her easy acceptance of every vice. But how essential it was to be led astray when Bay was doing the leading.

She had meant to say "don't." She had meant to say "no." Instead she had watched in a languorous stupor as Bay packed her belongings in a valise by candlelight. He carried it off before the Pig and Whistle locked its doors, with precise instructions to meet him the following day. He had obviously never doubted for a minute that he could convince her to join him, the devil. She found herself on Mr. Trumbull's doorstep the next morning, stammering that she had been summoned back to London again to see her sister. She rode the mail coach three towns over before Bay met her in the courtyard of the Grasshopper Inn. Even though she knew not a soul, she was as veiled as a freshly made widow. Bay had tossed that veil and the cap under it out of the window of his coach almost immediately. When she delved into her case when they stopped at the first of several inns on the journey to the coast, she had been irritated to discover that he had somehow misplaced all her other caps. But he had purchased her a lovely straw bonnet, telling her the blue ribbons were an exact match for her eyes, so she was on her way to forgiving him.

He had been restless the past hour, shifting in his seat as the driver bumped along a winding path along the cliffs, almost as if he were as nervous as she was. He had spoken about his house with pride, and she could see he had every reason. She counted numerous gables and chimneys on the Jacobean façade, noted the many-paned mullioned windows. A high stone wall covered in ivy and climbing roses sheltered his grandmother's garden at the east end of the house. Somewhere in his luggage were Mr. Trumbull's cuttings. Bay had been most particular wrapping the stems in wet cotton batting at each stop.

They had not passed another dwelling for some time, driving down a spit of land surrounded by the sea. Bay had hopped down from his dry perch, braving the weather to unlock the gates at the end of the drive. The carriage pushed forward a few meters, then Bay locked them back up "to discourage the random visitor," he said. Somehow Charlotte felt trapped, not that she wanted to risk her reputation and venture off the estate. There had been a village a mile or so back much like the one in which she had grown up, the Smugglers' Rest Pub proclaiming the previous pastime of some of the citizenry. Now that the wars were over, most free traders were forced to earn an honest living, depleting the little community. Bay had given Charlotte a very brief history of his section of the Dorset coast during their trip.

As a boy, Bay had a fascination for the local smugsmiths, which his grandmother had firmly squelched. His house itself had once been owned by a prominent family who had dabbled in the trade over the centuries. He'd watched the lights on the water for hours from his bedroom with his grandfather's spyglass. Things were now staid and settled, although there was still some remarkably good brandy in his cellars. He'd promised Charlotte a large tot of it once their feet were on the flagstone floors of Bayard Court.

The short journey had not agreed with her. She'd been queasy off and on for days. The roads were rutted and muddy, and the inclement weather had not helped, necessitating the closure of the carriage windows. She was trapped in the still air of Bay's carriage, although the scent of him—starched linen and vetiver and sex—was very pleasant. Charlotte had seen the sun shine for just one day in two weeks, and she had spent part of that day in Bay's arms with the curtains closed.

Her garden would be a shambles when she returned. Before she left Little Hyssop, she had pressed some money in Mr. Trumbull's arthritic hand, asking him to hire one or two of the local boys to work in both their gardens for the next month. The produce from her vegetable patch and fruit trees was to go to the poor. Richer by six thousand pounds, she could order hampers from Fortnum & Mason to fill her belly for the rest of her life.

Six thousand pounds for thirty days. Two hundred pounds per day. The sum was inconceivable, but Bay had assured her he wouldn't miss a single sovereign. Judging from his house, he was ridiculously rich. She wondered why he had gone into the army. As a baronet and only son, surely he could have stayed home and left the fighting to others.

And then she remembered Anne and his illegal marriage. Bay had gone off to get himself killed. Charlotte shivered. She hoped that woman was far away, her schemes for Bay thwarted by his loyal retainers.

Charlotte and Bay dashed from the carriage under an umbrella provided by a windblown Mr. Frazier. Mrs. Kelly beamed a welcome to them in the wide flagstone foyer. Evidently Charlotte had been forgiven for her earlier behavior and was now in the housekeeper's good books. Making his excuses, Bay disappeared with Mr. Frazier almost immediately, leaving Charlotte to tour the house without him.

If Jane Street had been lovely, Bay's true home was one hundred times more impressive. Intricate Jacobean oak paneling lined the walls. There was no evidence of Bay's art collection downstairs; assuredly it would have shocked his elderly grandmother. Mrs. Kelly said many of the rooms in the house were still shut up, had been so even when Lady Bayard was still alive, but everything Charlotte inspected was mellow, tasteful, shining, dust-free. Bay's little staff had been busy getting the house ready for what Charlotte was beginning to think of as the only honeymoon she would ever have. Instead of vows and a wedding ring, she would leave Bayard Court with the promise of economic independence and a priceless ruby necklace, which Bay had stubbornly insisted she keep. It was beneath her high-collared gray frock right now. The jewels were all he permitted her to wear at night in the modest inns they stopped at on the road. His letter had come to life at last with the wrong sister, but everything he had suggested became better than promised.

Charlotte was grateful most of the house was under Holland covers, as she did not think she'd get her bearings if she had to navigate through all of it. Mrs. Kelly was a bit breathless just from showing her the parlors, dining room, morning room, breakfast room, well-stocked library, and conservatory,

an exquisite glass extension that overlooked the walled garden and the pewter sea. The conservatory was empty now of
greenery, and rain tapped incessantly on the panes. Charlotte
could imagine frost and snow on the window while tropical
plants reached for the ceiling, but Bay's grandmother had cut
back on her hobby long ago.

Charlotte was winded herself when she entered her desig-
nated bedchamber. She was glad Mrs. Kelly and Irene had
not put her in Lady Bayard's bedroom, which still bore evidence of being a sickroom. Instead she followed Mrs. Kelly a
good ways down the hall.

"We've put you right next to Sir Michael. He never moved
into his grandfather's room when he inherited, of course. He
didn't want to disturb his old gran."

"Perhaps he will when he marries again," Charlotte said
softly.

Mrs. Kelly looked at her with some sympathy. The door to
Bay's suite stood open. The room, papered in a dark blue, was
unmistakably masculine. Charlotte couldn't restrain her cu-
riosity and stepped in. A massive bed faced the leaded windows that overlooked the sea. Charlotte had an immediate
image of lying on it, the blue brocade curtains concealing all
the wicked things that Bay would do to her.

"This was his boyhood room. Mr. Frazier told me his grandmother had it redecorated after he came back from the war."

Charlotte gazed through the wavy glass. "Bay told me he
used to watch for smugglers."

"Very likely. They were active on this part of the coast. My
sister used to send me lace when she could get hold of it."

"I make lace, Mrs. Kelly. Perhaps I'll have time to make
you some." She had purposefully brought her equipment with
her this time. She hated to be idle.

"Well! That would be lovely. I'd never say no to a bit of
lace. If you're ready?"

Charlotte would have ample opportunity to snoop into
Bay's things later. She followed Mrs. Kelly down three steps
into another wing.

He had the bigger bed, but her view was just as perfect. Drawn to the window, she plunked down on the cushioned window seat to watch the whitecaps dance rhythmically beyond the lawn. Charlotte thought she might be perfectly content staring at the water all the rest of the day.

Mrs. Kelly broke the spell. "Is there anything you need, Miss Fallon?"

Charlotte shook her head. She'd examine her new room more thoroughly later. Now all she wanted to do was revel in the luxury of being in Dorset again.

Irene had already unpacked her meager belongings. Mrs. Kelly encouraged Charlotte to rest and come downstairs for tea with the master in an hour. Too excited to sleep, she washed and changed from her traveling clothes without ringing for Irene. The maid was a lovely girl, but it had been so very long ago since Charlotte and Deb had shared a maid that she was quite used to doing for herself. She sewed her own simple clothes so that she could get in and out of them without too much difficulty.

She was in a fresh gray dress, her head feeling unnaturally naked without the comfort of one of her little spinster's caps. Of course, her neighbors in Little Hyssop thought she wore a widow's cap. She really would feel like a widow once Bay was finished with her. There were thirty days left to enjoy her pretend marriage.

Charlotte sighed. What she had with Bay right now was better than most marriages. People in the ton married for property and consequence. For titles and wealth. If one could endure being covered by one's husband once a week without too much revulsion, one could consider oneself lucky. Charlotte, on the other hand, could not wait to ditch her gray dress and tumble with Bay in his massive bed. She was fascinated by his conversation, loved studying his male beauty as he spoke. She could understand why Anne was so determined to have him again. Bay was the type of man one could not ever forget.

But forget him she must when she went back to reality and her little cottage.

Heavens. She could now afford something on a slightly grander scale. A house with a bigger garden. Her own conservatory, where she could make her lace in warmth and brilliant sunshine surrounded by the blooming plants she loved. She might even be forced to move from Little Hyssop if certain circumstances arose. Bay had promised to help her with investing her nest egg so that she could increase her new-found wealth.

But a financial bubble could burst, and then she'd be as badly off as her parents had been. She must be as careful and conservative with her treasure and heart as she'd been this past decade. Except for the next thirty days.

Charlotte removed the ruby necklace and wrapped it carefully in a lace-trimmed handkerchief. Leaving her room, she wished she had a trail of Hansel and Gretel crumbs to follow downstairs. After a few wrong turns, she bumped into Mrs. Kelly, who was wheeling a loaded tea trolley into one of the downstairs reception rooms. A fire burned in the grate to ward off the damp of the cavernous room. Bay was already seated in one of a pair of wing chairs in an alcove. The uncurtained French windows led out to the clipped lawn and the beach. Raindrops slid down the panes, but Bay's smile was as sunny as it could be. He rose and kissed her hand.

"I trust you've settled in and everything meets with your approval?"

"Yes, of course." She had nothing to complain about so far, except for the wretched weather, and there was nothing Bay could do about that. "Mrs. Kelly, thank you. This looks delightful. I'll take care of serving." Mrs. Kelly had even included a cut-glass bowl of raspberries, although Charlotte was not about to put them to their previous use. Truthfully, she wasn't hungry at all, but she busied herself pouring tea for them both and pushing a full plate toward Bay.

"Sorry I left you in the lurch earlier and disappeared. I had some business with Frazier." Bay wolfed down a sandwich and grabbed another as though they hadn't shared a breakfast and a substantial luncheon already today.

"And how is Mr. Frazier? As feisty as ever?"

Bay grinned. "I believe he's a bit bored after all the recent excitement."

"I cannot say the same. I am looking forward to a quiet sojourn in the country. Your home is lovely, by the way." She took a tiny bite of muffin for politeness's sake.

"All my grandmother's doing. This was her favorite spot in the afternoon. On a fine day the view is spectacular." He scooped a spoonful of berries onto his dish and raised a naughty eyebrow at her. Charlotte ignored him.

"I can imagine. Even now it's rather majestic." The wind whipped at the shrubbery and the waves frothed white.

"I like a good storm myself. Maybe that's why I like *you*." He winked at her impudently.

"I'll have you know until I met you I was most temperate. You are excessively provoking." She watched him swallow a mouthful of berries, enjoying them far too much. His tongue darted out to lick his lips. It was stained bright pink. Charlotte thought of that tongue tasting her.

"So I have been told. Come sit on my lap, Charlie. I'd like to provoke you right this minute."

Charlotte felt her blush wash over her. She supposed she must do as he asked. He was paying her more than enough. She slipped from her chair to his. His hand reached under her gown. Besides her caps, he had failed to pack any drawers. He was an absolute fiend.

"Ah," he sighed happily, finding her shamefully accessible. He set to strumming the center of her womanhood. She leaned back onto his shoulder, her eyes closed. There was nothing but his hands and her body. He held her still with one hand. With the other he made her loose, free. Unraveled. She was soon as wet as the windowpane, weeping onto his fingers. Wanting much more.

Half of her wondered if Mrs. Kelly would return for the tea cart; the other half was quivering under his concerted stroking. She was on the cusp of danger and delight. He held her in an iron grip as if he was afraid she'd run off. Impossible. She'd be mad to forgo this sensual abandonment. That would happen all too soon, and she'd be back in her little cottage, lonely and rich. Unhappy. Untouched.

Charlotte knew happiness was an illusion, but she'd settle for touch. She needed Bay's touch. Everywhere. Right now. She began by kissing the raspberry essence from his mouth. His lips were firm, his tongue wicked. It twinned with his fingers to subdue her worries and lull her into bliss. Just when she thought things could not be more perfect, he edged her over the cliff, catching her as she fell apart in his arms.

Her eyes were still closed as he shifted her and fumbled with his falls, keeping her reality in check. His shaft was adamantine against her bare buttocks. His broad hands raised her hips. She steadied herself on the arms of the chair as he gripped himself and filled her from behind. She sheathed him easily, feeling every glorious pulsing inch of him inside her. They both stilled, Bay's breath hitching in blissful agony.

And then she took control. She pushed herself up on the arms of the chair. Came down hard. He was buried deeper than ever, touching her in places previously forbidden. Exquisite sensation washed over them both, like the driving rain outdoors.

Touching. So basic. So elemental. So cleansing for the soul, so affirming that one was not truly alone in the universe. Charlotte felt each prickle of coppery hair on her skin, each imprint of his fingertips, each ragged breath against the back of her neck.

She nearly swooned with the glory of it, but she knew better. She was a very bad swooner, although this time she thought Bay might keep her safe in his arms. They were around her now, helping her to rise and fall, repeating the rhythm again and again until she thought she'd *die* of his touch, both inside and out. As he lost himself, his hand sought her center again. She joined him a jolt of breathless union, as fierce as the waves outside slapped against the rocks.

His hand splayed on her belly in ownership. Too sated to move, she leaned back against his heaving chest. His lips were at her neck, her ear, whispering words she couldn't make sense of. She couldn't make sense of anything. The man drove her completely mad. They had taken no precautions—again. Charlotte was playing a dangerous game, one she suspected she might have already lost.

She couldn't tell him. Wouldn't tell him that more than likely a few weeks ago—perhaps that very first night—they had made a new life. It was too soon to tell, but she was almost certain. Her courses had not come. Even if she had been off balance what with the kidnapping and gunplay, her body should have righted itself by now.

She could not think of any child as a mistake, for she had longed for motherhood even as she pushed away the few suitors she'd had over the years. Of course it meant she'd have to sell her cottage and move again, go to a new part of the country, this time as a widow bearing her late husband's child. She'd had years of experience playacting, although she did not look forward to trading her gray dresses for black ones again. It couldn't be helped.

There would be sufficient funds, and Lord knows she had sufficient love within her to raise a baby. She knew if she asked him, Bay would do right by his son or daughter, but the thought of tethering herself to him as a dependent for the next twenty years pierced her soul. He needed to marry some sweet young thing and have a normal life. She couldn't stand by in the shadows and watch that. She needed to disappear.

Perhaps it was all wishful thinking. His finger was at her cheek, wiping up a tear she hadn't planned to shed.

"I'm sorry I was such a beast, Charlie. Was I too rough?"

"Oh, no. It was perfect." She sniffled a bit, then found her tart tongue. "Perfect, as always, although your head will swell to the size of a hot-air balloon if I must keep complimenting you."

Bay chuckled. "A man cannot ever have too much praise over his sexual prowess, my love. Tell me more."

"I shall not!" She struggled to get up from his lap, but his arms were like iron bands across her chest, and his cock twitched with renewed interest inside her. "Do let me up. Mrs. Kelly could come back at any moment," she begged.

"I doubt it. But if she did, she would just see you sitting on my lap. Shocking, to be sure, but your front is completely undisturbed, more's the pity. I didn't have time to attend to your superb breasts in all the rush. I think," he said, his lips skimming her throat, causing her to shiver, "I should remedy that."

His hands made quick work of her buttons. He freed one breast easily from her bodice and then he bent to tease and suckle. She was tender, and the sensation was both torture and ecstasy. Suddenly his lips left their torment and he pushed her from his lap.

"What—why?"

He put a fingertip to her lip. "I want to watch you, Charlie. See your lovely face." He led her to a pillow-covered sofa. If he hadn't supported her across the carpet, her knees would have buckled beneath her. She was boneless and drunk with lust. Bay stripped her dress and underthings from her and laid her down on the velvet. She watched as he tossed his own clothing to the floor. There would be no disguising what was going on now should anyone come upon them, but Charlotte was too swept away to protest. She fell headlong into his dark gaze as he brought her ever closer to the storm.

What in God's name was the matter with him? True, his servants were well aware and accepted the fact that he was a lusty man. They didn't blink or flinch as he installed mistresses in the Jane Street house or flirted shamelessly and bedded racy widows in his townhouse. His French chef even had a standard romantic supper menu that never changed although Bay's female guests did. But it was rare that he'd be naked in daylight, rutting on parlor furniture, apparently incapable of controlling himself where Charlie was concerned. In the space of an hour he'd proudly brought her to orgasm too many times to count. She lay flushed and warm beneath him now, her white skin marbled with rose, her heavy dark hair falling from her pins to reach the carpet. He curled a strand around his fingers and brought it to his nose. He was reminded of orange peel. Lemons. As far as he knew she had no expensive scent, just some cakes of soap she'd tucked into a satchel for the trip. Soap she'd made herself with her own work-reddened hands.

At least she'd have a month free from care and worry. If this blasted weather ever let up, there would be walks on the beach. Picnics. Sailing. His little boat was tucked into the cove beneath the cliffs. It had been an age since he'd used it. Frazier had said it was still seaworthy. Frazier had said several things. But Bay wanted to let nothing disturb the peace of Charlie breathing beneath him.

Her eyes were closed, her lashes fluttering. They were tipped with tears again, but she didn't seem unhappy. Far from it. She seemed to cry more out of joyful release than any sorrow. Getting her here had been worth the slog through the mud and the tedium in the shut-up carriage, although Bay had sought to keep things lively by his constant attention to her physical comfort. Perhaps comfort wasn't the appropriate word. Satisfaction might be more accurate. He had discovered Charlie to be flexible and enthusiastic, even in the squabs of his coach. She was altogether an exceptional mistress, and worth the astronomical amount he had promised her.

He felt a twinge of guilt at his bribery. No sensible woman, no matter how vaunted her virtue, could turn away such a sum easily. But for a time Bay believed Charlie would do just that and give him his marching orders. There was no room for him and his proposal in her orderly, slightly shabby Little Stickup world. She had her pride, and her temper, too. But somehow over tea that Monday afternoon he had worn down her resistance and won a reprieve. He took advantage of her post-sex lethargy that night, packing most of her clothing in a valise—sad, sterile dresses which should be burned as he had done with her nasty caps. He wished he could furnish her with new gowns as he had done with Deborah, but rationalized he would have her out of her clothes as often as possible anyway. A month was not a very long time to endure the boring colors and styles of her "Widow Fallon" wardrobe.

A month might not be long enough, however, to get his need for her out of his system. He brushed his lips on her eyelids, tasting her tears. He watched as her teeth sank into her own plump bottom lip, as if she were preventing herself from speaking.

"Are you all right, Charlie?"

She fitted herself more snugly into his arms. "Quite." Her warm hand was over his heart, as if to inspect the effect she had upon him still. His blood surged in response. The velvet of the sofa back and the velvet of Charlie's perfect body cradled him, but he supposed they should make themselves presentable at some point. He hadn't even bothered to ask Mrs. Kelly to lock the parlor door, although he did not expect her to enter without knocking first. The tea was long cold, the crusts of the sandwiches curling up. The sky outside was darkening with thunderheads, rain spattered on the windows, and the wind-driven ocean roared. This was no ordinary mild June afternoon. It mirrored the war he was having within himself.

He kissed her quickly on her nose. There was a freckle there he hadn't noticed before, and a few more strands of silver shooting through her midnight hair. He pictured her in twenty years, one of her ghastly caps concealing pearl-white curls. She would age well, he thought, the cushion of her womanly body softening any wrinkle that would dare to appear. He wondered where she'd be in two decades, and with whom. Surely she was meant to be a wife and mother; her housewifery was apparent in her neat little cottage.

And where would he be? Likely right here. London would soon lose its allure—it was doing so already. There were several improvement projects at Bayard Court that he had been putting off, not wishing to disturb his grandmother. He knew he could sell the Jane Street property at a tidy profit. A mile of gentlemen were lined up waiting to purchase one of the dozen houses if it came on the market. And if his grumpy little Charlie was not there waiting for him upstairs, it was too annoying and arduous by half to have to replace her.

He didn't think he could push his luck and coax her back to Jane Street on any terms. She really was a vexingly upright citizen after all, despite her undeniably sinful body. He hoped she wouldn't ask to attend church while she was here—her presence would attract unwelcome attention. He was known not to have any female cousins. A man of his class did not have female "friends" who visited unchaperoned. Even if he passed her off as the widow of an army comrade, there would be talk. Charlie would not be safe. The fewer people who knew he was back, the better.

"You look dreadfully serious all of a sudden."

Her eyes were bright, but the tears had dried up. He smiled at her, pushing his concerns away. "It's this blasted weather. How am I to take you for a moonlit sail when we're likely to be blown all the way to France?"

"One can do nothing about the weather. I'm sure we'll find other amusements." She wiggled into him playfully. This was the Charlie he loved.

He kissed her again, savoring the taste of her. He could kiss her for hours, but the chiming hall clock had other ideas.

"I think, my dear, that we should help each other get dressed and help each other get undressed to change for dinner. If I know Mrs. Kelly, she's been slaving away in the kitchen with something tempting for us."

She sighed in relaxation in his arms. "I am beyond temptation. For food, at any rate."

"Minx. You hardly ate anything at tea. Don't be foolish and go on some sort of slimming regimen. I like your womanly curves." He brushed a hand across her belly for emphasis. She was round in all the right places. He'd never been one to admire a bony or waiflike female.

She slapped his hand away. "No tickling. Not again."

"Spoilsport." With a groan, he raised them both up to a

sitting position on the divan. Her nipples pebbled against his chest. "Cold?"

"It's supposed to be summer. How can I be?" She reached for a stocking on the carpet. "You've thrown my pins every-where. Just how am I to do my hair up so I can pass the ser-vants without them smirking?"

"All this sex has made me stupid. I completely forgot. We'll go up the secret stairs. There will be no need to even dress."

Charlie blinked. "There are secret stairs? Next you'll tell me there's a ghost."

"Nothing so predictable. But there is a passage leading from this room to one of the bedrooms upstairs. Not yours or mine, but I doubt we'll bump into anyone." He got off the sofa and scooped up the bundle of their clothes.

"I will *not* go upstairs naked."

"All right." He tossed her shift to her. "Put this on, Miss Prim. Now, if I can find the right panel . . ."

"Please, *please* put your trousers on at least."

"You're right. There might be spiders." He enjoyed her shudder as he stepped into his pants and boots. She sat back down and put her slippers on sans stockings. "This house is very old, you know, and it wasn't always in my family. My grandfather bought it when he made his fortune and changed its name."

"That's unlucky, isn't it?"

"It may well be, but my grandfather didn't believe in luck but hard work." He walked to a corner and started rapping. Charlie glided after him, interested.

"You're quite serious, aren't you. Will a door pop open?"

"If *I* get lucky. It's been years since I've been exploring here. The house was built by a family that was always in trouble with the church or the law. Hence a bolt-hole. There are stairs and a passage that leads to the beach. My father showed me when I was a boy, but then my grandmother absolutely for-bid me to use them once he died. She thought I'd disappear."

"And you were obedient."

Bay grinned. "When I had to be. I don't think I've used the stairs since my school days. It was always amusing to jump out at my friends in the middle of the night."

"I suppose you were wearing a sheet."

"On occasion. Ah!" He gave a shove with his shoulder and a narrow strip of aged wood creaked open.

Charlie peered into the cavity. "It's dark."

"Well, yes. Shall I light a candle, or do you want to parade before the staff in your chemise with your hair down your back? Not that you don't look very fetching."

"H-how long will it take us?"

"Not long. It's just a few dozen steps. I'll hold your hand and keep you safe." He lit a candle stub from the sputtering flames in the hearth and stuck it back in the candleholder. "You'll have to hold our clothes, though."

Charlotte clutched the assorted clothing to her chest. She was freezing now, the dampness between her legs adding to the chill. She wanted nothing more than a hot bath and a ray of sunshine. She most certainly did *not* want to be trapped in a dark cobwebby corridor. But Bay held her fast and pulled her up the well-worn wooden stairs. She screamed only once when something fluttered on her cheek.

"Hush. People will really believe the house is haunted," Bay teased. "Here we are."

There was an actual door with an actual knob. Bay turned it and led her into a room whose furniture was covered in dust sheets. She sniffed and sneezed.

"Mice," she said.

"No doubt. This wing has been closed off since before I went to war. The mice have probably evolved into rats by now."

"Urk." Charlotte felt invisible teeth nibbling at her ankles. The room was dim, the shutters closed. She scampered to the door and burst out into the hall. "Which way?"

"Turn right." She was almost running now, Bay chuckling a few steps behind her. "Right again. Here we are."

Charlotte was at her own door. "Would it be too much

trouble for the household if I ordered a bath before supper?" She was convinced an army of spiders was weaving an elaborate web in her hair.

"My dear, we live to serve you. I'll take care of it. Wrap up in your wretched gray elephant robe and wait patiently."

She stood up on tiptoe and kissed him. "Thank you, Bay. I haven't anything grand to dress in for dinner, you know."

"If I had my way, we'd dine naked in bed. You know how fond I am of that particular activity." He held up a hand to stop her complaint. "But not tonight. Tonight we'll be proper. But I can't promise propriety for the rest of our holiday."

Charlotte shut the door on his grinning face, grabbed a hairbrush, and tore it furiously through her hair. Every inch of her itched, ached, throbbed. And she supposed she would be subjected to more lovemaking tonight in Bay's enormous bed.

She took her robe out of the wardrobe and wrapped her arms around herself. A clap of thunder startled her, but she had already been struck by lightning.

Chapter 20

For a moment, Charlotte feared Bay would stay with her while she bathed, and then she would never get entirely clean. Or for that matter, dressed again. They would wind up supping in her room, or his, their appetites hungry for each other rather than Mrs. Kelly's cooking. He had helped orchestrate the little procession of maids who trundled up the stairs with hot water and fluffy towels, going so far as to carry an enormous sloshing, steaming pail himself, but then left them to their duties. Irene introduced the two maids, sisters Mary and Kitty Toothaker, and explained they came for the day only, going back to their village home each night.

Charlotte looked out her window. The sky was slate gray, the rain coming down in sheets.

"That won't do tonight, girls. Surely in a house this size there's room for you to sleep here."

"Our mam would worry, miss," said Kitty, the darker of the two. She was short, slight, and didn't even look strong enough to carry the pitcher of hot water she set down before the hearth. A good gust of wind might knock her right down. She might turn a thin ankle and roll into a ditch.

"I don't think she'd want you to walk all that way alone in the rain and dark."

"Mr. Frazier keeps us both company, Miss Fallon, and he's got a big lantern." Mary caught her sister's eye and giggled. Kitty blushed under the ruffled brim of her mobcap.

"Mr. Frazier?" Charlotte thought the explosive ex-soldier was the last man she would think of to go a-wooing. But Kitty was young, fresh-faced, and considerably shorter than the short Angus Frazier.

"Hush, Mary!" There's nothing going on, Miss Fallon! All Ang— All Mr. Frazier does is walk us home. He's been a perfect gentleman this week while we've been getting the house ready for you."

Charlotte bit back her smile. "I am acquainted with Mr. Frazier a little. He is very brave and loyal. Perhaps if you spend the night, you can get to know him better. Irene, please let Mrs. Kelly know my wishes." If it was true they were all there to serve her, she might as well take advantage of it.

"But our mam—"

Mary elbowed Kitty in the ribs. "She'll be asleep anyway and never miss us. She drinks, you know."

Kitty rolled her eyes at her sister's indiscretion but kept her lips shut tight.

Charlotte knew what it was like to have a mother who drank. A father, too. "That settles it. Irene, go downstairs with the girls and consult with Mrs. Kelly. As soon as you all have had your supper, you're free to do as you see fit. I won't need you until tomorrow, Irene."

"Not even to help you dress for dinner?"

Charlotte laughed. "Irene, dear, you've unpacked my clothes. I'm not getting into a court gown."

"You should have brought that red dress."

"Sir Michael packed for me and must have overlooked it." Charlotte had barely been able to see through her tears when she threw her belongings into her case at Jane Street the day she escaped from Anne Whitley. The object was to get out of town as quickly as possible. To go back to her cottage. To get on with her life, such as it was. But she had taken the impractical dress and Bay's letters. She was a romantic idiot.

When the girls left her, she sank into the tub and scrubbed herself vigorously with her special soap. The secret stairwell could have been worse, she supposed. Charlotte was not all that fond of dusty, shut-up spaces, but Bay had shouldered the cobwebs away as he dragged her up the steps. He was never going to induce her to enter the tunnel to the beach, however. Bayard Court had once been home to smugglers, its cellars full of contraband. That had appealed to Bay's grandfather, who was a big risk taker himself. He had bought the house for his child bride, then disappeared to make more money.

Charlotte thought Grace Bayard must have been lonely. She raised one son, then one grandson in this isolating splendor. The house could accommodate a dozen children easily with all its twisting and turning corridors. Charlotte could see why Bay had chosen a London life after he came back from the war—rippling waves and waving grasses had little conversation. It was far more amusing to surround himself with courtesans than watch his aging grandmother tend her rose garden, although she knew he had loved her deeply.

Charlotte washed and towel dried her hair, coiling the linen around her head. She was grateful for the brisk blaze in the fireplace. It would not surprise her one bit to see a snowflake out her window, even if it was June. She wondered if it were raining still in Little Hyssop, or if they had brought the bad weather with them. As the water was cooling, she rose from the tub and dried off in front of the fire. She shrugged into her robe again and combed the tangles in her hair with her fingers.

Her body was warm and relaxed now, its memory of Bay imprinted on every plane and fold. She hoped she could find the switch to turn off her feelings when the month was up. It would be the challenge of her life.

"Bah." Bay stood before the window in the morning room, watching the rain thunder down. Charlotte sat at a table, her hands flying with bobbins and thread. He had observed her, nearly growing dizzy at her dexterity. Her pattern was pinned to a little pillow. He would go cross-eyed trying to figure it all out. He'd never had the opportunity to think about lace, or many female occupations before, if it came to it. His grandmother's interests were limited to gardening and gossip. Tramping through the mud carrying a heavy kit to kill the enemy had been his priority for a decade. The wenching and gambling afterward were his peacetime reward.

"How did you come to make lace?" he asked, bending over her shoulder. He deliberately blew his breath on her neck.

Her clever hands paused, then resumed their effort. "There was a neighbor in Bexington. Deb and I would visit her when our parents were otherwise occupied." She looked up at him, her blue eyes somber. "They drank, you know. First as a lark, as everyone does. It was all merry fun—house parties and other entertainments. Trips to town while we stayed behind. They had scores of friends. My papa could charm the bark off a tree. My mama was the ultimate lady, always with admonishments to us girls about our deportment, but somewhere along the way her tea became spiked with brandy, and there was champagne at breakfast. Pictures started disappearing off the walls. Mr. Peachtree became a fixture in our life. Deb ran wild. And so, in the end, did I."

"Charlie." His voice was rough. "You were betrothed. Robert took advantage of you, the cur."

"Perhaps I took advantage of him." The bobbins clacked relentlessly. "I wanted to escape, you know. Deb had. I thought if I gave Robert my body, he'd marry me sooner. I was wrong."

He placed a hand on her shoulder and her hands finally stilled. No matter what she said, Charlie had been Robert's victim. It was a pity that a woman's purity was more important than a man's, but it was society's highest dictate. He was beginning to feel the injustice of it. Ten years ago, Charlie's black hair was not lit by silver. She had everything to hope for. She had acted in good faith, out of misplaced love, and look where it had gotten her—a solitary life working herself into premature old age. She deserved more. Much more.

Her shoulder shrugged beneath his palm. "It's old news anyway," she said lightly. "I'm well over it." The bobbins wove back and forth in her hand again at their furious pace.

Bay wondered how many years it had taken for her to

leave her guilt behind. The fact that she felt any was absurd—he had never regretted any sexual congress he'd ever undertaken, except perhaps with that Spanish camp follower who had raked his back like a frenzied panther. It had taken Frazier weeks of potions and ointments to get the swelling down, all the while mumbling that female fingernails would kill him sooner than a bayonet. Frazier never had much good to say about the fairer sex. But if what Charlie had said was true, he was now in the petticoat line courting one of the housemaids. It quite boggled the mind.

"You're right. No point in dwelling on the past. Now, how would you like to plan our future?"

The bobbins slipped through Charlie's hands. "Wh-what do you mean?"

"Our day. Obviously we can't go out in this muck. And I'll be damned if I sit here all day watching you make yards of lace, fascinating as it is."

"It's my livelihood, Bay." She snipped a string that had gone astray.

"It needn't be. Surely the stipend I've arranged for you will comfortably provide for you and all the charities you favor and all the stray cats you could ever choose to adopt. You can be a lady of leisure."

Her lower lip jutted out. He'd seen that stubborn look many times before and couldn't like it.

"It does not suit me to be idle."

"How do you know if you've never tried?"

"I'm not meant to be a wastrel like you."

Bay laid a hand over his heart. "A wastrel? I am mortally wounded."

"Sorry if the truth hurts. What do you do besides ensure your pleasure?"

She was looking at him as his old governess used to, all beetle-browed and pursed-lipped.

"I manage my investments! And I collect art."

Charlie snorted. "Art that is by its very nature suited to the advancement of your pleasure."

How did she know he'd gazed at his paintings a time or two, his cock firmly in hand? He felt his color mount. "You are forgetting I spent a decade serving His Majesty in conditions I can assure you were not at all pleasurable."

"Do not rest upon your laurels. What have you done lately?"

"I—I—" What *had* he done lately? Certainly he sent money to veterans' charities. He tithed although he rarely attended church. He was kind to small children and animals when they crossed his path. It didn't amount to much, not enough to brag on. "What do *you* think I should be doing?" he asked, turning the tables.

"What did you want to do when you were a boy? Besides be a smuggler."

He had wanted to be an artist. His cartoons at school had been dead-on until an upperclassman objected to his depiction as a bully and only proved it by beating a young Bay to a pulp behind the dining hall. After that Bay put away his brushes and charcoal and stuck to declining Latin verbs. Anne had posed for him when they married, but he had destroyed the pencil sketches years ago. Until Angelique insisted on the ceiling fresco, he'd spent years admiring art instead of creating it. A wicked thought crossed his mind.

"I'll show you. Stay right there."

He took the stairs two at a time to his room. In his dressing room was a battered trunk he'd had at boarding school. Within were some dried-up watercolors, several yellowing sketch pads, and some dull sticks of charcoal. He took out his knife and sharpened the points, nicking himself in the process. Not an auspicious beginning for the rejuvenation of his artistic career.

He made a quick detour into Charlie's room and was downstairs in minutes, the pads tucked under his arm. "Disrobe, my dear."

Charlotte looked up at him, startled. He flattered himself to think she looked interested in an après-breakfast interlude, as was he, but first things first.

"H-here in the morning room?" she faltered.

"The light, what there is of it through all this bloody rain, is excellent."

"Surely you know what I look like by now."

"Indeed I do, every lovely inch. Your body is exquisite. And I wish to immortalize it."

Charlotte seemed to notice the paper for the first time. "You want to *draw* me?" She made it sound as if he planned to roast her and feed her to wild animals.

"I cannot think of a more deserving subject. You give all my Italian ladies a run for their money."

"You're an artist." There was an unpleasant degree of doubt in her voice.

"You remember the ceiling on Jane Street. All the angels and clouds and whatnot."

"*You* painted it?"

Her openmouthed shock was comical. He didn't think it was because she thought he was the next Michelangelo, either. "The subject matter was not my first choice, and the execution a bit rusty, I admit. But we have all the time in the world. Twenty-nine days, anyhow. I'm prepared to practice until I get your likeness right. I'll even put wings on you, if you like."

"I'm certainly no angel." She abandoned her lace making and stood up. "Let me see your notebooks."

Bay shrugged. "I haven't touched them in years. Trust my grandmother to have squirreled everything away. She thought I had some promise." He handed her the oldest collection of drawings. She smiled when she saw the first, a pencil sketch of his old spaniel Homer. Perhaps he should consider getting a dog again. Dogs were diverting, and if he were to rattle around in this enormous house, he'd welcome some good company.

She picked through the pages carefully. "She was right. Why did you stop drawing?"

"I suppose I outgrew it. When I was in the army, every

now and again someone might ask me to sketch their horse or their portrait in a letter home, but there was little time for frivolity."

"Let me see the rest."

He gave her the second notebook. The pages were mostly empty, but it was clear that a large chunk had been torn away.

"What happened to the drawings?"

Bay swallowed the lump in his throat. He had hoped she wouldn't notice. "I'm afraid they were honeymoon drawings. Once the honeymoon and my marriage were over, it didn't seem right to keep them."

"Oh, Bay." She placed her hand on his sleeve. "I am sorry for you. How horrible it all must have been."

"It seemed so at the time. But now I begin to think I made a lucky escape." He looked down on her. Her hair was arranged too neatly on her head. Soon he would fix that.

"Lady Whitley might not have become unhinged if she had been Lady Bayard all these years."

"You are a warmhearted girl, Charlie." He bent to brush his lips against hers.

"Hardly a girl," she murmured. She responded to the kiss, deepening it artlessly. At this rate he might as well throw his drawing paper in the fire and bed her on the chaise. She aroused every bit of his lust, for all she was a short, shrewish thing.

He disengaged gently. "Later, my love. Let me stir up the fire. I shouldn't want you to catch a chill."

"You *are* serious about a life study. Why can't you draw me with my dress on?"

"Where's the fun in that? Besides, that dress is definitely not worthy of immortalization."

"I have nothing better. I need nothing better."

"'Tis a shame your sister stole all the clothes, but at least we have this." He took the ruby necklace out of his pocket and dangled it before her. She snatched it away.

"I hid it! How did you find it?"

"Sweetheart, nothing and no one escape me. I found you in Little Hurryup, didn't I?"

"You went through my things." There was a mulish set to her mouth. He wondered what else she had hidden from him.

"Just a pile of handkerchiefs and a stocking or two. I shall not trespass again, I promise. All your secrets are safe. Hold still." He began unhooking, unlacing, unpinning. Her cheeks flushed, her nipples puckered dark pink. Taking the rubies and diamonds from her slack hand, he fastened it around her throat. The center stone pointed its way to the pleasure of her. He stepped back. "Perfect."

"Hardly."

"Oh, don't fight with me now. You won't win." He rearranged the furniture, dragging the chaise to the bank of windows. He selected a comfortable chair for himself, then tore down a curtain.

"What on earth?"

"Some judicious draping."

"I'll sneeze my head off."

"Nonsense. I know for a fact all the curtains were taken down and cleaned this spring. I was here."

"Oh." She looked very uncertain without her own dowdy gray curtain covering her. "What do you want me to do?"

"Turn into pudding, all smooth and boneless. I'm going to have my hands all over you. Try not to flinch. Sit on the sofa, please."

He pushed her back deftly, his hands stroking satin. He was being wicked, he knew. He palmed a breast, flicked a nipple, watched the gooseflesh prickle across her limbs. He lifted a leg, stroked a foot, laid a bit of curtain across her hip.

"You can see everything! You haven't draped me at all," she complained.

"The next time. Now try to be quiet while I work." He pulled the charcoal from his pocket and set to sketch.

"That will not be difficult. I have nothing to say. You did lock the door, didn't you?"

"Um."

"Bay! Suppose one of the maids comes in to dust or something! Your staff is worldly-wise, but Kitty and Mary are practically children. Please lock the door this instant."

Bay's fingers were flying across the paper, the charcoal an extension of his vision. He was baffled as to how the creative process worked, only knew how restful it felt to be drawing again. Well, it would be restful of his subject didn't have such a scowl and wasn't making an effort to get up.

"Lie still. I'll lock up in a minute." He added a sweet curve of ankle, a toenail. The foot in question hit the floor. "All right, all right!"

He made a loud to-do at the door to assuage her, then was back to his seat. She was in position again, though there was a palpable tension to her body. "Relax."

"Much easier said than done. I feel like a bug under a magnifying glass."

"Oh, certainly you're not a bug. Perhaps a flower, though. A white rose."

"Well past its first bloom."

"In lush, full bloom, with plenty of days yet in the sun. Don't fish for compliments, Charlie. It doesn't become you."

"I was not fishing!" She made a cranky face at him.

Fine. He would show her just what she looked like. The drawing was quick and crude, but he was just warming up.

"My nose itches."

"It must be the spider from the curtain."

In a flash, she was off the chaise screaming, jumping up and down and wiping her face with both hands. He bit back his laughter as he appreciated her bouncing breasts and silky, swinging tendrils of hair as she shook her head free of imaginary insects.

"Don't just sit there! Get it off me!"

Tossing the pad to the floor, he enveloped her in his arms and kissed the tip of her nose. "There, all better."

Her eyes narrowed. "You fiend. There was no spider, was there?"

"I told you the curtains were cleaned," he said mildly. "I would never subject you to danger willingly. Now, shall we try again? You should have all the bugs out of your system." He grinned down at her.

"You really are impossible. How would you like it if you lay naked and I was staring at you?" She settled herself back down on the divan, clutching a pillow over her breasts. He wrestled it away from her and put her back into position.

"I would count myself lucky. You have an incredible amount of power over me, you know. I don't quite understand it myself."

She snorted and made one of her faces. "Here. You must stop looking so condescending." He picked up the drawing and showed it to her. "Lovely everywhere, except for your expression. It's as if you swallowed a lemon."

Charlie squinted at it. "Oh. Oh dear. I'm sorry I spoiled the picture. But I feel so—so very *awkward*."

"Pretend I'm not here." He sat back down in the chair and flipped to a clean page. "Imagine you're in the sultan's harem. The sun is blazing out of doors, but you're in a dark, cool zenana. You have every luxury at your fingertips, because you are the sultan's favorite, you know. He's given you those jewels to prove it."

Charlotte fingered the necklace. "Was I sold into slavery?"

"Oh, no. You are a princess of the first consequence. Your father the king received several goats for you, I believe." He ducked the pillow she flung at him. "It's true you have a terrible temper, but today you are happy. Ecstatic. Don't grimace so. I want to see a natural smile."

Charlie showed more teeth. "Why am I happy?"

"Because the sultan has granted your fondest wish. Yes, yes, that's the face I love. That little secret smile. Tell me, what did you ask for?"

"My freedom, of course. And the freedom of my sisters in the souk."

Bay shook his head. "Impossible. The sultan is very fond

of you, but he would never let you leave. Besides, where would you go?"

"I would capture a camel and ride off into the desert."

"Tsk. You would only be discovered by nomadic tribes-men. They would make your mangy camel smell like a flower garden by comparison. And their teeth?" Bay shuddered. "No, no. There's no escape, I'm afraid. Just lean back on the pillows and indulge your senses."

"I will not be some sultan's plaything."

"You're looking cross again. Remember, he prefers you to all the others. He sees to it personally that your dates are sweeter, your veils like gossamer, your jewels brighter. And the sultan is a fit, attractive man. A warrior."

"Brawn is all very well and good, but does he have a brain?"

"Of course. The poetry he's written praising your attrib-utes has all the other wives green with envy and Byron him-self suicidal, knowing he can never hope to measure up." Bay was enjoying this game, watching emotions flicker across Charlie's face. The cold rain outside drummed incessantly, but they were far away in a fictional sensual haven, warm, ex-otic, erotic. Charlie's lids dropped. Her hand was splayed across her mons veneris, but this act of modesty only made her more appealing. He could easily picture her as the sultan's fa-vored wife. He could easily picture her as *his* wife.

Lord, where were these thoughts coming from? He needed to dash out in the rain and wash some sense into himself. He concentrated on the drawing, adding a few improvements to the morning room setting. "There. Open your eyes."

Charlotte struggled up from her reclining position. She had begun to take Bay's words seriously, lulled by the heat of the fire and thoughts of endless opulence in some imaginary desert palace. When she had challenged his idleness earlier, she never expected to discover this hidden talent of his. She may not have appreciated Jane Street's insidious cupid ceiling, but Bay could definitely draw.

She examined the paper. A decadent concubine lay upon

the sofa, which had sprung up poles and tents of figured silk. A dish of sweetmeats lay upon a low ornate table, and she looked like she had indulged in several plates beforehand. Her body was ripe and bursting like a fig.

"I'm so fat!" she cried.

"Don't be ridiculous. You are perfect. Womanly."

Bay sounded offended, and Charlotte hurried, "I'm not criticizing your work. It's beautiful. Beyond beautiful. I just—I just didn't know I looked quite like this."

She didn't only look fat. She looked *sinful*. Her eyes were not quite open, and she had a cat-that-swallowed-a-canary smile. So smugly satisfied, as though she had just been plowed very thoroughly by the sultan, who was obviously a magnificent lover. Possibly the best lover in all of Dorset. Or rather, in the Ottoman Empire. "It—it's lovely. Very flattering."

Bay took it from her. "You don't like it."

"I do! It's marvelous, really. The detail is exceptional. It's just—this woman looks so *wicked*."

He raised a skeptical eyebrow. Charlotte blathered on. "I'm dull. Boring. Not a bit wicked. And surely my breasts are not quite so large."

Bay gazed down at the portrait and then at her chest. "Oh, I don't know. I think I was fairly accurate. But shall I try again?"

Charlotte knew she was blushing to the roots of her hair. She wished she could plead a headache to end this art experiment. Or hunger. But after the enormous breakfast she'd eaten, Bay would never believe it. She's risen from their bed, starving for a change. She soon would be even fatter than she was if she didn't push away from Mrs. Kelly's table.

"I want some drapery this time." She knew she sounded petulant, but couldn't help it. It was *not* natural to lie about naked in the middle of the day, a man smirking as he immortalized you.

"All right. Get yourself settled."

Charlotte padded barefoot to the sofa. She wrapped the curtain around her like a shroud and lay down.

"No and no and no." Bay tugged and pulled until her

breasts sprang free and half her belly was exposed. He propped her cheek up on a curled fist, tucked some pillows under her elbow, and fiddled with her hair. "Better. As you didn't care for the sultan story, you choose. Tell me who you are now."

"I'm Charlotte," she said, gritting her teeth. Her knuckles bit into her jaw.

"What, that dull, boring woman?"

"Don't be so vexing. I can't talk if my hand is to stay still." She stared out through the gray rain at the gray sky and the gray sea.

"Very well. You'll have to trust me on the next fantasy."

Out of the corner of her eye, she could see the fleet movement of Bay's hand as he propped the sketchbook on his knees.

"You are—you are a woman waiting for your man to return home from the sea. He's been gone a very long time. So long you're not certain he'll ever come back. There are some mornings when you awaken that you're too lonely to get out of bed."

Charlotte knew all too well what that felt like. The week before Bay turned up in church had been difficult.

"You've kept all his letters and read them when you're blue-deviled." She turned sharply to look at him, but Bay was absorbed in his work and didn't notice.

"Is he a sea captain?"

"A pirate, actually. Quite an infamous one."

"With a woman in every port, I imagine," Charlotte said dryly.

"Oh, no. he's quite devoted to you—a puritanical pirate, if you will. That ruby necklace—it was part of some buried treasure on a tropical island. He couldn't wait to sail home and give it to you."

"Where is he now? Drinking rum in the shade?"

"He's lost in a storm. The mast is broken and the sails torn asunder. He may never get back home."

"Oh, you are horrid! That's a terrible story!" She sat up and covered herself with the curtain. Bay joined her on the couch.

"Exactly. Perhaps you'll approve of this version of you."

This Charlotte no longer looked sated, but unbearably sad, searching out a window for her missing pirate's ship. There was much less of her on display, yet she was still embarrassingly lush.

"What do you think?"

"I think it's a sin you ever gave up your art. You are disgustingly talented."

"Why, thank you, I think. I'm not sure about the disgusting part." He ran smudged fingers through his hair. "Damn, but I need my hair trimmed. I wonder if I can get Frazier away from—is it Kitty or Mary?"

"Kitty. I could cut your hair." Although shearing off those incipient curls would be a shame.

"Aha! A Delilah in my house! Not a chance. I take my manhood seriously. I don't want to tempt you with sharp scissors."

"I would never hurt you—now," Charlotte said. She had learned her lesson the hard way. She would remember her poor mama's advice and count to ten before she lost her temper again.

"That's delightful to hear. Perhaps you should dress before luncheon. Here, let me help you."

He unwound the curtain from her body as if he were unwrapping a present, then looked toward the pile of clothes that Charlotte had neatly folded. "No," he said quietly. "Perhaps not quite yet."

He tipped her backward on the couch again, this time arranging her not for posterity but for pleasure. As was his wont, his mouth and fingers brought her to completion before he entered her with a patience she could only wonder at. She'd lost all control some time ago in the arms of her sultan-pirate. She now combined the desperate longing of the wistful wife with the sexual artistry of the houri, pressing herself against his hot, hard body, her legs locked around him, stretching and constricting her muscles until his seed spilled deep within her. There was nothing in the world but the two of them, their breaths ragged, their skin damp and fragrant. Charlotte blessed the cursed weather for keeping them indoors. She would never enjoy a rainstorm like this so well again.

"I know what you're thinking," Bay whispered.

"Silly." She ruffled his hair. "You cannot have the first idea."

"You are very happy you came back to Dorset."

"True, I am, but that was not foremost in my thoughts."

He pulled her even closer. "Tell me then."

Charlotte felt an irrepressible urge to laugh. "Don't be insulted, Bay, but I was thinking about the weather. I am a dull, boring Englishwoman, after all."

Chapter 21

It rained for over a week, days and days of damp, leaden skies and roiling ocean. Bay's hand became surer wielding his charcoal. He expanded to India ink and watercolors, sending to London for a fresh set of paints. He'd never be a master with oil paint, but he was determined to improve while he had such a radiant subject. Charlie had learned to relax, and their fantasies had expanded far beyond pirates and sultans. Each session ended with a satisfying foray in the art of love. Almost half of his time with Charlie was up, and he was missing her already.

But one morning a brilliant ray of sunshine pierced the cocoon of his bed hangings, and he pushed them aside. His bedroom was bathed in light so bright, Bay thought he'd be struck blind. In her sleep, Charlie turned from the glare with a little groan, exposing the length of her white back to him. He pulled the covers from her buttocks and was inspired to sketch her from this angle. She was as compelling as any odalisque he's seen in a museum, her jet hair ribboned across the pillows. He slipped from the bed to get his pad, then returned to draw her sweet curves.

She was beautifully fleshy. He pictured her buoyant in the sea like a mermaid, playful, teasing. Perhaps today they would have their picnic on the beach. There didn't seem to be a cloud in the sky.

If he counted correctly, there would be a full moon tonight. Even better to make love to her under its pearly glow, listening to the lap of each wave as they rode to their bliss together. He stiffened automatically and knew he couldn't wait for this afternoon or this evening to take her.

He cast the pad aside and returned to the bed. What position suited him this morning? He and Charlie had been creative exploring the house and each other. He decided to spoon against her, his cock bobbing against her lovely arse. He reached over her soft belly and buried his fingers in her nether curls, stroking her awake. She gasped and thrust back snugly as though she had been dreaming of just such a thing. He guided himself in with his other hand, interlocking the pieces of their sensual puzzle until her wet and heat surrounded him. Inflamed him. Completed him.

"Good morning," he whispered, and then made it so.

He kissed her shoulder, a poor substitute for her mouth, but he knew this position gave him easy access to her breasts and her clitoris. He cupped one full breast and circled the nipple, peaking it to perfection. She always came so alive in his hands. It was not so much his skill but her life force, long buried beneath gray dresses and linen caps. Charlie was meant for lust, even more so than her famous sister. Meant for love.

Now, where did that thought come from? His cock surged in possession. She was his absolutely. At least for now. Every smooth white surface, every curly dark hair. He smiled against her back. Even the silver ones. Her innocent blue eyes, her knowing mouth. Her small, work-worn hand, now pressing his as he rolled her clit between his fingers.

"Oh! I cannot bear much more. Please, Bay!"

"Please what?" He couldn't bear much more either, but couldn't bear the thought of stopping. Of withdrawing from her tight perfection. Never had any woman made him feel this way. Transcendent. Capable of nearly anything.

She uttered something, but it was more a growl than a word. Then her core shook him to his own, marking him. Making him lose control. His seed spilled inside her, as it so often did. He'd long since stopped worrying about consequences. He'd take care of her. Always, if he could.

When they were at last finished with each other for the time being, Charlotte squinted into the shafts of sunlight. "Can it possibly be? Is the sun really shining, or have you brought me to heaven?"

"Both," Bay chuckled. "As you have brought me." He kissed her mouth, tasting sleep and satisfaction. "And we should make the most of it before the clouds roll back in. Breakfast in bed first, though, I should think."

Charlotte shook her head. "I'm not at all hungry. Some tea perhaps. I think I could manage that."

Bay raised himself up on one elbow. Now that he could see her face, she did look pale. "Are you ill?"

"Oh, no. I'm fine. Mrs. Kelly's been spoiling me rotten with her cooking. I've overindulged, that's all."

"Charlie, I've told you a hundred times I love your body. And shown you, too. You'll not be so foolish to go without eating. I won't permit it."

"Really, you sound very bossy this morning, Major Sir Michael. I'm not one of your soldiers to be ordered about." She sat up quickly, and just as quickly dropped back into the pillows.

"Charlie! What is it?"

"A dizzy spell. It will pass."

"This is what come of going without food, you ninny," Bay thundered. "I'll go downstairs and bring up a tray myself, and you'll eat every bit."

He belted his robe and left the room. Charlotte scrambled out of bed and made it to the chamber pot just in time, then collapsed on the floor. "Blast." She felt too weak to pick up the pot and toss the evidence out the window, but she must before Bay returned. Staggering to the window, she heaved the mess onto the bushes below, gulping the fresh sea air. Sunlight sparkled on the water like a convocation of fireflies. She had to close her eyes.

There would be a baby. She had no doubt of it now. She was queasy at the thought of food, and not just at breakfast time. Her breasts were so swollen she struggled to lace them flat enough to fit into her gowns. Charlotte had spent years as Little Hyssop's helpful neighbor and was well aware of the symptoms of pregnancy. Bay might notice, too. As her sister Deborah once said, Bay was a noticing sort of fellow.

What would he do if he discovered her secret? She need only get through the next two weeks before she never had to see him again.

Which would tear her heart in two, for she loved him so.

She hadn't wanted to. For all his naughty, teasing barbs, he was the finest man she had ever met. He was thoughtful, and deeper than the rakish dilettante she first supposed him to be. Charlotte alternately cursed and thanked Deb for tricking her and running off with Arthur. How much easier her life would be if she'd never felt Bay's wicked kiss that morning on Jane Street.

She threw open all the bedroom windows to air out the room, then turned her attention to her own appearance. The pier glass on the wall told a grim tale. Charlotte splashed some water on her face, pinched her cheeks for color, and borrowed Bay's tooth powder to get the revolting taste out of her mouth. Before she put on her dressing gown, she turned to the side and examined her reflection. Her stomach, never flat to start with, seemed a little rounder. But perhaps she was just imagining things.

Hearing the rattle of the breakfast dishes, she sat down at the round table tucked into the corner of Bay's bedroom. She was not going to wind up in bed again, covered with jam and crumbs and clotted cream while Bay feasted.

"Here we go." The tray was heavy with covered dishes and condiments. Charlotte felt her stomach flip but willed the sensation away. Bay poured her a cup of tea and began to drop a sugar lump into it. He knew her sweet tooth, but today she wanted bitter, black, and harsh.

"No sugar this morning, please. I told you my stomach is

not quite settled from all the rich food last night." She pretended to take a sip. "Ah, isn't the day just beautiful?"

"The wind is brisk, a perfect day for a sail. I say, Charlie, our breakfast will blow away with all these windows open. Do you mind if I close some?"

"I'll do it." She leaped up to shut the window that overlooked the vomit-covered bushes, praying for more rain to wash away the stain. She was not at all sure her stomach was ready for a day spent in a boat, pitching and rolling about.

She came back to a plate loaded with ham, toast, and eggs and began to mince everything into miniscule pieces. "Do you really want to go out on the water? I haven't been on a boat since my parents died."

Bay looked stricken. Oh, she was evil, using such an excuse. If she did get ill, she could always chalk it up to plain seasickness.

"Not if you don't want to. I'm sorry, Charlie, I didn't think."

"Perhaps not today. But a walk along the beach would be lovely." She forked a tiny square of eggy toast into her mouth and chewed determinedly.

"That might put the roses back into your cheeks."

He was looking at her with speculative intensity. *He was a noticing sort of man.* She forced a smile. "If you didn't keep me up all hours of the night, you randy devil, I suppose I might look like less of a hag. A woman my age needs her beauty sleep, you know."

"I didn't hear any objection to my attentions, my dear. And I know from experience when you are not pleased, your wicked tongue can lacerate. All I can remember of last night's conversation was 'Please, please' and 'Oh, yes' and 'Oh, God.'" He slathered butter on a muffin and crunched away, looking pleased with himself.

"See? I must have been half-asleep if I confused you with the Lord."

Bay looked up at the coffered ceiling. "I'm waiting for lightning to strike."

"Not today." She took a deep breath of fresh air, reveling in the salty scent. "You must want to visit with your tenants now that it's not so grim."

Bay put his napkin down. His plate was clean, whereas she had barely touched a thing. "You know, I may just do that. You won't mind being alone for a few hours?"

"I welcome a respite from your wicked ways. I shall loll about like a lady of leisure."

"Good. You might do so in my grandmother's garden. Feel free to make any improvements. I expect to be inundated with bouquets when I return. I imagine it's a bit overgrown since I left."

"As my garden at home must be."

He got up and chucked her under her chin. "You sound wistful. Homesick. Have I bored you?"

"Don't be silly. You could never be boring." How she would miss him when she left. And how she would miss her cozy little cottage. The Widow Fallon could not stay in Little Hyssop and produce a child in seven months' time.

"We'll have a romantic picnic supper on the beach. Watch the sun set. How does that sound?"

Charlotte agreed that sounded like a perfect way to end the day. She watched as Bay moved efficiently around the room, his military bearing and training still evident. In a matter of minutes he was shaved and dressed for riding. Charlotte decided it was time to make a foray into cleanliness herself and rang for a bath in her own room. A good soak would help her think and plan more clearly.

She spent the rest of the day in blissful retreat within the high stone walls of Bay's grandmother's garden. The roses had rioted over their cages and trellises. Charlotte found an old pair of gloves and kept busy pruning and clipping, wondering if Bay had transplanted Mr. Trumbull's cuttings. She peered into the empty conservatory and saw four lonely jars on a wooden table. By next spring, the twigs they held would be ready to join the rest of the bushes. She stepped inside with her basket of flowers and shears, imagining the space as it must have been years ago, lush and redolent with plant life. The sun-heated bricks warmed the soles of her slippers. A solitary wicker chair listed in one corner, and she dragged it to the wall of glass so she could watch the ocean beyond the emerald lawn. It wouldn't do to become so mesmerized by the waves that she forgot to put the cut roses in water, but she couldn't resist watching the gulls wheeling over the white-caps. She supposed in a few hours she would be frolicking below like a fat water sprite, drunk on wine and Bay's attentions.

Sunlight slanted in through the glass roof, making her hot and drowsy. The girls could tend to the flowers. Charlotte rather thought she should have a nap to be ready for the night.

Bay had been busy since he returned home. His tenants had been glad to see him and had pressed all manner of tribute on him—tiny wild strawberries, a tin of biscuits, a thick wedge of Dorset Blue Vinny, a nut loaf fresh from the oven. Mrs. Kelly had augmented her baskets, and Bay sent Frazier and the maids to set up the picnic area sheltered by a crescent of rocks. He had half an idea to sleep under the stars with Charlie, so there was much to-ing and fro-ing with blankets and pillows and whatever else might come in handy. Once things were to Frazier's satisfaction, he was to walk the girls to the village and take the rest of the evening off. There was the pub—and Kitty's parlor, if Angus wished to brave the difficult Mrs. Toothaker.

He noted the hall was filled with roses, a sure sign that Charlie had been equally busy. He followed the scented trail to her bedroom. Her door was ajar, and he peeked in. A row of mismatched vases lined the mantel, filling the room with perfume. Charlie lay beneath the coverlet sound asleep under the cloud of fragrance. As tempting as it would be to crawl into bed with her, he reckoned he needed a bath to rid himself of the smell of sweat and horse which all the roses in the garden could not overcome.

He'd done a fair amount of thinking as he rode over his acreage, and had come to a surprising conclusion that had eluded him too long. His grandmother had been an excellent steward of the estate even at her advanced age, but there was no excuse now for him to fritter away any more time in London. His respectable army career was long over. If he hadn't conquered his demons by now with women and drink, he never would. It was past time he assume his responsibilities as magistrate in his own little corner of the world.

But he didn't want to live at Bayard Court alone.

In fact, he didn't want to live anywhere without Charlie.

He didn't know quite when her singular presence had become so necessary to him. She was a little shrew, and far past the age of biddability. He was unlikely to be Petrucchio to her Kate. In fact, it was she who had tamed him, bringing him back in touch with his boyhood home and ambition. His art was now paramount, and Charlie was his muse. Of course no one could ever set eyes on all the nudes he had done of her over the past weeks—it would be highly improper. Those drawings were for their pleasure alone. But they had warmed him up and unlocked the river of creativity which had been dammed up for a decade. He had plenty of money to indulge his hobby, and would have even more if he implemented improvements to his property. And surely she was not too old to bear him a child or two. His head was buzzing with possibilities. But foremost was securing Charlie permanently.

He would ask her to marry him this evening.

There truly could be no objection. Even if his grandmother had lived to give her opinion, Charlie was from a respectable gentry family, though they'd fallen on hard times. The fictitious Mrs. Fallon could easily disappear from Little Crackup and reappear here as a Dorset lamb come home. The Divine Deborah was now a dull married woman in distant Kent, too busy being Mrs. Bannister to bother them.

And Robert Chase would keep his mouth shut if he knew what was good for him. Bay was longing to smash him into the ground at the slightest provocation, the merest hint of a knowing smile or whispered word. He would never have the power to hurt Charlie again.

Bay whistled through his bath, pleased with his plans. The only fly in the ointment was Anne Whitley, who was not in France or any other foreign country, despite the fact that Bay had shoved her onto the packet himself weeks ago. He had learned from one of his tenant farmers today that she had been seen shopping in the village with her mother. The man obviously thought that Bay and Anne would be reunited now that the impediment of a living husband was overcome. Bay quickly disabused him of this notion. There would never be a second wedding ceremony for them in the village church no matter how many times Bay was kidnapped. He'd kill himself first.

Anne's parents' home was not very far from Bayard Court. She had been an object of his boyhood admiration for years before neighborliness turned to something more, and then something much less. He and Frazier had conferred on the matter this afternoon, and a few village lads were to be hired to repel unwanted guests, specifically Lady Whitley. If she caused him any further trouble, Bay was prepared to have her arrested. Charlie was apt to take matters in her own hands if she learned Anne was anywhere in the vicinity, and that was one encounter Bay could not permit.

He would marry Charlie by special license if he had to, just to make sure Anne got the point that they were finished for good. But tonight Bay had to make his own point with his future bride, a prospect that filled him with some trepidation. He'd always been much better on paper than in speech, writing poetic nonsense rather effortlessly. Charlie deserved some romantic blather, but Bay could see her stubborn chin and her incredulous look already. She was a practical woman who would no doubt disbelieve that he loved her.

He almost disbelieved it himself. He'd thought he was incapable of another grand passion until he'd been trapped indoors with Charlie through the rainiest summer in memory. Rather than chafing at the limitations, he had enjoyed every

moment spent in her company. Even when she was disagreeable about her placement across a sofa as he sketched her or
embarrassed by her expletives as he brought her to climax,
she was a delight to him. His grandmother would have loved
her, recognizing another woman who had the mettle to keep
him in line.

Bay had not wanted to fall in love, had indeed fought
against it, but Charlie with her honesty and incredible body
had vanquished him utterly. He'd realized it today as he met
with the humble farm families and felt jealous of their good
fortune. Their dwellings were not as grand as Bayard Court,
yet they had a shared purpose, children, affection. He would
soon have that, too. The next time he rode out to visit with
his tenants, she'd be with him, with bits of her lace and
bunches of flowers. There would be no more hiding.

He had nothing to pledge their troth with, however. When
his grandmother had passed on, he'd sent her jewels to his
bank in London for safekeeping. There was nothing left but
the ruby necklace, and he'd already convinced Charlie to keep
it. She could have whatever she wanted—more rubies and diamonds or sapphires to match her eyes. They would go to
Garrard's first thing when they returned to London, although
he was loath to break up their idyll to do so. However, something must be done about the house on Jane Street and his art
collection. Perhaps if he promised Charlie all his lovely Italian ladies could be housed in one empty room at Bayard
Court, she wouldn't protest too loudly. She put them all to
shame anyhow.

Feeling refreshed and confident, Bay stepped down the hall
to find Charlie. She was, he was surprised to see, still firmly
asleep, her hand curled under her chin like a child's—and
snoring just a bit. A delicate and ladylike snore, but a snore
nonetheless. He had tired her out every night for weeks, poor
thing, and would continue to do so for the rest of his life while
he still could. A wife like Charlie might keep him young forever.

He bent over her and blew a breath across her eyelids. Her

lashes fluttered, her eyebrows scrunched, but she continued to sleep. The sun would not dip behind the cliffs for hours yet, and he had every intention of seeing her naked in the foam before too long.

"Sweetheart, wake up."

She rolled away with a grunt.

"Charlie, it's still warm and beautiful outside. Let's enjoy the rest of the day together."

"Go away," she mumbled.

"Come on, sleepyhead." He tugged the covers from her. To his disappointment, she was in one of her prim white night-gowns, not an inch of her delicious skin visible save for her face and hands and toes. Her cheeks were sleep-rumpled and rosier than when he saw her last. The day in the garden and the nap had done her good. "I've got a supper fit for a princess down at the shore. Are you hungry?"

"Mmmf."

"I'll take that as a yes. I'll send Irene up to help you dress, unless you'd like me to play maid."

"As if you'd put clothes *on* me." She stretched like a lazy cat. "What time is it?"

"Just after six. I thought we could have a swim before we eat."

"I don't have a bathing costume."

Bay lifted an eyebrow but said nothing.

"Oh, but you're a fiend." She said the epithet mildly, as though she was very fond of fiends, him in particular.

"I'll meet you in the garden in thirty minutes. I want to see the wonders you worked."

"Mostly I just cut." She rubbed her hands together. Bay noticed a scratch and kissed it.

"It was worth the injury. The house smells wonderful, like it did when my grandmother was alive. She would have liked you."

"You can't know that."

"Oh, but I do. And even if she didn't, I like you enough for two or three people," he teased.

Charlie blushed. "Oh, go away and let me get dressed. I won't need Irene, either."

"As you wish." He kissed her hand again and then drew her to him, finding her lips warm and soft, a seductive promise of what was to come. "Don't be too long. I'm very anxious for our swimming lesson."

"Perhaps I'll teach you a trick or two," Charlie said, a naughty gleam in her blue eyes.

"Perhaps you will." Bay looked forward to it.

The sun hovered over the horizon, still a bold orange in the sky. Bay led her across the thick lawn to the beach below, holding her hand as they picked their way over a jumble of rocks. Charlotte was amazed to see a mock room set up in the curve of sheltering stones. There was an enormous moth-eaten carpet unrolled over the sand, two camp chairs, heaps of pillows placed here and there, blankets tented over poles to keep the wind away. A small freestanding stove was already alight, a tin bucket of coals next to it. Boxes and baskets of provisions anchored one corner of the rug and a flickering lantern was sunk into the sand. Bay—or someone—had thought of everything.

"This is lovely!"

"Not as lovely as you. Here, sit down." He indicated a flat rock.

Mystified, Charlotte did as she was told. Bay dropped to his knees and Charlotte's heart lurched. Surely he wasn't going to propose.

Assuredly, he wasn't. He began to unlace her boots with concentration.

"I can do that." She managed to sound quite normal after her scare. But it wasn't a scare, it was a dream. And a foolish one at that.

"Don't spoil my fun." She watched as his fingers slowly worked at the knot she'd so hastily tied so she could be ready for their picnic on time.

"Blast. You don't mind if I cut this, do you?"

"I certainly do! These are my only boots." Charlotte tried to tug her foot away, but Bay held on to her ankle.

"I'll buy you new ones. Or at the very least, new laces." He took a pocketknife out and sliced the stubborn knot. Once her foot was free, he tickled the bottom of her stocking.

She tapped him lightly on the head. "Oh, no. No tickling. You promised."

"So I did. I'll have to find another diversion." His hand smoothed up her calf to her garter. Sight unseen, he flicked it with a finger and it unraveled. He unrolled both stockings, paying far too much attention to her exposed flesh as he did so. Charlotte was reminded of raindrops slowly sliding down a window. Each fingertip left its trace.

He looked up at her, his smug grin revealing that he knew perfectly well the effect he was having on her. "There! Doesn't the sand feel good between your toes?"

Charlotte scrunched her feet into the sun-warmed sand. She hadn't gone barefoot on the beach since she was a child chasing after Deb. "It does. But don't ask me to remove your boots so you can say the same. I can't do it."

"Not a problem." He hopped up to rummage around in a basket and pulled out a bootjack. "Frazier is a nonpareil. I should give him a raise. Scoot over."

Charlotte made room for him on the rock. "You should. I think he's very smitten with Kitty. He should marry her."

"Marry!" Bay wrenched a boot off and tossed it to the rug. "He's that far gone, is he? What do you think of the girl?"

"She's very quiet. A hard worker. I think she'd be forever grateful to him."

Bay frowned. "Doesn't sound like a grand love affair to me."

"Girls like Kitty and Mary can't afford grand love affairs." *Or me, for that matter, she thought ruefully.* "She's very young. But I think she holds him in esteem. Her face turns as red as his hair when her sister teases her about him."

"So grizzled old Frazier is a Lothario, is he? I'll have to tell him I approve. There's plenty of work for them both in London."

Charlotte's breath caught. "So you won't be staying here at Bayard Court?"

Bay unwound his neckcloth. "I've urgent business to tend to once our month is up."

"Oh." Charlotte had envisioned Bay as lord of his manor, busy sketching and painting away. She supposed one of his urgent tasks was to secure another mistress for Jane Street. She was half tempted to tell him she could serve in that role as well as any other, but then she remembered the possibility of a baby. No man wanted a pregnant mistress. She didn't want Bay's pity or his charity. The sum he'd settled on her already was more than enough.

But soon she didn't have the wit to think or say anything. He was peeling back her gown, unlacing her corset, slipping her chemise down to suckle her breasts. The copper strands in his hair glinted in the waning sunlight, his long fingers were dark against the white of her skin. She closed her eyes to his beauty as he worked his lips around one nipple, then the other. Her limbs loosened as his warm, wet tongue unleashed its magic.

He stopped abruptly, his dark eyes unreadable. "W-what's wrong?" she asked.

"Not a thing. It occurs to me if we are to go swimming, we should do so now before the sun drops and the wind picks up. We'll continue this in the water."

Charlotte shivered in anticipation. They both shed their clothes and left them folded on the rock. Judging from Bay's jutting erection, he had every intention of taking her quickly. She couldn't imagine how this was to be accomplished, but was perfectly happy to be an experiment. Before she knew it, he had scooped her up and tossed her into the waves.

"It's freezing!" she shrieked. She had forgotten just how cold it was so early in the season.

"Only at first. Better to get it out of the way than to walk in inch by inch. You'll be warm in no time. Here, come to me." His arms encircled her as he brought her to his chest. His brave words were false—even *his* nipples were pebbled. He took down her hair, tossing the pins away.

"New pins, new boots," he said, warding off her criticism. "New everything. Kiss me, Charlie."

As if she could refuse. They were lost in each other for a spell, hands and mouths slippery and busy, the taste of salty skin and water sweet as wine. He finally lifted her up, fitting her to him. She slid onto his cock effortlessly, and then they drifted, caressed by the waves. The sensation of being anchored to him, yet absolutely free, was a novelty. Swirling at first in lazy circles, his hands clamped around her hips, she closed her eyes again and let bliss overtake her. His movements, so gentle yet inexorable, brought them both to climax.

She held fast, feeling his erratic pulse on her check. She would never forget this day.

"Mermaid," he whispered, toying with her hair. It floated around her like black satin ribbons. Charlotte wondered if the inestimable Frazier had packed a hairbrush, for she was likely to look more like Medusa than a mermaid when her hair dried.

She smiled up at him. "Shall I sing a song and bewitch you?"

"Unnecessary. You already have. I've crashed up against the rocks, shattered. Splintered. There's no hope. Take me to your kingdom at the bottom of the sea."

"Bah." Charlotte pushed away from him, treading water. "What good are you to me if you drown?"

"I? Drown?" Bay thrashed through the sea, his arms windmilling.

Charlotte was not about to be left behind. She kicked off and made a creditable attempt to catch up, ducking under the swells. Bay allowed her to reach him, and together, hand in hand, they floated on their backs, watching the sky turn turquoise and lavender, the clouds tinged silver-pink.

"It's beautiful here," Charlotte murmured.

"Mermaids and shipwrecked sailors cannot live on beauty alone. I'm starved."

"I wonder what mermaids eat. Certainly not fish. That doesn't seem right."

"Yes, rather like a cannibal eating his own feet. Speaking

of which—" He flipped over, grabbed her waist, and stood her upright. To her surprise, she felt sand and rocks

"This is so shallow!"

"A perfect spot to teach children to swim. You can go out quite a ways without fear. I practically lived at this cove when I was a boy. Camped out nearly every summer night with my friend Jamie. We slept rough, hoping to be carried off on a smugglers' adventure. It was," he said, a rueful expression on his face, "excellent training for the army. No tents or pillows or rugs for me then."

"Thank goodness you weren't kidnapped! Your grand-mother would have been frantic!"

Bay laughed. "You don't know the half of it. She set up a camp bed at the end of the tunnel just in case. I never found out until the butler told me years later. Either she or he or an-other poor servant kept vigil in the cave to watch over us."

"Oh, she must have loved you so."

"Yes. Spoiled me rotten, as you can see. Come on, I'll show you her hiding place."

They splashed to the shore. Once out of the water, Char-lotte shook with cold. Bay opened a battered trunk and pulled out a thick towel and led her to stand before the little stove. He scrubbed her down thoroughly, taking more time than was absolutely necessary with every nook and cranny. Char-lotte submitted, wondering how she would be able to live without his touch. Then he wrapped her in a dark blue cash-mere robe that felt like a warm cloud against her skin.

Charlotte's hand traced the soft folds. "Goodness! What else is in that trunk?"

Bay bent over, still perfectly naked. "A robe for me. I sup-pose you'll want this." He tossed her a tortoiseshell comb. "Some slippers for both of us. Odds and ends. I hoped you'd agree to spend the night with me under the stars."

Charlotte gasped when she saw what he pulled out of the trunk next.

"In case of smugglers. Or Jamie. No one is welcome to in-trude on us this evening."

She stared at the pistol, her stomach twisting nervously. The last time she had seen such a weapon was still too fresh in her mind.

"I thought you said the smugglers have gone straight hereabouts."

"So they have. Frazier, God bless him, is a worrywart. Plans for every eventuality. I hope Kitty settles him down. It's a wonder he didn't pack a rapier." Bay put the gun back and pulled a banyan over his head, a colorful striped affair that made him look reckless and rakish. "Let me comb out your hair, and then we'll go a-caving."

Charlotte sat down obediently on a folding camp chair. There was no fear of the pocketknife this time. Bay was efficient in unknotting knots and untangling tangles. She suspected he had lots of practice combing women's hair and felt a flare of jealousy. Soon some other lucky dark-haired blue-eyed girl would be his companion, unless he changed his ways and made her his wife. There were probably a slew of seventeen-year-old brunettes lined up at Almack's just waiting for him to get back. She pushed her disagreeable thoughts away and concentrated on the moment. The sky was turning smoky purple, and orange and pink clouds hung low on the horizon. The ocean glittered with the last of the light, the regular rush of the waves as soothing as the strokes through her hair. Her body felt heavy with relaxation, but she remembered exploration and supper were still ahead.

Apparently satisfied with his results, Bay tossed the comb onto the old carpet. Charlotte could see it once had been a thing of true beauty. Scarlet poppies and palm fronds formed an elaborate border around a midnight blue field covered with golden birds. There was a substantial rip in the center, with loose threads sticking up everywhere.

"This rug—I've never seen anything like it."

"My grandfather sent it back from India. It was in my grandmother's bedchamber for years until she kept tripping on the worn spots. I made her retire it but she didn't have the heart to throw it away. It does lend some class to our camp-out."

"I haven't agreed to spend the night out here with you, you know. I've never done such a thing."

Bay nuzzled her neck. "I'll keep the fire going. There is a chamber pot nearby, if that's what you're worrying about."

Charlotte felt heat course through her. How very cavalier he was about her bodily functions. There were still some things she was too shy to speak of or do anywhere in his vicinity.

"I've seen it all, you know. There weren't privies in Portugal," he reminded her, as if sensing her objection.

"Well, we are in England, and my mama would *die* if she weren't dead already that we are even having this conversation." Charlotte fastened the robe more securely around her waist. Her mama would certainly not approve of her current attire or recent activities either. "Speaking of which, let's change the subject. Take me to your cave."

Bay picked up the lantern and offered her an arm. "You know the hidden passage in the parlor. Turn left and you're up the stairs. Turn right and there's another set of stairs that leads to the cellars and an underground tunnel, very convenient when you're unloading contraband from the beach. Right through here—"

He pointed to a narrow seam between two boulders.

"Goodness! Your contraband couldn't be very wide, could it?"

"Ye of little faith."

Bay placed his hand in an indentation and the rock, which wasn't really a rock at all, pushed open with a screech of hinges. The rock had been sliced and affixed to a wooden panel. They were now standing in a small stone-lined chamber. There was indeed a fraying canvas cot, an abandoned rusty lantern, and a gleaming white chamber pot with neatly folded linen rags beside it.

"See? Nothing to worry about. Frazier is incomparable."

Charlotte laughed. "What about the bats and spiders?"

"Gone. They wouldn't dare linger. Now, my mermaid, what say you? Are you ready to spend a night counting stars with me?"

To do the job properly would take an infinite number of nights, but Charlotte knew she had just one.

"I am."

Chapter 22

Bay watched her as she unselfconsciously licked apple tart crumbs from her fingers in the shimmering glow of the lantern. Her glorious hair corkscrewed down her shoulders. The robe had come undone, and each time she had leaned forward to pick another treat from the basket in the center of the carpet, Bay caught a glimpse of plump white breast. The moon had risen, casting a silver stripe on the sea. The sky was spattered with stars and a sultry breeze billowed the makeshift tent. If this wasn't the perfect time to propose, there would never be one.

He'd moderated his wine intake, wanting to be clear-headed when he made the most decisive declaration of his life. Charlie had no such scruples. She was a bit tipsy, delightfully so. Gone was the cap-wearing solemn spinster of old. In her place was a saucy temptress, whose every movement aroused his unbridled lust.

But he felt more than that. Much more. And hoped to find the words to tell her.

He didn't think she'd believe him, not after their distinctly rocky beginning and tempestuous middle.

It's not as if he'd had much practice proposing either, not like his old army friend and fellow baronet Sir Harry Chalmers. Harry had been engaged four or five times. He'd been spectacularly unlucky in love, but the man at least had an initial way with women and words. Harry seemed to propose every time he popped out of bed. A little advice might prove useful right about now.

Of course, Bay had proposed once himself, thirteen long years ago. He couldn't quite recall what he'd said to Anne to convince her to marry him, but in any event wouldn't want to repeat *that* experience. He'd been a callow youth with years' worth of worshipping her from afar, and she'd been a lonely young widow itching to get out of her parents' house again. Anyone might have done for her back then, he thought sourly, except somehow she had become as fixated on him now as he was once with her. The fact that Anne had not stayed abroad was worrisome, but he shook his head free of those details. Now was not the time to be ruing the past and recent present. Now was the time to sweep Charlie off her feet with romance and enchantment.

Charlie was already off her feet, lounging in innocent seduction on a stack of cushions. Her eyes were half closed, her lashes casting long shadows on her cheeks in the flickering light. Her alabaster skin glowed, and her lips were stained from the berries and the fine port that Frazier had packed. Bay wanted to kiss those lips, taste the berries and the wine and the tart and Charlie, so he did. She snuggled against him with a sigh.

"This has been perfect."

He caressed her hand, bringing her knuckles to his lips. "The best is yet to come."

"What? Have you arranged for some entertainment? Dancing girls from your harem, perhaps? This all does remind me of an Oriental dream—the tent, the carpet, dining on pillows."

"I wouldn't insult you with any other women, Charlie. You are the only one I need."

He felt her stiffen beneath him. Just pretty, insincere words, she'd be thinking. It was now or never.

"Charlie, there's something I want to talk to you about." He ran a hand through his too-long hair. By God, he was nervous. "I'm not sure where to start."

She rolled back on the rug, tucking her legs beneath the dark robe. Her face was covered now with a jet curtain of hair. Just when he wished most to see her, she was drenched in shadow.

"Charlie, look at me. I promise it's not so terrible. You might even like it."

"Don't spoil it, Bay." Her voice was brittle. "Just let me have tonight. We can discuss me leaving tomorrow."

"Leaving! What the devil are you talking about?"

"This—this holiday or whatever you wish to call it. Our time together is almost up. But I can go home sooner. Lord knows I have plenty of work ahead of me. Why, my garden is probably a jungle! Those village boys won't know—"

He kissed her again to shut her up. She fought every parry and thrust. Just when he thought he had softened her, she broke away with surprising strength. Tears glistened like diamonds on her cheeks.

"Charlie, sweetheart, don't cry. Please don't cry."

He should have written the words beforehand and read them. Always was handy with the ladies in a letter, each missive full of flights of fancy and romantic nonsense. But he'd never meant much by them—they were just a way to smooth his way into their beds. Tonight was different, and it was clear Charlie had no idea what was on his mind.

"Marry me," he blurted.

"What?"

She looked at him with her mouth flapping open, rather like a dazed fish who has realized life as he knew it was over.

"Will you do me the honor of becoming my wife, Charlotte Fallon?" He smiled. There. That was much better.

"*What?*"

"Good lord, Charlie, you're making this difficult. You haven't got water in your ears, have you?"

"Water?"

Well, that was an improvement over "what," though they sounded rather alike. He took her hands in his. "Charlie, I am proposing marriage to you. It's not something I do every day, mind you, and no doubt I've gone about it the wrong way. But you wouldn't like it if I'd had years of practice and a past littered with wives and fiancées, would you? One is bad enough. And now," he said, catching sight of her black eyebrows knitting together, "I've reminded you of Anne, which I'd hoped never to do. Blast."

Charlie seemed less fishlike, but her hands were cold as ice. "Let's get closer to the little stove, shall we? You're chilled." He dragged her across the carpet and settled her in front of the camp stove. What he wouldn't have given for one of these on the Peninsula. There were times he thought he'd freeze to death, but here he was, still alive, making a mess of the most important night of his life.

"You want to marry me."

She sounded as if she were in some sort of trance, but at least she was talking sense. "Yes," he said firmly. "Yes, I do."

"W-why?"

"Because." She'd have to settle for that. He hadn't quite worked it through his own mind. Oh, he could go on about her delicious sinful body and her wicked sharp tongue, but taken together they didn't add up. And he wasn't about to babble on that he loved her. That she bespelled him. She'd think him an imbecile.

"Because why?"

Lord, she was stubborn. Here he'd offered her a life of comparative luxury and she was bedeviling him with questions. He cleared his throat and fixed his eye on the smiling face of the Man in the Moon. That fellow didn't have to explain, just be and beam down. "We suit, you and I. You must agree we've gotten on great guns the weeks we've been here. I know you like Bayard Court, and it needs a chatelaine. I've decided to retire to the country, and you can keep me company."

"That's *it*?"

"Isn't it enough? I can settle more money upon you if you like, although I won't be a cheese-paring ogre. You'll have whatever you need, and then some. And you love to garden.

We can set up the conservatory again with all the plants in the kingdom."

"I'm not going to marry you because of *plants*," she said, her voice rising. "Or housekeeping. Or money, you stupid man! Do you—do you *love* me?" She was practically screaming now.

Bay reminded himself her tongue was a part of her body that he did in fact love. What harm would it do to tell her? She wasn't Anne, about to control and subjugate him for his weakness. Charlie was a completely different soul. But he would keep the upper hand at all costs.

"Whatever love is. I hold you in the deepest affection. You are not at all the woman I first thought you to be."

Bay suddenly found himself sprawled on his arse in the sand. Charlie was above him, shaking a little fist very close to his nose. He knew she was perfectly capable of using it, so he scrambled away. "What have I said? Of course I love you, you little shrew! Why else would I ask you to marry me? You haven't any money, and you're old! Mature, I mean, past your first season," he said hastily, crawling sideways like a crab.

"You utter fiend! How dare you!" Her hair lifted wildly in the breeze, making Bay think of a frenzy of black snakes. Snakes that seemed ready to inject their venom in him with glee.

"Well, let's be honest. You're on the shelf," he tried to reason. "We both have unfortunate pasts, but together we can make a good life." He ducked too late as she flung sand at his face. "There's no need of that." He spat out a mouthful of grit, grateful her aim wasn't higher. His sight was important to him, and right now Charlie was a vision as the High Priestess of Passion. The belt of her robe trailed in the sand, and she seemed unaware that her body was fully exposed to him in the moonlight. Her nipples were puckered with anger and cold, making him very interested in soothing them. "Sweetheart," he attempted, "perhaps my choice of words was clumsy, but—"

"Clumsy! What an understatement! Where is the man who wrote 'I dream of you, despairing when the sun wakes me. For in the darkness you are near, your lips a crimson butterfly dancing from one end of me to another, delighting in my nectar'?"

The words were absurd, yet somehow familiar. "What rubbish! What the hell are you talking about?"

"Oh!" She twirled around in pique, swirling up a storm of sand. "I should have known better, truly I should. You're right—I *am* 'mature,' old enough to know better. If you think I want some marriage of convenience—*your* convenience—you have another think coming!"

"You silly woman! I just told you I loved you! What more do you want? Fealty? A blood oath? Find me a knife in the basket and it's done." He instantly regretted his words. An armed Charlie was not someone to be taken lightly. She could slice out his liver and serve it to him for a midnight snack without a qualm.

So much for sleeping peacefully under the stars. Charlie was stomping off in the direction of the tunnel, tripping on her loose robe. He heard her snort of disgust and watched her tie herself up tight again. Just as well she went into the cool cave to cool down. He'd have to think up something brilliant when she came out to pacify her.

Obviously the elaborate romantic setting had not been enough, and perhaps his statements had been less than heroic. One never reminded a woman of her age if one could help it. But how could Charlie not know how he felt about her? One didn't do all they did together when one felt indifferent. Dispassionate. He pushed himself off the damp sand, brushing off his backside. He'd like to swat Charlie's bum for tossing him down, the little baggage. Her temper was uncertain at the best of times. Why on earth did he want to saddle himself with her for eternity?

Bay knew the answer. It was lodged like a chubby little fist in his heart. Charlie's fist. He truly was putty in her hands, at her mercy, and that was no way to spend the rest of his years. But he could no more dislodge her fist than rip out his heart. They were one.

He settled himself back on the old rug, supine and, yes, vulnerable, wondering what was taking her so long. She'd left the lantern behind, but he hadn't heard her curse the darkness. He'd give her time. Privacy. He tucked a pillow under his head and gazed at the cloudless velvet sky. Thousands of stars twinkled above, dimmed a bit by the brightness of the full moon. From his position, he could see the stone door ajar. Surely she wouldn't bumble in the dark through the passage up to the house—he'd only had Frazier clear the little room free of dust and cobwebs for the makeshift necessary room, and she would get unpleasant surprises if she were so foolish. In a minute or two he'd pick up the lantern, casually stroll up to the cave, and inquire as to her health. After all, she had drunk a fair amount of three kinds of wine. He'd like to think her choler was caused by overindulgence, but he knew he'd bungled his offer of marriage.

The waves lapped in hypnotizing rhythm yards away, though Bay was alert to the nuances of the night. An owl flew slow and low over the beach in search of prey, its wingspan startling. There were encouraging hoots in the distance as the creature inspected Bay in a lazy loop.

Bay tossed a crust onto the sand. "Go away. We need the rest for breakfast." The owl couldn't be bothered, but two sandpipers darted from the dunes and fought an energetic battle over the crumbs. Bay sat up to watch the racket, then pulled a watch from the pocket of his robe, a habit from the army he'd never broken. He needed to know what time it was, although he had nothing in particular to do but woo the woman he wanted to marry. A shadow intervened. Smiling his most charming smile, he turned.

"Frazier told me where to find you."

Bay kept his smile in place, but his throat constricted. Lady Anne Whitley, cloaked from head to toe in widows' black, edged up to the carpet, the silver barrel of her gun glinting. Bay took a deep breath, confirming his fears. The weapon had been fired recently, but he'd heard nothing out here except the birds, the waves, and the wind.

"He didn't want to tell me. Loyal to a fault, he is."

"I hope you haven't done something foolish, Anne." He kept his voice steady, but as loud as he dared, praying that Charlie would stay put.

She shrugged, the hood of her cloak falling back. "He'll live, if those stupid girls have their way. It was just a scratch."

Frazier would have been on the road to the village, walking the Toothaker sisters home. Perhaps between the two of them they had helped him to safety and then had the presence of mind to send someone after Anne before she shot the second man of her evening. If something happened to Frazier—

Or to Charlie—

Bay would kill Anne himself.

He couldn't think twice about it. The woman he had loved once had disappeared.

He watched the gun waver. She was as nervous as he was.

"Where is she?" Vitriol dripped from each word.

"Where is who?" he bluffed.

"Your whore, Bay. The little slut you ran off to Dorset with. That Charlotte." She spat out the name as though its taste was foul. "You tricked me in London, Bay, sent me away. But I came back."

He would never be free of her. Charlie would never be safe from her. Did Anne's parents know the lengths to which she'd gone? Could they keep her confined before she did something desperate? Deadly? They had an aversion to scandal, had done their best to hush up Anne's bigamy, turned a blind eye when Anne had complained of Whitley's treatment of her. She'd had no one to turn to for years, except him, stolen moments in a broken life.

"We had a disagreement. She's gone off somewhere. Surely you heard?"

"I'm sorry to have missed that." She looked around at the little seraglio he'd created. "Very romantic. Wasted on a tart like her. You never learn, do you? Silly letters, extravagant gestures."

The letters! That's where the whole butterfly-nectar tripe

came from, all those letters he wrote to Deb to keep her sweet. Charlie must have read more than the one about the necklace. He pictured her in a starched white cap, a frown on her face, poring over the little bundle that had been tied with a blue ribbon. At least she'd have them if he died, words that weren't even written to her but had meant something just the same.

Bay flopped back on the carpet, inching toward the trunk that held his pistol. They had used it as a dinner table, the bottle of port and two glasses still resting on the surface.

"Do you mean to shoot me, Anne? I say, I'd much rather share the rest of this wine with you. If I'm about to meet my Maker, or more likely go to the devil, at least the pain of it will be dulled."

"What good are you to me dead?"

"None, I should think. Do you still wish to go forward with your procreation plan? If so, holding a gun on a man is somewhat suppressive of any ardor he might manage. I confess despite the romantic setting, I'm limp as a willow branch at the moment. Not my best night, I'm afraid. What with the little whore lacerating me with her fishwife's tongue and you threatening me with that pistol, my willy's awfully weak."

"You won't fool me again, Bay. Don't bother. Lie back." Cocking the pistol, she smirked in triumph at him.

"Oh, Anne." He failed to keep the despair out of his voice.

He could try to do as she wished, hoping she'd be so distracted Charlie would somehow emerge from the cave and run up to the house for help, if there was any to be found. He'd kept them short-staffed on purpose, protecting Charlie's reputation. There was Mrs Kelly. Irene. A scrawny kitchen boy if he remembered correctly. Frazier was wounded, and with luck being tended to in the village. Two stable lads, callow youths with spots, probably sound asleep. His old coachman. Reinforcements were coming tomorrow, too late to save him from this calumny tonight. "You'll deny me that glass of wine?"

He could topple the bottle, make a pretense of getting another inside the trunk, seize the weapon.

And then shoot her. Perhaps not to kill after all, but to send her own weapon flying into the sand. It was a good plan, the best he could come up with on short notice.

"You've had enough. Undo your breeches, Bay. Now."

Charlotte stood in the oblong of moonlight watching, her heart in her throat.

She had done her business earlier, quite furious after the worst proposal in the history of mankind. Stewing a bit in the dark, she contemplated turning back into the hidden passage to reach the house, but it was pitch-black and the route was unfamiliar. She hadn't the luxury of playing hide-and-seek and pirates in the tunnel to know where she was. Bay had said he and the servants had brought everything down to the beach over the lawn, so it would be most unwise of her to brave through decades of cobwebs to reach an equally dark cellar.

So she had sat on the swept floor to think, wrapping the cashmere robe around her. Bay didn't know about the baby, yet he still had asked her to marry him. That was a good thing, she reckoned. There was no talk of duty or guilt. She might be old, but not too old to have his child. He'd be surprised when she told him, but she wouldn't tell him yet. Not tonight. Tonight was supposed to be hers. She'd go out there and make him re-propose, this time with a few high-flown phrases, something a woman could cherish on a cold night when the silver in her hair outnumbered the ebony and her bright blue eyes were cloudy and gray. Perhaps she should ask him to write it in one of his infamous letters—his pen was much prettier than his tongue. Although his tongue had its uses. She had shivered with remembrance.

And then she had risen, gone to the secret door, and seen a menacing black wraith standing over Bay with a moonlit silver gun. Heard Bay's bravado. Saw as he cleverly lounged toward the trunk and the disappointing result. Heard the ominous click of the pistol. The voices were subdued now, carried off by the wind.

There had been an old lantern in the corner. Silently Charlotte backed back along the wall, extending her bare foot. There. She touched cold metal. As she bent to pick it up, the handle came off in her hand and the lantern clattered to the floor, splintering, its echo sounding like cannon fire. Please God that Anne didn't hear it and come to investigate. Charlotte didn't doubt that Lady Whitley would shoot her dead without thought. But maybe the sound of the ocean and the gulls and Anne's black beating heart obscured the noise.

Charlotte picked up a curved scrap. Could she use the lantern shards like a knife? She really didn't think she had the strength to plunge a bit of broken metal into another human, no matter how worthy there were of dismemberment. But she had to do *something*.

She wouldn't have time to delve into the trunk and get the gun, not that she would know what to do with it to begin with. She'd probably shoot Bay by accident and then she'd want to shoot herself. She had the belt to her robe—a garrote? The thought of strangling Anne was remarkably appealing, but Charlotte knew she'd lose her will or her footing, and the gun might go off. There was nothing for it. She returned for the chamber pot, tipping the contents into the bladed beach grass, using one of the linen rags to dry it out as best she could with trembling hands. Bay was prone now, the striped robe pulled up from his legs, the soles of his bare feet curiously innocent. Anne appeared to be sitting on him, her back straight, the gun not visible but undoubtedly trained on him. Anne was *sick*. Deranged and obsessed. And if anyone deserved to be crowned with a chamber pot, it was Anne Whitley.

Charlotte waited. There was murmuring, awkward shifting, then regular movement. She froze, realizing the full extent of what she was watching. But she needed to find her courage, find the right time to interrupt this hellish display when Anne would be too preoccupied to expect anything other than fulfillment of her obscene fantasy.

Charlotte clutched the porcelain bowl with both hands, gliding across the evening-damp sand. The Man in the Moon winked and grinned down at her. If she succeeded, the story would be too good to ever tell, a joke she would share with the full moon and her husband. If she failed, the clouds would blot out all the light in her life.

She was so near. As was Anne, moaning, her dark hair blowing in the breeze. Charlotte was now close enough to see Bay's pale face, his eyes shut, his mouth a grim straight line. Good. If he had been enjoying himself, she might have had to brain him as well. Raising her arms, she dropped the pot down with all her might. Anne swayed for a harrowing moment, then toppled to her side, a deafening roar following.

The gun had discharged harmlessly into the sand. Charlotte picked it up and flung it underhanded into the encroaching waves.

"Nice to see you. Excellent aim. On both counts." Despite his blinding smile, Bay's rough voice betrayed his anxiety. He was scrambling up, pulling the striped banyan down over a rather flaccid cock.

"I'll marry you," Charlotte said, her eyes suddenly moist. "But I want a proper proposal. The last one was rubbish."

"I'll do better tomorrow." He pulled a long length of rope from the trunk and efficiently trussed up Anne's arms. Squelching the desire to roll her into the sea, he tied her securely to one of the tent poles. Someone else would have to deal with her. He was done.

And a good thing too. For his brave Charlie had fainted, pitching backward onto the rug with an alarming thud, just like the first day he met her. This time he knew she wasn't faking. He scooped her up and carried her back over the rocks and grass, heedless of his bare feet, shouldering his way into the closest room, which was the empty conservatory. The moon and stars shone through the glass ceiling, bathing the room in ghostly light. He laid her out on one of the wooden worktables and gently patted her cheeks.

"Wake up, Sleeping Beauty. Your prince is here, and I will never, ever let you go."

Chapter 23

Charlotte woke to the morning rhythms of Bayard Court, the rattle of a coal bucket, whispers and laughter on the stairs. The other side of the mattress showed no signs of disturbance. Bay had not ever come to the bed he'd tucked her into around midnight. He'd left her with a warm brick, a tot of brandy, and a kiss, off to the village to check on Frazier and see that Anne Whitley got more than a lump on her head. Gingerly, Charlotte touched her own goose egg. Her mama would have been disappointed that, once again, she'd failed to faint with grace.

She tried to rise, but quickly sank back onto the feather pillows. Dizzy and nauseous, and not just because of last night's commotion. She felt weak as a kitten, although she was proud that she found the necessary strength last night to do the dirty work of dispatching Anne Whitley.

Lord, but her head hurt, but probably Anne's was worse. Charlotte rolled carefully to reach the bellpull, then shut her eyes to ward away the dancing spots. She'd drunk altogether too much wine last night. Feeling her stomach lurch, she willed herself to lie still and wait.

It didn't take Irene long to tap on the door and enter. Charlotte was relieved to see the maid brought two pitchers of water, one for drinking and one for washing up. Irene hadn't said a word, but knew that Charlotte had been too sick first thing in the morning to swallow anything but Adam's ale.

"Good morning, Miss Fallon! Such excitement last night! You're a proper heroine, you are." The girl poured Charlotte a tall glass of water and brought it to her bedside. "My, but you're looking peaky. A bit green. Do you want a basin?"

"Not yet. Did you bring any crackers?"

Irene reached into her apron pocket and pulled out a linen napkin. "Here you are. Sir Michael says you're not to worry yourself about getting up. I'm to bring breakfast to you when you want it."

Charlotte took a deep swallow. "Where is he?"

"He's downstairs with Mr. and Mrs. Buckland. Lady Whitley's parents, you know."

Charlotte shuddered. "And where is *she*?"

"Dr. Dixfield's house in the village. You're not to worry about her either. He's got her under lock and key. Drugged her, too," Irene said, her eyes lighting with satisfaction. "After what she did to poor Angus, he's not letting her out of his sight."

"Mr. Frazier will be all right, won't he?"

"Oh, aye. He's back home already, and Kitty is spinning in circles waiting on him hand and foot. The doctor said it was just a flesh wound. On his arm. Angus said it would take more than one crazy woman to kill him when the Frogs couldn't. Everything will be all right, Miss Fallon, you'll see."

"I hope so." She bit into a soda cracker and took another sip of water. Charlotte didn't think Bay would want any of last night to become public knowledge. But the Toothaker sisters were witnesses to Anne's desperation—how quiet could they keep? "Sir Michael hasn't slept at all, has he?"

Irene shook her head. "I don't believe so. He was busy with you, then getting the stable lads to watch over Lady Whitley while he went into the village to see about Angus and get word to the Bucklands. And then he came back and took that woman away. The boys are to take turns guarding the doctor's house today. They said Lady Whitley screamed like a banshee all night long. Scared them silly, she did, cursing and whatnot. They'll

have something to talk about in the pub for years to come."
Irene opened the drapes and threw open the casement window.
A fresh sea breeze wafted in. It looked to be another beauti-
ful summer day.

And now the stable boys were involved, and hardly the
strapping guards as would be needed to protect the world
from Anne Whitley. Poor Bay. What a scandal it would be.
Even if no one ever found out exactly how Anne spent her
last unfettered minutes, the gossip would be relentless. Charlotte knew only too well its power. How could she and Bay
marry and find peace at Bayard Court when they lived only a
few miles from the Bucklands?

Charlotte made a second unwise attempt to get out of bed
and was grateful when Irene caught her before she tumbled
to the floor.

"Now, you stay put. Let me wash you up and do your hair,
Miss Fallon. According to my mam, you'll feel better in a
month or two." Irene blushed, lowering her eyes. "I hope I
haven't got ahead of myself, but I did notice."

Charlotte blushed right back. "You haven't said anything
to Sir Michael, have you? I—I'm not sure yet, you know."

Irene dipped a sponge into the warm water and proceeded
to scrub Charlotte's hot face. "'Course not. Nor to Mrs. Kelly
either, but I think she knows. She always knows everything."

Charlotte was quiet as Irene brushed and braided her hair,
remembering Bay's attentions yesterday after their swim. She
really should wash the sea salt from her hair. Her body itched
a bit, too. "I think I'd better have a bath this morning, Irene,
if it's not too much trouble for you girls. Don't take Kitty
away from Mr. Frazier, though. Goodness, the Toothaker sisters must be done in. Frightened, too."

"Oh, we'll be glad of our beds later. But you don't know!
In the shock of the shooting and all, Angus proposed to Kitty,
so she's more than happy. And Sir Michael has given everyone the day off tomorrow, and cash bonuses besides."

Charlotte smiled, imagining tough Angus Frazier pouring

his heart out. She hoped he did a better job of it than his master. "Please tell Sir Michael to come up here when he can, Irene. And don't bother with my breakfast for a while yet. Just the bathwater."

"Yes, miss. Right away."

Charlotte waited until Irene disappeared before she spewed her water and cracker crumbs into the chamber pot. If she had to endure two more months of this, it would be hard going. But worth every unpleasantness. She rested a hand on her belly, imagining the tiny child within, a child that was actually going to have a father once Bay got his proposal right.

Summoning up her energy, she limped to the window to toss the contents out onto the bush below, then leaned out to swallow up the day. That poor bush wouldn't thank her for the regular morning insult. Friendly puffy white clouds shadowed the sea's dazzling surface as they blew across the sky. The wind caught the tail end of Charlotte's braid. It was a perfect day for a sail, if she dared trust her stomach. But Bay would probably spend the day in bed in well-deserved rest once he had tidied up the business of Anne Whitley.

What would become of her? Charlotte decided she could not feel sorry for the woman, despite things Bay had told her as he quickly wrapped her in the coverlet last night. No matter what the viscountess had suffered at the hands of Viscount Whitley, she had gone beyond the pale. Kidnapping, attempted murder, virtual rape, if a woman could actually rape a man. Charlotte had not thought it possible until she had seen it with her own eyes. Thankfully it had been too dark for details.

If Anne were not imprisoned somewhere, they would never be free of her. She posed a danger to them—and this baby. Charlotte had horrific visions of a figure in black, tossing the child into the sea.

Her hand gripped the windowsill. If she had to, she would leave Bayard Court, and all the worthy proposals in the world would not be enough to stop her.

*   *   *

Bay half listened in exhaustion as Mr. Buckland continued to sputter inarticulate inanities. Mrs. Buckland was silent, looking gray, her skin and hair blending into the gray dress she'd donned so hastily in the night. They had both seen their daughter for themselves in Dr. Dixfield's study. Bay had had to pry her off once again when she threw herself at him in hysterics, then restrain her as she began to throw medical textbooks and bric-a-brac with abandon. The Bucklands had watched in relief when Jamie Dixfield forced her to swallow an opiate while Bay held her still, then watched in alarm as the doctor restrained her in his spare bedroom.

Bay had known Jamie Dixfield all his life. They were of an age, played together, drank together, even wenched together. As boys they both had worshipped the slightly older Anne Buckland from afar. "Young" Dr. Dixfield, who had succeeded his father, "Old" Dr. Dixfield, had looked about as sick as Bay felt during that fiendish hour as Anne thrashed about his study.

Her parents had seen most of it. Why were they so blatantly resistant to the truth? Impatiently, Bay pulled his shirt from his breeches and lifted it. Four inches shy of his navel was a perfectly round bruise. Mrs. Buckland switched from gray to bright pink.

"Cover yourself, man!" Mr. Buckland said, shocked.

"See this? It's from the barrel of Anne's gun. Probably one of yours, sir, but sorry, it was pitched into the sea. This is the method she persuaded me with last night when she chose to couple with me. I should be grateful. Last time she hired four men who kidnapped me and beat me senseless. You cannot keep making excuses for her, sir. They dishonor you and diminish Anne's problem."

"Her only problem is you! First disgracing her with that hasty marriage—why, she wasn't even out of mourning—and then never leaving her alone! You—you forced her to break her wedding vows!"

Anne's mother spoke, finally. She had progressed from pink to vermillion. Bay gave her a twisted smile. "Which ones? Mine or Whitley's? I assure you I meant mine as much as he did. And I would have been kinder to her than he ever was. Look to yourselves—I know Anne came to you time and time again when he made her suffer. And you both did nothing."

"He was a viscount," Anne's ambitious father said, as if that explained everything.

"And I am a mere baronet. Rich, though. I can pay for Anne's treatment. Dixfield might know of a place—"

"No!" Mrs. Buckland's face was white now. "She'll be with *mad* people. She won't be safe."

"Madam, I and my fiancée Miss Fallon—indeed my entire household staff—will not be safe unless Anne's locked away. She can't keep shooting my valet. Eventually, he won't stand for it. Should harm befall Charlotte, I would have to take matters into my own hands."

He stared down Mrs. Buckland, leaving no doubt of his threatened intentions. The woman looked away. "I'll discuss it with Dixfield. You need do nothing more than—than sign the papers."

Both the Bucklands suddenly looked their age. Anne was their only child, born to them when they had given up hope of ever having children. She had been spoiled from the instant she opened her blue eyes in her bassinet. They had wanted nothing but the best for her—which unfortunately included marriage at sixteen to a viscount with a vast estate and a predilection for cruelty. Anne had spent nearly twenty years paying for her parents' willful blindness.

Mr. Buckland nodded. "Very well. Tell Dixfield—tell Dixfield we'll cooperate."

"Kenneth! Couldn't we keep her at home? Hire s-someone?"

Her husband touched her gently, as if he knew she was already broken. "Marjorie, you know he's right. It's been an uncomfortable few weeks having her home again. You must agree." He turned to Bay. "Thank you, Sir Michael. I'm sorry things have turned out the way they have. If I had known—well, there's no use crying over spilt milk. Tell Jamie Dixfield to do his best. It won't be easy."

No, it wouldn't be. But if anyone had a hope with Anne, it might be the other lad who had loved her, too.

Bay wanted nothing more than his bed, with Charlotte beside him. Seeing Irene standing discreetly in the hallway as he saw the Bucklands out the door, his heart stuttered. "Is she all right?"

Irene blushed. "Yes, sir. A bit tired. She's having a bath and would like to see you as soon as it's convenient."

Bay supposed Jamie Dixfield could wait a while. He'd lent the doctor the two stable boys for the day to serve in shifts as needed, and secured Mrs. Kelly's niece, who lived in the village, to assist the doctor's elderly housekeeper in the care of his difficult new patient. The man had access to drugs and restraints, so he was better equipped to deal with Anne Whitley than most.

He pictured Charlie in the bathtub. It was almost as large as the tub on Jane Street. He'd lost his neckcloth somewhere during the hazardous evening, but began to unbutton his shirt as he mounted the stairs. Hot water. The satin of Charlie's clean skin against his heart. His pace quickened.

He didn't bother to tap on the door but went straight to the little dressing room. Charlie's back was slick with soap bubbles, her hair piled up in a hasty knot atop her head. With a flick of his wrist, he removed the pins and watched it tumble down.

"Oh! I didn't hear you! You might have given me apoplexy," she said, looking up at him, the tender skin beneath her blue eyes a perfect match for them.

"You did sleep a bit, didn't you?" he asked, concerned.

"Off and on. I missed you." She extended a hand of welcome. Bay dropped his wrinkled trousers and slipped gratefully into the water.

"I was rather busy."

For a few minutes there was silence between them as Charlie lathered his torso, her wicked fingers teasing the hair
under his arms and tracing the muscles of his chest. She made
no mention of the purple circle at the base of his ribs, but
brushed by it with a featherlight caress. What could she think
of his honor and intentions, when she had found him with
Anne last night? He stilled her hand. He had to tell her. Now,
when the words were foaming up to the surface like soap
bubbles. Words he was too stupid to say yesterday. "I love
you, Charlie, and only you. You saved my life last night. If I
had gotten the gun away from Anne, I think I would have
shot myself. It was the only way to stop her." He watched all
color leach from her face; even her lips seemed bloodless. "I
can't kill her. Oh, I think about it, I've even talked about it,
threatened her parents with it, but I can't. There's too much
history. And pity. But if you can forgive me, I'll make last
night up to you for the rest of our lives. Please marry me,
Charlie. I can't live without you."

She blinked, or perhaps he did. There were tears in his
eyes, tears of frustration and impossible yearning. He hadn't
cried in quite some time; it simply wasn't done. But all he
wanted to do was hold Charlie's beautiful wet body to him
and weep into her sea-scented hair. He was so tired, so very,
very tired.

He heard her sigh and then whisper the word he needed to
hear. And then the problem of Anne seemed to float out of
range as the miracle of Charlie's love washed over him. Her
kiss was so innocent. So hopeful. So hard to resist, and he
would never have to. Why had it taken him so long to realize
that love could be separated from obsession and defeat? Charlie would never collar him and tug at his leash on a whim. She
would give herself to him without reservation, and he to her.
Anne as an obstacle was removed from his heart and their path.

Her finger stroked the raised scar on his cheek, a permanent reminder of his stupidity. But he would brave any sword if it meant a future with Charlie. Perhaps every single stumble had led him right here where he should be, in cooling bathwater with this stubborn, loving woman. A woman who saved his life with a chamber pot. In the middle of the most delicious, the most disarming kiss, he began to laugh.

He couldn't stop. Relief coursed through his blood like the richest wine. Charlie's eyes flew open, her dark brows beetled. She looked as prim as if she had one of her ridiculous lacy caps on her head. She smacked his chest.

"You simply cannot get the hang of this proposing business. Just what is so amusing?"

"Oh, my love. Think about it. A short while ago I entered a dark house to commit the sin of seriously mistaking your identity. You must admit we got off to a most dubious beginning. I seem to remember candlesticks and kidnapping and a bite or two. But there's no doubt. None. You were made just for me, and I thank God for it."

"Well." She seemed somewhat mollified by his explanation and just a bit speechless. He tangled his fingers in her hair and she winced.

"How is your head?"

"Sore. My poor mama's fainting lessons were unsuccessful, I'm afraid."

Bay grinned. "You had fainting lessons? Just what else did your mother try to teach you?"

"I was a poor study. She would be horrified to see what Deb and I have come to."

"Now, now. Your sister is a respectable married woman and you are about to be."

She leveled a clear blue gaze at him. "You *really* want to marry me?"

"Have I not proposed awkwardly twice already? If you tell me the third time's the charm I shall endeavor to do it better, but only once more. A man can only debase himself so much."

Charlie scooted back, sloshing water onto the carpet. "Debase? Is that how you think of it? Lowering yourself to my level?"

"You quite mistake me. I'm on my knees, Charlie, and damned uncomfortable."

Charlie glanced down, and just as quickly looked into his face. His erect shaft pierced the water like a rigid fish.

"I n-need to wash my hair," she stammered.

Bay leaned in closer. "I'll do it for you, if you do something for me."

"Anything," she whispered. "You know I'll do anything for you."

There was an urgent tapping on the bedroom door. Charlotte disentangled herself from the covers and Bay's sleep-heavy arm and threw on her gray robe. Running her hands through her hair, she wished Bay had allowed it to dry before he fell upon her like a starving man. But a few knots were nothing to the saturated bliss of her body. She cracked the door open.

A pale Frazier stood there, his arm in a sling.

"What are you doing up? Oh, that sounds awful, but I thought you weren't to be disturbed. How are you, Mr. Frazier?"

"I've never been better, Miss Fallon. Miss Kitty Toothaker has agreed to be my bride." The man grinned like an idiot, and the gruff old Scot completely disappeared. "But Sir Michael's wanted below. It's Dr. Dixfield come to call, and he seems a mite agitated."

"What time is it? Oh, good Lord. Lady Whitley hasn't escaped, has she?" Charlotte looked down the hall behind him as if she expected to see the Black Widow any second.

"Just on four. And no. That was the first thing I asked. He says she's got plenty of protection at the house and he felt confident enough to leave her."

Charlotte hoped the doctor didn't have any spare firearms

lying around. "If you give us a few minutes, I'll wake Sir Michael and we'll get dressed and be right down. Have Mrs. Kelly do up a tea tray. I'm actually hungry." They had slept right through lunch. No, not slept.

Angus Frazier gave her a beatific smile. "Yes, yes. You should eat more in your condition."

Charlotte shut the door. Did everyone in the entire household know her secret? Everyone but Bay.

What if she wasn't pregnant, but coming to the end of her child-bearing years? She knew of women her age who got sick and whose flow had stopped. She also knew women who bore offspring well into their forties. Mrs. King in Little Hyssop even had a babe at fifty-one, the same year one of her daughters gave birth to her seventh grandchild. Perhaps she should see a doctor.

Well, there was one waiting downstairs. She leaned over her lover, sprawled like Gulliver across the linens, his cock rampant, a sleep-sweetened smile on his face. She would be interrupting a very pleasant dream.

"Bay, wake up. Dr. Dixfield is here."

"Unh." He rolled over, giving her a very fine view of his bottom. It was a beautiful bottom to be sure, white, tight, just the right curvature to fill out his pantaloons properly, but she needed to see his dark eyes. Wide open.

"Bay!" Sharper now. He sat bolt upright, reaching for an invisible weapon. Realization dawned and he gave her a sexy smile. "Sorry I fell asleep. Come back to bed and we'll take up where we left off."

"Bay, you need to get dressed. Dr. Dixfield is below."

"Damnation! Has she run off?" He was stuffing a leg in his ruined pants before she had a chance to even walk to the wardrobe.

"He says not. I've ordered tea and sandwiches. You haven't eaten a thing."

Bay gave her a sardonic look, and she felt the blush spread from her nose to her toes. Bay had been very, very thorough, "proposing" to her again and again until there was absolutely no question she would agree to be his wife. No wonder losing him had deranged Anne Whitley.

He stuck a comb in the tepid basin and slicked back his coppery hair. The longer it grew, the more it seemed to turn autumnal. Even with a day's growth of beard, he was so handsome the breath left her.

He gave her a quick kiss. "Take your time. I won't decide anything important without you."

And he was gone.

Jamie Dixfield was one of his oldest friends. Bay had mentioned him numerous times over the past few weeks, recalling one boyhood stunt or another. He had entrusted Anne to Jamie's care, and not only because he was a doctor. Charlotte wished to make a good impression, but was faced with her dull dresses. Gray or brown? She pulled a pale ashy muslin dress over her head, quickly braided her hair, pinched her cheeks, and bit her lips. That would have to do.

She needn't have worried. When she reached the parlor, neither man even glanced her way. Both of them were standing before the bank of windows, not enjoying that view either but emanating a certain menace toward each other. The tea table was untouched. Nervous, Charlotte cleared her throat.

The doctor was the first to break away from Bay's glare. He was an attractive man, if somewhat disheveled, with curling fair hair and an angular face. He looked like he'd been wrestling alligators on the Nile, but she supposed he had only wrestled a distraught Anne Whitley all day. Smiling, he revealed even, white teeth. "You must be Charlie. May I be one of the first to offer my wishes for your future happiness?"

His hands on hers were long, elegant, and warm. Good, safe hands for a doctor. "Charlotte, actually. No one calls me Charlie anymore, except for Bay." And her sister, but there was no point in bringing her into this. "How do you do, Dr. Dixfield?"

"It's just Jamie, but if you must be Charlotte, I can be

James." He winked at her. Out of the corner of her own eye she saw Bay flex his fists as if he longed to thrash his oldest friend for displaying such charm to his fiancée.

"What is going on?" Charlotte asked baldly. "Whatever it is, you'll both do better with some tea and a sandwich. Won't you sit down and join me?"

"Tea won't solve this," Bay bit out.

"Very likely not." Jamie smiled at her again, but the smile didn't reach his sober gray eyes. "I'm afraid my old friend and I are having a rather fundamental disagreement. As lovely as it is to meet you, perhaps we can become better acquainted another time."

"You'll not order Charlie out of *my* parlor in *my* house!"

"No, indeed. I'd never interfere with the woman you love." Dixfield sat on the edge of the nearest chair, inspecting a loose button on his wrinkled jacket.

"Love!" Charlotte sat down quickly as Bay stalked about the room, waving his arms about like a windup toy. She had never seen him so ruffled, not even when his life had been in danger. "Don't talk to me of love! You're as unhinged as she is!"

"I beg your pardon," Charlotte said with feeling, "but just because I agreed to marry you does not mean I'm unhinged."

"Not you," both men spoke at once.

"Oh, do sit down, Bay, you're making me dizzy. What do you take in your tea, Jamie?"

"You can't turn this debacle into a tea party, Charlie. It won't work." But at least Bay landed on a sofa, too far away to have tea or any sort of plate passed to him.

"Sugar please, no milk or lemon." The men were quiet while she poured a cup, her hand shaking just a trifle, and passed it to the doctor. She served herself, adding a huge dollop of milk for the baby.

"Now," she said after taking a bracing sip, "suppose one of you tells me what this is all about."

The mantel clock ticked a full minute before Bay spoke, his voice dripping sarcasm. "It seems the doctor here has a peculiar plan to bring Lady Whitley back to some semblance of sanity. Why don't you tell her, Jamie? I find I'm unequal to the task."

Charlotte had heard of asylums for those afflicted with mental impairment. Some people in the ton even went so far as to visit the inmates—in Bedlam, for example—for sheer amusement. Such cruelty. Surely this kind, friendly man didn't plan on subjecting Anne Whitley, no matter what she'd done, to such a fate.

And he didn't. What he said next was far more frightening.

"It seems love is in the air—first for Angus Frazier, then for you and Bay, and now for me. I've asked Lady Whitley to marry me."

Charlotte dropped her cup to the floor. Its contents fell on her slippers and it rolled harmlessly on the thick Aubusson carpet. She was too shocked to remark on the hot tea finding its way between her toes.

"You see? Unhinged," said Bay grimly.

"I have loved Anne Buckland since I was a boy. Bay had his turn with her, and now it's mine. We talked for hours when she woke up, Anne and I. She just wants what all women want: a home, children, a man she can depend on. She can depend on me. I've had my chances with the ladies, but I never married. It's always been Anne. When I heard her husband died, I was getting my courage up to go see her, but then she came back home."

"But—but—" Once she found her tongue, she revealed their shameful recent history. Charlotte was fairly sure she mentioned the word gun a few times. Bay chimed in about the brutes who kidnapped him. Nothing would shake Jamie Dixfield's certainty that he could make Anne Whitley happy. His eyes shone as he pleaded his case.

"But I realize it would be awkward if I kept my practice here. My father has retired, but he's still got some good days left in him, long enough to train a new doctor for these parts.

Bay has more money than God, you know, more than he'll ever need. I've come for a loan. He can set me up in another town where no one knows Anne or the trouble she's had. I heard about a situation not long ago from a doctor friend of mine up in Scotland. A new country. A new start."

Bay looked shattered. "If I thought it could work, I'd give you my whole fortune, Jamie, but you don't know what she's like now."

"Oh, I believe I do. I was there this morning when she had her little fit, remember? She's told me everything, Bay—what her husband did to her and what she did to survive it. She wants a baby so badly that it's clouded her judgment. That happens to some women. I've seen it before."

"I wager you've never been at the business end of a gun over it," Bay snapped.

"No. She didn't need to hold a gun on me. I was most willing." Dixfield flushed, realizing what he'd just revealed. Bay stared at him, slack jawed. "I'll marry her, whether you approve or not, whether you can give me any money or not."

"Good God. She was drugged, Jamie. I watched you dose her myself. You can't count on anything she said or did."

"It was just honey and brandy. I knew she needed to sleep, and she did. She's sorry, Bay, truly sorry for causing you both such trouble. It's as if she was under some kind of spell and now she's snapped out of it."

"You're the one who's under a spell, man!" Bay returned to pacing the room, running his hand through his hair every seventh step. Charlotte counted—he was as regular as a metronome.

"You're right," Dixfield said. "And you of all people know what it's like. You've moved on, Bay, and found your happiness. Don't deny me mine."

Bay snorted in disgust. He pulled open a French door and slammed it shut. Charlotte watched him lope down the green lawn toward the beach, leaving her alone with the love-struck doctor.

"I know Anne just sees me as a port in the storm," he said softly. "But I have hope she'll come to care for me, even love me. She—she was very responsive. Physically." His cheeks were crimson but he continued the unwanted confession. "She's had a hard life. Her only true peace was her brief time with Bay. Not even six months. Then she played her games. I know she hurt Bay terribly, but I swear she won't bother you again."

Charlotte's mouth was dry. "How can you know that?"

"Because I mean to get her with child, children if we're so lucky, and she'll be too busy to think about the past. I've waited for her more than half my life."

Apart from her obvious beauty, Charlotte could see no reason why any man should fall in love with Anne Whitley. Yet these two old friends had, and for most of two decades. Perhaps her judgment was clouded as well, and they knew a different Anne, one who was not shrill and dangerous. "I can't trust her," Charlotte said at last. "Especially not now."

"Then convince Bay to lend me the blunt so we can go to Scotland. We'll marry at Gretna Green on the way up. Once my practice here sells, I can pay him back."

"I don't think his reservation is about the money. Bay's the most generous man I know. Don't you see? You're his best friend. He doesn't want Anne to use you."

Dixfield smiled. "I want to be used, Charlotte. Sad, isn't it? Here I've got looks and skill—no false modesty for me. I know my worth—but all I want is that madwoman in my house. She's all I ever wanted. I thought my heart would turn black and curdle with jealousy when Bay married her. I was glad when her husband came back from the dead—*glad* that my friend couldn't have her either. You're the only person I've ever told that to."

Charlotte felt sympathy for the man, but Anne's problems surely were too complicated to be solved by honey and brandy and one afternoon in bed with Jamie Dixfield. From the state of his clothing he hadn't even bothered to get undressed. Charlotte scrubbed her mind of the unwelcome images.

"I will talk to him, but I can't promise anything."

Dixfield rose. "Thank you. I'm going to bring Anne back home to her parents. It's not proper that she stay with me."

Oh, God. A fist of fear clutched her heart. Anne would come after them again, and next time she might be successful. Bay's child would be at risk as long as Anne was not confined. Charlotte stumbled over her good-byes and stared at the deceptively calm sea. She had to do something—*something*—but she couldn't think what.

Chapter 24

He'd walked on the shingle until he reached the tumble of unclimbable cliffs, then turned back into the wind to head for home. Still too enervated to go back to the house, Bay perched on a sun-soaked rock, surveying the abandoned seduction site. The tent poles had collapsed, the basket of food overturned and picked clean by swooping gulls. A long dark stain of wine had dried on the ruined carpet.

And then there was the chamber pot, glistening white in the afternoon light. Bay's lips twitched, remembering. But the seriousness of his situation brought a quick halt to his amusement. Jamie was as mad as Anne if he thought to marry her and run off to Scotland. What Anne's parents would think was anyone's guess. Life as a doctor's wife was quite a comedown from life as a viscountess, but nevertheless an improvement over being an inmate in an asylum, no matter how humane.

At the heart of it, he couldn't imagine Anne turning from him to Jamie in less than twenty-four hours. It smacked of the kind of desperation only possible if one was completely unbalanced. How could Jamie settle for a wife like that, far from the home he grew up in, away from his elderly father and friends? Both he and Anne were tethered to their obsessions.

Bay knew what it was like to crave Anne's touch. In losing

her he had lost years of his life, put himself at needless risk, frozen his heart to new possibilities. Charlie had thawed it with the heat of her tongue and body. Now he couldn't imagine his life without her.

And he had left her alone at the house to sort out his mess. He was a craven fool.

The glass door to the back parlor was still open as he left it. His instinct had been to slam it when he stormed out of the room earlier, but his better self had prevailed. Charlie sat at the tea table, its starched linen cloth wafting in the light breeze. A dried-up sandwich sat untouched on her gilt-edged plate.

"I'm sorry," he offered before she could say anything. "I shouldn't have run away and left you with Jamie. I was just so—so—flummoxed."

"Bay, I want to go home. To Little Hyssop. It's almost time anyway."

He couldn't have heard her correctly. He reached for a hand that was fisted tightly in her lap, but she clutched the fold of her dress. "Why?"

"Jamie says he's taking Anne back to the Bucklands until we get all this sorted. I think you should give him the money and send them away. Far away. Until you do, I just can't stay here."

"I'll protect you, I swear. Frazier and I were in the process of hiring some men from the village to patrol the grounds round-the-clock."

"Too late." Her blue eyes were bright with tears. He cursed himself for leaving her by herself to worry and placing her in danger. Anne could be walking up the drive right now, armed with one of Jamie's bedpans to return the favor.

He didn't want her to leave. He didn't even want her as far away as the next room. But it was clear from her stricken expression she was scared half to death. "You're right. I'll send Frazier with you. And Kitty, I suppose."

"Frazier! Is he fit enough?"

"Angus Frazier's a tough old bird. Believe me, he's marched miles with worse. It's just a superficial wound. I think he wears the sling to garner sympathy from his bride-to-be."

Her smile was wobbly. "You must think I'm an awful coward."

"No, my love, you are a sensible, respectable woman, as you've reminded me time and time again. And anyone with the grit to use a chamber pot as a weapon is a force to be reckoned with. You are the bravest woman I know."

"She could have shot you. When the gun went off—" She swallowed back a sob.

He pulled her up against him quickly, the china on the tea table clattering. Yes, she had fainted last night, but the enormity of everything was finally hitting her in all its grim glory. He'd seen some of his troops go through stages such as this—functioning because they had to, then suddenly going to pieces. Bay couldn't bear to see her hurt or uncertain. He would deal with Jamie and Anne, then claim Charlie at last.

"Hush, hush," he whispered into her temple as she wept. "It will be all right. Everything will be all right. I'll see to it, and then I'll come for you. You can leave tonight, as soon as we can get you packed up. Frazier will think he's on holiday, two pretty girls to ride with. Let me go talk to my coachman. He's an old army man, too—used to moving on short notice." He murmured comforting nonsense as she slowly stilled in his arms. Whatever it took to calm her fears, he was prepared to do. He acknowledged his own fears were elevated as well. Until he saw Anne for himself, he would doubt any solution Jamie proposed.

He wouldn't be separated from Charlie forever, just long enough for him to find a permanent solution to the problem of Anne Whitley. Charlie would never have reason to worry about anything ever again, save what to order for dinner or what color to repaint the parlor. An idea was even now beginning to form, taking amorphous hold on his imagination, but he wouldn't speak of it until he could explore it further. In the meantime, the woman in his embrace needed kissing in the very worst way, something he was eminently qualified to do.

From the corner of the coach, Charlotte had observed the blushes and the giggles, the secret glances, the "accidental" touches of her companions as the carriage rolled through the countryside bounce after bounce. She definitely felt like a fifth wheel as Angus Frazier and his Kitty were thick in the throes of their love affair. She couldn't begrudge them their euphoria; if things had been different, she would be similarly enraptured by Bay. It was in fact amusing to see the gruff Frazier as besotted as a schoolboy with the tiny maid. Charlotte was quite looking forward to their wedding as well as her own.

But right now she had a more pressing problem than wedding arrangements. She simply didn't know where she was going to put Mr. Frazier and Kitty when they got to her little cottage. It was not as though she had servants' quarters, or even the need for servants. The upstairs rooms were crammed to the ceiling with Deborah's spoils from her years as a courtesan. Kitty would just have to share Charlotte's bed, and Mr. Frazier was doomed to sleep on the lumpy sofa, poor man. Bay would not hear of them returning with the coachman and the carriage once she was safely back in Little Hyssop. She was to have the security of Angus Frazier's protection until Bay decided otherwise.

Throughout the trip, Mr. Frazier had taken his guard duties seriously, but the farther away from Bayard Court they travelled, the more relaxed Charlotte became. It was unlikely that Anne would somehow discover their whereabouts. If it wasn't for the baby, Charlotte would feel craven for leaving Bay behind. She missed him fiercely, especially when confronted with the two cooing lovebirds opposite.

She had almost—*almost*—told him what she suspected when they parted. But she had been so very desperate to leave. She'd been irrational, really, now that there was distance in both miles and days to reflect. If Bay resolved the Anne entanglement quickly as he promised, he would know soon enough.

The carriage rumbled over the last bridge and into the village proper. Charlotte felt a sense of peace as she viewed the familiar stone buildings, their flower boxes overflowing, their front steps swept spotless. Bay's driver knew just where to go from his last visit, when he brought his horticulturally challenged master on his "garden tour." But the carriage stopped short on the lane.

"Bother. This is Mr. Trumbull's house. Mr. Frazier, could you hop out and tell John to go down to the end?"

Frazier did as requested, but was back in seconds. "There's a cart blocking the road, Miss Fallon. Piled high with furniture and boxes it is. Have ye been evicted?"

"Certainly not! I own my cottage free and clear." It couldn't be thieves, could it, taking advantage of her absence to empty out her home? "Kitty, you stay here." Charlotte stepped down from the coach, grateful that Angus Frazier would be at her side to confront whoever was stealing her possessions. Not that she had anything of value, except for her broken jar of money and Deb's things.

Deb! Her sister came flying out the open door, covered in one of Charlotte's own aprons, and, remarkably, one of Charlotte's caps affixed to her glossy dark hair.

"There you are! Do you know I've been worried sick? I wrote letter after letter. When I didn't hear from you, I persuaded Arthur to let me come down to see what was wrong. And then that old man next door told me you were visiting me, which you most assuredly were not, because why would I be looking for you if you were with me in Kent? Careful with that!" she interrupted herself, speaking to a pair of men balancing a mirror between them. "That really should be wrapped in a blanket. I say, Charlie, you wouldn't have a spare one I could borrow? I should hate to have seven years of bad luck, just when my luck has turned. Charlie, I'm the happiest woman in the world. You'll never guess! The most amazing thing! I'm going to have a baby! And Arthur's home is delightful, but it will be ever so much better with my lovely things in it. His uncle didn't have much taste, I'm afraid." Just then Arthur came out the door clutching the hideous stuffed parrot. "No, not that, darling. I've changed my mind. Charlie, I want you to keep this. As a token of my affection. Now where have you been, you sly puss? And with whom?" She cast a somewhat disparaging eye on Angus Frazier, who stared right back at her, his mouth hanging open.

Charlotte was quite sure she gave off a similar sense of shock. While Mr. Frazier was probably surprised at her resemblance to her sister, Charlotte was stunned to see Deborah in domestic garb, chattering like a magpie, and pleased to be pregnant. Not only had luck turned, but the world had turned and was tilting on its axis. Charlotte thought any minute now she'd drop off and be tossed off into the firmament.

Deb pulled her close in a hug, temporarily tethering her to earth, and whispered in her ear. "Well, say something! Stop gawping like a looby. Don't ever tell me that this man is your protector. I left you set for life with Bay."

"It's complicated." Charlotte escaped the embrace. She wasn't sure Deb was ready to hear all about the last several months, nor was she ready to explain the recent past with any lucidity. Art theft, imprisonment, kidnapping, armed sexual assault, and insanity were not typical topics of conversation. "Congratulations on your marriage, Arthur, and your good news."

Arthur turned quite pink. "Thank you, Charlotte. Deborah, sweetheart, come inside and sit down. I don't want you to tire yourself out."

From what Charlotte had seen already, the only thing apt to be tired was Deb's tongue. A small battalion of men moved to and fro up and down the stairs, loading the cart. "Mr. Frazier, perhaps you and Kitty and the coachman can refresh yourselves at the Pig and Whistle. They do a very nice lunch."

"Are you sure, Miss Fallon?" He seemed suspicious of Deborah, having heard all of Mrs. Kelly's and Irene's tirades against her. Deb had not made herself popular in her brief tenure on Jane Street.

"Perfectly. You might do a bit of shopping as well, after. We'll need something for dinner and breakfast."

"I don't like to leave you alone with these people," Frazier mumbled for her ears only.

"I'll be fine," Charlotte said stoutly. Arthur could always hit any intruder in the head with the parrot.

"I know you've been sitting a spell, but you haven't been sleeping well. You take care of yourself, too." Frazier warned.

Charlotte *was* tired. She missed the length of Bay's body against her in the night. Sleeping with Kitty in inns was not the same at all. Arthur tucked the parrot awkwardly under one arm and assisted Deb back into the cottage as though she were made of spun sugar. Following, Charlotte bit her lip as Deb milked her maternal status for all it was worth.

Mercifully, everything in the parlor was just as Charlotte had left it, except now Arthur propped the parrot on the mantel. Its malevolent beady eyes took in the comfortably shabby room, no doubt wishing for her sister's more familiar exalted objets d'art. Deb kicked off her fancy embroidered slippers and lay back on the sofa, putting her feet up on a cushion.

"Be a dear and massage my feet, Arthur. Now, tell me. Who was that funny-looking red-haired man? And who is Kitty? Never tell me you were travelling with one of your cats. What a nuisance they've been, by the way, yowling at all hours ever since we arrived, getting underfoot of the removal men. Nasty creatures. I don't see how you can stand the little beggars."

"Prefer a dog, myself," Arthur interjected as his hands smoothed over Deb's stockings. "A nice beagle. Had one when I was a boy."

"Yes, yes." Deb waved her hand vaguely. "You may have one when we get back to Bard's End, but it is not to come into my house and mess on my carpets. Nor will it nip my precious baby. Arthur, you must see to its training."

"Yes, my love."

Charlotte suppressed a giggle. For all Deb's domesticity, she had not lost imperious sway over her husband. Arthur was completely in her thrall, no doubt pinching himself several times a day that he was actually married to London's most sought-after courtesan.

"What has happened, Charlie? I even stopped at Jane Street and inquired of your neighbor Lady Christie. What an elegant woman she is, even if her life's a scandal. I do wish I'd gotten to know her when I was there. She told me you simply disappeared, the house was shut up, and if I was to find you to send her felicitations. Oh! And she said she bought a red dress and her husband was apoplectic. Very odd, that. Anyway, tell me everything."

"Well." Charlotte wondered about Deb's reaction when she told her about the engagement. Arthur compared rather unfavorably to Sir Michael Xavier Bayard, and Deb would think if she had played her cards patiently, she might have been Lady Bayard instead of Mrs. Bannister. She might as well get it over with. "I was with Bay at his estate in Dorset. He's asked me to marry him, and I've said yes."

Deb jerked her foot out of her husband's hand. "Don't be ridiculous, you tease. Where have you been really?"

"I've just said, Deb."

Deb sat up. "I can't believe it! Where is your ring?"

Charlotte looked at her naked hands. "I—I don't have one yet. A ring isn't the important thing anyway."

"Oh, you are so naive. Look what Arthur gave me." She leaned over and thrust a good-sized winking sapphire under Charlotte's nose.

Charlotte felt a twinge of spite. She untied her fichu, revealing the magnificent ruby necklace.

"My necklace!" cried Deb.

"*My* necklace," countered Charlotte. "And you know you took it without permission."

"It was an accident. I was in such a hurry to marry my Arthur I didn't pay attention when I was packing. What a lot of trouble the silly thing caused. That man who interrupted our blissful honeymoon at Patrice's chateau put a damper on us for days. It looks very nice on you," Deb said grudgingly. "But that dress—don't you have anything more suitable?"

"You know I don't. Look, Deb, I'm happy for you. Please be happy for me."

"Why shouldn't I be? I have everything I've ever wanted—a house of my own and a child on the way." This was news to Charlotte, but she held her tongue. After a pregnant pause, an embarrassed Arthur cleared his throat. "And you, of course, Arthur! That goes without saying. But Charlie, are you sure Bay will marry you? He's not a marrying kind of man."

"I'm sure," Charlotte said, praying that it was true.

The next hour passed as Deb gave orders from the couch while Charlotte brewed up tea and a fierce backache. Charlotte breathed a sigh of relief when the cart rattled off, taking the clomping, stomping men with it. Arthur and Deb repaired to the relative luxury of the Pig and Whistle, saying their good-byes as they were making for Kent with all the treasure at first light. Charlotte was spared sharing her supper with them—fresh bread, ham, and beans from her garden, which were running riot up over the poles. She and Kitty and Angus had dined in the cozy kitchen together, and the couple was now readying the two cleared-out attic rooms for nightfall, although Charlotte imagined just one of the pallets would be slept on tonight. Frazier's arm was fully healed, and there was no reason why he could not consummate his engagement. Charlotte had no objection, as long as they weren't too noisy. She was looking forward to sleeping undisturbed in her own bed beneath her own worn quilts.

By now Little Hyssop's rumor mill was working overtime. First there had been Charlotte's sudden departure, then her sister's arrival and the removal of a king's ransom worth of oddities from the tiny cottage, then Charlotte's return with two servants in tow. She'd have a lot of explaining to do in the morning and needed all the rest she could get.

She went into her little back bedroom off the kitchen and

opened the window to the summer night. Her hollyhocks had grown up taller than she was and mostly blocked her view of the stars. But she made her wish anyway, undressed, and crawled into bed. Fingering the heavy necklace still at her throat, she was reassured. She may not have a ring, but she had something better—a man who swore he loved her and would protect her always.

She woke in the middle of the night to loud growls. The sound was not at all catlike, and it came from indoors, not out. Frightened, she grabbed a trusty candlestick and tiptoed through the dark to the parlor. Angus Frazier had angled the sofa against the hall entryway, and was guarding her noisily against nighttime visitors in his sleep. Either that, or Kitty had thrown him out for the ruckus. Charlotte noted on her way back to bed that the kitchen door was blocked with a chair. No Little Hyssopian would gain access to her cottage tonight. She fell back asleep with a smile on her face, and woke to the smell of frying bacon, which gave her stomach only a minor lurch. It was to be one of the good mornings. She pulled on her gray robe and stepped into the kitchen.

Sunlight streamed in through the open back door. A jar of fresh-cut flowers was centered on the set table, and Kitty was in total control. A pan of eggs bubbled on the stove, and bread had already been buttered. "Good morning, miss! Did you sleep well?"

"Like the dead. This looks lovely, Kitty. The food and the flowers. Thank you." She sat down like a true lady of leisure as Kitty poured her a cup of tea.

"Oh, your garden is a wonder, Miss Fallon. I could be happy living in a cottage like this. It's just perfect."

"It is, rather. Not fancy, but I've been happy here."

Or as happy as one could be, lonely and more or less poor.

She would miss her cottage when Bay came for her, silly as that was. Bayard Court was beautiful, and she was sure his house in town was as well, with its fabled French chef, but Little Hyssop had been her home for a decade. Charlotte looked at Kitty's shining face as she stirred the eggs. "I say, I'd like to make a wedding present of it for you, when Sir Michael and I marry."

Kitty dropped the wooden spoon. "You're joking!"

"I'm not. But perhaps I spoke too soon. Mr. Frazier might not like it. I don't know what he could do to keep busy in Little Hyssop."

"Oh, now that he's got Sir Michael settled with you, he'd love to retire. He gets a small pension from the army, you know. Enough for us to live on. And I'm sure Sir Michael would be generous. He owes Angus his life. Saved him single-handed from a band of rogue Frenchies, he did. Bad 'uns. They killed them all."

Charlotte shuddered. It was difficult to imagine Bay using his artist's hands to willfully kill other human beings. But of course he had. It was his job, or he would not be here today.

Of course, he wasn't *here*. But perhaps there was a letter from him. He had promised to write. Charlotte ate her breakfast quickly, washed up, and braved the walk into the village. Her walk should have taken just five minutes. However, it seemed every one of her neighbors had work to do in their front gardens this morning, and her trip down the lane was a slow but steady one. She deflected most questions to their obvious disappointment, stuck faithfully to comments about the weather, and found herself in the tiny tobacco shop that doubled as Little Hyssop's post office after most of half an hour had passed. Mr. Forrest's eyes lit up as she entered, the bell jangling behind her.

"There you are! I've got a passel of mail for you, what with the month you've been gone. Your sister was in here yesterday, accusing me of withholding her letters, because she'd not heard from you. Off on a secret adventure, eh?"

"You might say that. I'll take my mail, and a few ounces of pipe tobacco. You pick it—something not too strong but aromatic." Mr. Frazier might as well benefit from her gauntlet.

"Don't tell me a fine lady like you has taken up that habit." He waited expectantly, but Charlotte simply shook her head, rifling through the letters. Her sister's hand was on most of them, but one brought a smile to her lips.

A letter from Bay! To her, not to her sister. Charlotte slipped the letters into her reticule, then paid for the tobacco and practically ran home. Let the neighbors talk. She went directly to the back garden bench beneath a trellis of roses that were past their prime but still fragrant and carefully broke the seal.

Dearest Charlie,

You haven't even been gone a day, but I miss you more than I can put into words. Wish me luck. I have an appointment tomorrow with the Bucklands and Jamie. If things go my way, we should have everything settled within a month or two. Until then, I shall dream of you every night. All my love,

Bay

Charlotte leaned back, then reread the few lines. It wasn't half as romantic as she'd hoped, and vague to boot. Although it was gratifying he'd written before she'd even exited Dorset's borders.

And two months! It was an eternity. Getting Jamie and Anne to Scotland couldn't possibly take that long. She wanted to write right back to him, but was distracted when one of the stray cats rubbed up against her stocking with unusual affection. Hungry again, even after Kitty put the breakfast leavings out. Sighing, she went inside to inspect her larder. But first, she pressed Bay's letter between the pages of her Bible, right where her marriage lines would be written. Someday.

Chapter 25

Charlotte had quite a collection of letters now, which she kept in the drawer by her bedside. To her dismay, there was little talk of scarlet butterflies sucking nectar or rubies glimmering in the candlelight, but each missive was treasured nonetheless. The letters were altogether more like what a *husband* might write to a *wife*, although she and Bay were still the only unmarried couple of their extraordinary summer. Unfortunately Bay had missed the Fraziers' wedding last week. Mr. Kemble had presided. But even though Angus and Kitty had been relative strangers to Little Hyssop, everyone turned out for the occasion under the unusually hot late September sky.

Bay had approved of her deeding her cottage to the happy couple, and was supplementing it with a monetary gift of his own. The newlyweds were on a brief honeymoon trip to Scotland now to visit Mr. Frazier's ancient mother and slightly less ancient brothers. Charlotte thought it was rather nice to have her house back, although clearly Kitty now thought of it as her own. She had moved around the kitchen crockery to suit herself and Charlotte had difficulty finding things. But soon, God willing, she'd be in Dorset.

Bay had left absolutely nothing to chance. His last letter had brought hope to her heart.

Dearest Charlie,

An entire ocean will separate us from the Dixfields as soon as I personally pack them on a vessel heading to Boston. They were married last Saturday in the village church, after three of the longest weeks of banns-reading in history. I kept expecting Anne to pop up herself to object each time, but her father and mother sat on either side of her and must have pinched her still. I stood as Jamie's best man, if you can believe it. He whispered at the altar that Anne has missed her monthly, so perhaps our waiting all these weeks was worth it. I know Jamie was most diligent in his "treatment" of his fiancée. You'll be happy to know that Anne did not give me a second look, which was a bit hard on my pride.

So soon, my darling, I will be knocking at your door, fresh from the docks, travel-worn and needy. I know you'll provide the succor I require.

All my love,
Bay

Somehow Bay had fixed it for Jamie to be a doctor in the new state of Maine in America, and his gift to the bride was a fur cloak to weather the uncompromising winters. Charlotte didn't know how Bay had arranged it all or how much it had cost him, but she was anxious to arrange her own wedding. She laid a hand on her growing belly and tried to get comfortable in her bed. Good thing her dresses were old and unfashionable—the high waists still concealed her condition from the world. But it was too hot tonight to wear clothes of any kind. A regular Indian summer had descended on Little Hyssop, confusing her spring bulbs—Kitty's now—into sprouting up. Her night rail hung neatly in the cupboard and she was shamelessly naked under a thin sheet.

She was nearly asleep when she heard a muffled thud.

Snatching the candlestick from the nightstand, she put it down when she heard the familiar curse and smiled. Kitty *did* have to move that chair from its perfectly good spot for the intruder to trip over. This was one intruder Charlotte wanted to intrude, and intrude deeply. She feigned sleep, pulling the sheet down so one very full breast was exposed in the moonlight. The sight might give him ideas.

Charlotte heard him shed his clothes with each step. Her old mattress listed. How brave he was to stretch out beside her, when she so easily could bean him on the head as he set it down on her pillow. She waited to feel his touch, but instead was rewarded with a nearly immediate light snore.

The fiend! She didn't care how tired he was, or how long he'd traveled, or what time of night it was. They had been apart for *centuries*, and he was not going to sleep without intruding. She turned on her side, studying his chest, lifting and falling with each breath. Touching a flat copper nipple was not quite enough, so she fastened her lips around it and sucked.

"Unh."

He lay still, too still. Charlotte snaked a hand down his belly to his cock, which was awake even if he was not. Unless he was pretending, although the snores sounded reasonably authentic. She climbed atop him and licked along the seam of his lips, coaxing them open until she thrust inside to his warmth. He gave her the merest nip, and she knew then what he was doing.

This was a re-creation of their first night. He was the innocent, sleep-laden and nearly virginal. She was the aggressor. Experienced. Hungry. Desperate. *She* was the fiend.

It had not taken her long to fully participate then. Bay was just as irresistible all those nights ago as he was now. The mistake he made resulted in the greatest blessings of her life. She knew love, and love grew within her. But had she left it too late to tell him?

She wouldn't think about that right now. No, it was time to seduce the seducer. She deepened the kiss, trailed her fingers slowly down his chest to his erection again. He was, impossibly, harder than a few minutes ago. Her hand curved around him and lured him to her folds.

He groaned. She wondered if he would continue to feign sleep or master her as he always had. She didn't have long to wait. His black eyes snapped open and a feral grin split his face. He was her pirate tonight, home from his long quest at sea. It did not take him any time at all to grab her hips, slide into her center, and find his treasure. Their connection was instant and insistent. True.

"Welcome home," she whispered. He watched as she rode him hard, oblivious to heat or vanity. He would see her, all of her, in the moonlight. He was a noticing sort of man. His hands wove through her hair, cupped her swollen breasts, stroked everywhere, finally coming to rest on her stomach. The moment he realized, Bay's hand stilled, the touch so gentle she thought she'd weep. He smiled slowly, his cock pulsating inside her.

And then he held her in place, his orgasm fierce, almost frenzied. She came along with him, grateful.

His hand returned to her belly in wonder. "My God! Charlie, why didn't you tell me?"

"You're not angry?" She attempted to move, but he wouldn't let her. The warmth of his protective palms went straight to her heart.

"Of course not! But why go through this alone?"

She pushed a tangle of hair behind her ear. "I wanted to tell you, the day I left. But I wasn't really sure then, and so frightened, and I didn't think you'd let me leave if you knew. I was sure she'd do something, and I had to get away." The words rushed out, but she couldn't say Anne's name. No matter that she was married and on a boat half an ocean away, there would always be residual fear of Anne Whitley.

"Oh, sweetheart." Bay brought her down to his chest, his arms strong around her. "You're safe. Our baby is safe. You just don't know how much I've hoped for this day. I've even got a special license, you know. No banns for us. When?"

"The doctor thinks February. It must have happened right at the first."

"When I didn't know you. But I know you now. Thank God for it. I'll go see Vicar Kemble in the morning." He kissed her forehead, both cheeks. Then her mouth, spending a bit more time on that consummate kiss. A kiss that promised their future happiness. Oh, she would be cross and he would be fiendish, but she loved him enough to believe in the possibility. "You don't want a big Little Burpup wedding do you?"

"We just had one. I did the flowers. They were lovely. You truly aren't angry?"

He squeezed her tighter. "I would have been wild with impatience getting everything settled had I known. A madman. As it was, it was sheer hell. I'll tell you about it sometime. God, I missed you so, Charlie. I even missed you yelling at me."

"I can do that if you want." She snuggled into his shoulder.

"Tomorrow, my love. We've got tomorrow and the rest of our lives for you to yell at me. Right now, all I want to do is sleep with you in my arms."

"I suppose that's as good a plan as any."

All those weeks of waiting, over. She'd sleep very well tonight. She was drifting when he spoke again. "I do have just one request, however."

She yawned. "Just one?"

"Those caps of yours."

"Don't worry, Kitty and Angus will take care of the cats."

"No, no. the *caps*. Those silly lace things. You're not to bring them to Dorset. I won't stand for them."

"They're very proper."

"But you are not. My wife is the most improper woman in Dorset. See?" He nudged her hip with his stiff cock. "See what you do to me. I think the plan to sleep has changed."

Here's a sneak peek at UNDONE, the historical romance anthology featuring Susan Johnson, Terri Brisbin, and Mary Wine. Turn the page for a preview of Susan's story, "As You Wish."

Fortunately for the earl's pressing schedule, the night was overcast. Not a hint of moonlight broke through to expose his athletic form as he scaled the old, fist-thick wisteria vines wrapped around the pillars of the terrace pergola. The house to which the pergola was attached was quiet, the ground floor dark save for the porter's light in the entrance hall. Either the Belvoirs were out or already in bed. More likely the latter with only a single flambeau outside the door.

He'd best take care.

Kit had described the position of Miss Belvoir's bedchamber—hence Albion's ascent of the wisteria. Once he gained the roof joists of the Chinoiserie pergola, he would have access to the windows of the main floor corridor. From there he could make his way to the second floor bedchambers, the easternmost that of Miss Belvoir, where, according to Kit, she'd been cloistered for the last month, being polished by her stepmother into a state of refined elegance for her bow into society a few weeks hence.

Which refinements, in his estimation, only served to make every young lady into the same boring martinet without an original thought in her head or a jot of conversation worth listening to.

He hoped there wouldn't be much conversation tonight. If he had his way there wouldn't be any. He hoped as well that she wouldn't prove stubborn, but should she, he'd stuff his handkerchief in her mouth to muffle her screams, tie her up if necessary, and carry her down the back stairs and out the servants' entrance. It was more likely though—with all due modesty—that his much-practiced charm would win the day.

Pulling himself over the fretwork balustrade embellishing the pergola, he stood for a moment balanced on a joist contemplating which window would best offer him ingress. His mind made up, he brushed himself off, navigated the vine-draped timbers, and reached the window. Taking a knife from his coat pocket, he snapped open the blade, slipped it under the lower sash, and pried it up enough to gain a fingerhold.

Moments later, he stood motionless in the dark corridor. The stairs were to the right if Kit's description was correct. After listening for a few moments and hearing nothing, he quietly made his way down the plush carpet and up the stairs. A single candle on a console table dimly illuminated the hallway onto which the bedrooms opened. Pausing to listen once again and distinguishing no undue sounds, he silently traversed the carpeted passageway to the last door on his right.

It shouldn't be locked. Servants required access if the bell-pull by the bed was rung. For a brief moment he stood utterly still, wondering what in blazes he was doing here about to abduct some untried maid in order to seduce her. As if there weren't women enough in London who would welcome him to their beds with open arms. Considerable brandy was to blame, he supposed, and the rackety company of his friends, who had too much idle time on their hands in which to conjure up wild wagers like this.

Bloody hell. He felt the complete absence of any desire to be where he was.

Then again, he recalled with a short exhalation, he'd bet twenty thousand on this foolishness.

Now it was play or pay.

He reached for the latch, pressed down, and quietly opened the door.

As he stepped over the threshold he was greeted by a ripple of scent and a cheerful female voice. "I thought you'd changed your mind."

The hairs on the back of his neck rose.

His first thought was that he was unarmed.

His second was that it was a trap.

But when the same genial voice said, "Don't worry, no one's at home but me. Do come in and shut the door." His pulse rate lessened and he scanned the candlelit interior for the source of the invitation.

"Miss Belvoir, I presume," he murmured, taking note of a young woman with hair more gold than red standing across the room near the foot of the bed. *She was quite beautiful. How nice. And if no one was home, nicer still.* Shutting the door behind him, he offered her a graceful bow.

"A pleasant good evening, Albion. Gossip preceded you." *He was breathtakingly handsome at close range. Now to convince him to take her away.* "I have a proposition for you."

He smiled. "A coincidence. I have one for you." This was going to be easier than he thought. Then he saw her luggage. "You first," he said guardedly.

"I understand you have twenty thousand to lose."

"Or not."

"Such arrogance, Albion. You forget, the decision is mine."

"Not entirely," he softly replied.

"Because you've done this before."

"Not this. But something enough like it to know."

"I see," she murmured. "But then I'm not inclined to be instantly infatuated with your handsome self or your prodigal repute. I have more important matters on my mind."

"More important than twenty thousand?" he asked with a small smile.

"I like to think so."

He recognized the seriousness of her tone. "Then we must come to some agreement. What do you want?"

"To strike a bargain."

"Consider me agreeable to most anything," he smoothly replied.

"My luggage caused you a certain apprehension, I noticed," she said, amusement in her gaze. "Let me allay your fears. I have no plans to elope with you. Did you think I did?"

"The thought crossed my mind." He wasn't entirely sure yet that some trap wasn't about to be sprung. She was the picture of innocence in white muslin—all the rage thanks to Marie Antoinette's penchant for the faux rustic life.

"I understand that women stand in line for your amorous skills, but rest assured—you're not my type. Licentiousness is your raison d'être I hear—a very superficial existence I should think."

His brows rose. He wondered if she'd heard about Sally's when she mentioned women standing in line. She also had the distinction of being the first woman to find him lacking. "You mistake my raison d'être. Perhaps if you knew me better you'd change your mind," he pleasantly suggested.

"I very much doubt it," she replied with equal amiability. "You're quite beautiful, I'll give you that, and I understand you're unrivaled in the boudoir. But my interests, unlike yours, aren't focused on sex. What I do need from you, however, is an escort to my aunt's house in Edinburgh."

"And for that my twenty thousand is won?" His voice was velvet soft.

"Such tact, my lord."

"I can be blunt if you prefer."

"Please do. I've heard so much about your ready charm. I'm wondering how you're going to ask."

"I hadn't planned on asking."

"Because you never have to."

He smiled. "To date at least."

"So I may be the exception."

"If you didn't need an escort to Edinburgh," he mildly observed. "Your move."

"You see this as a game?"

"In a manner of speaking."

"And I'm the trophy or reward, or how do young bucks describe a sportive venture like this?"

"How do young ladies describe the snaring of a husband?"

She laughed. "Touché. I have no need of a husband though. Does that calm your fears?"

"I have none in that regard. Nothing could induce me to marry."

"Then we are in complete agreement. Now tell me, how precisely does a libertine persuade a young lady to succumb to his blandishments?"

"Not like this," he drily said. "Come with me and I'll show you."

"We strike our bargain first. Like you, I have much at stake."

"Then, Miss Belvoir," he said with well-bred grace, "if you would be willing to relinquish your virginity tonight, I'd be delighted to escort you to Edinburgh."

"In the morning. Or later tonight if we can deal with this denouement expeditiously."

"At week's end," he countered. "After the Spring Meet in Newmarket."

"I'm sorry. That's not acceptable."

He didn't answer for so long she thought he might be willing to lose twenty thousand. He was rich enough.

"We can talk about it at my place."

"No."

Another protracted silence ensued, only the crackle of the fire on the hearth audible.

"Would you be willing to accompany me to Newmarket," he finally said. "I can assure you anonymity at my race box. Once the Spring Meet is over, I'll take you to Edinburgh." He blew out a small breath. "I've a fortune wagered on my horses. I don't suppose you'd understand."

This time she was the one who didn't immediately respond, and when she did, her voice held a hint of melancholy. "I do understand. My mother owned the Langley stud."

"That was your mother's? By God—the Langley stud was legendary. Tattersalls was mobbed when it was sold. You *do* know how I feel about my racers then." He grinned. "They're all going to win at Newmarket. I'll give you a share if you like—to help set you up in Edinburgh."

Her expression brightened and her voice took on a teasing intonation. "Are you trying to buy my acquiescence?"

"Why not? You only need give me a few days of your time. Come with me. You'll enjoy the races."

"I mustn't be seen."

Ah—capitulation. "Then we'll see that you aren't. Good Lord—the Langley stud. I'm bloody impressed. Let me get your luggage."

Try HOT SOUTHERN NIGHTS, the latest from
Dianne Castell, out now from Brava . . .

"Where are you going now?"

"To get my grandmother."

"She's at my place and she's doing just fine. She's probably sleeping by now."

"But she's *my* grandmother." Cal kept walking till Churchill caught up to him and took his arm, the unexpected light touch stopping him faster than any hard punch. She could still do that after so many years. What was it about Churchill that got to him? Auburn hair pulled back in a loose knot and held in place by a pencil? Her slim figure under the simple skirt and blouse? Her long legs? All of it, dammit, all of it. The whole uptight librarian package drove him nuts because he knew somewhere under all that uptightness there was something a little reckless and hot as hell.

"She's fine. I tried to call you about what happened, but with all the racket coming out of that heap you call a car the world could have exploded and you wouldn't have heard a thing. Miss Ellie thinks I'm out getting dog food, so I better get back in case she wakes up." Church let out a sigh and let go of Cal's arm. "That's not a lie. Seems I always have to get dog food except when he won't eat dog food and I have to fry chicken or scramble an egg or make quiche."

"You cook quiche for a dog?"

"He has separation anxiety. He liked Jersey." She didn't say anything for a moment and stared at him. Her blue eyes suddenly went dark and soft and too damn sensual for a hot summer night in Savannah with no one around but the two of them. "Did you take Dodd's money?"

He had to bring an end to the conversation before her damn questions and her ability to turn him upside down made him say something he'd regret and mess up everything he set in motion. "You want to know why the police hauled me in? One of the guys who worked pit here at the track three years ago wound up dead. They think I had something to do with it. I'm a felon, and that means any crime within a fifty-mile radius has my name on it. That should answer your question."

"Why would your robbery have anything to do with the dead person?"

"You aren't nearly as smart as people say you are, Ace."

She didn't scare off easy, he'd give her that. Bet those Jersey boys had their hands full when Little Miss Know It All showed up wanting her car back. Churchill McKenzie didn't do "I don't know" well. "Go home." He walked across the track. "Thanks for taking care of Miss Ellie," he added without turning around. He slid through the open window of Mud Monkey and gunned the engine to drown out any other questions or comments Churchill had. She shook her head at him and walked away till Killer ran ahead, nearly pulling her off her feet. Who was taking who for a walk? He stifled a laugh making him feel better than he had since . . . since he kissed her. Damn that kiss, why did he do that? Why did she have to be there? Why couldn't she have kept her job in Jersey? Everything was going okay, he had everything under control for a long time now and then Churchill came back to Savannah and talked to Miss Ellie. Cal had a bad feeling things would not end with one talk. He had to keep a clear head and stop her before she got involved.

Trouble was, when it came to Ace McKenzie there was

not one thing clear at all. He was attracted to her and shouldn't be for a grocery list of reasons. They were opposites on every front, the librarian and the jailbird. The darling of Savannah—just ask anyone—and the devil—just ask anyone.

Mark your calendars! BEAST BEHAVING BADLY, the newest Shelly Laurenston book in the Pride series, comes out next month!

Bo shot through the goal crease and slammed the puck into the net.

"Morning!"

That voice cut through his focus and, without breaking his stride, Bo changed direction and skated over to the rink entrance. He stopped hard, ice spraying out from his skates, and stood in front of the wolfdog.

He stared down at her and she stared up at him. She kept smiling even when he didn't. Finally he asked, "What time did we agree on?"

"Seven," she replied with a cheery note that put his teeth on edge.

"And what time is it?"

"Uh . . ." She dug into her jeans and pulled out a cell phone. The fact that she still had on that damn, useless watch made his head want to explode. How did one function—as an adult anyway—without a goddamn watch?

Grinning so that he could see all those perfectly aligned teeth, she said, "Six-forty-five!"

"And what time did we agree on?"

She blinked and her smile faded. After a moment, "Seven."

"Is it seven?"

"No." When he only continued to stare at her, she softly asked, "What to meet me at the track at seven?"

He continued to stare at her until she nodded and said, "Okay."

She walked out and Bo went back to work.

Fifteen minutes later, Bo walked into the small arena at seven a.m. Blayne, looking comfortable in dark blue leggings, sweatshirt, and skates, turned to face him. He expected her to be mad at him or, even worse, for her to get that wounded look he often got from people when he was blatantly direct. But having to deal with either of those scenarios was a price Bo was always willing to pay to ensure that the people in his life understood how he worked from the beginning. This way, there were no surprises later. It was called "boundaries," and he read about it in a book.

Yet when Blayne saw him, she grinned and held up a Starbucks cup. "Coffee," she said when he got close. "I got you the house brand because I had no idea what you would like. And they had cinnamon twists, so I got you a few of those."

He took the coffee, watching her close. Where was it? The anger? The resentment? Was she plotting something?

Blayne held the bag of sweets out for him and Bo took them. "Thank you," he said, still suspicious even as he sipped his perfectly brewed coffee.

"You're welcome." And there went that grin again. Big and brighter than the damn sun. "And I get it. Seven means seven. Eight means eight, etc., etc. Got it, and I'm on it. It won't happen again." She said all that without a trace of bitterness and annoyance, dazzling Bo with her understanding more than she'd dazzled him with those legs.

"So," she put her hands on her hips, "what do you want me to do first?"

Marry me? Wait. No, no. Incorrect response. It'll just weird her out and make her run again. Normal. Be normal. You can do this. You're not just a great skater. You're a normal great skater.

When Bo knew he had his shit together, he said, "Let's work on your focus first. And, um, should I ask what happened to your face?" She had a bunch of cuts on her cheeks. Gouges. Like something small had pawed at her.

"Nope!" she chirped, pulling off her sweatshirt. She wore a worn blue T-shirt underneath with B&G PLUMBING scrawled across it. With sweatshirt in hand, Blayne skated over to the bleachers, stopped, shook her head, skated over to another section of bleachers, stopped, looked at the sweatshirt, turned around, and skated over to the railing. "I should leave it here," she explained, "In case I get chilly."

It occurred to Bo he'd just lost two minutes of his life watching her try and figure out where to place a damn sweatshirt. Two minutes that he'd never get back.

"Woo-hoo!" she called out once she hit the track. "Let's go!"

She was skating backward as she urged him to join her with both hands.

He pointed behind her. "Watch the—"

"Ow!"

"—pole."

Christ, what had he gotten himself into?

Christ almighty, what had she gotten herself into?

Twenty minutes in and she wanted to smash the man's head against a wall. She wanted to go back in time and kick the shit out of Genghis Khan before turning on his brothers, Larry and Moe. Okay. That wasn't their names, but she could barley remember Genghis's name on a good day, how the hell was she supposed to remember his brothers'? But whatever the Khan kin's names may be, Blayne wanted to hurt them all for cursing her world with this . . . this . . . Visigoth!

Even worse, she knew he didn't even take what she did seriously. He insisted on calling it a chick sport. If he were a sexist pig across the board, Blayne could overlook it as a mere flaw in his upbringing. But, she soon discovered, Novikov had a very high degree of respect for female athletes . . . as long as they were athletes and not just "hot chicks in cute outfits, roughing each other up. All you guys need is some hot oil or mud and you'd have a real moneymaker on your hands."

And yet, even while he didn't respect her sport as a sport, he still worked her like he was getting her ready for the Olympics.

After thirty minutes she wanted nothing more but to lie on her side and pant. She doubted the hybrid would let her get away with that, though.

Shooting around the track, Novikov stopped her in a way that she was finding extremely annoying—by grabbing her head with that big hand of his and holding her in place.

He shoved her back with one good push, and Blayne fought not to fall on her ass at that speed. When someone shoved her like that, they were usually pissed. He wasn't.

"I need to see something," he said, still nursing that cup of coffee. He'd finished off the cinnamon twists in less than five minutes while she was warming up. "Come at me as hard as you can."

"Are you sure?" she asked, looking him over. He didn't have any of his protective gear on, somehow managing to change into sweatpants and T-shirt and still make it down to the track exactly at seven. "I don't want to hurt you," she told him honesty.

The laughter that followed, however, made her think she did want to hurt him. She wanted to hurt him a lot. When he realized she wasn't laughing with him—or, in this case, laughing at *herself* since he was obviously laughing *at* her—Novikov blinked and said, "Oh. You're not kidding."

"No. I'm not kidding."

"Oh. Oh! Um . . . I'll be fine. Hit me with your best shot."

"Like Pat Benatar?" she joked, but when he only stared at her, she said, "Forget it."

Blayne sized up the behemoth in front of her and decided to move back a few more feet so she could get a really fast start. She got into position and took one more scrutinizing look. It was a skill her father had taught her. To size up weakness. Whether the weakness of a person or a building or whatever. Of course, Blayne often used this skill for good, finding out

someone's weakness and then working to help them overcome it. Her father, however, used it to destroy.

Lowering her body, Blayne took a breath, tightened her
fists, and took off. She lost some speed on the turn but picked it
up as she cut inside. As Blayne approached Novikov, she sized
him up one more time as he stood there casually, sipping his
coffee and watching her move around the track. Based on
that last assessing look, she slightly adjusted her position and
slammed into him with everything she had.

And, yeah, she knocked herself out cold, but it was totally
worth it when the behemoth went down with her.

GREAT BOOKS,
GREAT SAVINGS!

When You Visit Our Website:
www.kensingtonbooks.com
You Can Save Money Off The Retail Price
Of Any Book You Purchase!

- **All Your Favorite Kensington Authors**
- **New Releases & Timeless Classics**
- **Overnight Shipping Available**
- **eBooks Available For Many Titles**
- **All Major Credit Cards Accepted**

Visit Us Today To Start Saving!
www.kensingtonbooks.com

All Orders Are Subject To Availability.
Shipping and Handling Charges Apply.
Offers and Prices Subject To Change Without Notice.